Dr. Ahmed Al Sinani is a medical doctor with an avid interest in science fiction that started from a young age of 7. He has shown his passion with his book, *From Ashes to Flames*, and his ultimate dream is to transform this into a mega franchise of bestseller science fiction series.

Dedicated to my mother and father who have been instrumental in inspiring this book, and my mentors, teachers, advisors and loving family members for their continuous support and advice that brought this book to life.

Dr. Ahmed Al Sinani

FROM ASHES TO FLAMES

Austin Macauley Publishers™
LONDON * CAMBRIDGE * NEW YORK * SHARJAH

Copyright © Dr. Ahmed Al Sinani 2022

The right of Dr. Ahmed Al Sinani to be identified as author of this work has been asserted by the author in accordance with Federal Law No. (7) of UAE, Year 2002, Concerning Copyrights and Neighboring Rights.

All rights reserved. No part of this publication may be reproduced, stored in a retrieval system, or transmitted in any form or by any means, electronic, mechanical, photocopying, recording, or otherwise, without the prior permission of the publishers.

Any person who commits any unauthorized act in relation to this publication may be liable to legal prosecution and civil claims for damages.

This is a work of fiction. Names, characters, businesses, places, events, locales, and incidents are either the products of the author's imagination or used in a fictitious manner. Any resemblance to actual persons, living or dead, or actual events is purely coincidental.

The age group that matches the content of the books has been classified according to the age classification system issued by the National Media Council.

ISBN – 9789948825579 – (Paperback)
ISBN – 9789948825562 – (E-Book)

Application Number: MC-10-01-9313640
Age Classification: 13+

Printer Name: iPrint Global Ltd
Printer Address: Witchford, England

First Published 2022
AUSTIN MACAULEY PUBLISHERS FZE
Sharjah Publishing City
P.O Box [519201]
Sharjah, UAE
www.austinmacauley.ae
+971 655 95 202

Thanks to Rama Al Saman, the book's illustrator.

Chapter 1
A Strange Encounter

The space port of Nebula 1 is bustling with buyers; a sight that is common to this area of the planet. Especially since today is market day. The streets are filled with every humanoid species imaginable, both outsiders and locals making purchases. You can hear them haggling with the vendors as they strain to find a price that they both agree on. However, the markets of Nebula are distinguished by their aromas. Spices from all over the universe can be found here that suit the purposes of every traveler.

However, for Ranthor, this is not the case. He seeks something else that is far more valuable. The jewels of Nebula are the object of his desire. The jewels are said to be worth billions of kruats. For this young bounty hunter, it would ensure a very luxurious life. It would put him in a position of power in his home planet Creed, far away in the Beta 3 galaxy. It would certainly restore his position in his father's court.

He was once part of the royal family in his home planet, but his arrogance has led him to lose the battle of Tartuga. He led his troops into a trap. Even as his advisors tried to warn him, he did not take their heed and decided to plunge straight into battle. He entered through the tunnels and found that his enemies predicted his every move. They intercepted him and killed all of his troops. He was the only one to survive. Ranthor returned to his father's court bloodied, misshapen, and disgraced. The attack had terribly scarred his face, he had to cover most of it. His father welcomed him home with a cold stare, disgraced by his son's failure. He decided

to exile his only son into the far reaches of the universe. He was an outcast in the eyes of his people for as long as he can remember.

The once pampered prince was condemned to live the life of a pauper, living off whatever his bounty hunter's job can afford him. His anger at his father's decision had not yet subsided. Even though the years passed by since his exile, the wounds and scars of his soul still bleed raw. His bitterness fresh and strengthened as the days pass by, with every passing moment. The memory of his humiliation, always reminding him of his own failure. It still haunts in his dreams.

Ranthor began his search in the markets of the space port questioning a couple of the civilians about the legend of the jewels and gathering any form of intel about them. From what the locals say, the jewels possess some hidden powers that they will bestow upon their bearers. It is said that they give their wearer the power to alter time, psychokinetic control over moving objects; the ability to move them with their minds. This would mean that whoever finds them can have control over the galaxy. *I understand why father wants this object so badly*, Ranthor thought to himself. This would definitely be his way back to his father's court.

Legend has it that it is hidden in a cave on the darkest side of the planet. The locals warned him that the ones that ventured into this cave never came back, not in one piece anyway. Despite that, he was determined to find the place and was going to head to it at the break of dawn. Meanwhile he retreated to a local inn where he booked a room for the night. He ate a meal from the inn, some local mystery meat, and drank ale from a metallic flask. He had left to his room afterwards to sleep and prepare for the long journey that lay ahead.

Ranthor was surprised to find an intruder in his room. A reptilian alien, around 4 feet tall, was playing with his gun. He quickly snatched it from the little thief's hand and held him by his neck. He started questioning him about his reasons for entering the room.

"Listen you little vermin. You have about five seconds to tell me why you're here in my room, trying to steal my gun or I'll blow your brains out with it," Ranthor raged.

"I was m-merely admiring it young master," stammered the reptilian humanoid.

"False! Get ready to taste hot plasma vermin scum," replied Ranthor in fury.

"Okay, I was sent here to spy on you and follow you to the location of the jewels and find where they are. Please don't kill me, I'll help you. I can be your guide in these treacherous deserts," offered the reptilian humanoid. "My name is Ooger," he added.

Ranthor agreed after realizing that he neither had a map nor a guide to that dark region of the planet and Ooger could help him navigate his way through the area. He had to be careful of him though. He could not let his sense of wariness to slip or wander around aimlessly, he cannot trust this 'guide's' motives yet. He is very wary of this shady little thief. He was able to sneak into his room unnoticed, who knows what he may do next.

He made Ooger pack his own tent so that they don't have to share the same tent. Surprisingly, he came prepared. Apparently, he had it before when he was preparing his stake out to spy on Ranthor the other night. *How resourceful*, thought Ranthor. This creature could be of immense help in finding the elusive Nebula jewels.

They left the space port at 5:30 am, having packed all their gear, including ropes and rock-climbing equipment. The journey to the dark side of the planet was a very strenuous one, filled with a series of mountains that have to be traversed to get to the caves guarding the jewels.

Ranthor learned that he has to reach the city of Omnivora 1, which lies close to the mountains which they were bound to climb. He also learned from his guide Ooger that the citizens of this city are paranoid, and do not take kindly to outsiders questioning them. Luckily, the guide is familiar with the customs of this city, being a citizen himself. Ooger began briefing him with the customs and mannerisms of this unwelcoming city. He had also taken the liberty of purchasing an outfit for him, one worn by most people, so that he could be disguised as a local. They took the road east of the space port and headed for the city.

They arrived at Omnivora 1 at 8:00 am to find the city nearly deserted by its citizens. This is odd, the city being one of the most densely populated cities in Nebula 1 and the heart of its commerce, after the space port of course. Usually on a day like market day there would be a lot of space vendors and flying markets flying to and from the planet. They would adjust their ships to the planet's gravity and set up their floating shops. You could smell their different herbs from the anywhere in the planet, their intoxicating aromas urging you to buy them. The sound of vendor clerks booming on their speakers and the larger-than-life holo-screen projectors starting at dawn was annoying, yet almost mesmerizing. The silence was all too suspicious for Ranthor's liking. The eerie silence indicated an incoming ambush. Ranthor's instincts were telling him to be cautious; he was a trained bounty hunter after all. They're bound to be suspicious.

Unfortunately, the bounty hunter's instincts did not betray him; there were indeed bandits waiting for them at the end of the road, blocking their entry to the city. A tall, dark, and strongly built alien with a serpentine face was riding a Banshee. He wore a malicious smile, indicating he was prepared for a fight. His ion beam sword at hand and holo-gun in its sheath, an ominous sign of trouble that was soon to come. Ranthor pulled his own sword from its sheath and prepared for confrontation. Ooger hid behind a close by rock to avoid being hit by the gunfire or the clash of swords.

The serpentine aliens approached them; sword raised in a combat stance signaling battle. Both swords clashed with such force that the heat from the beams scorched the surrounding grass and other flora within its range. Both warriors were seasoned fighters; each blow that was landed was countered by the opposing warrior that the fight seemed endless. Both warriors were not fatigued at all.

The fight seemed to drag on forever as both beams crossed and clashed that they cancelled each other. Eventually, both fighters seemed to show signs of exhaustion. Until, finally, the bandit's defense fell, and he was struck by Ranthor. The cut severed him in half, showing the scorch marks left by the fatal blow. Ooger finally came out of hiding, his face stricken with fear as he saw the alien brute laying their motionless and split in half. They left him there to be hacked at by any scavenging creature that might still find interest in his decaying corpse. They continued their journey to the heart of the city where they were going to ask the locals about the jewels.

They arrived at the heart of the city of Omnivora 1, fatigued and exhausted from the battle with the alien bandit. Ooger headed to a nearby space inn to book a room for them. Since they were going to stay here for a while, they might as well get adjusted and rested for the journey that lay ahead. Since he is familiar with the local dialect; it seemed more appropriate that he made the reservation. An outsider would arouse suspicion and would make their quest of finding the jewels a lot harder than it seemed. Ooger finally completed the reservation. While he was in the inn, he also learned that the entrance to the mountains was heavily guarded by the local forces. They needed to arm themselves in case they had to force their entry. Ooger also managed to find ropes and harnesses for the climb to the mountain. He turned out to be very useful in this journey, realized Ranthor.

After they managed to acquire all the supplies for the journey they headed to the mountain. The climb turned out to be challenging and drained them of all their energy, after all Ranthor sustained a lot of battle wounds from the last confrontation with the alien. Nonetheless, they progressed through the mountains; they neared the site of the cave with every stride. They were weary, restless, and exhausted. They hoped that they would not encounter any beast on their slippery slope. They were tired and were on the verge of defeat. Their only hope of survival was to hide in the nearby crevices. It was humiliating for the young warrior prince, but he had to adhere to these new terms, and accept the reality of his situation.

They were only a few steps from the cave now. Their hopes of finding the jewels grew with every step. As they reached the entrance to the cave, they were relieved that their journey was drawing to an end. It was finally going to be over. This sordid, humiliating experience made him a laughingstock in his father's court. He will return to his former glory, stronger and much wiser.

He could not have been more wrong. For the unwary travels did not know that this was only the beginning of their journey.

The realization hit Ranthor at once, when he found out that there were no jewels in the cave. They kept searching for hours and hours. Whoever came here before them must have taken the jewels and ran away. But the situation was far more complicated than that. It appeared that they were ambushed. Two strongly built, armed mercenaries were blocking the entrance to the cave. A mysterious hooded figure stood between them. He was not really standing but rather he was floating slightly above them. He spoke in a raspy, metallic voice, "prepare to die vermin," and then he motioned to the mercenaries to attack. They approached Ranthor and drew their blades. The inscription on the blades seemed familiar to the warrior, although he didn't remember where he saw it. He drew his own blade and prepared for battle.

The blades of the warriors clashed with precision and strength. Their strikes were calculated and planned unlike the blind flurry of swords that was usually seen in mercenary combat. Ranthor's suspicion grew even more, and he started to realize that these mercenaries may have been led by someone he knew. There is a person out there trying to assassinate him and that made him even angrier than he already was. Some unknown person was trying to prevent him from getting back his position in the court. If this person gets the jewels, he might even replace him. He was not going to let that happen. He must defeat these mercenaries at any cost, or he will be stuck as a bounty hunter forever.

The strong mercenaries seemed undefeated; they didn't seem to have any weakness at all. This was very frustrating; the person who ambushed him was on his way to his father with the jewels. He kept striking them but with no use. Finally, he found a weakness, an Achilles tendon, the warriors seemed to focus on precision leaving a gap of time where the unarmed part of their suit was exposed. He had a window of time to strike, and he had to be quick, if he had any chance of survival. He waited for the perfect moment and when the time came, he struck with raging fury. The blow was so strong that it severed the warrior's torso from his legs. The other two suffered the same fate. They just lay there in the welcoming embraces of death. Their faces retorted in a single expression, utmost fear. It was engraved onto their faces, just like the crevices and openings that were carved in the caves that lay close to them.

After this strenuous duel with the warriors, Ranthor headed to the opening of the cave followed by Ooger whose face was as white as snow. He had never seen such a powerful display of force like the one Ranthor had shown in battle. What was even more frightening was that the reptilian warrior had no wounds scarring his scaly body. He was glad that he was not the one to cross paths with such a formidable opponent. Despite his nagging fear that urged him to escape, he ventured with him further into the cave.

The journey through the cave seemed endless; Ooger could have sworn that he passed the same stone carving for the tenth time. Did Ranthor get lost in this endless labyrinth? But this seemed to be the least of their fears. They just hit a dead end. The cave seemed to end in a hollow abyss, an endless pit that made it impossible to cross to the other side.

Just as they were about to lose hope, Ranthor spotted something. There was an inscription carved on the wall. He tried to read the passage, but it was in a language that he was not familiar with. The prince was well read and had received an excellent education in linguistics by his tutors in the palace. Yet, this language seemed somehow different. Judging by the inscription patterns, it looked archaic. A message left by the first inhabitants of this cave to the travelers hoping to reach it. A warning, perhaps, or maybe a sign to lead them through the labyrinth?

"Illumination is the key to your success; search the darkness to find the path of light borne within," cried Ooger.

"What are you ranting on about?" asked Ranthor.

"This inscription is written in Krulian, an old language used in Nebula many millennia ago. My grandfather taught it to me," explained Ooger.

"Grandfather, you mean there's more of you?" asked Ranthor.

"Yeah, my clan lives in the surrounding mountains," replied Ooger, rather enthusiastically.

"Oh great, more trouble!" sighed Ranthor.

The moment he said that a sound was heard at the entrance of the cave. The sound of around 50 steel boots hitting the solid floor. Their movements were very coordinated and meticulous, which could only indicate one thing; they were military troops. And they were heading straight for them.

The troops were approaching the caverns. The rhythmic hum of their boots was becoming louder and louder, they were nearly halfway through by now. This made Ooger very apprehensive. His face was pale, and his breath was shallow. Ranthor on the other hand showed no sign of fear. His face is calm and serene as if he had been anticipating this moment for a long time. If there was any hint of fear in his face, then it was clearly not visible in his expressions. The sound grew louder with each passing moment, yet Ranthor's expressions did not betray him. His face was as calm as ever. With a swift motion, he drew his sword from its sheath and adjusted himself into a stance.

The troops reached the entrance to the cavern. Their eyes were set on Ranthor, they were analyzing him, wondering if he would pose a possible threat to them. The latter was doing the same. His focus was locked onto the soldiers, assessing their strengths and weaknesses. They kept eyeing each other for a long time, it seemed that it was more of a duel of wit more than of strength.

Finally, the captain of the infantry decided to break the wall of silence. He approached Ranthor with incredible agility and began talking in a military tone:

"This cave is a property of the emperor of Nebula. Your presence here is a violation of our planetary law. Leave this place or we will open fire!"

"And what if we say no?" challenged Ranthor.

"I warn you, what you are doing is treason and will be punishable by death. The troopers will open fire if you do not leave immediately," roared the captain.

"Your bullets do not scare us," yelled Ranthor.

"Talk about yourself Ranthor. For all I know, you've been blasted by many bullets that your brain already got accustomed to it. But I haven't, so I suggest we leave now. Please, spare us! You can take him if you want," cried Ooger.

"Silence pest, your mere presence makes my skin crawl. If there's anyone who's dying today, it's going to be you. So, if I were you, I'd better say my prayers," shouted Ranthor.

"As for you captain, I'd suggest you take your troops home because we're not moving an inch. So, unless you are here to provide entertainment for our little excursion, I'd suggest you leave this cave," bellowed Ranthor in rage.

"Artillery! Prepare to fire!" answered the captain.

"Ranthor, do you enjoy getting us killed?" asked Ooger.

"I have faith that we will leave here unscathed. Well, I think that's what you're supposed to say in a crisis. See, I wasn't really pious so I can't promise anything. Best of luck!" Joked Ranthor.

And on that last comment, Ranthor decided to dive headfirst into battle. He charged through the hordes of troopers as if they were mist, evading their line of fire. He almost got shot, but he managed to deflect it with his blaster. The shot landed on the roof of the cave and sent a row of stalagmites flying, only to land on a group of soldiers, flattening them. The second group was ordered to come to the front. Many of them hesitated at first, but knowing the rules of the imperial army, that cowardice is punishable by death, made it clear to them that they can either kill them or be killed in the process.

The troopers readied their blasters. This time, they used a sonic wave gun to blast through the rock, creating a makeshift barrier. They then aimed their blasters; all of the guns had their laser beams aimed at Ranthor's head. Yet Ranthor did not even grimace. His eyes were locked on the troopers, daring them to fire their blasters.

"Soldiers, fire at this worthless bounty hunter, and his rat," cried the captain.

"Hey! Who are you calling a rat you…"

Before Ooger managed to finish his sentence, a shot was fired so close to him that it actually shaved the hair on his hand. His face turned ashen, and he wasn't able to utter another word. He just stood there, paralyzed by fear. The effect of the paralysis only lasted for a short while before he made his way to the entrance of the cave. He was followed later by a barrage of gun fire. He was barely dodging the shots, with each one coming closer to hitting its target. The imperial army of Nebula did not joke when it came to recruiting marksmen. They went through a rigorous training program. Many of them die during these training sessions. The ones that remained are the elite of the elite. And these soldiers did not joke around when it came to plotting an assassination.

Ranthor was next, the marksmen's eyes were focused on him, following his every move like heat seeking missiles picking up a thermal signal. Their shots came at him like a whirlwind, bringing the roof of the cave crashing.

Their sounds raged near the cave like booming thunder. The shots of the imperial army were met by Ranthor's eternal fury slashing through the air and creating rifts in time itself. The warrior was trained in the art of death as were the soldiers. It was as if two titans were battling in this eternal duel, their resolve was unbroken and their strength so formidable that it seemed the entire cave was about to be blown to another realm. One of the soldiers of the imperial army was cunning enough that he managed to slip from the battle scene. He found a secret back entrance in the cave that bypassed the battle arena and lunged at Ranthor from the back. He slashed at his face with incredible force that he opened a gaping wound near Ranthor's cheek. Immediately warm crimson blood started oozing from the wound and evaporated as it contacted the ionic beam of the soldier's sword. Luckily for Ranthor, the wound was not deep, and he quickly covered it with a rag that he made by cutting the fabric of his coat. Then he immediately leapt from harm's way and prepared to attack the assailant.

Ranthor was instantly searching in his mind for a plan to attack his assailant. He decided to confront him with the same guile and trickery that his opponent displayed. After all, this is war, an art of craftsmanship and strength. At last, after all that pondering, he found his opening. He drew from his belt a crystal orb. It looked like some sort of sonic wave transducer. He pressed on it, immediately it gave him a reddish glow and sprang to life. He threw it onto the roof of the cave, and it shrieked violently sending shards of rock flying in all directions. One of them hit the soldier in his neck and opened a hole in it. Blood was trickling. The soldier tried to staunch the wound but unfortunately it was too deep for him to stop the bleeding. Eventually, he collapsed in a pool of blood. Ranthor emerged victorious, but the wound in his face was still drawing a lot of blood and he started to feel dizzy.

The imperial troops began to notice that too as the heat of the battle subsided. They were attracted to him like a Nebula flesh-eating banshee. They were nearing him now and with every step closer, he felt desperation drawing closer to him. Then, something unexpected happened. Ooger emerged from the shadows with a pulse beam bomb that he must have stolen from their previous victim. Well, it didn't seem that he will be trying to get it back from them anytime soon. He removed its trigger and quickly threw it at the troops. It detonated with a powerful blast that sent the soldiers flying to the rocks and they immediately met their end.

Ranthor tried to lift himself from the rubble that he was in but found that he could not even lift his feet off the ground. He felt dizzy and disoriented and immediately began to lose consciousness. He succumbed to sleep and lay there motionless. Ooger saw him in that state and hurried to his aid. At that moment, his mind began racing. Different thoughts were racing through his mind at this time, many conflicting thoughts. Should he just leave Ranthor to his doom and leave with to find the jewels on his own or stay to help his newly-found friend, if that is what he is. How could he trust that Ranthor was not leading him to the edge of the abyss and will not involve him in his everlasting struggle with his father or worse still what if at the end of this journey he may realize that Ooger's existence is unnecessary and finish him off; he is mercenary and will do anything for the benefit? If there is a time for escaping, it would have to be now because Ranthor is losing a lot of blood and soon enough death will be his only friend. *What should I do?* thought Ooger to himself.

Then it suddenly hit him. There was no way that Ooger could escape this mountain without the aid of Ranthor. The rocks were too steep and carrying the rock-climbing gear would be too difficult as it was heavy. Besides, he did not know how to climb, and Ranthor had helped him the last time. He decided to find something to stop the bleed. The cave was empty and lifeless, and it seemed impossible that he would find anything in it. He looked for a long time for anything that resembled silk or fabric that was durable and will stop the bleed without folding under the weight of the blood. At last, he found a material that resembled gauze, some kind of fiber that a worm-like creature was producing in the cave. With the knife that he had, he slayed the creature and procured this material from it. He quickly wove it into gauze and went back to Ranthor. Surprisingly, this material was very malleable; it felt like clay. He could shape it into whatever he wanted and then it becomes hard again. He quickly wrapped it around Ranthor's cheek. It had an immediate soothing effect on him, a strange medicinal quality that nursed him back to health. *Well, at least to an acceptable level of consciousness*, thought Ooger (we would not want to exaggerate, would we?). Ranthor began waking up, everything felt a little hazy in the beginning and at first Ooger thought that he was going back to his comatose state. Luckily, he got back on his feet and managed to support himself on one of the rock pillars that surrounded the cave. He called to Ooger, but his voice was still weak. Ooger was frightened and tried to make a run for it.

"Relax you buffoon, I merely wanted to thank you. Hahaha, I never thought that a thieving rascal like you could pull off a stunt like this. Still, this doesn't mean that I will be sharing with you any of my jewels. I am not that sentimental; I simply know when thanks are due. After all you did save my life, surprisingly," called Ranthor.

"Phew! I thought it was my throat that you were coming after. With you, I can never be so sure. As for my cut, I expect a sum of money to be handed to me for my services. I will also send you a bill for my heroic services today and any that may come up during this long, arduous journey. Hahaha," laughed Ooger heartily.

Both of them were laughing so hard as if they were old friends that were reunited and were re-living their oldest, funniest memories. Ranthor was laughing so hard until he noticed that the laughter was making his stomach growl. Ooger also noticed that he too was hungry. They forgot that they hadn't eaten anything ever since they left the space inn. They needed to replenish their energy before they can search the cave. At this time, Ooger decided to surprise Ranthor with another thing. This crafty thief has managed to steal yet another thing, he had taken almost a dozen loafs of bread from the inn that they had left and almost 3 pounds of ground beef, two cans of venison stew, supplies that would keep them alive for at least a week before they needed to find another source of food. They decided it was about time that they made camp and they had their tents set up. They also found wood to light a fire. The flames brought them warmth at least for the night, it was one of the coldest winters that they have ever seen in this planet according to Ooger. They were both shivering; the realization only hit them as they were preparing the camp. Winter was coming and when it hit, it hit you badly. They also decided after having their meal that it was time to sleep, they have not slept for at least a few days now, they couldn't recall how many it was.

They were going to take shifts guarding the place. They tossed a coin, and it was Ooger's turn first. Ranthor decided to sleep with his eyes open. Even with the newly found friendship with his companion, he could not be sure of his motives for saving him yet.

The night was long, and hours passed by before it was Ranthor's turn to guard the place. During that time Ooger was pacing the place back and forth. He was contemplating his decision to keep Ranthor alive, would it be helpful in the coming days, or will he meet his fate by Ranthor's blade as soon as he was of no use? Would Ranthor spare him and even be kind as to give him something in return for helping him? He could never know for certain with this guy. Ranthor's people were always known for their cruelty and lack of compassion to what they viewed as creatures lesser than themselves. But maybe Ranthor was not like them, maybe he is different, or it could be that his betrayal by one of his own people softened his heart towards other races. Still, he could not rest his safety on blind faith or Ranthor's change in demeanor. This person was still dangerous and capable of doing anything, this was evidenced by the opponents that he defeated, who were left in a condition far worse than death. Their brutal massacre is a testament to the strength of Ranthor and his cunningness when it came to killing someone. Ooger was restless but he decided to go with his feelings and see this journey through to its end. When it was time for Ranthor to take the shift, Ooger also did the same as his partner and slept with his eyes open. Both noticed the tension that was still to some extent between them and decided to be careful of what the other might do.

Morning at last came after what might have been an eternity. The sun rose lazily with a dull glow in the beginning but soon it was bathing them with its warm welcoming rays. It was a cool morning, and the breeze was ruffling their hairs. Ranthor woke up first and he was glad that he did so. He looked at Ooger and he saw that he was sleeping peacefully. He did not want to wake him up yet. He wandered around the cave, scanning every nook and crevice looking for a clue on how to find the jewels. The inscription that they found earlier in the cave talked about illumination and light borne from within. It also talked about finding the path in the darkness. All of this did not make any sense; he had to find a way to put all of this together. Just as he was looking through the carvings in the cave, he noticed that one of them was glowing. He did not notice this opening the night before. It seemed that it began glowing with the rising of the sun. He peered through the opening and saw that the light was shining in the center of the room. It was showing a pedestal with a weird looking object that was not discernible from this distance. Could it be the jewel? It was not likely. Many people came to this cave, the writings showed that many tribes may have inhabited this cave for many centuries; the writings on each chamber were from a different time period. How could they all have missed it? But then again, so did he. He only saw it this morning. This was not a mere coincidence. Maybe it was destined for him to see it and seize the jewels. It was as if a heavenly light was being shone around him. Could it be that this is the moment of his redemption? Would he walk back into his father's court? This might be the moment of his second coronation, a new birth of the once-exiled prince to return to glory and sneer at those that once betrayed him and now believe that he is gone for good. He needed to wake Ooger and tell him of his new discovery. He immediately went on to wake him. It was not welcomed well by his friend. He was tossing and turning, trying to avoid Ranthor's hand that was attempting to pull him away from sleep's warm embrace. At last, he yielded and decided to wake up. Ranthor was angry at him and decided to whack him with the hilt of his sword.

"Oww, what'd you do that for. I was about to wake up peacefully," said Ooger sourly.

"You idiot, I have found the answer to all of our questions. I think I have found where the jewels are stored," replied Ranthor, showing a trace of excitement.

"This place is exactly like fits the phrase that was inscribed on that wall we found. Light shines on it and from within it there is illumination in the midst of darkness. I saw it when I woke up in the morning. We finally may be able to put this issue to rest and I can finally don the clothes of a prince again," continued Ranthor.

"Well, what are we doing here then? Let's go to this place and discover what lies within," said Ooger enthusiastically.

"Hold on a minute, you'd think we'll still be talking if I could actually reach it. There is a catch. It's only a small opening in the cave, enough for the eye to peep through but not enough to enter through it and I'm out of bombes to blast through it," replied Ranthor, in a matter-of-fact way.

"Here is the part of where I come into play. That bomb that I snatched from the serpentine soldier you killed wasn't the only one. I took his entire satchel. I recon he had about half a dozen of 'em at the time. I figured they might still be useful," said Ooger, rather proud of himself.

"I have got to be wary of you Ooger, you are cunning devil. I guess size really does not really matter. Who knew you had brains, huh?" Chuckled Ranthor.

"Hey!" Replied Ooger, who was offended by the comment.

They left to the site where Ranthor had found the hole in the cave. Ooger gave the bomb to Ranthor and decided to keep the rest to himself for safe measure, which Ranthor did not find very comforting. Yet, he had to hand it to him; the little fellow did help him on several occasions and was not likely to betray him this time. The rocks shattered and the opening grew wider as the bomb exploded. The entrance to the room was beckoning them to enter. There was pedestal with the mysterious object perched on top of it. Ooger's eyes were immediately set on it. The bright light that shone from it was strong. This was strange, since the light from the sun was only faint and this place is in a secluded area of the cave. This only made them more suspicious that there is more to this place than meets the eye. It won't be this easy to reach the jewels and just grab them from the pedestal. Still, they marched to the cave entrance to find out what was there.

Chapter 2
The Light from Within

Ranthor and Ooger made their way to the cave. The place was so dark that Ranthor had to use the beam of light from his sword to find his way around. Ooger followed quietly around and tried to keep pace with his companion, otherwise he would be engulfed by the darkness. The pedestal was still glowing with its celestial light; the source of it was still unknown. It challenged them to come close to it. Ranthor noticed that and turned towards it. He was treading with care, checking for any traps that may have been set up by the place's previous visitors. An object of such great value would not just be lying their unprotected, displayed on a pedestal like some prize to be taken. He scanned the floors for any hidden beams, pressure-sensitive pads or any reader of some sort that can detect his thermal energy. There was no such apparatus in the place, and it came up clean after a very thorough scan. This made even more apprehensive than he was already. Just because he didn't find anything doesn't mean that there aren't any traps. If it could mean anything, it just suggests that whoever lived here before is even more meticulous and crafty than he is. He felt very exposed in this place and soon found that beads of sweat were pouring from his face. Ooger noticed that too and began feeling rather nervous himself. When he asked Ranthor about what he was afraid of, he reassured him by telling him that the place was very hot and since it was in the depths of the cave; it didn't cool down by the wind. He agreed, reluctantly, and made his way with his friend to the pedestal.

They finally reached the place, but they found, to their dismay, a note was placed on the pedestal. It had a golden seal attached to it. That must have been what was glowing in the morning when he woke up, thought Ranthor. He stamped his foot in rage and was cursing loudly at everything. He could not contain his anger. This was going to be his break. His chance of finding peace with himself at last and most importantly go home. He was yearning to go home and be back again to the comfort of his palace. He knew it would not be as easy as finding the object of his desires gift wrapped and handed to him with a golden ribbon. Even in his moment of anger, he knew that it was no coincidence that he found this letter. It may lead him to something. He went to the pedestal and retrieved the letter. He broke the seal and began reading it:

Congratulations reader, you have reached the hall of coronation. Alas, the place is not like what it was before, but it will still guide you to what you seek the most. Follow the trail of the river that once ran through here. At its origin you will see what you once were, what you have become and what you will soon be. The answer lies there, seek illumination from the darkness within.

"That line comes up each time, what illumination is it talking about exactly," said Ranthor, truly feeling perplexed.

"Maybe if you found the River Ranthor, we will have some answers at least. Come on, let us go," replied Ooger.

They continued their trail in search of this mysterious river. It was an impossible search, whatever ran through this place if indeed it was a river did run its course. If there was a river, many animals would have been drinking from it already. How could Ranthor make sure that no one was playing a game with them? Something aroused his suspicion. How did all these people suddenly know that he was on a quest to find the jewels of Nebula? Also, many of the warriors seemed to have something in common. The way they were fighting was peculiar, he had seen it before. Could it be that someone from his past was trying to assassinate him? He had many enemies, if he had to choose someone it would be difficult as he would have to look through an extremely long list. The planets that he had conquered during his years as a loyal commander of his father forces numbered in the thousands. His race was known to enslave a lot of others. They were merciless. Someone must have been left alive, driven by hatred and vengeance and was plotting to kill him. But he still found that unlikely. The people that he has attacked were not half as skilled as these people that he met. This seemed to be someone from the inside, someone that he knew. There was no time for him to ponder on who would plot against him, he had to find these jewels. For that, he had to find this river and plan on how to proceed from there onwards.

Meanwhile Ooger was focused on his own dilemma. He was just looking at the road leading away from the pedestal when he noticed that the road had a side turn that sloped downwards. The road here was slightly rougher and it seemed that it had seen better days; it was withered as if something had eaten through it. It was also strange because the marks left by the rocks all pointed in the same direction toward one point. He followed the path that they made and soon he found himself near an incline. He climbed upwards and soon he found, to his surprise, that a lake was there. How couldn't anyone spot it? It must have been feeding the river that was mentioned in the letter. That would explain that he had found below. But why would the river just stop flowing? That didn't make any sense. The lake was still there, it didn't just run dry. This seemed very odd. He wanted to call Ranthor to tell him of his discovery, but he was nowhere to be found. Where could he have wandered off to? This was seriously not the time for him to go on one of his solo expeditions. If this was his way of punishing him for not waking up early in the morning, then he clearly got the message because he is feeling afraid that he was left alone. Who knows what could be lurking in these dark caves, waiting for someone as small as him to come along? Well, he'd let them know that he can fight off any creature that will come in his way. He was used to the life of being the oppressed victim. He would not take to being tossed around by people just because of his size.

The search for Ranthor proved to be a long one indeed. He tried to retrace his steps, following any footprint that he had left but it was to no avail. Ranthor was as skilled in making himself invisible as he was with swordplay. After searching the corners of the cave for hours he finally found himself looking at some strange rune tablet that was left in this cave. By the looks of it, it seemed as if it was cast millennia ago, probably by the first inhabitants of this cave and maybe even this planet. At least the first sentient beings. The writings on the tablet told the story of a king, once loved by his people. He was a just ruler and kind to his people. They lived in a kingdom far away in the stars or so the story told anyway. An ailment had swept through his kingdom, one that he cannot treat. In his search for a cure for this mysterious illness, he met an old man that told him that this disease was caused by vanity. The king, kind as he is to his people, treated other sovereign nations with malice and evil. In his vain efforts to seek glory, he enslaved many of them, forcing them to work in his palaces either as servants or entertainers. The less fortunate of them were sent to the gallows either because they did not wish to work for him or simply because he was bored with them. These people plotted against him and decided to cast a plague upon him and his people. They poisoned all their food and drink and left them to die. The king and his family were the only ones to survive. Some of them were hit with this disease but hope was not yet lost for them. The old man told them to leave their planet and come to a cave far away in the reaches of Omnivora 1. In it was a river that could heal all ailments. It was going to be the king's salvation.

As soon as they arrived at the planet, the king began his search for the cave and soon he found it. Finding the cave was also not very difficult as the entrance to it was not closed. They all drank from it and soon he found that those from his family that were diseased began feeling healthy again. Happiness was returning to his family. The grieving had stopped and was replaced with joy. He was glad to have that curse lifted from him. Little did he know that the river, although it healed his family, it demanded a price for the gifts that it bestowed upon them. It was beginning to draw from their energies to keep it running. They drank from it with impunity, as if it would day become dry. The happiness they got from it was almost intoxicating that it was difficult to stop drinking from it. Then it all hit him afterwards, his wife and children were beginning to age prematurely, their hair were thinning, and their bones were growing weak. Finally, they succumbed to death and the river stopped flowing. In its place was a dry basin that was waiting to be filled again.

Ranthor was just thinking of this river that was being mentioned over and over again. What could its significance be? He was lost in his own thoughts that he didn't notice Ooger spinning around him excitedly, waiting for him to notice his presence. He finally awoke from his stupor and saw that he was still looking at him with his big, beaded black eyes that gleamed with hope.

"What is it pest, be out with it," demanded Ranthor.

"You won't believe me when I say it, but I have found the river that you are looking for. Now I know this is not a small feat and I expect my fees to be higher. But..." He was interrupted by Ranthor's fist clenched around his throat, tightening around it.

"Listen you imbecile, I have no time to humor you. Either you show me this place, or I end your life here. And if I find that you are lying, then I will show you no mercy at all. Do you understand?" Shouted Ranthor.

Ooger nodded obediently and led Ranthor all the way to where he found the lake. They climbed to it and Ranthor found, to his surprise, that this place did indeed fit the description. He scanned it with his eyes in search for any clues that may help his search. There wasn't anything to be found. It seemed like a useless search. But how could it be? This place was exactly like the one the letter talked about and the one described in the rune. This seemed like a dead end. This was not the time to despair. He has already gone a long way to find these jewels. He was not going to ruin what might be his only chance at finding absolution just because he can't find anything. He had to search this place thoroughly. It is practically the only lake in this damned cave. All the traces lead to it. He couldn't help feeling frustrated. And he couldn't blame Ooger either. He was truly trying to help. Although he regrets to say it, Ooger is the only friend that he has left ever since the attack of his troops. Strangely enough, that made him feel relieved.

They were both searching the place around the lake for any sign of anything strange that might help them. Anything that is out of place that might be interpreted as a clue. The place was abandoned; nothing in it could help them in any way. They decided to head back to their camp site and try to think this thing through. Night was approaching and they were both exhausted from the search. Ranthor needed to examine the passage written in that letter and cross check with the story in the rune. They're bound to have something in common. Maybe he can find something hidden in them. People who usually leave trails are bound to hide them in plain sight. It must have something obvious that he missed in his search. Examining all the information he had so far will shed some light to the whereabouts of these jewels. He kept search for any hidden meaning within these words but unfortunately, he did not find anything. Eventually, he had to give in to sleep and rest for the night. It was around 3 am when he finally yielded.

He woke up the next day with the same thoughts that were haunting his mind last night. He had to find the meaning of the words in the passage in the letter. How would the river show him his past, present and future? Where is this river's origin that will lead him to all this? All of these writings talk about one single thing, illumination is the key. He always thought it was some figurative term referring to the fact that he had to find his own path. Maybe its meaning is more literal? It seemed that in the previous searches, light has aided him in finding this part of the cave. It might also lead him to the river's origin. But where would light shine in that place, which was in the midst of all that darkness. He tried to search his mind for anything that he may have seen the previous night that would point towards something. It seemed that the further he searched for an answer, the further he was from finding the answer. Out of all the riddles that he had tackled, this was by far the most difficult. He was out of ideas for the time being. Maybe if he searched the site where the river once flowed, he might find his answer there. He picked up his gear and left for the place and Ooger, seeing

Ranthor leaving, followed suit. They arrived at the place and quickly began searching the area. The place was just as barren and empty as they left it the night before. It was very unlikely that they would find anything here. Yet, they were both adamant and did not leave any rock unturned. Ooger was not feeling well. His stomach was rumbling. He did not eat last night because he spent most of the day looking for Ranthor. He had left his food in the camp, and he decided that he had to go and get it. It was unbearable to withstand all this hunger. He left Ranthor's company for the camp.

Ooger tried to retrace all the steps to the camp site, but he was still very confused from the hunger. As he was heading back to the camp, he noticed that the trail that he had taken bifurcated. He did not know which way to take. He decided to take the one on the left after much thinking. He thought this area seemed familiar, so he continued on that trail. As he was walking, he was hearing a faint voice that came from the end of the pass. The voice grew with every step that he took towards it. At first it sounded muffled but soon the voice sounded more like that of a humanoid. It was angry and this was clearly evident to Ooger because it became much louder now, as if it was issuing a warning to someone. When he finally reached, there was no one there but he could still hear the voice and he was able to make out the words now.

"Why do you disturb my sleep travelers, you have angered the souls that dwell in this cave. We have come before you and we hold claim of the river that flows here. What you seek is long gone. There is nothing for you here in this place. Leave now or you will suffer our wrath!" Shrieked the voice.

"W-who are you?" Stammered Ooger, who at this point just wanted to flee the place.

"I am King Aldor, my family used to live in this place after we have been cast away from our home planet. We have been the victims of vengeance from those who were once our slaves. We have fled our home only to killed by another poison, this blasted river took away from me my wife and children and left me, a wandering spirit to ward off any unwanted presence from these caves. Alas, I cannot not do anything now. Nothing will bring them back," said King Aldor who was weeping now.

"Well, perhaps you could at least help us with one thing. My friend, see, he is trying to find the jewels of Nebula and he is having trouble finding the river's origin. It will help him a lot if you could lead us to where it is," replied Ooger.

"Why should I help you with anything? This river only brought me sadness and sorrow. If I help you find where it started, then it will only prolong my misery. However, maybe you can help me lift this curse that has been cast on me. If you can do that, then I might be able help you with your little predicament. I might even recall where this place is," answered the king.

"We will aid with whatever you ask of us. Rest assured we will lift this curse from you, but you have to give us your assurance that you will indeed help us in finding this place. So will you do that?" asked Ooger.

"That depends on you. I will keep my part of the bargain, if you do too," said Aldor.

When the voice finally faded away, Ooger felt relieved. He was extremely afraid of King Aldor and was surprised that he was composed and had managed to bargain with this evidently angry spirit. After he recovered from his surprise, he realized he still had to tell Ranthor of his discovery. He was still there in that empty basin where he found him, looking for clues. As soon as he arrived at the place, he told Ranthor of what the spirit told him. Ranthor was suspicious about this new spirit that had appeared out of nowhere. He had to be careful how to approach it. What benefit would it get from helping them? If it is this king that the story in the tablet mentioned indeed. This could be some imposter trying to lead them on to an ambush. It may even be their pursuer. He needed to tread with care in this place. There is more to it than raving spirits looking for salvation. Ooger may be quick to believe the story of a king that wanted to be at peace with himself, but Ranthor was not gullible. He knew what it was like to be led into an ambush and he was not going to let that happen to him again. He managed to leave unscathed last time. Who knew what was in store for him this time?

Ranthor followed Ooger to the place where he had last seen the spirit. They both waited there for something to happen. If what Ooger said is true, Ranthor thought, then this elusive point that they have been trying to locate would soon be within their reach. The wait was long, and it seemed like this fabled spirit was not going to show up. Then out of nowhere, a thunderous voice began speaking. The words were not clear in the beginning but then they took on human form and it was clear that he was addressing them.

"So, travelers, have we reached a settlement? Are you going to help with my quest to rid myself of this curse? If not, then be gone or I will unleash my wrath upon you," said Aldor in rage.

"Even if what you say is true, we don't even know how to lift this curse off you. How do you propose we begin?" Answered Ranthor with a hint of sarcasm in his voice.

"The answer lies in the lake, beyond where the river was. In it, you will find a chalice. I used to use it when I drank from the river. It was a ritual of sorts that a wise man once told me is needed to cure my family and I from our ailment. After I had passed away, it sank in the depths of the lake. I need you to recover it for me and perform the ritual. But do not drink it as the water in the lake is as lethal as it was when it took my life. I need you to draw a circle around this place. It is here where I will materialize and then I will guide you to what you seek the most," replied Aldor.

"Fine, we agree to your terms. But if you double cross us, trust me, my retribution will be swift and merciless," warned him Ranthor.

Ranthor headed immediately to the lake, sparing no time to wonder whether this 'spirit' was telling them the truth. If there was any chance of finding the place, then he would follow any trail no matter how dangerous it was. No matter how perilous the road this spirit may lead him to, it was worth trying if it meant that he would be at least a step closer to finding the jewels of Nebula and forsake this miserable life that he has been living all these years. Meanwhile, Ooger was finding it incredibly difficult to keep pace with Ranthor. His legs were too short to keep up with Ranthor's long strides. He was already out of breath midway. Ranthor had noticed it too, but he couldn't stop now. He had to know if this king was being honest with them or not. Ooger was doing all his best to keep up. He was glad when they finally reached the place. His face was blue, and he breathed heavily. He was also scared that they were being led to the edge of the abyss, but he was powerless against Ranthor's unending determination.

They reached the lake at last. They were both very exhausted, but Ranthor was determined not to show any signs of fatigue to his friend. His goal was to find this chalice. As soon as he arrived, he removed his coat and plunged into the cold water in search of the chalice. Ooger was very surprised that Ranthor just jumped into the water without any second thought. As soon as he recovered from his sudden shock, he tried to locate him in the water. The lake was murky, and it was extremely difficult to see anything from the surface. Ooger was scared for his friend. Who knew what the water may do to him? Even though he did not drink from it, what if the mere contact with this poisoned water may be lethal in itself? But he could not know that for sure, only time will tell. He was just hoping that his friend will come out alive.

Ranthor, in the meantime, was finding it difficult to locate anything in the lake. The water was so cloudy that it was blinding his eyes. Something else also felt weird with the water. He was experiencing visions while he was in the lake. There was this one scene that was playing in his mind. At first, the place was blurred but then, gradually, it took on form. He saw his old palace, with his father on his throne. He was there too!! This lake was showing him old memories. What purpose would this serve? He did not need to be reminded of his failure. The scene is always being playing in his mind, day by day he would reminisce on times where he was once feared. Soon, soon this will be a reality once again.

The scene shifted now. It was showing him being led in chains, brought into the palace for questioning. His father's face was red with anger, his rage knew no boundaries. Yet, he saw something that he didn't notice before. In the midst of all that anger and frustration, he saw a father that was looking at his son with grieving eyes, knowing that he must banish his only son to the far reaches of the universe. He never saw his father this concerned, even in the days when he used to rule by his side. At that moment, he felt that all that resentment that he felt towards him had evaporated. He wanted to meet him again so that he can explain to him that it wasn't his fault that their war was lost. But would he believe him though? Years had passed since the incident, if his father had any compassion towards him, it would have been lost. For all he knew, his son was dead; he ceased to exist for him. He would have been over him by now.

He finally woke up from the memory. It seemed that a long time had elapsed since he had jumped into the lake. He was still breathing though. Did he hold his breath for all that time? It was almost as if time had stopped. This lake was playing tricks with him, and he didn't like that. He wasn't accustomed to being anyone's prey. If King Aldor had sent him on a fool's errand, then he will surely pay for this. There was no sign of the chalice. He knew it; this blasted thing did not even exist. The lake started bubbling and frothing, *that's strange*, thought Ranthor. Another vision started materializing. This time, he did not leave the lake. A light shot through the water and the cloudiness that enshrouded it began to fade away and disappear. He could clearly see Ooger now. He was sitting there alone, tossing a few pebbles at the lake. He looked concerned. Ooger was looking at the water, waiting for Ranthor to ascend to the surface with the chalice. Ranthor looked at him, wondering why he couldn't see him now that there was light shining through the lake. He was beginning to wander if this was light, or an image created by the lake to distract him from finding his goal. What was the source of these illusions though? What was creating all these visions? Unfortunately, he could not answer all of these questions. This only made him feel uneasy. These visions were not random. Someone is watching him and has been doing so ever since he left the space port of Nebula. After he would find this chalice, which he was almost convinced that it does not exist, he will make it his business to find out who is tracking him. They may even lead him to where the jewels are hidden.

Ooger was immersed in the new hobby he made for himself. There seemed to be no shortage of pebbles near the lake. It was getting late and Ranthor did not resurface yet. Ooger was wondering how he survived all this long underwater. Then he remembered that Ranthor's people had accessory gills and can breathe underwater. They have both sets of breathing apparatuses; this has always been an advantage for them. They did not only conquer nations that lived on land, but their kingdom also spanned many oceans in galaxies far away. That was not Ooger's focus on the time being. Ranthor's triumphs are not important now. Who knew what his friend was facing down there? The fact that he did not hear anything from him was not reassuring. He found it strange that Ranthor did not emerge with the chalice already. The lake was small and Ranthor is a skilled tracker. This is supposed to be an easy job, unless this chalice was not there. He was wrong to trust that spirit. He may have put his friend's life in jeopardy just because he was so eager to help. If he remained in the lake any longer, then he would jump after him. It was dangerous, he knew that, but he got them into this predicament, and he had to get them out of it.

The air around the lake was strange. It was ominous as if it indicated some hidden danger about to come. Ranthor did not yet emerge from the lake and night was already upon them. *What is taking him so long*, wondered Ooger? He wanted to swim after him but was afraid. Unlike Ranthor's people, his race tended to avoid the water. Although they were surrounded by seas, they lived closer to land, and they hardly even looked towards the sea. He was caught between helping his friend and his fear of water. He wondered what Ranthor was doing at this time. Little did he know that the lake was showing his friend yet another vision.

Ranthor was struggling now to find balance. The lake started bubbling violently and he was caught in the middle. *I guess it's time for another vision,* mused Ranthor. This time the vision was different. The setting was unfamiliar to him. He wasn't in any place in particular. Was he floating in the sky? He was flying in the night's sky, looking down at the world below. This was strange, what would this vision show him? Suddenly, another figure appeared out of thin air. He had a long grey beard and wore a crown made of emerald. He was tall and strongly built yet he looked very old. When he spoke, his voice was deep and bellowing.

"Welcome Ranthor to my realm. I am King Aldor. I thank you for meeting me here. I apologize that I wasn't entirely honest with you. There is no chalice in this lake. I only wanted to test if you were the right person for the task of finding the jewels. They are an object of tremendous power and if they fell in the wrong hands, they would wreak havoc to the universe. Alas, your journey is still far from over. It has only begun. I have every faith that you will protect us. I will reveal to you where you have to look for the next clue. Follow the trail that I have set for you. The light will not fail you," said Aldor, and with that he disappeared. He burst into many tiny specks of light.

Ranthor awoke from the vision. As soon as he woke up, the lake began forming many small whirlpools. Eventually, all of them coalesced into one huge whirlpool and the water was sucked into the bottom of the earth. It was almost as if had just disappeared from there. In its place emerged a staircase cast from the rocks in the cave. Ranthor was too shocked to say anything. Ooger noticed that too and he too stood still as a statue, watching in awe as this secret passage revealed itself. They both realized what they had to do next. The way was shown to them by the spirit. They only had to walk through the path. They were more than glad to leave this cave. They longed for fresh air and freedom. Besides, they didn't notice it at the time, but they already ate through most of their supplies, and it was time to restock. It only became apparent to them when they felt their stomachs rumbling. They were in that lake for almost a day and Ooger's stomach was protesting. He could not walk another step without eating anything. They had already left the cave. They left the mountain and were near some meadow. They stopped and sat in the grass. Ooger unpacked the food satchel and took out whatever was left from the supplies. There were a few bread loaves left. They ate through them like ravenous crows. They left the meadow to find a place to set camp for the night. It wasn't difficult to find a warm place. It was not very cold tonight. They found a few twigs and lit a small campfire. They both slept soundly. They were equally exhausted and as soon as they hit the bed, they embraced sleep's welcoming hands.

Chapter 3
The Unwelcomed Visitor

Ranthor and Ooger were sleeping soundly in the warmth of the campfire. They were so tired that even if a barge vessel, with its deafening sirens, passed by them they wouldn't even flinch. They were easy targets for any marauder and thief within sight and there were plenty of them lurking nearby. Alas, it would be disappointing for any thief to rob them in this state as they had nothing worth stealing. They barely had enough food to last the night. Stealing from them would be a fool's errand. And there were many fools around this place. One of them was approaching the camp site. Her movements were as sleek as a fox. She moved around without making a sound, not even a single twig snapped. Even the leaves were not rustling as if the wind stopped and submitted itself to her. Nature had been bent to her will. She came very close to Ranthor so much that she could smell his breath which was tainted with the smell of stale bread and port wine. She grabbed him from behind and before he could move his hands, she tied both of them and stuffed a cloth inside his mouth and tied it too. It was Ooger's turn next. Both were subdued easily with not a single sign of struggle. She rummaged through their belongings looking for anything of value. She was disappointed to find nothing.

The mysterious assailant was cursing her luck. She shouted all kinds of profanities in multiple languages. Ranthor could understand only a few of them and that didn't in any way help him identify her identity. She wore a veil around her face so that her eyes could be seen. She had big almond shaped hazel-colored eyes with big eyelashes that beat wildly and defiantly. She had a lean and attractive figure. It wasn't only Ranthor's body that was subdued. His heartbeat with a different cadence. The beats were increasing in crescendo. He was in shock that he was feeling that way towards his captor, but he could not help it. It was tugging at him with a force so powerful that it seemed the ropes tied to him would cut into his flesh if he pushed any further. His thoughts were racing thinking of how to escape but at the same time he didn't want to escape this feeling. She must have felt it too because she was approaching him too, blade in hand. With one swift motion she cut the rope tied to his mouth and removed the cloth she gagged him with and held him by the mouth. When she released him, the first thing he asked was, "Who the hell do you think you are to capture us like this?" Shouted Ranthor in rage.

"You were easy prey. Capturing you was really easy considering that you didn't even put up a fight. It is almost humiliating to capture you like that," answered the stranger in a matter-of-fact tone.

"You took advantage of the fact that we were fatigued from previous battles to attack us. That is too low even for a lowly bandit such as yourself," said Ranthor.

"Even now when you have every opportunity to attack me you lower your guard for me. I am intrigued as to why you are doing that. You don't look like any of the weary travelers I usually attack," challenged the stranger.

Truth be told, neither did Ranthor. A force much bigger and more powerful than him was pulling him down. He was at a loss for words and the veiled stranger could clearly see that. He could have easily escaped given the chance to do so. Yet there he was staring at her eyes. Those big intoxicating eyes lured him in and he was sinking deep into the well of lust. Ooger could see that his partner was lost, and he barely stifled his laugh. Who knew a brute like Ranthor could fall in love? Well miracles happen even in this sodden part of the world. I guess that started to make Ooger a believer. He was looking at his friend in astonishment wondering if he should be afraid or happy for him.

Ranthor quickly awoke from his stupor and was working to untie himself and his tiny friend from their shackles. Meanwhile, the stranger was busy scanning the perimeter for signs of other thieves that might try to snatch her victims from her. Each time she would look back and make sure that Ranthor did not escape from his bonds. She did not pay the slightest attention to Ooger. It was as if the ropes she tied Ranthor with symbolized some other bond. She could have killed them as soon as she had found nothing on them. That's what she used to do to all her other victims. Were these two somehow different? She sensed that they were sitting on a big secret, one that could ensure incredible wealth for her. She decided to bargain with them but before she could find a chance to do that, they had already freed themselves and this time they pointed at her neck.

"So now that the tides have changed, do you wish to say anything to us? Or do all your 'easy prey' do that to you," sneered Ranthor.

"I could help you; you know with whatever you are looking for. I am an excellent scout and I certainly know the area better than anyone around these parts," replied the bandit.

"What makes you think we can't do on our own? And besides I am sure we can trust someone that tied us like livestock and threatened us with a knife," said Ooger angrily.

"Well, it could make our lives easier if we had a guide. Even if she tries anything on us, we will stick a knife behind her back. Backstab the backstabber so to speak," answered Ranthor.

"That's a fair deal," said the bandit.

"You are going to get us killed or worse you buffoon," said Ooger in rage.

"In order to trust we must first know your name," said Ranthor, ignoring his partner completely.

"My name is Kendra. Follow me," answered Kendra.

"Lover boy has lost it," said Ooger under his breath.

That last remark got him a violent kick in the back. He was swearing angrily at Ranthor. They strode along to the nearest town. Ranthor was wary of this mysterious woman, but his instinct told him that she won't cause them any further trouble. But then again, he wasn't sure of anything anymore. The predictability that surrounded him before ended when he was removed as prince. Although he left that life behind him a lifetime ago, he still aches for it again. He was born a ruler and he would see to it that he dies as one and that means risking everything, he had even his life.

They arrived at the town after two long hours of walking; they were tired, thirsty, and sleepy. As soon as they arrived, they went to find a nearby inn to rest and regain energy. The inn wasn't difficult to find as there were many in town. They settled in and booked two rooms, one for Ranthor and Ooger, the other for Kendra. The room was simple with two beds, a bedside lamp and a glass-paneled window. They slept until dusk when they were woken up by a barrage of gun fire that was coming outside the town hall. Kendra was the first to wake up. The others followed suit and soon they found themselves in the middle of town hall where half a dozen people lay there dead. The killer already left the scene of the crime and law enforcement just arrived at the scene of the crime. They were trying to prevent the pile-up of curious citizens who were gathering there to view what happened. Many were asking questions, but no one offered any answers. From the looks of it, it appeared to be a simple robbery as the deceased were richly dressed and adorned with all kinds of expensive jewelry. Still, something didn't feel right about all this, thought Ranthor. *Why would the killer kill all these victims in public let alone leave most of their belongings intact?* If they indeed were thieves, then these people would have been stripped bare of any valuable items they had. One of the victim's family members told the police that a key was stolen from one of his relatives.

This sounded very peculiar to all of them, and Kendra suggested that this might be a clue. They decided to follow the trail. Who knew where it would lead them? Ranthor didn't even know how exactly it could lead to them to the jewels but it's as good a clue as any. He only told Kendra a few things about the jewels, only that it was a family heirloom and he needed it so that his father could forgive him for losing them. It was too soon for him to trust her yet. She proved to be a lot of help so far as she managed to bargain some of their belongings for food and drink that would last for at least a month. She also managed to lift the assailant's prints which led to the plains south of town. They headed in that direction where they found an abandoned house. Ooger was feeling suspicious, Kendra proved to be too useful to them. The fact that she knew everything that was happening at the time that it was happening was too ideal for his taste. Hopefully this would not be an ambush. He prayed to all the gods he knew that they would not be killed on this day.

They finally entered the house. The doors creaked and groaned as they were opened, *This place must be very old*, thought Ranthor. Who knew when it was last inhabited by living hosts? Even the spirits tread carefully around these parts. Rumors say that the grounds around this house were used as mass execution sites for convicted criminals. People still believe that their spirits still roam the place in search of victims to haunt. They say the desire to kill stays with you even beyond the grave. It is in this that they find their everlasting peace. But Ranthor was never a believer and these stories never seemed to bother him. He only cared about matters of the material world. He was a bounty hunter and not a mystic in search of spirits. They counted their steps as they walked around the house. Both of them looked for signs of the killer. Kendra walked straight as if she had no fear in the world. She had her head held up high as if she had not a care in the world. The place was very quiet. This was a very bad omen. The only sound that came out was the groans of the decaying floorboard that looks like it had seen better days. Ooger wondered why anyone would build a house far away from any sign of civilization. Maybe it belonged to a writer looking for a quiet retreat away from people or a hermit trying to isolate himself from the pleasures of the world trying to live a life of simplicity and serenity.

They opened the door to one of the rooms. It appeared to be a child's room as it had a crib and many toys. Eerily enough, there was a song being played in the background. It was a lullaby that was coming from one of the toys. It was set to play continuously. That was odd because no one turned it off which meant whoever turned it on either had left the place abruptly or had been killed. It didn't seem to be the latter as there weren't any signs of murder, no corpse or at least the bones of the victims. They looked around the room for any clue. They found a letter in the child's crib. It was apparently addressed to the child, probably from the parents.

Dearest Gideon,

We're sorry to have to leave you my precious child. We apologize to have left you alone my dearest as we can no longer provide for you. We hoped that someday a kind stranger will find you and take you in their arms to raise you as their own. At least then you would not starve. We have left to a place far away in search of work so that we can one day take you back my sweet angel. Your father and I hope that one day you will find it in your heart to forgive us as we were left with no other choice. My heart aches as a piece of it was stripped off from it. It waits for the day where it will reunite with its lost piece as do I. I am sure that you will come back to this house again and once this letter finds you, we hope that you try to find us. The town we live in is two hundred leagues north of this house. It is a farming town.

Love,
Mother

"I wonder where this child, Gideon, has left off to? Where do we suppose we find him?" Asked Ranthor.

"It beats me. I haven't heard of the name before. It is not common to our town as there is no citizen by that name," replied Kendra.

"We will have to look for other clues that might tell us where he lives," added Ooger.

There were looking around the house for clues but there wasn't anything of value there. If there was, it would have probably been taken by the person who adopted the child. There weren't even holo-images of the child anywhere in the nursery to give them a clue as to how he would look like. Besides even if there were any who knew how many years had passed since the time the parents left him. They were at a dead end.

Just as they were about to lose hope Kendra stumbled upon something in the parents' room. It looked like a locket of some sorts. When they opened it, it displayed a holo-picture of the child. He appeared to be around 2 years old with dark brown eyes and ginger colored hair that measured till his shoulders. He had a pink complexion with a few freckles. He seemed sad in the photo as if he knew the fate that was written for him. The locket was a little bit rusty which suggested that it was a bit old. It could have at least been around for 30 years. This meant that the child in the photo must be in their early to mid-thirties. Ranthor wondered if he had ever visited the house but that didn't seem very likely as the place didn't look like it was inhabited by anyone for a really long time.

They all stood in the middle of the living room trying to take in all the pieces of information that they had gathered. Everyone seemed lost in their own world. It didn't seem apparent how the search for this mysterious child would help any of them with their quest but somehow things were usually linked together. They were all weaved into the seams of the universe that connected this motley group. Still, even though no one said anything, they were all afraid that this little expedition would lead them further away from their goal. They weren't sure if they were taking a step forward or a step back.

The first thing that Ranthor thought of was to go to town and ask people if they ever saw this child. They headed out to the town square to ask the locals. The streets weren't very busy. There were a few shops open but not many people seemed bothered about buying anything. It was a slow day, and it didn't seem likely that the market was picking up pace. The vendors themselves didn't seem interested in selling anything. Even the few shoppers that came to the stalls were not given any attention. Ranthor approached one of the souvenir shops and was asking the guy questions. He did not have a clue about the boy's identity, and even if he did it didn't look like he was interested in sharing any information.

They continued onwards with their search, interrogating every citizen in the hopes of getting an answer. No one seems to know the family or have interacted with them in any way, shape or form. They have gone as far as asking the village elders who did not have a clue about them. They then tried to ask the bakers, spice vendors, and pet shop owners to see if they would know about the whereabouts of this mysterious orphan child but, alas, to no avail.

Just as they were about to lose hope they were approached by a shrouded woman, wearing a purple silk veil. She claimed to have known the mother and that she was the boy's aunt. Her name was Aleoli. She was florist living at the far end of the street with her husband and four children. The parents had contacted her prior to leaving their home and made her and the husband the boy's godparents. Shortly after entrusting the boy to them, they left him in the trust of a local orphanage as they were also struck with poverty. They were barely providing for their own children.

The orphanage was located in meadow street, along the banks of the river tallow. She gave him the directions and told him that the boy must be around 13 years of age. His hair was as golden as the sun, had rosy cheeks, an olive complexion and had hazel eyes. He was 2 years old when had left their home. She also told him to ask for the orphan master named Torvus. The man was well into his sixties and glowed with kindness. He was the boy's current caretaker. She also gave him a locket with a photo of the child and his parents to help gaining his trust. He took it along with the letter and headed to meadow street.

It was to locate the orphanage, which was situated between an apothecary and a baker's shop. The front lawn was covered with gardenias and lilacs. It seemed like a very welcoming place. It was noon and by the time they had arrived the road was filled with buyers that were coming and going out of the shops next door.

They approached the orphanage door and Ranthor knocked on the brass handle. A creaking noise sounded, and the door was swung open. A kind old man welcomed them with his back hunched and with a warm smile. This was Torvus, who was very puzzled as to why they were asking about Gideon. He showed them into his office and offered them chamomile tea and raspberry-hibiscus biscuits. He listened very intently to their story and asked a series of questions.

"This is the first time someone came looking for Gideon. He was delivered to my doorstep in the middle of the night by a young couple. I took him into the orphanage and raised him for the past 11 years. He kept asking about his parents, and, alas, I did not know much about them to answer his questions," said Torvus.

"I talked to the boy's aunt, and she showed me this locket. I also have a letter from the child's parents explaining while they had to leave and their circumstances. Perhaps you could give it to him. It may also help him in getting the deed to their house, should he be interested in living in it," replied Ranthor.

He showed him both items and checked their authenticity. Torvus was quite astonished to discover them and was keen on showing them to the boy. Some of his questions would finally be answered. His eyes were shimmering with happiness, and he told his assistant to go and fetch Gideon. He hobbled at once and went searching for him in the courtyard. He came back ten minutes later with the boy. He looked just as his aunt had described.

He looked utterly bewildered and ambivalent about meeting these two new strangers who claimed to have some knowledge about his past. His face was guarded, and he approached them in a very cautious manner. At first, he kept listening to the conversation that went between his caretaker and the newcomers. He did not utter a word and kept observing them with keen eyes. Then he finally spoke to Ranthor.

"Could you please tell how this letter and locket came to your possession? This is the first time I've seen them," asked Gideon warily.

"I had retrieved this letter from your parents' house and in it they had mentioned your name. Then I went back to the town and asked about your whereabouts. They pointed me to your aunt's house, and she gave me the locket to hand over to you," replied Ranthor.

"I did not know that I still have family. Torvus, why did you not mention this to me before? And why did they never come look for me, after all these years? Did they think I was a burden to them?" Gideon asked in a very agitated manner.

"My dear I am as puzzled as you are. I did speak to your aunt, and she told me their financial situation was difficult. She had left in hurry and did not leave any contact details to trace them with. I did not wish to trouble you with this story as they were long gone and untraceable. I am very sorry that you had to find out like this," Torvus answered solemnly.

There was an air of tension clouding the room and neither the old man nor the others knew what to say. Gideon was reading the letter addressed to him, tears rolling from his cheeks. His face was as pale as snow and was shaking with anger. He felt very betrayed and was at a loss for words. But he felt somewhat relieved in knowing that his aunt lived close by and wanted to know answers regarding his family. He was excited to join Ranthor on his journey, provided they would first visit his aunt and learn more from her about his parents.

They both rode across the fields to the town center. Finally, they reached the aunt's house. Gideon met with his aunt, and he went inside. He had so many questions to ask and was not sure how to ask them. He was greeted by hugs and kisses from his aunt. She apologized for leaving him at the orphanage. She then recounted the story of how he ended up with them and why his parents had to leave town. She told him they were threatened by the local authorities. They were artifact collectors and they had recently stumbled upon rare jewels from one of their mining expeditions while on a trip to silver gorge, a mining town 50 miles from the town's center.

They had gone initially to find silver coins dating back to the mining era, which dated back to 700 years ago. It was rumored to be in silver gorge. They were very priceless, and many buyers and auctioneers were purchasing them for millions of Kruats.

They prepared for their journey and purchased maps of the mines. Their journey started in the mining town, and they had already set their camp. A local guide helped them maneuver the many traps set by the miners. Finally, they had reached the main cistern and were shocked to find the jewels. They had heard of the Nebula jewels of course but they thought it was the stuff of legends. There was barely any literature about them and most of the stories were from local folklore.

They had managed to keep them and were keen on showing them to the king or giving them to a museum. They left town and headed to the capital to meet with the king. However, their journey was halted by bandits in the planet Orion delta, their last location known was Silicon town. The planet was 20 million light years from them. It was littered with thieves, outcasts, and pardoned criminals. No one in their right minds would go there. Gideon's parents were captured while orbiting close to the planet.

However, these bandits were known to recruit their victims to serve them. That means that they were alive and could be reached. They left to the town center and prepared their ship to leave for Orion. They finally had a clue to find the Nebula jewels. Ranthor was beside himself with joy. He was one step closer to finding them. Kendra was scared of traversing that planet and expressed her concerns to Ranthor.

"How can we even be sure the jewels are there? For all we know, they already sold them and enslaved their captives. Besides, how can we be sure that they are still alive after all this time?" Asked Kendra nervously.

"This is our only lead and unless you have another brilliant alternative, we are headed there. You can leave using the pod if you don't feel comfortable. I am not forcing anyone to stay," snarled Ranthor angrily.

Everyone was quiet and Kendra finally agreed to go with them. They journeyed on. The suspense was palpable in the air. Everyone was tired and broken done from the last encounter. Ranthor mustered all the power he had and managed to find the easiest route to the planet. It would take them 2 days to reach the planet.

Gideon was glad to finally leave the orphanage. This was his first time outside the planet, and he was excited about the journey. He did not seem to mind the strange company he had ended up with and seemed to have made friends with Kendra. As they approached the planet his anxiety grew more and more knowing that he would finally meet his birth parents.

As they left the star system, their ship was hit by a barrage of ion guns from the Dicer ship fleet which came out of nowhere. Their hull was painted with red and white serpents, the emblem of the knights of Cravu, one of many soldiers under the employ of the planet Stratus, the nearest planet to them. The ships were circling them and there was no way of escaping them. They decided to stop and attempt communication with their leader via intercom.

"My name is Captain Salvado, leader of the nights of Cravu. You are trespassing on our territory, and I demand that contact your leader. Contact us at once or risk being vaporized by our ion cannons. If you are friends of ours, we will let you go," bellowed captain Salvado.

"My name is Ranthor. I am the leader of this expedition. Apologies for trespassing on your territory. We have not intended to come here but our travels have led us here on our way to planet Orion. We mean you no harm. Please let us go and we will do as you desire," answered Ranthor.

"I am afraid that we have to detain you and question you further. Our rulers will meet you and a council will decide your fate. We will escort you there at once. Please prepare to be boarded by our soldiers," stated the captain in a matter-of-fact tone.

The intercom stuttered and the captain ended his conversation and soon the soldiers boarded their ship. They were geared with Cruvian steel, their visors reading their vitals and their cold stare gazing upon them. The cadence of their boots with every approaching step sent chills down our heroes' spines. Each of these soldiers were towering at a 2-meter height. They clearly were not human, and they did not want to find what they were either.

No one dared to confront these strangers and they complied with their every command. Their ship was steered towards planet Stratus. The soldiers were pacing up and down searching the ships for evidence of weapons and contraband. They questioned all the passengers about their plans and their intentions. They did not find anything of value in the ship and were content. They informed Ranthor that after the search they were free to go back to their quest.

They finally reached the capital city of Narsea, and the ship was docked in the imperial hanger. They were driven to the royal palace and an appointment was made to meet with King Aldus Bane. He welcomed them into the ballroom, where he and his wife took them to the main study. She was very beautiful, dressed in silver and golden robes and a crown made of diamonds and white gold. The king wore a suit of adamantium armor and wore an equally splendid crown. He was quite interested in learning the story of our travelers.

"I am king Aldus Bane ruler of Stratus, and this is my wife Queen Caleiopi. We have summoned you here to determine your reason of travelling to our solar system. We require that you comply with our rules, and we shall be lenient with you," King Aldus spoke confidently.

"My name is Ranthor, and I am the leader of this group. We are traversing your system on our way to planet Orion. There is an object there that we desire. It was stolen from our friends, and we wish to recover it," answered Ranthor.

The king had a few more questions. He seemed to believe their story but was still pressing on with questions. He demanded to know more about this peculiar object and was not satisfied with Ranthor's answers.

"What is this object that you speak of? And most importantly, why is it so important that you would risk going to that dangerous planet in order to recover it?" He asked persistently.

"It is a relic that belongs to my father, dear king. A family heirloom that I wish to bring back. Jewels owned by my family for centuries," replied Ranthor.

The king was quite fascinated to learn of the existence of the Nebula jewels. He had learned about them years back from his advisors and wished to obtain them to gain an alliance with Ranthor's father. He agreed to let them go, provided that they take his advisors with him. Ranthor agreed and with that their shackles were removed.

Later that evening they dined with the king in his ballroom. The room was adorned with gold and silver statues. Many paintings and murals filled the hall gracing it. A beautiful mahogany table was laid out in the middle with seven golden chairs laid out. The king and his wife were at the head end of the table, dressed very elegantly. His advisor was on his right and the guests filled the other chairs.

The plates were laid out by the servants and entrees were brought to the table. Quail panache and veal cutlets were served. They were paired with Chablis wine brought in golden goblets and served to the guest in diamond crusted trays. Their napkins were folded like swans. The air was burning with incense and melancholic music was played by a harpist in the background.

The king was pleased to see his guests seated and amazed with the food. He thanked them for attending and welcomed them to his banquet. Ooger was gnawing away at the food, taking several cutlets in his mouth at once. Kendra ate slowly and was worried about poisoning. Gideon was talking to the advisor, Simeoni, and getting to know her better.

As they continued their conversations, the king leaned closer to Ranthor and started asking him about his father. He learned that Ranthor was no longer enjoying the company of his father and was living as a bounty hunter. He seemed sympathetic to his cause and assured him of his desire to help. By that time, the main course had arrived. The servants brought trays of pheasant steaks paired with gravy and cherry tomatoes. It was served with glasses of mead. Finally, dessert was brought. It was white chocolate souffle and blueberries.

The guests enjoyed their meal and were finally led to the study where they were talking to the king and queen. They then strolled on to the royal gardens and had tea there. The evening was drawing to a close and they were shown to their living quarters for the night.

Tomorrow, they would be embarking on their journey to Orion with their new friends. Kendra was not happy with this pairing. She was pacing her room nervously and was unable to sleep. Meanwhile, the others were fast asleep and comfortable. They were happy to receive the king's assistance and hoping it would help them with the difficulties that lay ahead. Still, it was strange to be offered help at seemingly minimal costs. Ranthor was also beginning to suspect that this might be a trap.

As they woke up early morning, they prepared their luggage for travel. They were leaving and thought they might be able to sneak unnoticed. Simeoni was already prepared to meet them by the gardens, much to their astonishment. She welcomed them and informed them that she will be the one to leave with them in search of the jewels.

She was joined by two guards who stood at the helm of the ship. Luggage, provisions and maps were being loaded onto it. They were astonished as to how quickly they were prepared. The ship was taking off and the coordinates were entered in preparation for their travel. Simeoni was also familiar with the local language of planet Orion, the terrain and the inhabitants of the bandits. She proved to be a valuable asset in their quest.

As they left the planet, they again were welcomed by the emptiness of space. And again, they were back on the jewels' trail. This time, the journey was much easier, and they did not run into any interruptions. They cruised through the planet system effortlessly, stopping only to refuel the ship and gather supplies.

They finally reached near the orbit of planet Orion, its surface looking very menacing. The outer rim was protected by dozens of pirate ships. All of them equipped with ion beam cannons and protected by many layers of armor that was ion beam proof. Aboard each ship was a war generals and pirates armed with the deadliest weapons. There was no easy way to get past them and get access to land on the surface of the planet.

They approached very cautiously and tried to stealthily get in. They noticed that the ships communicated with each other via four control towers scattered across the outer rim. They figured that if they disable them, then it would ease their passage without being spotted. The nearest was 2 kilometers to their right. They managed to reach it easily. Ranthor left the ship and entered the control tower.

He took out the first set of guards with his blaster and made his way to the tower's main computer. There, he was faced with a dozen pirates. However, he managed to defeat them with multiple blows of his sword and gain entry to the computer. Simeoni was by his side and managed to enter the mainframe. She then disabled the first tower, thereby blocking communication from the eastern part of the outer rim. They were now clear to move on to the next tower.

The next tower was placed centrally and was the most difficult to enter. It was protected by three pirate ships. They had managed to attack one of the pirate ships, however, the other two were alerted to their presence and were aiming at their ship. The first blow from their ion beam shook their hull and pierced through it. They managed to swerve from the remaining shots. Ooger found a weak spot at the tail end of the pirate ship. They targeted it and with one blow managed to gain entry to the ship. Ranthor and Gideon boarded the ship and took out the remaining pirates. The other ship managed to flee and join the remainder of the fleet.

They reached the second tower and once again it was dismantled. Similarly, the other two were shut down and they made their way to the surface of the planet.

The pirate ship reached the remainder of the fleet and alerted them to the presence of intruders. Ranthor turned on the cloaking device and began their descent towards the planet's surface. The pirates were circling the outer rim of the planet and attempting to restore the control towers. They had a few minutes to land before they would be discovered. They worked quickly to land the ship and landed quickly on the planet's surface.

They landed on Orion delta and were set out to start exploring. The area they landed on was a barren land. Ahead of them were a few pirate camps and in the center of town there was a tall bronze building—the headquarters of the pirate leader Amadeus. He was the most ruthless creature in this star system. His cruelty only matched by his unforgiving demeanor. None of the pirates dared throw a mutiny or protest to any of his rulings. He held public executions to show his soldiers that he was not to be held in contempt.

They managed to cross the pirate camps without being detected. There was no one in sight. This was strange, as the town was usually heavily guarded. This sent an eerie feeling down Ranthor's spine. He was not sure if this was just a coincidence, or an ambush had been set into place. As they continued to venture into town, he felt more and more suspicious. The others felt equally perturbed and were on the lookout for a patrol squad. Nothing was within sight, and so they continued on their journey and were planning to enter Amadeus's castle, hoping that there would be some clues as to the whereabouts of the jewels.

Finally, they reached castle and suddenly the drawbridge was opened for them. Everyone was feeling guarded and preparing for a possible attack. One of the pirates came out of the castle and headed in their direction. He was unarmed and was holding a key in his right hand. He was middle age, moderately built, and reeked of rum. His hair was greying, and his beard was neatly trimmed. He wore many rings on his fingers and walked with a limp.

"My name is Amadeus. Welcome to my humble abode dear strangers. To what to do I owe the pleasure of this visit?" Announced Amadeus.

"We come here in search of two travelers that came here 10 years ago. They were friends ours who were captured by your clan of bandits. I'm interested to find them and recover a priceless family heirloom that was stolen from them," replied Ranthor.

Amadeus gestured for them to enter the castle. They walked around gingerly, awaiting a sudden attack. He opened the doors and led them to the main hall. It was filled with priceless statues, paintings, and vases. The floor was covered with carpets made from the hides of every species imaginable. Chandeliers rose from the ceiling, gold, and silver spires surrounded the main castle. Music was playing in the courtyard, and a banquet was laid out for them in the main hall.

"Today you dine with me friends. I will tell you all about the travelers that came before you once you are settled and fed. For the time being, enjoy the wine and music. I hope that what we have to offer is pleasurable," said Amadeus jovially.

The servants started bringing trays of caviar and wine. Amadeus ate first, gesturing that the food was not poisoned. The others felt at ease and joined in. Candles were lit and the servants brought the remainder of the food. Assorted meats, pickled herring, and duck confit was laid out on the table. Dessert was served as well, a beautiful raspberry pecan tart which paired with an assortment of beverages. Everyone enjoyed the meal.

Shortly afterwards, they noticed that they were starting to get drowsy. The pirates managed to drag them and shackle them to the chains in the dungeon of the castle. Ranthor and the others were captured and there was nothing much that could be done. He finally woke up, groggy and disoriented. He just realized what had happened. He was boiling with raging and was hacking at the chains, trying to break free. Kendra soon woke up and realized what had happened to them. Her face was pale and ashen. The worst part was that they were stripped of their weapons and did not have any means of breaking out of these chains. Gideon was the last to wake up. He lay there motionless, looking bewildered and stunned.

When he finally woke up from his stupor, he realized that the pirates forgot to strip him clean of his possessions. He managed to get his pouch from his belt, and he found a small dagger. He managed to rotate it around the lock and pick it. He managed to free himself and the others. They escaped the dungeon and were making their way to the main castle. They managed to intercept the group of pirates guarding the dungeons and got hold of their weapons. They interrogated them thoroughly and found out that the pirate king's quarters were in the eastern spire. It was heavily guarded and if they crossed the main hall, they would be easily discovered.

They found a pathway through the courtyard that led to the eastern spire. It wasn't as heavily protected. Ranthor and Kendra single-handedly took the guards with their swords and paved a path to the spire. Just as they were about to enter their path was blocked by a large metallic wolf-like creature. The king had placed it there as a final protection mechanism. It was snarling at them menacingly and prepared its giant metallic claws for a fight.

It swung at Ranthor with its claw and managed to tear some flesh from his right arm. Blood gushed and experienced searing pain. He tore a cloth from his bag and made a torniquet to control the blood loss. He was starting to feel dizzy from the blood loss. However, his resolve was still strong, and he managed to unsheathe his sword and prepare for a fight. The hit did not pierce the metallic armor of this beast.

Kendra leapt and prepared to join the fight. She threw her mace at the wolf and managed to tear a hole in his armor. It started to howl and lunged at her. She ducked the attack and managed to get another attack which shattered the wolf's torso. It was leaking oil, writhing in agony, and feeling defeated. A final blow destroyed its skull and it lay there motionless. It was finally destroyed. Ranthor was semi-conscious at this point. He was starting to recover from his wound.

Gideon carried him on top of him and hauled across the hallway. They entered the eastern spire and were making their way on top of the stairs. This part of the castle was even more expensively furnished than the main hall. The windows were made from purple crystals, each window had statues on either side, and soldiers adorned in golden armor.

There were many rooms in the eastern spire. None of them knew which one was the king's room. At this point they were avoiding being detected. Simeoni guided them across the hallway and managed to find the room. It was the one at the end of the hallway. The crest of Amadeus hung on top of the room. They entered the chambers and made their way to Amadeus. He was sitting in the main study and was expecting them. He surrounded himself by pirate guards.

"Welcome to my spire. I was hoping that you would not kill Cerberus, I stole that wolf from the nights of Cravu. I relied on him to protect my spires and you were the only ones who escaped without being torn to shreds," bellowed Amadeus.

"We are tired of these games you keep playing with us. Tell us where my parents are at once or risk being killed. As you can see, we outnumber you. Surrender at once," screamed Gideon.

A battle broke between Gideon, Kendra, and the pirate guards of Amadeus. Swords were clashing with maces and the guards were being picked off one by one. They had put a fight and managed to injure Gideon and Kendra. Ranthor was still weak from the last fight and sat out this battle. He regretted not being able to fight these pirates. However, it looked that Gideon fared well and managed to keep them off.

Finally, they killed the last of the guards and were making their way to Amadeus. He fell at their feet and was begging for mercy. He told them that they could take anything they wanted as long as they spared his life. Trembling with fear, he did not know what to do. He took them to the inner chamber of his spire. He was finally willing to let them know what happened to Gideon's parents. There were many maps hung on the ceiling.

He explained to them that the travelers had managed to escape their captivity. They ran off with some of his maps. He tortured them thoroughly and managed to learn that they were looking for the jewels of Nebula.

"Wait, so you mean to say that they did not have the jewels in their possession? What a waste of time," shouted Ranthor.

"Not necessarily, their last coordinates and the maps they took led to planet Orion Theta. It is part of the same solar system. Perhaps we will find them there," Kendra reassured him.

They made their way out of the castle and managed to take Amadeus captive. He would be a valuable asset to them on this system. Ranthor entered the coordinates for planet Orion Theta, and they prepared their ship for ascent. Ammunitions and rations were stolen from the castle to aid them with their journey.

Gideon was glad that they have finally found a clue to his parent's whereabouts. Hopefully, this would not lead them on some wild goose chase. He was excited to meet his birth parents and learn more about them. He was deprived of this for 13 years and would finally reunite with them. He had a lot of questions to ask. Ranthor was excited to find the jewels and finally be back in his home planet. Once again, he would be heralded as prince and can finally live the life that he was destined to live.

Chapter 4
Orion's Hollow

They managed to leave the outer rim of Orion delta and were headed for the next planet in the solar system. The vastness of space surrounded them as they geared themselves for what lay ahead. Amadeus lay quiet in his cabin, contemplating his current situation and hoping he would be rescued by his guards. There was no sign of them, and he was unable to call for reinforcements. Finally, he decided to adjust to his current situation as there was nothing much to be done.

Ranthor was recovering slowly from his wounds, his conscious level improved and he managed to regain his strength. The others had also recovered and were sharing a meal. Ooger was fast asleep in his cabin. Kendra was talking to Gideon about their upcoming journey, discussing combat strategies and praising him on managing to help them with their previous mission. She told him that she too was an orphan and understood what it felt to be separated from family.

There were approaching planet Theta and the ship was being prepared for descent. The planet's toxic fumes of sulphur and methane shrouded its surface. Luckily, they came prepared with masks and oxygen cylinders for the journey. As they landed the ship, they noticed that its propeller caught on fire on contacting the poisonous fumes. However, they managed to land safely and were going to tackle this issue once they searched the planet.

There were no living creatures within sight. No flora or fauna within miles of their landing point could be seen. This was not surprising considering that the planet was not inhabitable by any species due to tis extreme living conditions. A settlement was seen at a distance. Gideon and Kendra rushed to find out who was living there. The others followed them cautiously and soon reached the nearby camp.

Unsurprisingly, they found it deserted. There was no campfire and no trace of any recent activity here. The tents were searched thoroughly and nothing of value could be found. Gideon managed to find a beaded purse in one of the tents. He searched its contents and managed to find another letter; the handwriting matched the one on the letter addressed to him. From the looks of it, the letter was recent. It described the location of some underground caves that the parents wished to explore. These were located in the western corner of the planet. The letter had the coordinates of this place and enclosed in it was a map.

They followed the map to the location of the caves. It was not difficult to find, and they managed to enter the underground cisterns. It was a very system of tunnels built by the first inhabitants of the planet. Prior to being filled with toxic fumes, this planet was a safe haven to many species of the galaxy. The brightest minds settled here and built their civilization. It was the hub of trade for this solar system, the center of research and machinery that created the latest inventions and gadgets. Soon, it succumbed to the toxic fumes from the factories. The citizens protested but the greed of their rulers and their decision to make more money blinded them. Eventually, no one survived, and the only relic of this once great civilization is this system of mines underneath the planet's surface.

The mines were still lit and did not look abandoned. Most of the machinery was still in good working condition. Ranthor was wondering if someone recently came here. There were also trails of footsteps which were estimated to be a few days old. It might belong to Gideon's parents. They decided to follow the trail of the footsteps and hoped that it would lead them to their goal.

The trail finally ended in the main cistern but there was no one to be found. The cave was deserted and there was no trace of any living creature. Gideon and Kendra continued to search for further clues, but they did not find anything meaningful. Whoever was here was good at hiding any evidence of their existence. The trails were wiped clean and there was no evidence of any camps set up.

Just as they were about to lose hope, they managed to find a room in the middle of the cave that was filled with mysterious artifacts. Many animal skeletons lay there, urns with runes written on them and several gold and silver coins that dated back 200 years ago. Everyone looked puzzled as to why these items lay hidden here. Amongst the rubble, a letter was found and was written in the same handwriting as the previous letter.

This letter oddly enough was addressed to Gideon. His parents are happy that he found their letters and urge him to venture further into the cave and find where have made their camp. Ooger picking the golden coins and hiding them in his bag and stuffed a few urns there as well. He was quite mesmerized with this room and when it time to go, he had to be forcefully removed in order to continue with the trail.

They went deeper into the cave and soon they reached an area with a subterranean pool of water. In the middle was a passage carved from rocks which led to the inner chamber of the cave. Through it a fire could be seen burning and the muffled voices of people talking could be heard. They followed that path to reach the inner chamber. Gideon's heart was pounding heavily in his chest. He was not able to contain his excitement. The others also wanted to know who these mysterious people were and most importantly what were they still doing in these caves.

They entered the chamber and found two people huddled by the campfire. They were thin built and malnourished. A man and a woman in their mid-thirties, tired and shivering lay in front of them. They looked at them, unsure what to say and terrified of these newcomers. They got up to their feet and it looked as if they were preparing to escape. Gideon approached them and wanted to talk. He raised his hand and reassured them that they meant them no harm. The two calmed down and sat back again in their places. At first, no one said anything, and the air was filled with silence. The tension kept building up until finally Gideon decided to end the silence.

"May I know who you two are please? My name is Gideon Erlin. I came here to search for my birth parents. They sent me a letter which led me to this place," said Gideon.

"Oh Gideon, I cannot believe that it is you. My name is Aelina Erlin and this Eodor. We are your parents and we have been living here in this cave for the past year. We were trapped here after fleeing from the pirates. They had found where we hid the jewels and we had to flee with them. Alas, they were captured though," replied Aelina.

Tears were flowing onto her cheeks. She embraced Gideon tightly and never let go of him. His father did the same. They apologized profusely for abandoning him and explained that it was for his safety. They were being hunted and had to leave him in the entrust of godparents to prevent any harm to him. Gideon had so many questions to ask them but there was no time to do so.

Ranthor interrupted him and wished to speak to them and learn about the recent location of the jewels. He was very anxious to find them and recover them. This was finally going to be his opportunity to get back in his father's good graces. He was ecstatic and besides himself with joy. His journey was coming to an end and he was regretting leaving the company he had made behind.

He asked about the last location of the jewels of Nebula. They told him that they had lost the jewels while leaving from Orion Delta. They had exchanged them for safe passage out of the planet and they now lay in the clutches of some local bandits around Orion's orbit. This is the last location they have seen him. His name was Dargus. He was the one of the most ruthless pirates ever to cross this solar system. No one dared cross his territory. He was also a known smuggler and helped people leave Orion undetected.

Aelina showed them the rest of the cave system and prepared living quarters for them to spend the night. She spent most of the day talking to her son, combing his hair, and making him any food he desired. They had so much to catch up with and very little time. Gideon was happy to see his parents and at the same time angry at them for leaving him alone. Even though he understood their reason for leaving him, he still felt overwhelming emotions towards them. He also wondered why they never tried to communicate with him all these years.

His father Eodor was also happy to meet his son. He was still shocked that they managed to find them and excited about this reunion. He had so much to tell his son of the adventures that they have had and the worlds they have seen. The first thing he wanted was to leave with his son out of this planet and back to their home, to establish their family and live happily again. He was planning on buying a big house with a farm and a pool. He had saved up money and the coming of his son was just the thing he needed in order to achieve that.

Kendra watched as this scene unfold and wondered about what would happen to their little group. Everyone was now searching for a different object and this was going to make things difficult. She needed to talk to both Ranthor and Gideon so that she can understand what is to happen next. She went over to Ranthor and talked to him to ascertain his next plan. He told her that they will meet with the bounty hunter and try to find the jewels. Afterwards, they will head back to Omnivora 1 to transport Gideon and his parents back home.

They went over to Eodor and informed him about their plan. He agreed to go with them and help gather the jewels. He knew the location of the bounty and gave them the coordinates for his ship. They left the caves and prepared for a journey back to the ship. They finally reached the ship by night-time and prepared to leave the planet. This journey to get the jewels proved to be very daunting and little did they know of the dangers that would befall them on the remainder of the journey.

They were already on their way to the ships orbiting Orion's space and Dargus's ship was within sight. It was surrounded by a dozen pirate ships circling it and protecting it. It was virtually impenetrable. Ranthor was thinking of a plan to penetrate through the fleet and gain access to the pirate leader's ship. He devised a way to access the ship's intercom system and command the pirates to leave the ship so that he can gain access.

He entered between the ships and attacked the first ship, managing to penetrate its shield and gain access to the computer's mainframe. Simeoni managed to gain access into the computer's mainframe and was able to command the intercom. He instructed the ship's commander to send a message to his fellow comrades to abandon their current post and intercept a possible invasion in Orion Delta. They followed suit and prepared to leave for the planet. The way was clearing up for them to access Dargus and communicate with him.

They powered through with full engine throttle. Finally managing to reach the ship and be able communicate with their commander. They asked for permission to board the ship and were granted access. Their weapons were holstered, and their swords were prepared for battle. Gideon was nervous about meeting this pirate leader. He was still not confident about direct contact and kept asking Kendra for advice. She assured him that he was excellent and offered to train him after the fight was over.

The ship's doors opened, and they entered it. They were welcomed in by two armed soldiers who ushered them into the control room where Dragus was patiently waiting for them. He didn't expect Ranthor at all and at first thought his commander came to debrief him on their latest update about the invasion of the Orion system. His blaster was ready at his hip and his sword was unsheathed. But first, he wanted to know what purpose brought these unlikely guests aboard his ship in the first place.

"What brings you to my ship? And why did you attack my commander and steal a ship from my fleet? I really do hope you have a good reason or else you I will be forced to gut you like the swine you are!" Asked Dragus angrily.

"We are here to retrieve the jewels of Nebula. The ones you stole from my friends over here and get them to back to their rightful owner. Give them to us and no harm shall befall you. Fail to do so and I am afraid I will have no other alternative but to kill you," answered Ranthor defiantly.

"I am afraid that I have already sold them to a wealthy traveler, he lives in planet Odelphius which is 2 million light years away. That is as far as I know. His name is Luther. He owns a chain of museums in the planet and wanted them for one of his exhibits. However, since you came here unannounced, I'm afraid I would have to get rid of you. Guards! Kill these intruders!" Dragus shouted furiously.

The guards swooped on them at once and were preparing their blasters to kill the intruders. Shots were fired everywhere. Kendra ducked just in time to avoid a ricochet of ion bolts. She managed to attack and kill one of the soldiers. He fell with one strike of her sword, and he lay there motionless. She managed to take hold of his blaster and began shooting at the remaining guards. Her aim was impeccable, and she managed to kill two other guards. Gideon and Simeoni took the remaining blasters and took a few other guards.

Now that the tide of battle had shifted in their favor, Ranthor felt less anxious and made his way to Dragus. He cut his way through the guards and made it to their leader. With one strike, he managed to slit his throat open and finish him off. He managed to steal a map from his pocket which contained the location of the museum. Apparently, Dragus was attempting to steal back the jewels and knew where they were hidden.

Kendra and the others left ship and were making their way back to their own vessel. They prepared to leave for Odelphius. The coordinates were entered into the computer and the ship sped through the solar system. Gideon was reading the map and felt like he had seen it somewhere before. Then he remembered that he had visited the museum before as part of a trip arranged by the orphanage. The museum of Space History was a well-known landmark in this solar system for its collection of rare ancient artifacts and magical runes.

He remembered being mesmerized by the many artifacts and paintings that adorned the walls of the museum. He was 8 years at the time and can still remember every smell, image, and emotion he had experienced that day. This place brought back so many memories of his childhood. And now he was going to make new memories there with his family. He was encouraged to visit the place and was going to show his parents the place he so much adored.

They reached the surface of the planet Odelphius, and they were making their descent. They landed in a nearby hangar 30 miles from the center of the city. Gideon started scouting the area and was followed by Ranthor and Kendra. Odelphius was known to be the metropolitan center of the solar system. It was the artistic and commercial capital and housed many humans as well humanoid species both residents and frequent guests. The museum was in the capital hub and was open most days of the week. Today was the busiest day of the year, considering that the coronation festival was being held this year for king Julius.

The streets are covered with carnations and roses are blooming in the nearby trees. Lights were hung on every street and golden red banister with the king's emblem were laid out on the streets. People were headed to the bakeries and buying sweets for the carnival. The children were out and playing with the games that were being set up in the festival. Music concerts were being held in the local square near the museum. The place was looking very cheerful and glee. Everyone was jovial and looked forward to this occasion every year.

The king usually came to the festival to start the event, surrounded by his entourage and the royal guard. He was going to hand out several awards to many of the distinguished dignitaries and ambassadors that helped maintaining the peace of his planet. People flew in from all around the galaxy to attend this prestigious event. Vendors were selling all sorts of foods, flowers, gadgets, and anything you could possibly think of. It was a chance for businesses to thrive and some of them made as profit to cover 6 consecutive months.

The crowds were teeming with excitement, and it was no longer difficult to contain it. They were waiting patiently for the king's arrival. Finally, the royal chariot arrived, and the king was welcomed with bouquets of roses and a golden scissor to cut the ribbon for the event.

The state senators and ambassadors trailed behind him dressed in their finest silk robes. They too came in majestic sport vehicles and were welcomed warmly by the welcoming committee. They were handed over an arrangement of flowers and a red carpet was laid out for them. The king made way to the center of the courtyard and prepared to make his speech to the citizens. He was dressed in full regalia and his crown was shimmering in the afternoon sun. He faced the crowds and was welcomed with a thunderous clap as he made his way to the stage in the center.

"Dearest citizens of Odelphius. I welcome you to our annual summer festival. Today we will be celebrating our distinguished senators and ambassadors for maintaining the peace of our beautiful planet. As you all know, war is being waged all around us in pursuit of power and glory. We are blessed to live in our little utopia oblivious to the terror of war and famine. Thank you all for attending today and showing your support to our noble statesmen. May the festival begin and may your days all be filled with peace," announced the king joyously.

The first event was the flower parade, which was being led by the town's maidens. They had arranged a beautiful arrangement of blue, gold, and red flowers. They marched into the center of town, and as they did doves were released from their cages. The trumpets blowed and the ambassadors were welcomed onto the stage in preparation to receive their awards.

People were cheering them on and were genuinely happy with the festivities. Ranthor was mesmerized by the scene and watched intently as each man was handed his or her award. He was reminded by similar events that happened back home and this brought tears to his eyes. He still continued to watch as the ceremony drew to a close. The man then left the stage and made their way to a banquet arranged by the king. Tables were laid out in a nearby lawn and the servants had arranged the food.

Ranthor and Gideon made their way close to observe what was happening. They visited the stalls and tried to get information from the vendors about the event. The king held these events annually to celebrate the coming of peace. It was one of the few times he let himself be seen by the public. His family ruled this planet for the past 300 years and the people seemed to like him. This year was important to him as it about reaffirming the people's faith in him. He too had learned about the whereabout of the jewels and wanted them for himself. However, the curator of the museum was refusing to hand them over to the crown.

King Julius was about to expand his control of the Orion system, and as soon as he did that, he would be an emperor. The jewels were fabled to hold great power and would be the key in establishing his control of that solar system. This coalition of politicians was helping him in fostering the relationships with neighboring planets in an attempt to rally them against Orion and gain control over them.

The lunch was going to be smoothly, and the king was forming many alliances. The ambassadors were interested learning about the jewels and each of was promised an improvement in status and wealth more than they had dreamed for. They swore allegiance to the king and were willing to do his bidding.

The award ceremony of the festival concluded, and the citizens were headed to the stalls to purchase the delicious baked goods famous in this part of the planet. Everyone was excited to have festival food and enjoy the carousel rides. There was also a firework show towards the evening that being put in place. Kendra went and bought barbeque meat for everyone. Gideon was enjoying this meal with his parents. He took them to various stalls and explained to them the history of the festival.

Gideon was excited to finally be with his parents, and most importantly, enjoying his favorite event of the year with them. They bought pretzels and went on a carousel ride by the riverbank. The others were also enjoying the festivities, and as they made their way to more stalls, they purchased more street food. Ranthor decided that this was a much welcome break from all the hardship they have endured on their journey. He spent the remainder of the day planning tomorrow's trip to the museum.

He gathered more information about the museum and its curator from the citizens. The museum was established over 6 years ago and held a vast collection of ancient runes and artifacts. It was the most visited building in the entire planet. Guests from all around and from all walks of life visited it on a daily basis. Every year the museum's curator holds an annual philanthropic event the night following the festival to celebrate the opening of a new wing in the museum. He had recently purchased a new set of runes, and as such prepared to launch his new wing to celebrate this new addition to his museum.

The king had promised to attend the event tomorrow and donate to his new wing. It was a gesture from the crown to support the culture and arts. It would strengthen his position with his allies, and most importantly, bring more prosperity to his rule. The event will be attended by many foreign rulers. It was a chance to socialize with them and build more alliances to expand his rule over this solar system. Julius was excited to find out what the curator bought. He asked for a private tour prior to the commencement of the event.

Ranthor was going to use this opportunity to meet with the curator of the museum and talk to him about the Nebula jewels. Perhaps he would be able to get them by making a lucrative deal with him. His father owned a lot of prized possessions, and he would give some to him in exchange for the jewels. He had planned to introduce himself to him and offer him his friendship and a possible meeting with his father to learn more about their kingdom.

Gideon was still exploring the festival with his parents and getting to know more about them. They were excited to see this part of his life and be introduced to his world, his interests and deepest desires. In the meantime, Kendra was also doing her fair share of exploration. She was in the western corner of the festival picking out roses. She wanted an audience with the king to discuss a few things. She was planning to meet him tomorrow at the museum event and introduce herself. She knew that after this journey was over that she will end up with little to do. Joining forces with Julius would help her gain a strong ally. One that could make all her dreams come true and bring her happiness and success.

The festival was about to conclude by the end of the evening. Fireworks were flying across the night sky and the children were mesmerized by the sight. Everyone clapped for the wonderful performance and welcomed the night. They were fed and happy, nothing could make this evening lose its sparkle. Today the rich and poor united to make this day wonderful for all. Children were singing and the birds were chirping. Everyone had put their differences aside and join forces to make the event memorable. This was the night that everyone kept speaking about and tomorrow the event would continue the festivities.

Kendra was making her way out the crowds and was meeting up with Gideon and his parents. She purchased dinner for everyone, and they were gleefully feasting in the gardens by the lake. Today everyone was talking and sharing stories about their life and their past. Gideon introduced his parents to Kendra, and they talked about their adventures reaching them. He told them about life in the orphanage. Now that they were reunited, they were never going to leave each other again. He dreamed about the kind of life he will have now with them and the new adventures he will experience.

The sun shined bright over the Odelphian sky, marking the starting of a new day. The birds were chirping, and the children were dancing and singing in the streets. Everyone prepared for today's museum function. New dresses and suits were steam pressed and readied to be worn. The men bought the tickets for the events and the women dressed in their finest dresses and adorned with the best jewelry. The houses were covered in gold and red banisters in preparation for the function welcoming the king.

Kendra and Gideon also dressed up in their outfits and prepared to interact with the people of this town. They wanted to know more about the curator. Kendra was going to the market to ask more about the event. She gathered some information about tonight's philanthropic function. It was for the instalment of a new wing to celebrate the ancient runes of Odelphius. They were discovered in a mine 200 kilometers from the center of town. The runes dated to at least 800 years according to known literature.

She also discovered that the king would be opening the new wing as a friendly gesture. He was also donating some ancient artifacts from his own treasury to the wing. The king's advisors were also invited to the event. A table was laid out in the middle of the hall and a red carpet was brought to welcome them. The event also attracted many foreign dignitaries from all over the galaxy. The guests were making they're onto the museum. The event was starting, and the museum's lights were turned. Banners were erected in front of the main entrance.

The king's chariot arrived at the center of the museum. He was welcomed by the curator of the museum. He headed to the museum's entrance and was shown around to the newest wing of the museum. A red ribbon was covering the entrance of the new wing. A set of ceremonial scissors were brought to commemorate the event. The king cut the ribbon and was preparing himself for a photo with the curator of the museum. He was welcomed into a private room where the curator was explaining the purpose of the new wing. There was presentation set up to explain the history of the runes, their origin, and the story they had to tell. The curator brought a sample of one of the runes to further help the king understand the importance of this new wing.

The town was all present at the opening ceremony of the museum's newest wing. They were making their way into the wing and admiring the newest additions to the museum. The runes were fascinating, and they had a lot of history to tell according to the plaques that were in front of the exhibits. All of them moved from one exhibit to the next and were admiring the paintings and murals next to the runes. The chandeliers were decorated and there were waiters serving entrees and champagne to guests.

It seemed as if the entire town was at the museum. They all dressed in their finest silk gowns and tuxedos. Everyone was enjoying the food and drinks, socializing with each other and discussing the new exhibit. They were fascinated by the newest collection of runes, paintings, and murals which lined the exhibit. The king was amazed by the exhibit and was brimming with joy. He was seated with the curator in his private quarters discussing the expansion of the museum and the possible purchase of another building for a new museum.

Ranthor waited for the curator to finish his private meeting with the king before attempting to contact him. He was headed into the center of the gala ball and prepared to make an entrance. The curator was talking to the ambassador of Orion and getting to know about their collection of ancient artifacts. He was planning to buy them to fill his new exhibit. A deal was struck between the two and the artifacts were going to arrive in a week's time. The curator was moving from one guest to the next and making small talk. He wanted to get their feedback about the new exhibit. The reviews made him happy, and he was teeming with pride.

Ranthor and Kendra finally managed to meet with the curator. They told him about their search for the jewels and their intention about buying them. He was not willing to separate with his prized jewels and informed them that they were not for sale. They increased the asking price, but he still did not budge. He told them that they were the main attraction in the museum and that losing them meant a decrease in the attendance of most the guests. The other artifacts were not as interesting to the visitors and most of the revenue was generated by the jewels.

The curator still honored their wish to see the jewels at least. He took them to the wing where they were situated. Ranthor was very excited to see the jewels again. He was at least going to see them. It was an answer to all his prayers. He did not know how to react when he saw the jewels. Gideon was also excited about this too. The jewels were a known fable back home and they were not seen for many years. They finally reached the exhibit and were shown into the central chamber where the jewels were housed. The curator opened the doors, and the room came into life. He ushered them into the room and was preparing the exhibit for them.

The lights shined on the jewels. It was a beautiful sight to behold. The jewels were glowing and shimmering as bright as sunlight. Ranthor was amazed by them and yet something seemed amiss. He remembered that they were slightly bigger than this and that their color was slightly different. The jewels he remembered were turquoise while these were emerald green. He asked the curator where had found them and he told it was in the mines of Orion Delta. They were placed there more than a century ago. These definitely were not the Nebula jewels. He was beside himself with fury.

Ranthor was pacing up and down the halls with rage. He did not know what to do at this point. They had just hit a dead end in their journey. He did not know even if there were any new leads to follow. Kendra came to comfort him and offer her support. She would try to find some information from the crowds in the museum. Surely, someone would know about the locations of the real jewels of Nebula. She asked whoever she could find but did not find any useful answers.

No one knew any useful information about the jewels. All the village elders did not know much about them and even the curator did not offer any new information.

They looked around in the museum hoping to find some information from the ancient artifacts and runes. Ooger was reading the writings on the artifacts but could not decipher much from them. He did find a rune that talked about ancient jewels though. It was said that they were somewhere near planet Talinus. However, their ship was not equipped to travel to that solar system. It would require new propellors to take them there. Luckily, there was a mechanic opposite the museum that could help upgrade their ship. They were planning to go to him tomorrow and fix the ship in preparation for travel.

For the time being, they enjoyed dining in the capital's finest cuisine and talking to the guest. Kendra was headed over to the king's quarters, but she was promptly stopped by the guards. They informed that the king did not wish to be disturbed. She would have to schedule an audience with him upon his return to the royal palace. She walked back over to her friends filled with dismay. However, there was a bigger task at hand, and she figured that helping acquire the jewel will bring her closer to Ranthor's father and possibly an invitation to the royal court.

They headed over to an inn nearby and called it a night. They woke next morning and made their journey to the repair shop. Gideon spoke to the owner and told him that they needed to upgrade their propellor in order to travel to planet Talinus. He agreed to help them for a small fee. He received his money and immediately started working on the ship. He told them the job would take at least 2 days to use the time and explore the town. Their first stop was by the riverbank where they had breakfast in a nearby patisserie. They enjoyed their food and from there they headed to the wrestling arena to see today's match.

Ranthor bid on one of the wrestlers and the odds were to his favor. His fighter managed to win the first 3 rounds consecutively and he gained 10 thousand kruats. He decided to stop and was content with watching the remainder of the competition. The others also were enjoying the show. Different humanoid species were fighting each other for the season cup. Each was hellbent on winning the competition and progressing into the next match. All of them were the most brutal fighters in the system. A few were local mercenaries, some pardoned prisoners, and few were professional fighters who grew old for other competitions.

It was time for the final match and people were getting out of their seats to see who was going to win the next match. Both of the contestants were returning champions. They were as big as boulders and from the way they walked just as bright. They had so many blows to the head and concussions it was surprising they could still walk upright and talk at the same time. The arena was packed with people who bet their life savings on this match.

Ranthor left the arena content with the money that he had earned from the match. It was already night by the time they had left. They walked to the nearest diner and grabbed dinner. Everyone ate a bison burger and chili fries. They ate heartily and enjoyed every bite of their meals. It was a welcome change from blasters and close encounters. They managed to get their much-needed break in their long and arduous journey. What was about to come was probably worse than anything they had faced. They still didn't gather anything useful about the jewels and were headed blindly into yet another chase.

Upon returning to the inn, everyone retired to their rooms and slept comfortably. Ranthor, however, was tossing and turning in his sheets knowing that their journey so far had been a complete and utter failure. He was afraid that the jewels were long lost and that he never will see his family again. The very idea scared, and he decided finally that it would be best to sleep and find out what tomorrow was going to offer. He didn't expect much.

He woke up restless at the break of dawn and made his way out of the inn before anyone woke up. He made his way to the river and decided to take a swim. The water was ice cold, and he nearly froze to death, but still he continued to swim. Back home swimming was always comforting for him and managed to clear his head and help him plan his invasions and strategic takeovers of other worlds. He gathered his thought and managed to plan for his next trip. He returned to the inn an hour later and decided to have breakfast.

The others were still fast asleep. Oblivious to what was going to happen to them next. But then again, none of them really had any stake in this wild adventure and they accompanied Ranthor merely for the sum of money he had offered them in exchange for helping him. Gideon had found his parents and Kendra was interested in the prospect of working in the royal palace. For them, the jewels were not as important to them and in fact they doubted their very existence.

Kendra was the first to wake up at 8 am. She walked over to the other and woke them up. Everyone got prepared and then headed to have breakfast. They were all surprised to see that Ranthor was already awake and not in his room. They searched for him, and they were told by the inn keeper that he was outside waiting for them. They had breakfast at the diner and then went to the gardens for a stroll. Today was somewhat quieter than the rest of the days. Afterwards, they decided to visit the garage. The ship was already fixed, and they were glad that they were finally going to leave the planet.

They prepared the coordinates for their trip to planet Talinus. They were very frustrated and hoped that we finally find some clues as to where the jewels were. They were all starting to think that they were just a hoax. All of them were on edge and tired from travelling planet to planet and find nothing. Gideon wanted to go back with his parents but finally decided to stay and help out with the mission. He was curious about it was going to unfold. His parents, however, had to return home and were given a pod to travel home. Before they left, they gave Gideon their permanent address and a key to the house. They told him that he was welcome to join them anytime. He could not wait till this adventure was over so that he can finally settle down with his parents and live the remainder of his childhood with them.

Chapter 5
A Warrior's Tomb

Ranthor was again welcomed by the emptiness of space. He did not know what was in store for him in this planet, and so far, his frustration was growing by the day. The crew soon became annoyed at his out outbursts. He apologized later and promised them that their reward would be a hefty one. This managed to settle the dispute between them for the time being. They too grew restless of this endless adventure and wanted to return back to their normal lives. The life of a space bandit was not well suited for them. Their travels so far were proof of this.

The journey to planet Talinus was going to take at least 3 days. It was very far from the current solar system, and they would have to stop in the middle to refuel. They made use of their time and decided to search the maps they had to pinpoint the possible location of the jewels. Everyone was hard at work at deciphering the runes. All of the evidence pointed to a small crater near the planet's surface. It held the first clue to finding the jewels. They marked the location and prepared the gear required for this part of the journey.

Gideon managed to set up a communication link with his parents and was updating them on the progress of their journey. He was at least happy that he could talk to them again. He spent most of the afternoon talking to them about preparing his room back at home. He told them about the posters of the famous bands he wants to hang. He also mentioned that they need to come with him to meet the orphanage caretaker and sign the papers to release him into their custody. They were happy that he wanted to come back to them. They did not know what to expect, especially that they had left him for several years.

Kendra was also pondering what to do when she would be back. She was thinking of the money that she would get and what would that mean for her. She decided to buy a nice home with it in Odelphius and maybe purchase a small shop and start an investigative business. She managed to gain a few ambassador friends on their previous journey and was planning to contact them as soon as this was over. Her last visit did not prove to be a total loss of effort. The connections that she had made would ensure a very luxurious life for her when she returned.

No one knew exactly what Ooger wanted, not even him. He probably planned on returning to his home and opening a business, a legal one this time. He would open a restaurant and try to recreate some of the food he had the pleasure of eating. Perhaps this would be his big break, and then later he would expand and open a chain of restaurants. He too was daydreaming about the rewards and how it would change his life.

As they ventured into the unknown, they were feeling more uncomfortable with their journey. They did not know what was in store for them next. As long as they avoided a clash with pirates, soldiers, or beast they were fine. Another fight was not something they were looking forward to. Half of them did not get involved in a fight prior to them joining this trip. Gideon had never even seen a sword. The caretaker of the orphanage taught them that violence was the way of cowards. He encouraged them to find inner peace and focus on helping one another achieve it. He managed to stock his orphanage with books so that the children will be well educated. He himself was a teacher, as were many of the faculty working with him.

Ranthor finally spoke and addressed everyone in the ship.

"Thank you all for helping with finding the jewels of Nebula. I understand that this has come at great personal cost and most of you are afraid of what it is to come. I will make to reward you for this, do not despair," spoke Ranthor confidently.

Everyone nodded in agreement, although none of them were very convinced. They finally managed to exit the Orion system and were headed into the next star system. They were approaching their goal. The first day has passed since they left Odelphius, and so far, everything was going smoothly. They were not intercepted by pirates or thieves. They could finally breathe knowing that they at least were not followed by anyone. Simeoni lay there quietly in her corner and was listening intently to the conversations that were held by other members of the crew.

She quietly slid back into her compartment and turned on her intercom device. She began speaking into it and updating her people about the progress they had made so far. Little did they know that she was planning to ambush

Ranthor and his friends as soon as they found the jewels. For now, she was biding her time and silently planning to take the jewels. She was a very skilled adversary, and she was more skilled at being at a double agent. The king understood this quality and utilized it to his advantage.

Gideon managed to leave his cabin just Simeoni exited hers. He managed to hear part of her intercom conversation and decided he would confront her. It's just that this was not the time for it. For all he knew, she was armed and would probably call for reinforcements. They could not afford an attack right now. Not when they were so close to achieving their dream. He decided that he will expose her in due time. However, he wanted to continue spying on her and learn about her plan so that when it came to foiling the plan, he would know what to do. He turned away just in time to avoid any suspicious glare from her.

Ranthor was leaning towards starboard and holding a drink in his hand. He was contemplating their current situation and preparing himself for the next step of the trip. He dreamed of this day for so long, and now it was finally coming to an end. He would finally realize his dream and be rid of this ridiculous way of living forever. Still, he wondered what would make him return to a father that abandoned him in his hour of need. Why should swear allegiance to someone who thought his worth was in his tactical prowess?

His life was so much better without the entourage and the attention. He enjoyed living a simple life and had gotten so much used to it. He also wondered if his father would recognize him after all this time. He found the entire encounter to be stressful and focused all his energy at finding the jewels. The rest would have to wait till later. The crew was his only priority at this moment and taking them to planet Talinus safely was crucial to this mission.

They had managed to cross yet another solar system. Planet Talinus was just a day's journey away now. The crew was exhausted from the journey and the fuel gauge was blinking red. It was time for a pit stop to refuel the ship, and most importantly, to have some decent food. Planet Zinzara was the nearest planet with a docking station. Refueling was possible now. They prepared for their descent into the planet's surface. The first thing they managed to do was get fuel for the ship. After that, they visited a nearby pub and managed to get some food.

The planet looked deserted. There was no living thing within reach. The crew was very suspicious at the lack of inhabitants. The only people they saw were the ones in the pub, and most of them were travelers from other planets. Kendra asked the bartender about the lack of people. He said that most of them were gone for the holidays. The planet was usually deserted this time of year. This was not a convincing excuse, so she decided to find out by herself.

The first thing she did was visit a nearby square, she managed to find a few people there and managed to talk to them. Apparently, most of the previous inhabitants did flee the planet due to the oppressive regime of their new sovereign. Most ended up as refugees at Odelphius and the remainder left to Talinus. Gideon came and told that they did not need to get involved in this drama. On that note, they decided to leave the planet and make their way to planet Talinus.

Gideon was glad that they left that awful planet. He did not trust any of the inhabitants and felt that most of them were bandits. They were lucky that none of them were robbed. Kendra was still perplexed as to why the current inhabitants were putting up with their ruler. She decided her first order of business after their mission was to liberate this miserable planet from their ruler. She did not stand tyranny, and she took a vow upon herself to rid the galaxy of all tyrants.

The ship was finally close to planet Talinu's orbit. They were able to see its faint silhouette in the distance. Ranthor was approaching the cockpit and preparing the landing sequence as soon as they reached. Gideon was relieved that they were close to achieving their objective. Kendra was looking out of the window at their next destination, she was fascinated by this planet. Her father once told her tales about his excavations in planet Talinus and various missions there while being in the king's service. The planet's rough terrain deterred most people from coming here. Little did they know that it contained a lot of rare earth metals and gems. All this fueled the industrial sector and provided for more than fifty percent of the jobs.

Ranthor entered the landing sequence and prepared to land the ship. Gideon was not feeling very comfortable about the expedition. Chills were running down his spine and he felt knots being tied in his stomach. He wished that could be back home with his parents. Although, he had already promised that he would be part of the journey. Just as they were making their descent, the ship was hit by a violent tempest and was swaying violently. Ranthor managed to steer them out of it, and avoid it careening into a certain death. His hands were visibly trembling, and he barely was able to control his apprehension. He finally managed to calm himself and turned the automatic landing feature of the ship. He reclined onto his chair and rested there comfortably.

The ship landed in a nearby deserted landing strip. Luckily, there was no one there to ambush them. They were at least relieved about this, but no one can be too cautious. Hence, Ranthor turned on the ship's cloaking device, therefore, effectively concealing the ship from any predator. They walked cautiously counting every step and burying any lead that could be traced.

The planet was packed with every species imaginable, and the roads were barely accessible. Speeders, racers, and big commercial ships were all making their way to their regular business routes. Everyone was in a hurry to make ends meet. They were all headed to the commercial center of the planet. Some ships even had inbuilt shops in them so that they could cater to people on the road. Some even had diners and bookstores that were fully equipped. It was home to a lot of thieves and pickpockets who made a living from scams and robberies.

Finally, they managed to reach the city center and were already looking for possible clues about the possible location of the jewels. Ranthor was questioning the vendors and the nearby citizens. As usual, they all denied any knowledge and insisted that it was just a myth. Some brushed him off and did not want to even interact with him. They feared the barrage of questions that would later follow from the troops patrolling the streets. Everything was censored in this city, and the king liked to keep an iron grip on his citizens. No one dared oppose his rulings.

The soldiers already were out and ready to inflict terror, emphasizing that the king was not to be trifled with. They closed one of the shops and arrested one of the citizens right in front of them. A few of his shirts were confiscated as they were deemed to incite rebellion. The shop owner was begging and pleading the soldier. He was convincing them that these were only inspirational phrases, and that he held the king in the highest regard. They did not listen to him, and instead beat him to pulp. They took him into their vehicle, battered and bruised. He was thin built and very frail.

Kendra was fuming with rage. Before she knew it, she felt an urge to march towards the soldiers and free the man. Ranthor took her hand and yanked her out of their way. He warned her that they needed not alert them to their presence. He did not need a full-scale upheaval before they even managed to get any useful information. He promised her that after they managed to find the jewels, they would do something about this situation. This ruthless ruler's days were numbered, and he was about to meet his match.

King Serpeo Kahin was the current ruler of Talinus, his family ruled for almost seven centuries, and most of their stories that told of their rise to power were written in blood. Their tyranny was only matched with their greed and love for power. Their people did not dare oppose them, and they sowed seeds of distrust among them. No one knew who to trust and who was a spy for the king. Spies were handsomely paid. It was one of the most lucrative and sought-after jobs in the capital. They were also people that spread propaganda and told tales of how the king worked effortlessly to benefit the land. They were loathed more than the spies.

The town was impeccably clean and well maintained. It wasn't clearly because of the upstanding hygiene of the citizens, but rather due to the penalties issued to combat littering. At first, it seemed that people were doing well, and that the king ensured financial prosperity. Later, they learned that the people they saw were from the affluent class. More than a third of the citizens lived below the poverty line and resorted to scavenging to sustain themselves. Most lurked in the shadows, and only made their way if a target was close by that could easily be robbed. They lived in deplorable conditions.

Kendra found them a place to eat and also managed to gather some intel at the same time. It was the local pub where most of the citizens came, and valuable information was traded. It was also a place where many drug deals took place.

There was veil separating the section where the richer citizens were dining. A better selection of wines and spirit was offered to them. It was also where most of the power deals, where crime bosses and government officials made their deals. Corruption was at its peak, and information was being leaked from the royal palace for the right price. Kendra and Ranthor were sitting at table besides a few of the local politicians trying to hear what they were saying. They managed to purchase a few cloaks to avoid suspicion. They also dressed elegantly to fit it with the crowd.

The men in the table were very careful and only indulged in trivial conversations. They were discussing the local weather, the stock exchange, and the upcoming harvest. Nothing so far seemed suspicious, and it seemed for a while that nothing amiss was going on. Gideon was starting to get restless and bored. He kept telling Ranthor of how this was a bad idea. Kendra nudged to stop talking as it would alert others to their presence.

The men then lowered their voices and started talking in muffled voices. The only thing they could manage to hear was the word local exchange. The men then decided to leave the crowded bar. They left and shortly after the crew followed. The politicians kept looking back and forth making sure they were not being followed. They were very apprehensive about being discovered. Clearly, this was not an official business for the royal crown. They also removed all traces of them and made sure to split so that if one was found the others would alert their leader of their compromised position.

Ranthor was making sure not to be discovered. He also managed to split his crew, half of them left with the other group of politicians and chased after them. It was very likely that one group went to a false location to lose the trail of any possible bandits. They finally reached an abandoned warehouse 50 kilometers away from the center of the city. A huge bald man exited from the door and welcomed them inside the warehouse. He checked their coast and searched them thoroughly for any wires, devices, and weapons. He then stood guard while they were inside to make sure that were not being followed. He towered over the entrance and stood between them and any chance of getting inside the building.

Kendra was devising a plan to takeout the guard. She would pose as an interested accomplice of the politician, claiming that she was here to offer companionship to the politicians. She'd try to seduce the guard and get the keys off him. Meanwhile, Ranthor would approach him from behind and take him out with a single blow on the head. The most important part of the plan was that it should be done stealthily. Otherwise, whoever was there in the warehouse would be alerted to their presence and would make their escape. Gideon and Ooger were asked to stay hidden and not alert anyone to their presence. It was deemed that their presence was not necessary, and more than likely would compromise them. They agreed in silence and managed to find shelter behind a nearby tree.

Kendra approached the guard and introduced herself to him. He seemed suspicious and asked her a few questions.

"Who the hell are you, and what are you doing here? I was not informed that our guests requested entertainment. I would suggest that you leave quietly before I make my mind about feeding you bullets for breakfast," bellowed the guard angrily.

"You look very charming. Perhaps I could entertain you for a bit before offering my services to the fine gentleman that you work for. Honey, you have wonderful arms, do you work out?" Spoke Kendra in a sultry voice.

"Perhaps you could come in after all. Although I will have to thoroughly search you for any weapons that would have in your possession," answered the guard ecstatically.

Kendra resented the idea of this oversized ape laying his hairy hands on her, but there was nothing much she can do to protest. Ranthor approached from behind and was aiming the hilt of his sword at the brute's head. He struck him hard with his sword, and shortly after he succumbed to a comatose state. Kendra was glad that this nightmare was over, and quickly slid her hand into the guard's back pocket and managed to extract the keys to the warehouse.

Both of them managed to enter undetected and made their way through the back passages of the warehouse. They could hear the faint sound of the exchange happening. The weird thing is that the place was not armed. There were no armed soldiers in any of the passages, which was very strange for a possible drug exchange. They finally managed to reach the room where the politicians stayed. Ranthor stood behind the door and was trying to catch glimpses of what was happening from the window. Luckily, the room was not soundproof and most of the conversation could easily be heard.

Their leader was a burly man with a short, webbed neck and a bushy uncombed beard. He was in his mid-forties, and his hair was starting to grey. He welcomed the new members of the group and made his way to the podium to begin his speech. He was dressed in a purple robe and so were the others. All of this was weird and did not do anything to reassure Kendra. These people looked dangerous despite not being armed. A priest accompanied the group and brought a ceremonial robe for each of the new guests. This seemed to be a sort of initiation ceremony to welcome the possible cult members. This was most definitely a cult by the rituals and robes.

She wondered who the red-haired woman was in the middle of the ceremonial hall. The other men were circling around her and chanting weird phrases and dancing. They brought a small black box, which was wrapped in a golden cloth. It was being placed on top of a pedestal in the middle of the room. A matching black key was brought, and the leader held the key for the members to see and was preparing to open the mysterious box. He finally opened it and removed a glowing object that was wrapped in a similar golden cloth. It shone as bright as the sun, showering the room with a green incandescent light. He removed the cloth and they realized that it was a jewel. Ranthor realized that it was one the Nebula Jewels.

The leader was passing it from member to member and they were chanting a weird phrase as they kept shuffling from one pair of hands to the other. He returned the jewel back into its box and sealed it carefully. The mysterious hooded figures sat in a nearby table and were ready to start their meeting. Kendra pressed her ear next to the handle of the door and was listening intently to their conversation. She managed to hear some of the conversation and was leaning in closer to catch the remainder of it.

The woman was pacing the room back and forth looking very agitated. She removed her hood, and to Kendra's surprise she recognized the hooded figure behind it. Her hair was as golden as maize, and she walked with a slight limp. She began throwing things violently in the room and tossing priceless pieces of furniture. Kendra recognized this woman because she was her long-lost sister Casseopi. They had been separated almost 10 years back and she was taken by her stepfather when their parents were divorced. They left the planet immediately and removed any trace of their existence from there.

"What is taking this extraction process so long? I cannot believe that we only managed to find a single jewel. The moment I find the thief that took the remainder of the jewels, I will skin him and distribute the hide among the ware sellers of this planet," Casseopi's face contorted in anger.

"Don't worry my dear. The jewel will lead us to the location of its sister jewels, the ancient civilization that made them ensured this was possible to safeguard them and ensure their immediate return to their rightful owner. We will soon have our rising, and our orders will once again rise like a phoenix from the ashes," replied a mysterious voice soothingly.

Casseopi was quiet now and was deeply pondering their next plan to extract the jewels. Her insides were burning like lava, her resolve did not weaken, and she would hunt down the remainder of the jewels. She was determined to find them and strengthen her position in the guild. She was currently being evaluated by the members, and if found to be ready will be receiving the rank of master. The guild of Rhineheart does not look kindly upon failure. Her mentor was understanding and helped her in whatever way her could. He also explained that the jewels resonate more strongly when the other jewels were nearby. This was going to aid them in the search for the remainder of the jewels.

She was Kendra's elder sister and the apple of her father's eye. Kendra was closer to her mother and opted to stay with her. Casseopi was 5 years older than Kendra and is fluent in many languages the neighboring states. She was introduced to the guild by her father, a prominent member and one of the founders. Euphalys was a powerful guild member and a strong adversary that no one would wish to encounter. He ruled the guild's faction in this planet and held control over the governorate elections and ruling family. He knows most of the political candidates and the local police answered to him.

The guild was well known in the planet, and people heard stories of the initiation ceremonies that took place in their halls. Recently, many influential members flocked to them in order to help gaining more support and power. It was rumored that they were the reason the current king was in control. It was also suspected that the king was a member of the guild, and one of the founding fathers. However, the royal guards spent countless days spreading propaganda to prove the opposite. This ensured that the people still favored him and prevented an uprising.

Other members of the guild were coming now, and another new member prepared himself for the anointing process. A silver urn was brought and in it was a tarry black liquid. The guild elders hovered around it, and each dabbed a cloth into it. They covered the newest member's face with this strange liquid. It started peeling the skin on his face and he writhed in agony. Still, he maintained his composure and held his ground. Finally, he was handed a bejeweled ring with the guild's insignia and was welcomed into their ranks.

The man was in his mid-thirties. His face and torso were covered in tattoos. His hair was ash colored and he had an olive complexion. He was still in agony, but he did not want to show any sign of weakness. His name was Sirius Moghaven, a man recently elected to be the head of the city's chamber of commerce. This job was facilitated by the guild. He was not keen on joining, but he soon discovered that this was not a viable option. He was attacked in the middle of the night and was brought here against his will. He was told that he would be stripped of his position and publicly shamed if he decided to leave the guild. Sadly, he complied with their commands and was initiated into their ranks.

Kendra kept listening to the ongoing discussion between the guild members. She thought that it was best that they don't storm their meeting, and instead figure out where they were headed next and plan an ambush for them. Ranthor agreed with her plan and pressed his ear closer to the door to listen. The jewel was going to be hidden in Casseopi's manor for the time being. They will prepare for their journey in two days' time. The location was going to be announced at the manor. New members had to attend all meetings but were forbidden from participating. Sirius did not want to involve himself anyway in this messy business.

They all parted ways and he was headed to his quarters to spend the night. Kendra was tailing him and made sure not to be discovered. He kept looking back and forth as if expecting that he would be followed. He knew the guild would be suspicious of him as evidenced by the way he was brought to the meeting. He did not want an altercation and decided to comply with whatever they had asked him to do. He knew that they would protect him from any legal actions. After all, they owned the planet and were able to do as they please.

Kendra managed to sneak up behind him and tie his hands. She was preparing to interrogate him and was taking him to their ship. He tried to resist initially but then gave up and decided to accept his fate. He did not even utter a single word due to fear of death. He was perplexed as to why the guild would kidnap him another time. He did not even suspect that it was another bystander. The ship doors opened, and he was hoisted on top of the landing strip. He entered the main chamber and sat on a stool.

The lights were dimmed, and the blinds were removed. He gazed in horror as he finally met with his kidnappers. His face was paralyzed with fear, and his insides were churning. He was mortified that he had become a target for kidnapping and contemplated if this job was ultimately worth the risk he placed under. His soul was sold to the devil, and payment was yet to be settled. Kendra was pacing the room and angrily stared at him. She threatened to murder him if he did not comply with her orders.

"Listen to me scum and pay close attention to what I am about to tell you. I need you to spy for me and gather as much information you can get about the jewels. Fail to do so and your house will burn like kindling, understood?" Kendra said menacingly.

Sirius stood there and nodded silently in agreement. He was overcome with fear and could not utter a single word. He knew that his life would not be the same anymore. Kendra left and he immediately locked the door behind him. He was not able to sleep that night. Visions of death welcomed themselves into his head. By the time he was able to shake them off the sun was rising. He prepared himself for work and boiled a kettle of tea to calm himself.

Gideon was starting to wake up. He was feeling groggy from the previous night. As the sun was rising, he woke up and faced the coming of the new day. He longed for the warm embrace of his mother. He waited anxiously for the return of Ranthor and Kendra from their latest expedition. Gideon was glad that he was not involved in their meeting with the guild. As they returned and recounted the events of yesterday, he felt a shiver run down the back of his spine. He wanted to leave this planet as soon as possible and get rid of the memories. Ranthor equally hated the prospect of staying here and wanted this meeting to be over soon.

Kendra was still shocked that she finally got to see her sister. However, she was not shocked to learn that she was part of the guild, especially knowing that her own father was one of its founding members. This has got to be one of the worst family reunions in the history of dysfunctional family reunions. She did not want anything to do with them anymore, and if it came to it, she would not hesitate to put a bullet between their heads. The others were surprised at her resolve and told her that it would be okay if she sat the remainder of the journey out. She insisted, nonetheless, and vowed to rid the planet of this evil seed.

The market was closing, and all the stalls were covered to avoid any robberies. The shop owners headed to their homes. The only businesses that were open at this time were the pubs and diners, their inhabitants were the depressed and the depraved souls wondering around town aimlessly in the hope of finding salvation. There were also the politicians that sought the services of the mistresses of the night. Longing for companionship while avoiding the gazing eyes of the public. They managed to keep this going discreetly. Especially, since whoever knew about it was either bribed or was six feet under.

The pubs had their fair share of customers, and sometimes were more packed than the market on harvest day. The regulars were always there to pay homage to their habitual drinking habits. They also longed for the companionship and comfort of their friends. Most of them were retired sailors and washed-up politicians that refused to honor the current regime. They were stripped from their positions and forced to leave office. They found their only solace in drinking and drowning their sorrows.

Ranthor was told that the next meeting was happening today, and he decided to visit one of the pubs to gather information about the location of the house the politicians would meet. He covered his face with a shroud and entered the pub. The place reeked of bourbon and mead. Even after their eventual demise, the politicians decided that they still would drink the same drinks they would while in office. These drunks were spilling more secrets than drinks and leaked a lot of information about their previous work. However, none of them dared to talk about the guild for fear of execution.

The pub was almost deserted except for a couple of men who were feasting and drinking. Most of them were above sixty years of age. They had seen their fair share of trouble and did not wish to interact with anyone this evening. They were huddled in the booth at the far end of the pub and were dining silently. Clearly, whatever they were whispering was something of great importance. Ranthor decided to sit at the table adjacent to theirs and try to gather some information. He could barely hear what they were saying, but still managed to understand that the meeting was going to be held at counsellor Paulus's house tomorrow evening. It was by the riverbank and was usually heavily guarded.

They decided to stay and have a meal at the pub. The night air was calm, and no one was around to disturb their peace. Kendra and Gideon were grateful to finally be able to have a meal. Their stomachs growled and the sound filled the room. It was as if a beast was devouring its prey slowly. They ate a plate of venison steak and drank corn broth. The food was delicious despite preconceived expectations. The atmosphere was quiet, and they were not disturbed by anyone. The previous customers left, and they were free to enjoy their meal privately. Afterwards, they had the chocolate mousse and enjoyed the remainder of their evening.

The journey to the ship was similarly uneventful. Ooger was glad to reach the ship and sleep after this mighty meal. He entered his chambers and was out like a light bulb. The others were surprised at the ease at which he managed to succumb to sleep. It was as if he never cared for a single thing. He slept soundly under the covers and not even the purring of the engine woke him up. Kendra, on the other hand, was unable to close her eyes. She kept imagining the encounter that she would eventually have with her sister, her disappointment at her and that she would have to face her in combat.

Gideon was also tossing and turning. He did not like staying in this planet, and with every passing day found less joy here. He was no longer able to distract himself with the promise of uniting with his family. He was thinking of stealing the escape pod and leaving the others behind. After all, this was not his battle, and he did not wish to become collateral damage in any blood shed that would eventually occur. He opened the compartment and was reassured that there was one pod ship remaining. He would wait for the day when the others would be busy at the meeting to make his move.

His parents had sent a message the previous day. He kept playing it over and over again on the monitor. He enjoyed listening to their voices. It was one of the few things that had kept him sane so far. He was worried of being killed on this dangerous mission. Also, there was no more any benefit of him staying. He was a child stuck in a mess created by the adults around him. The world would be better off if they stopped their petty grievances. He wondered as to how the king was not yet killed. He was hated by almost everyone, including most of his royal guard. He then realized that he managed to sow discord among them and pit them against each other.

Ooger was feeling neglected. He went over to Ranthor to see if he needed any help. Lately, he felt that his role as trusted companion was diminished and wanted to contribute to the current adventure. He managed to convince him to take him along on the next mission. He would act as their scout and would alert them to the presence of any intruders. He was especially adept at sneaking around in tight spaces. He scurried back to his quarters and lay there waiting for the break of dawn. The night was long, and the cold was piercing his bones. He wrapped multiple blankets around him, but despite that he felt the frost penetrate his bones.

The ship's cloaking device was turned on to avoid any bandits. This area was littered with thieves, and they did not want to wake up with their feet dangling upside down. Kendra walked to Gideon and was trying to comfort him. She had just realized that he was starting to feel despair. She could not imagine how leaving his parents behind after finally finding them had made him feel. She was going to speak to Ranthor tomorrow and let him release him to go with his family.

The day finally arrived, bringing with it a new uncertainty. Kendra prepared herself to face the challenges of today's meeting with the guild. She would finally get her chance to learn more about their plans and hopefully foil them. This meeting is going to help them in finding the remainder of the jewels and ending this hellish journey. The meeting today was going to point them to the direction of the rest of the jewels. The journey is finally going to become easier, with the green jewel increasing their chances of finding the other jewels. The guild was holding their meeting at the house of counsellor Paulus. He was the advisor to the king and owner of several properties in the capital. They were meeting at one of the properties on the outskirts of town, away from prying eyes. The meeting was going to start at midnight, and it was being attended by the highest officials of the guild.

Gideon was pacing the ship back and forth trying to figure a way to reach home using the pod. He didn't really know how to operate it and was worried about getting lost in space. Perhaps he would enlist the help of Ooger. He too was not keen to be on this journey and felt left out. He wanted to talk to him today and see if he was going to attempt an escape. However, if he fails to persuade him, then he was going to be in a lot of trouble with the others. Still, it was better than wandering aimlessly in space. He was faced with a lot of difficult decisions and he starting to feel the walls closing in on him.

Life was getting out of control, and Gideon felt that the odds were not in his favor. He was gazing into the planets and counting the hours and days till he got back home. He was not going to waste any further time contemplating his future. He went into the main chamber looking for Ooger, but he was surprised to find that he had left the ship. He then learned that he was looking for more information regarding the meeting. Ranthor told him to gather more details from the citizens of the city. He wanted to be prepared in the event that the place was heavily protected, which is most likely the case. He also wanted to know if he could get to know the identity of the other members of the guild.

The jewel was currently being held in the meeting place. It was securely kept in place and guarded heavily. No one was allowed to go in or out of the holding place. Paulus did not like the idea of the security detail, but he did not dare defy the decision of the guild. Their support for him throughout the years had meant that they could ask him for favors anytime. He had to cater for their every wish and demand, even when he did not like it. However, he decided to not only help but actually spent his resources protecting the jewel. This mission was going to help push his career forward. From what Ooger gathered, he was going to be elected as the high commissioner of the king's council. This meant that he would have more influence and power.

Ranthor was mentally preparing himself for today's mission. He wanted to make sure that this encounter would be bloodless. He finally was on the right track to finding the jewels. However, he also wanted to protect Kendra from having to make the difficult decision of having to choose between her family and this mission. Even though she was committed to their cause, he knew it would be difficult for her. He wanted to spare her the difficulty of having to make the decision. No one should ever have to go through this ordeal. Despite agreeing to wait and let the guild take them to the jewels, he wanted to take the jewels and use them to locate the other jewels. However, he decided finally to honor his end of the bargain and respect Kendra's wishes.

Gideon headed outside the ship to the nearest restaurant to have his lunch. He figured it would at least distract him from the difficult decision he would have to make today. There was not much time before the others would leave for the mission. He didn't have much time to decide. But for the time being, he would forget about all that and enjoy a nice meal without thinking about anything. The food in the restaurant was surprisingly good. He forgot about all his sorrows and was holding on to this one moment in his life. He thought about how courageous he was and how much his life had improved. This wouldn't have been possible without the efforts of his friends. This was the first time he thought of this group of misfits as friends.

He realized that he could not betray Ranthor's trust, even if it was for a reunion with his family. This was a man who had rescued him from life at the orphanage and helped solve his lifelong mystery. He was going to stick with him till the end of his mission and help him reunite with his father in the same way he reunited him with his. It was fair to do, and with that his resolve to stay was strong. He finished his food and decided to take a stroll around the river. The weather was beautiful for a picnic and the town was empty. He could walk at ease without being disturbed by anyone.

Meanwhile, Ooger was trying to find his way in a nearby market without being stepped on. His small frame avoided him being detected, but at the same time people almost squashed him without realizing that he was there. He moved from stall to stall trying to gather intel for the upcoming mission. The house of commons was around 500 meters from the market. Politicians would eventually leave their offices and make their way to the market to buy bagels for their afternoon break. Deals were made during these small breaks and information was passed on without the risk of being detected in the middle of the house of commons.

It was already noon, and the politicians were ready to leave their offices. The ovens were being heated to make freshly baked goods and bagels were set up at the counters. Cakes from all across the planet were there to accommodate for every taste. Coffee was brewed and any chocolate patisserie ever imagined was being crafted by the skilled bakers of town. The politicians were piling in by the dozens and were making their way into the shops. The place was packed, and coffee was served. It was rush hour, the time when the coffee houses made the maximum amount of revenue. Important discussions were being held and plans were set in place. The counsellor was sitting alone at his table and was looking at his watch as if waiting for a meeting. His guest was running late, and he did not like being kept waiting.

He was eyeing his watch when finally, his guest arrived. He was scolded by the counsellor who was not amused . The man apologized profusely and offered to pay for the entire meal. He did not spare time making small talk and went straight into the purpose of the meeting. He held in his hand the map where the location of the next jewel was located. It was supposed to be in the Ventu system, a nearby solar system. They were yet to locate the planet hosting the next jewel, but it was only a matter of time before they found it. Scouts were already sent in its trail, and the mission so far was yielding good results. Paulus was happy with the current progress and rewarded the messenger for his efforts. The next jewel was almost within his grasp, and his quest for power and wealth was becoming more of a reality as the days went by.

The day was finally drawing to an end and the night sky was a powder blue color. It was a full moon night, and the star were shining brightly. Ranthor and his crew made their way across the city to the house where the meeting was supposed to be held and hid behind the bushes. The only thing they had to do now was to wait until midnight when the politicians made their way. The night was quiet, and the breeze cut the tension in the air. It was strange that the entrance was not guarded by anyone. There were no locks on the door. It was as if the person setting up the meeting was beckoning them to eavesdrop. No one came within sight for hours, and everyone was getting bored of waiting.

Finally, the hour struck midnight and just like clockwork the counsellor was the first to arrive. His timing was flawless. He was dressed in traditional guild robes and wore a silver amulet. He opened the door and was preparing the rooms for the meeting. Others soon followed suit and the meeting started. The members were seated, and the waiters rushed in with appetizers and wine. Half of the guests were hooded and there was no way to recognize them. The leaders of the guild were the ones wearing amulets. The rest only wore the ceremonial robes and hats. They enjoyed the food and were listening intently to the counsellor's plan to extract the jewels.

They were all mesmerized by the presentation. Each of them gazed as they imagined their futures, and they were all imagining the power and wealth that was going to rain down on them. This would permanently improve their futures and gain them the trust of several solar system leaders. Perhaps, even an appearance at the royal court. There was a rumor that the king was on the search for the jewels, and whoever found them was going to be highly favored. A bright future awaited the one who delivered the jewels to him. The people in the room were mortal enemies, united only by greed and capitalism. As soon as this mission was over, they will be back at each other's throat to fight for the ultimate seat of power.

The counsellor was showing them the schematics for the next jewel's location. Time seemed to stop outside the walls of this room. Ranthor was surprised that many people knew about the king's announcement regarding the jewels. He thought he was the only one seeking them. He assumed that the politicians wanted them to gain the king's favor It was more likely that they did not know much about the jewels, or the power they wielded. Otherwise, they would not consider handing them over to the king. The counsellor, a power-hungry political devil, would use the power to be the next king of the land. He was an even more ruthless dictator than the king, and people have attempted assassinating him for several years.

Kendra was searching the room for Casseopi. She did not find her sister anywhere. She kept searching the room for any signs of her. Her elder sister was late to the meeting and this did not bode well for her. Casseopi was tasked with monitoring the grounds for intruders. She approached them from behind and was preparing to remove her holster. She pointed her blaster at Ranthor and ordered him to kneel down.

"You have two seconds to tell me who you are or else I will pump you full of plasma. How dare you intrude in our meeting! I will kill you all and leave you to the beasts. But first, Kendra it is a surprise to see you after all these years. I apologize in advance for your murder," snarled Casseopi.

Chapter 6
The Devil's Advocate

Kendra turned around to see who had uttered this warning. She realized that it was none other than her own sister. She fought the urge to break free, especially since she knew that would risk having the others shot. Casseopi began tying them one by one to nearby trees. The moment she reached Kendra, she grasped her strongly by the hand and hoisted her over the overpass. She decided to save her so that she avoids the confrontation. Kendra was truly perplexed as this act would jeopardize her sister's mission. However, she immediately woke up from her trance and made her way to the trees as soon as her sister left. She untied the others, and they made their way to the back of the house. They would now have to sneak more discreetly as their position was definitely compromised.

Casseopi returned back from her stroll, surprised to see that her prisoners were no longer in their places. She immediately entered the manor and alerted the others that there were intruders approaching the manor. Guards approached the main chamber and were surrounding the four points of entry to prevent any eavesdropping. Even if the intruders managed to enter, they would not be able to listen in on the conversation. Luckily, they had their mole on the inside, and they would therefore be able to get information from him. They have arranged a meeting with him the following day. They only came here as a precautionary measure to ensure that he was trustable.

All of the members were seated in their chairs and were listening to instructions from the counsellor. A few of the members were then selected to participate in the search for the jewels. The mission's plan was laid out for them, and no one dared object. One of the leaders was going to head the expedition and ensure the safe return of the next jewel. Kendra's father was selected for the mission. He would be tasked with training the new recruits and ensuring their safe return to the planet. He was remarkably skilled as a training sergeant and had never failed a mission before.

The meeting continued and further briefing was done to inform the recruits about their identities while on mission. All of them were given different travel documents with a new identity. This was done to ensure if they were captured, their political affiliation would not be compromised, and this would point all the attention away from the royal palace. The king did not want to be publicly associated with the guild. Despite being a prominent member of the organization, he had remained to conceal his identity well and provide extensive support while serving in the royal palace. The guild members formed the majority of his cabinet and security detail.

The meeting was now concluded, and the members remained in the mansion overnight to avoid suspicion that would result from them sneaking outside late at night. Their rooms were already prepared by the servants. However, most of them stayed in the foyer to enjoy brandy and the mixed assortment of fruits brought by the servants. They used the opportunity to tend to their other political matters. Alliances were being forged between the members for the next round of election. This ensured the continuity of this line of politicians. The guild protected their members and made sure that they would remain in their respective offices. They also managed to bury their scandals despite the overwhelming mountain of truth that was behind them.

All of the politicians finally made their way back to their rooms. Ranthor could finally exit the manor without arousing suspicion. He and his crew snuck outside without triggering any alarms. He was happy that he was now armed with knowledge of the location of the next jewel. However, it was not yet time to act. They would remain in this planet for a few more days and wait for the guild to send its members on their mission. They would then follow them and intercept the ship before it landed on the planet. The jewel would be extracted, and the search would begin to locate the other jewel. Gideon was still on board the ship the following day and was waiting eagerly for them in anticipation.

Ranthor lay in his bunk and decided to take a nap. He was content knowing that he was close to achieving his dream. The jewel was within his grasp, and soon all the others were going to be with him. He longed for this moment and spent countless nights dreaming of the possibilities. At one point, he had given up hope entirely and considered continuing with his current profession as a bounty hunter. Despite its meagre rewards, it was actually rewarding to perform most of the tasks of the job. He was also very good at locating treasures, people and secret documents should the mission require it. He was well reputed and was known to be reliable.

He had already forgotten how to behave like a prince. They were so many rigorous protocols and meetings. He would rarely get the opportunity to move out and about in town. Therefore, he used the opportunity now to explore the city. He woke up, showered and headed into the market to enjoy his meal before venturing into the woods. The grounds near the capital were filled with different kinds of flora and fauna. There were species that were long extinct in other systems due to the mining industry and industrialization. These woods were not touched by anyone. This was mainly because the king owned these woods. They were his personal hunting grounds, and he had outlawed hunting some of the creatures due to their rarity. The other animals were used to make hides and rugs for the king's castle.

A beautiful wooden trail was laid out so that the king would enjoy his evening stroll whenever he desired. He would rarely come nowadays due to fear of assassination. The grounds were heavily covered with plants and any trespasser would be easily missed. Besides, he enjoyed spending more time in his study in the company of his books. He owned a collection of rare books bigger than person could imagine. His personal library housed every encyclopedia and journal ever written. He was also a fan of the theatre and kept various musical records and instruments. He enjoyed having the harp played for him during his reading sessions. He had found it to be quite soothing.

The royal guards were stationed across the woods today and Ranthor made sure not to run into them. This was strange, especially, since the king had a meeting with the town's people in town hall today to discuss the issuance of a new royal decree. Many of the town people were going to be there to protest the recent unjust rules. He enjoyed attending these events that dismiss all notions of a fair ruling. It was surprising that he would be walking in the woods at such a time. Perhaps, there would be an unofficial meeting with Paulus. Rumor has it that a strong alliance was forming between them. The counsellor was seen more frequently in the royal palace. The local town people took to name him the king's hemorrhoid problem. This was on account of his close and very personal relationship with the king. However, no one dared to utter these words publicly due to fear of the king's wrath.

Ranthor left the woods and was making his way to a nearby stream to bathe. He enjoyed a quiet swim and enjoyed the view of the mountains. He enjoyed his current state of freedom, one that he will never regain after joining the royal guard. As captain of the royal guard, he rarely had any free time and if he did, he was summoned by his father to handle his political affairs. He was being groomed to be the next king. His father wanted to ensure that he would carry on with his legacy. With him now gone, the next in line would be his cousin Brevis. He was as stubborn as a bull and probably just as bright. His father spent more time training him than he did ruling the kingdom.

A masked figure approached the ship and entered the main chamber. Luckily, Gideon was awake and managed to intercept the intruder. He struck him with the hilt of his sword and unmasked him. He was a man in his mid-thirties who he immediately recognized as the spy Ranthor talked about. He had come to share some information and unfortunately was kidnapped for the third time during this week. He realized his first order of business upon completing the mission was to hire a security detail. He dropped off the map with Gideon and instructed him to give it to Ranthor.

He then made his way out of the ship and disappeared into the crowd. Gideon also made his way out of the ship. He went to a nearby diner and ordered breakfast. The place looked deserted and was extremely quiet. The food was delicious and was fresh out of the oven. The boy enjoyed his meal in silence and then left the diner. After strolling along the banks of the river, he was on his way to explore further. He entered a field of maize and walked across it as taking in the beautiful scenery. This was the first time since he arrived that he had started to appreciate the beauty of this place. Perhaps, it was not that bad after all.

Gideon was surprised to see that most of the workers tended to the barns rather than harvesting the fields. Despite it being maize season, no one was around to collect any corn. Still, he was relieved as this provided him with the opportunity to explore the place and enjoy time out in the open. He rarely got to do that as he was always within the confines of the orphanage. The place lacked funding and the ground was very salty to grow anything on. He was mesmerized by the beauty of the farm and did not want to leave at all. However, he realized that the workers were coming out to the fields and decided to finally leave to avoid being detected.

Ranthor was still enjoying his swim. He found the activity quite liberating, and it made him forget all the worries that he had in his life. He was wondering if it was really worth it to return to his previous life. There was nothing much for him to do in the royal court. Also, he was not sure that he was ready to forgive his father for his abandonment. What kind of father would disown his only son because of a failed mission? He was clearly not someone to be admired or cared about. Furthermore, he was not sure how long the peace between them would last. After all, his father was already preparing another heir to the throne, and he wanted to steer clear of any scandal. To the kingdom, Ranthor was officially pronounced dead to avoid his father being villainized.

It was amazing at the lengths this man would go to avoid causing a scandal. His father cared about his reputation more than he did care about his family. Nothing was going to stand in the way of his rule, not even his own son. He did not care for anyone but himself and he would crush anyone that would stand in his way. Ranthor was not prepared to forgive this man, but still he wanted to return so that he may live his previous life for the sake of serving his people.

The market was starting to be filled with people from all parts of town. It was lunch hour, and everyone was making their way to grab food to eat. The vendors had already prepared the food and were only waiting for orders to start so that they could arrange them. It was the same customers over and over again. All of them made their way to the same diner at the exact same time of the day. It was like clockwork, their love for return was both profitable and utterly boring. Nothing changed in this city and if it did it would soon lead to a protest. The citizens were content with the lack of change that surrounded them.

Ranthor made his way back to the ship. He enjoyed the welcome change from this little expedition. It took the edge of the journey and the accumulated stress from his mind. His mind was clearer, and his resolve was much stronger now than ever. There was still some left, so he decided to go to a nearby pub and enjoy a drink. The place was quiet except for the sound of the band playing in the background. The bartender poured him a whiskey and he enjoyed his drink in silence. He also managed to eat a snack to quench his hunger. It felt as if time had stopped. He was wishing that it would go faster so that they can finish their mission and head back.

The others were feeling equally frustrated. Each one of them was confined to a part of town, wandering endless in search of meaningless activities to engage in to pass the time. Kendra was also taking a stroll across town. She was wondering around aimlessly in the town center. She realized eventually she was walking in circles for the better part of an hour. This town was the most boring place that she had ever set foot in. There was barely any sign of life. People were dull and very much stuck in their ways. Everyone was trapped in despair and hopelessness. It was as if the joy was sucked out of every single one of them, including the children. She wished that there was something that she could do to help them.

On the other hand, Gideon managed to distract himself from his ordeal and was finding joy in spending time by himself. It gave him the opportunity to reflect and gather his thoughts. His life had changed drastically over the past couple of weeks, and it was not going to be the same anymore. He found his family and was reunited with them at last. He was on his way to fulfill his dreams. The boy was already making plans for his future. He thought of running for political office in the future. At least, he wanted to do so to help create a better future. His journey showed him that there was a lot of injustice in many of the planets he had visited. All of them were gripped by the powerful clutches of corruption.

Meanwhile, counsellor Paulus was preparing for their next mission. He commissioned ships for the politicians to travel in. Travel maps and gear were laid out and loaded onto the ships. Their fleet was assembled, and the guards were selected to travel with them on their mission. He also managed to appoint a deputy to serve his duties in the planet. They would be leaving by tomorrow morning. He alerted his office that he would travel on official duty on behalf of the king. Therefore, he was not able to disclose in full detail the nature of the mission that he was embarking on. It was the perfect cover, and no one suspected a thing. In the meantime, his replacement would govern in his absence and was already given clear instructions on how to conduct himself. The other politicians made similar arrangements for their offices so that things would go smoothly. The ships were kept in their hangars and were already fueled in preparation for the upcoming mission.

The night sky was glowing from the light of the thousand stars and the moon was full, it cast its shadow over the ships. The engines were revved up and every politician's luggage was loaded onto their ships. Everyone was ready to depart the planet. Paulus was in his ship and his butler prepared his meals and drinks. His quarters were lavishly stocked with the finest carpets and rare urns. The main chamber of the ship looked immaculate. It was a place fit to house a king. Perhaps, the jewels were going to help him in his dream to rule the planet. It was only a matter of time before he found the remainder of the jewels. The world was going to be his oyster and every wish of his was going to be granted.

Ranthor already prepared his ship and managed to trace the route the counsellor's ship was embarking on. He turned on the cloaking device of his ship and started the engine. The ship began its ascent away from the planet and into the vastness of space. The others were sound asleep as the ship went into autopilot. He was not able to sleep at night. Especially since the jewels were almost within sight. He was not going to let the counsellor gain an advantage over him. Kendra was similarly unable to sleep. She dreaded another encounter with her sister. Worst of all, meeting with her father was even going to be worse. She did not know what she had to say to him. After all, she still loved him. She kept remembering when her little hands were held by him as he helped her cross the street.

However, he was no longer her father, but rather a villain that was threatening the very fabric of the universe. The Order he served and operated was spreading tyranny and fear throughout the universe. The man she knew was no longer inhabiting that body. Instead, a demon had made him his puppet. This no longer was her father and she no longer owed him anything. Still, she felt very conflicted about the encounter. Hopefully, she was going to convince him to join them and leave the mission. But she knew that this was not going to happen.

The ship was now close to planet Alvinus. Its radiant glow was very mesmerizing. The jewel started to shimmer brighter than ever and resonated loudly. The counsellor was thrilled to learn of the location of the next jewel. He ordered the ships to descend and communicated the order to the others via intercom. They began their descent into the planet's surface and landed. Ranthor landed his ship as well and prepared to disembark. He waited for them to make their camp and then trailed behind them. The ship was still cloaked to avoid any suspicion. Gideon decided to opt out of the mission and stay inside the ship. The jewel was guiding them to the location of its sister jewel. With every step they made it shimmered more brightly and stronger than ever. They were nearing their goal, and nothing was going to stand in their way.

Casseopi was carrying the jewel in her hands. She could feel its immense power pulsating in her chest. She could only imagine the collective strength of the collection of jewels. The power it held was rumored to control galaxies. Their legend was as old as time itself, and their power was handed down from ruler to ruler. Battles were fought for them, and they always ended up in the hands of thieves. Kings were crowned and wars were waged because of the power the jewels bestowed upon them. No one knew anything about their creator, but it was rumored that he held power equal to the jewels themselves. The only thing known is that he was called the sculptor. He was one of the master creators that crafted the powerful jewels, amongst other weapons.

Planet Alvinus was teeming with a variety of predatory wildlife. It hosted many carnivorous species that tore up anyone who dared enter their lairs. There were no human inhabitants and there were no other humanoid species living here. This world is one of the most hostile and least visited. It was surprising that the jewel found its way here. Casseopi found her way to the ship and managed to place the jewel there. The counsellor wanted this mission to be over quickly. He did not like the atmosphere in this planet. He almost got attacked by one of the creatures. Luckily, his guards managed to kill it and avoid any massacre. He never left the ship without the protection of his guards. Alvinus used to have many inhabitants, but after fights with the creatures they were extinct. No civilization managed to inhabit the planet for more than 500 years.

Ranthor was also not fond of staying in this planet. However, his quest for the jewels was more important and therefore he ventured through. He managed to spot the first jewel being carried by Casseopi. It resonated near a mountain in the center of the planet. Casseopi had marked this location as the potential site of the second jewel. The mountain was covered with snow at this time of year. It was a safe haven for many birds of prey and was surrounded by a wide assortment of the planet's fauna. The cave system in the planet was the most likely location of where the jewel was housed. It was also home of the feathered bats. The bats were indigenous species of the planet and were not found anywhere else.

There was little known about the mountain. People rarely visited them on account of the bats. They were the most vicious of the predatory creatures in this planet. Planet Alvinus also possessed a lot of natural gems and fields of orchids. There was an industrial complex left by the previous inhabitants of the planet. Many of the other rulers were in search of these gems in the hope of increasing their wealth. However, none of them managed to acquire the gems. They were fiercely protected by the bats who prevented anyone from laying their hands on them. The jewel was in the central chamber of the cave and was heavily guarded by the bats. No one dared to enter the caves for fear of death.

The ship was still cloaked, and Gideon was pondering if he could lend a hand to Ranthor. He realized that perhaps he could do something to help. He wanted to join the search for the jewels so that he can hasten the search. His parents had already prepared his room at the house and filled it with the things he enjoyed the most. He was excited about returning to his home planet and living with his parents. However, he started to like the adventure and the opportunity to harvest the jewels' power with his crew. He started to grow fond of them and might even miss them upon his departure. This was the first company he had for a long time. At the orphanage he was lonely and did not have any friends. He was finally fitting in and had a role to play. Ranthor and Kendra were his friends and he wanted to help them in the best way he could.

Ranthor made his way to the mountain with Kendra. Both of them treaded carefully to avoid attracting any beasts. Luckily, they were not approached by anything on their way to the mountain. They finally managed to reach the mountain and were making their way up on the trail. The trail was treacherous and difficult to maneuver. It was difficult to traverse the trail and Kendra found it extremely difficult to get on top. Ranthor helped her gain footing and they managed to reach midway. The best part, however, was the fact that the politicians were not anywhere nearby and did not have a chance to thwart them. Kendra was not keen on meeting her sister just yet.

They finally reached the summit of the mountain. Kendra was gasping and could barely manage a smile as she realized she conquered the trail. Ranthor on the other hand was feeling relieved that he could finally find the jewels. He ushered her into the caves, and they made their way into the mountains. The bats were asleep and they made sure not to disturb them as they made their way onto the inner chamber of the cave. They searched the place for hours but did not find a trace of the jewels. Kendra was wondering if Casseopi already made her way here and took them for herself. However, if that were the case their ship would not still be here. Perhaps it was in on the of the other chambers. They left the central chamber and were on their way exploring the other chambers. Unfortunately, the bats there were wide awake and getting through them was going to be a challenge.

The bats made their way to Kendra and were preparing for an attack. She drew here sword and sliced the oncoming bats. The others escaped and made their way onto the other chambers. She entered the chamber and was searching for the jewel. There was nothing in this chamber either. She searched every nook and crevice but did manage to find anything. There were a few gems, but they did not resemble in any way the jewels of Nebula. She decided to take a few as she knew they were valuable and could be exchanged for a hefty sum of money.

She made her way into the next chamber where another group of bats lay there waiting for them.

This chamber was different than the others. It was filled with many vases and precious golden urns. There were more bats here than in the other chambers. It was heavily guarded for some odd reason. Perhaps this was the chamber that housed the jewel. Again, the bats tried to attack them, but they were cut down by Ranthor and Kendra. They then made their way into the chamber and searched for the jewel. They finally discovered a shimmering purple jewel. It shone brightly like its sister jewel and was deeply resonating. Kendra took it in her hands and wrapped it in a cloth. They made their way out of the cave and prepared to leave to their ship. Their next plan was to confront the politicians and steal the second jewel.

The politicians' tent was close to their ship. They managed to reach it by midnight and were preparing a stealth mission to steal the jewels. They did not anticipate that Casseopi lay there wide awake. She saw Kendra and prepared her sword in anticipation. The others soon woke up and prepared themselves for the battle. Her father was surprised to see Kendra and was unsure if he wanted to attack his daughter. Despite their differences, Kendra was his daughter and he remembered holding her in his hands when she was little. Perhaps he could sway her to his cause and get the jewel from her. He decided to try this approach and enlisted the help of Casseopi.

"Kendra, father and I wish that you join us on our quest. We do not wish to harm you sister. Please consider joining us and gain the power of the jewels. After all, we are your family and do not wish to harm you. However, if you decide to join this team of bandits then we will be forced to attack you despite the pain it would cause us to do so," bellowed Casseopi.

"Casseopi, I am not about to join your guild. You have terrorized this universe for quite a long time. Your rulers are spreading tyranny in it. This is the very thing that I am fighting. So be it, if I have to strike you down to achieve peace then it shall be done. It pains me too, but I will not let evil make its way here," answered Kendra.

The two dueled with their swords which clashed violently. The others were fighting the other politicians and tried to pry their hands from the jewels. The politicians were surprisingly good at wielding the swords. Ranthor was injured by his opponent. Luckily, it was a superficial wound. He fought back and managed to strike his opponent. Ranthor made his way to the jewel and attempted to snatch it out of Casseopi's hand. She fought him and did not allow him to get close to the jewel. Kendra was exhausted from battle. She did not even manage to dent her sister's sword. She was an expert swordswoman and managed to best her in every way possible. She, on the other hand, was used to fire pistols and rarely used her sword. Despite that, she was a worthy adversary and managed to hold off her sister.

    The battle seemed to go on forever. Ranthor managed to strike yet another politician. He was now dueling with Kendra's father who was an equally skilled swordsman. He fought Ranthor and managed to knock the wind out of him. Ranthor held his ground without being struck. He was finding it difficult to fend off the attacks. He could barely keep up with his opponent. It was only a matter of time before he was going to lose. Finally, he managed to parry the attack and strike him. The attack hit him square in the chest and a gush of crimson blood shot out. His opponent was writhing in agony from his injury. He did not expect to be bested by Ranthor. He managed to retreat just in time to avoid being killed. He left the caves and was preparing to leave to his ship. Kendra also managed to strike Casseopi and disarm her sword. She took the jewel from her and then cut her down. Casseopi lay there dead amidst her warriors.

    The battle was finally won. Ranthor and Kendra prepared to make their way out of the caves. Kendra was still awestruck that she had just killed her sister. A streak of tears was pouring onto her cheeks. Despite their differences, she had once loved her sister and wished to have a life with her and her father. Still, she did not want tyranny to reign over the castle and she was going to do anything to stop that from happening. Ranthor tried to comfort her and tell her that he was going to help her. She was calm now and managed to make her way out of the mountain. The second jewel was now within their grasp and was going to help in their quest to find the remainder of the jewels. Their quest was becoming clearer and the path to the jewels lead them to closer to finding the rest. At least they now would know where they are headed.

    They managed to leave the mountain and made their way back to the ship. The path to the remaining jewels was now much clearer. Finally, they were going to leave this uninhabitable planet and make their way to their next location. They also were going to do so without the meddling of the guild. The ship's cloaking device was lifted and the coordinates for the next planet were entered into the ship's mainframe. They made their ascent into space. Ranthor was excited to find the next jewel. He could almost imagine his father's joy at this discovery and the way he would welcome back his son into his kingdom. He would be the next in line to rule the planet. Most importantly, he would abandon being a bounty hunter. He would no longer rely on the meagre scraps to make ends meet. He would finally return to the power and authority that he had once commanded.

Gideon was also glad that this brought him close to connecting with his parents. His goal was now within reach. He also might benefit from the jewels. His wishes would be granted. He was looking forward to being back in his room and away from the loneliness of the orphanage. That place ate away at his soul. He was finally on his way to having a family. It was something he had always dreamt of.

They were again surrounded by the emptiness of the galaxy. The ship was cruising its way into the next planet system. Another long journey was waiting for them and another tyrant that was holding the next jewel. Their last encounter with the counsellor and his politicians left them with several injuries. Ranthor started training and improving his sword stances in preparation for the upcoming battles ahead. Kendra did the same thing. The last battle knocked the wind out of them, their opponents were skilled at swordsmanship. They were armed with two jewels and had the advantage of locating the next jewel. However, the politicians managed to locate the third jewel earlier and had already mapped out its location.

The two jewels were mesmerizing in their beauty. They did still not resonate but a faint glow was coming off them. The crew ventured further into the solar system in search of the next jewel. The glow was becoming stronger, indicating that they were on their way to the next jewel. Kendra was relieved that they were on their way. However, she was still feeling empty inside after having to kill Casseopi. She kept imagining the previous encounter with her sister. She could not imagine doing the same thing to her father. He was the only remaining family member that she had. Still, she did not want the guild to take hold of the jewels. The king of Alvinus would be unstoppable with the jewels and would further spread his tyranny. At least she can now thwart his attempts at power and might even defeat him bringing peace to the people of the land.

A fleet of pirate ships was blocking their way. They circled around the ship and prepared to shoot them. The leader of the pirates was making his way to Ranthor, and his ship collided with them in an attempt to dock. Ranthor shot him with his ion beam and managed to pierce a gaping hole into it. The leader decided to avoid him and prepared to leave. However, Ranthor blasted him again destroying the ship. The other ships were soon destroyed. However, one of the ships managed to escape and made its way onto the surface of a nearby planet. Hopefully, he would not call for reinforcements. Kendra returned to her post and took control of the ship. She sped through the field of asteroids and made her way further into the next solar system.

Ranthor was glad that they defeated their opponent. His ship was speeding through in an attempt to reach the planet housing the jewel. He could not imagine finding the next jewel. It was a dream come true for him. The next solar system was the Omega system. Planet Slovari was the one housing the next jewel. The jewels were now resonating as they made their way into the Omega system. The planet was at the end of the solar system. It was a pirate safe haven. Hopefully, they would not encounter a lot of trouble acquiring it. If these pirates were the same as the ones they encountered then the job to acquire the jewels would be easy. They would not suffer the same wounds that the politicians caused them.

Planet Slovari was the crown jewel of the solar system. It used to be the capital of the galaxy and the home of a proud race of warriors. The pirates however managed to take hold of it and kill its inhabitants. The remainder were sold as slaves. The warriors did not stand a chance against the pirates in battle. Their home was the center of trade for the planet. Many species would come and enjoy the beauty of the planet. The pirates used it as one of their outposts and abandoned the markets. It soon fell to decay and there was now no trace of the proud civilization that once inhabited it. The jewel was probably in the chamber of the pirate king. It was an object of immense power, this much was known to the pirates. The jewel would grant them control over the other pirate clans and would help them in their conquest.

Ranthor finally managed to reach planet Slovari. He managed to find a landing strip away from the pirate outpost. He landed the ship and then engaged the cloaking device. He exited the ship and was cautiously exploring his surrounding and trying to find where the king's palace would be. He planned to attack the pirates and wear their uniform. Disguised as pirates, he would be able to infiltrate the palace stealthily. He would therefore avoid any encounter with the army that surrounded the palace. He could not take any further injuries at this point. His wounds from the previous battle just managed to heal. He was trying to avoid any bloodshed at this point. The king's palace was heavily protected, and stealth was going to be their best chance at acquiring the jewel.

Gideon requested Ranthor to join them on the mission. However, Ranthor reminded him of the dangers of this mission and the need for stealth. He advised him to remain on the ship and be available as look out to avoid detection by the guards. Gideon agreed and decided to remain aboard the ship. The others were dressing in white gowns and cloaked to avoid any suspicion. They made their way across the planet in search of pirates. Kendra was holding a blade in her hands. She was prepared to capture the pirates and dress as them. Ranthor held a club in his hand and decided that he would beat his opponent. They would then take them to the ship to avoid them being discovered, and therefore foil their plan.

Ooger was also instructed to remain in the ship. He would not pass for a pirate and hence was going to blow their cover. He was instructed to protect Gideon and help him with surveillance. He was happy that he was not headed to the castle. The pirate king was known to be ruthless, and he did not wish to have an encounter with him. He made his way into his quarters and slept peacefully. Gideon on the other hand was reading the maps of the planet. He wanted to see where the jewel was located in the palace. He would at least help Ranthor, and Kendra find the jewel quickly. He also found an intercom device which could help him communicate with them while they were in the castle.

The castle was now within their reach. They had managed to find two guards near the perimeter. They attacked the two guards and then donned their uniforms. They blended easily and were allowed to enter the castle. The place was lit by thousands of candles hung on the chandeliers. Guards surrounded the rooms of the castle and the king was nowhere to be seen. They learned that he was occupied in his study. The jewel was most likely there. The guards were not privy to the location of the jewel. None of them knew that it was being held in the castle. The king did not trust them with its safekeeping. He was the only one who knew about its whereabouts. The only thing he instructed them was to guard the study with their lives. They figured something valuable was there, but they did not dare to ask him what was housed there. He kept it locked in a vault in the middle of the study. The vault was sealed by twelve locks. The keys were given to twelve guards, and each key-wielding guard was guarded by several guard units. A few guards also carried fake keys in the event that they would try to open the vaults themselves.

The king warned the guards that the penalty of opening the vault would be death. Therefore, none of them approached the vault and decided to ignore it all together. They kept a lookout for intruders. Ranthor was looking for the vault and decided to make his way to the study. Some of the guards eyed him suspiciously, but after a while averted their attention from him. None of them recall seeing him or Kendra. They ignored them and decided that they were probably new recruits to replace the guards that were killed by the king. Meanwhile, the king was in his study admiring the vault and making sure the jewel is safely stowed inside. Ranthor made his way to the king and prepared to steal the jewel from him.

Simeoni also headed with them to the castle. She had managed to update her leader about the current location of the jewels. They were preparing to come to the planet and extract the jewels. However, they would do so after the pirates were dealt with. They thanked her for her efforts and assured her that she would be gifted with a promotion for her efforts. She made sure not to be seen contacting her clan. Gideon was the only one that suspected they would enter. He did not know, however, that they were making their way here as they speak. The pirates were making it difficult for Ranthor to enter the study. He had to find a way to distract them in order to gain an audience with the king.

He also realized that some of the guards were carrying keys. He figured that they were important and therefore he decided to steal the keys before he made his way to the study. He managed to pickpocket the first key from the guard without being detected. He then made his way to the others and managed to gather a few keys. The remaining guards would be difficult to pickpocket as their keys were in the pocket of their vest. However, he noticed that they occasionally remove them and place them on their tables.

The guards were scattered around the perimeter of the castle. Ranthor would have to cross them in order to gain access to the keys. The first guard was eying him suspiciously. He figured that he was staring at him and that made him very suspicious. He looked at his key and kept it very close to him. He then placed on top of the table and did not leave it alone. He made sure to hide it away from Ranthor. A friend of his called him and he made his way to him leaving the key unattended. Ranthor managed to take the key and left immediately to the next location. The guard did not return and therefore he was not alerted to the loss of his key. Ranthor collected the remainder of the keys and made his way to the study.

He told the head guard that he found a few intruders that wanted to steal the vault and was planning to warn the king about them. The head guard instructed him to head to the study and alert the king. He made his way to the study and was trying to find the king. The king was guarding the vault and made sure that no one had access to it. Ranthor came up to him and told him that the counsellor was here to steal the vault. The king was alarmed and decided that Ranthor should thwart the counsellor's attempt to find the vault. He then made his way to the inner chamber of the study and retired to his bed.

Ranthor picked the locks of the vault and opened it. He found the jewel and stowed it in his pocket. He then locked the vault to avoid suspicion that it was stolen. The king was already asleep and did not attempt to come to the vault. He then left the study and made his way to the castle. He informed Kendra that he had taken the jewel and both of them prepared to leave. The king finally woke up and decided to open the vault. He was furious that the jewel was no longer in its place. He called the guards and told them that someone had taken what was in the vault. They were searching for Ranthor and Kendra to regain the contents of the vault.

Kendra was hidden in the courtyard of the castle. They realized that the guards were now on their tail and would soon try to kill them. Ranthor managed to leave the courtyard and make his way to the entrance of the castle. The guards were guarding the entrance and would have to be taken out in order for them to exit the castle.

Kendra was already attacking the guards. She struck them with her sword and managed to injure one of the guards. She ducked as soon as he tried to do the same. The guard was injured heavily, and he decided to leave battle and avoid being killed. The others were attacked by Ranthor and were injured as well. However, the guard managed to bring reinforcements. The other guards were making their way to the entrance in order for them to catch Ranthor. They were many guards and outnumbered Ranthor and Kendra. However, Ranthor managed to find a hiding place to avoid being detected by the guards. They looked everywhere in search of them and did not find any evidence of their whereabouts. They split into groups and searched for them. They then attacked the groups individually and took care of the guards.

The exit of the castle was now unguarded and Ranthor made his way out. Kendra followed suit and soon both of them had left the castle. The king cursed the remaining guard who had escaped the initial encounter. Ranthor and Kendra were already in the countryside and had the jewel in their possession. It was the third jewel of Nebula. They were almost halfway done collecting the jewels. Nothing was going to stand in their way. The remainder of the jewels were scattered in other corners of the universe. Finding them would not be hard now considering the other jewels acted like a tracker. It was important to avoid any pirates as the king most likely alerted them to the missing contents of the vault.

They managed to find an abandoned hut outside the castle. It had a few cloaks and pistols. They wore the cloaks to disguise themselves from any onlooking passengers. The pistols were loaded and would help them in the event they were outnumbered with guards. They then headed to a nearby marsh and decided to swim to their ship to avoid being caught by the guards. This way they avoid the main road, where most of the guards were stationed. The guards were nowhere to be seen at this point. The king instructed them to head to the ship and ambush Ranthor. They carried with them wands that enabled them to disable cloaking devices. They used to scour the area in search of the ship. Meanwhile, Gideon and Ooger were on lookout duty and saw that the guards on their way. They communicated with Ranthor on the intercom and let him know that the guards were there.

Ranthor prepared himself for an upcoming ambush. He realized that the guards were not on the main road for a reason. He finally made his way to the ship and was surprised to find that more than a dozen guards had removed the cloaking device from his ship. They had taken their friends captive and threatened to kill them in the event Ranthor attacked them. He decided to drop his sword. However, he still had his pistol and managed to shoot the guards. Kendra shot the remainder of the guards and disabled the wand. Gideon hurried back to the ship and prepared for their departure. He was happy to see that the third jewel had been acquired. They entered the new coordinates and prepared for their ascent into space. Kendra was exhausted from their latest encounter. She headed to her bed and laid there in silence. Ranthor was also tired and headed to his chambers. The ship was on autopilot and had disappeared into the vastness of space. Gideon was looking at the maps and trying to figure out the location of the fourth jewel. Their journey was finally getting them what they had desired. It was soon going to be the end and he would be reunited with his parents again.

There was nothing preventing them from reaching the next planet. They were guided by the resonance from the jewels and were making their way into yet another adventure. The four remaining jewels were going to be within their reach and away from the grasp of the guild. The fourth jewel was going to be tricky to find. There was another guild outpost where the jewel is rumored to be at. It was a place that was heavily guarded and filled with guild agents. The jewel was in the entrust of their leader. Furthermore, the planet was two solar systems away and the journey to it was a treacherous one. It felt like an eternity traversing the vastness of space. Kendra decided to take rest and sleep in her quarters. Gideon was daydreaming about his reunion with his parents. Ranthor, however, was waiting anxiously for the fourth jewel. He would do anything to reach the outpost and take it from the guild. Nothing could stop him from achieving this, especially since his goal was so close to completion.

He was pacing the ship back and forth searching all the maps for clues to the location of the jewel. He also learned about this guild faction and their leader. He wanted to know how they operated in order to understand the placement of the guards and how the leader operated his planet. He wanted to make sure that they would not be bested by them. The last group of pirates proved to be challenging to them and he did not want a repeat of that scenario. He learned everything there is to know about the guild. This helped in planning how to travel the planet. He knew the access points to the guild's castle and the location of the jewel within it. Ranthor also knew the number of guards within the castle grounds and the lock combination that opened the jewels.

This mission was planned to perfection. There was nothing left to do except wait for its execution. Still, Ranthor knew that his adversary would be difficult to defeat. The guild employed several crafty members who were very versatile in combat. This guild member would not surrender his jewel easily. The chances are that some of the information he gathered was falsely misleading and was designed to derail unintended bounty hunters from finding the jewel. The guild was amongst the most powerful clans in the solar system. No one dared steal anything from them. They also had a habit of getting the thieves to become new recruits. This helped them gain a number of guards and increase the security around the jewels. They also had the support of the king and his army. That meant that they had more guards to summon. It was rumored that the king was part of the guild, but there was little proof to this. He was certainly a powerful ally and one that they always enlisted the help of.

They finally managed to enter the castle. It was left unguarded, which was strange for Ranthor. He knew that this was a trap to convince them that there is a lack of security. The moment they stepped inside they realized that the guards were stationed in the inner chamber and around the corners of the castle. Furthermore, they realize that more than six vaults were laid out. Five vaults had gems and the sixth housed the Nebula jewel. This was done to prevent the thieves from acquiring the jewel. Each guard carried a key for the vaults, and it had to pried away from him to open the vault. The guards were expecting Ranthor to come. They had learned about his previous expedition finding the other jewel and were expecting him.

The leader of the guards was not the one with the jewel. The jewel was with one of the guard groups. Ranthor assumed that the leader would have it and headed there first. He killed a few of the guards and opened the vault when the king left his station. To his dismay, he did not find the jewel and instead found one of the gems. He locked the vault and kept the gem inside. He then searched the other vaults for evidence of the jewel. The jewel was nowhere to be seen. He finally reached the last vault and opened it. Again, the jewel was not there. Instead, another gem was kept in its place. He realized that the king must have a hidden vault somewhere. He searched the place in the hopes of finding the hidden vault. Nothing could be seen within sight. The room did not have an additional vault. The only thing that resembled it was a sarcophagus with a similar lock system. He realized that this must be the last vault. He headed there to attempt opening the sarcophagus.

The keys were placed on top of the sarcophagus. He picked up the keys and opened the sarcophagus. He managed to locate the jewel and he took it with him. The guards were alerted to his presence. Soon, he was swarmed with a dozen guards that were attacking him. He managed to strike the first guard and kill him. He was outnumbered and could barely keep up with the guards. Kendra joined him and was also attacking the guards. She managed to strike another guard and pin him down. She then attacked the remainder of the guards and soon they were all down. Ranthor made his way out of the castle and was preparing to leave. The king, however, decided to ambush them by attacking them from the rear. The king swung his sword at Ranthor and managed to injure him. Ranthor was limping so Kendra went after the king. She managed to kill him. The guards however were difficult for her, so she was aided by Ranthor who despite his injury managed to attack them.

The two of them managed to defeat the guards. Luckily, the place was now empty and there was no one to attack them. Both of them were badly injured and could not cope with another attack. They left the halls of the castle and made their way outside. They had finally managed to acquire the fourth jewel. It was shining and resonating, indicating that another jewel was nearby. Ranthor approached the ship and was happy that there was no one to trail them. Kendra was looking out for any guards and prepared for any encounter. There was no one to tail them and they soon were close to the ship. Gideon smiled when he realized that the fourth jewel was found. He realized that they would finally be able to leave the planet in search of the next jewel.

The ship doors opened, and they were welcomed by Simeoni. Another ship just landed near them. They realized that it was Simeoni's clan. She had called for reinforcements, and they had just arrived to claim the jewels. Ranthor was livid with rage after realizing that he was ambushed and could did not have the strength nor the stamina to fight. Gideon opted to join Kendra in battle. Ranthor agreed and he retired to his chamber to tend to his wounds. He was worried about sending Gideon into battle, but he had no choice. Besides, the boy was good at combat. He had helped them before and proved that he was a worthy adversary. Simeoni had betrayed by doing this and they were surprised as to how she managed to do it while she was with them. She explained to them that she had managed to do this while they were on their little expedition. Kendra struck Simeoni with her bullet and she collapsed in agony.

Gideon and Kendra made their way to the other ship to fight their foes. They breached the hull of the ship and managed to kill the guards that were protecting it. They also managed to reach the king and fight him. The pirates were very skilled and proved to be strong opponents. It was difficult to fend them off. They were about to make their way into the ship and escape with the jewels. Gideon managed to kill one of them and Kendra did the same. Finally, they were left with the king who decided to surrender to them. He offered to join them; however, they did not want a repeat of what happened to Simeoni, so they killed him. The jewels were now in safe possession.

The ship left the orbit of the planet and was making its way to the location of the next jewel. Ranthor was praising Gideon for his excellent dueling skills. He realized that the boy had a lot of potential in battle. He told him that they would use him in their next battles. Gideon was thrilled that he could contribute to gathering the jewels. This would help make their journey quicker and therefore he would be back home. Kendra was also pleased that they were not as likely to be injured with him fighting in their midst. Their last fight was exceedingly difficult and had left Ranthor injured. She almost met the same fate had it not been for her cunning intellect. The fifth jewel was going to be exceedingly hard to find. Their journey was not going to be easy. Many challenges would be in their way to prevent them from acquiring the jewels of Nebula.

Space welcomed them into yet another treacherous solar system. The jewels were shimmering brightly as they approached the neighboring planets. The guild was now disbanded and there were very few of them left to attack them. However, there were many foes searching for the fabled jewels. They were probably stronger than the guild and well equipped to kill them. Who knew what danger lurked for them on their way to the next jewel?

However, their resolve was very strong, and they were sure that they were going to get all of the jewels. Ranthor felt the power of the jewels course through his veins. The four jewels that were with them gave the strength and resolve to continue with this journey. The others were equally empowered to continue. The journey that lay ahead of them was not going to be easy, but then again, they proved yet again that they were worthy adversaries that were not to be contended with.

Ooger was eying the jewels and was enchanted with their beauty. He had never seen the Nebula jewels up close. He was wondering what powers they would grant him once all of them were found. He would finally be free of being a useless scavenger. Perhaps, he would join Ranthor in his father's royal court and serve the king. He would no longer be just a common thief. He would help Ranthor in his quest for power. He wondered though if Ranthor would help him use the jewel's power. He might not indulge this, and would instead resort to sending him back home. After all, Ranthor was the one seeking the power of the jewels, and if it could be granted to one person then it would definitely be him. None of them if the jewels would help a single person or the entire group. All of them were daydreaming about the powers that the jewels would bestow upon them. However, Ranthor was the only one entitled to their power.

Kendra woke up from her sleep and realized that they had just crossed the outer rim of the solar system. They were now in the next solar system, Beta. It was most likely that the jewel was in one of these planets. The jewels were now shimmering. They knew the next jewel was bound to be here somewhere. However, they did not start to resonate yet. Perhaps, they would be in a neighboring solar system. She was glad to have defeated the guild and Casseopi. It pained her to see her family as tyrants, threatening the very order of the universe. Killing Casseopi still weighed heavily on her. She kept reminiscing about the time her sword killed her sister. She cried continuously and was angry at the guild for enlisting her sister.

The ship's fuel was running low, so they decided to head to the nearest planet to refuel their ship. Planet Alveron was the nearest planet. They managed to reach the docking station and were preparing to fuel their ship. The planet looked peaceful enough and did not show any signs of pirate inhabitants. The citizens were gathered in the marketplace, the bakery and the town center purchasing whatever goods they desired. There was no sign of any nefarious activity.

Planet Alveron was the crown jewel of the planet's solar system. There were visitors from all of the galaxy coming here to trade. It was rich in natural oils, gems and different kinds of agricultural products. The planet also had streams which were used to build amusement parks for the children. It was a famous travel destination due to its rich history and the abundance of natural resorts. It had all the amenities for both the rich and regular travelers to enjoy. The casino scene was enjoyed by most of the adult travelers. The planet was home to a variety of humanoid species, all of which were working in the hospitality sector. They managed to get a lot of revenue this time of year from the oncoming tourists. Business was booming and it made them extremely rich. The market was bustling with visitors.

Ranthor managed to find the docking station to fuel his ship. He refueled the ship and decided to explore the area while the ship was being refueled. He and Gideon managed to visit a nearby restaurant and dine there. The place was crowded with every humanoid species available. Most of them enjoyed their drinks at the bar and had the restaurant's famous bison steak. There were a few regular customers who were always present. The place was full, and business was booming. Ranthor decided to order the steak and was happily enjoying his meal. Gideon ordered the duck confit and was enjoying his meal. They ate in silence and waited for the ship to refuel so that they can leave the planet. The restaurant was very quiet as this despite the abundance of inhabitants. Everyone was happily digging into his meal and was busy to start any conversation.

They finished their meal and decided to visit the nearby marketplace. They walked along the banks of the river and enjoyed the scenery. The planet had a lot of rivers and streams which attracted visitors form far and wide. They also had a wide collection of rare minerals which were sold at extremely high prices. The planet was a regular hub for merchants and thieves alike. The abundance of natural resources also made it a regular spot for politicians to exert their control. For Ranthor however, all that mattered to him now was refueling his ship and getting out in order to gather the remainder of the jewels. Although he felt that he could really settle in this planet. He enjoyed the atmosphere here and so did Gideon. The food was amazing, and the weather was moderate unlike the extremes of temperature in both of their planets. This planet was a safe haven to most of the travelers coming to it.

The ship had completed refueling and Ranthor was making his way towards the ship. Gideon was buying some pearls to gift his parents upon his return. His mother had told him that she was fond of them, and he decided to bring some for her. He soon joined Ranthor back to the ship and prepared for departure from the planet. It was nighttime and most of the restaurants and shops were closing. Ranthor prepared the ship for departure. He entered the coordinates for the next planet system and the ship was leaving the planet's atmosphere. One of the guests at the restaurants had overheard their conversation and decided to trail them to find the jewels.

Her name was Amara. She was a bounty hunter also tasked with finding the jewels. The king had wanted them for himself to gain power over his court. She was going to be rewarded heavily if she found the jewels. She learned the location from overhearing the conversation that went between Ranthor and Gideon. She prepared her ship and decided to stalk them and gather the remainder of the jewels. She was adamant to find them all and procure them for her king. She was interested to gain the reward that was going to be given by the king. This will also strengthen her reputation amongst the bounty hunters. The jewels were requested by many, and she might even give it to the highest bidder.

Gideon was facinated by the beads of pearls that he had bought for his mother. He wanted to surprise her with them and could not wait to finish the mission so that he could give them to her. He contacted his parents regularly and they showed the room they had prepared for him. They too were very eager to have him back. His mother told him that she would prepare his favorite food and his father was going to teach him to hunt. They were finally reunited at last, and nothing was going to separate them again. The path to the jewels was becoming easier. Only five jewels remain to be found.

Kendra was glad that they were back in action. She was annoyed that they had to make a little pit stop. They would soon be headed to the next planet to find the jewel. She was still mourning the death of Casseopi and could not imagine her encounter with her father. She told Ranthor that she preferred it if he dueled with her father. She could not bring herself to harm him and feared that this would jeopardize the mission. He agreed to do it and reassured her that what she did was not making her a bad person. He comforted her and reassured her that he understood the pain of turning his back on family. Kendra felt glad that she would avoid the encounter with her father. She can now focus on the mission at hand and help in gathering the next jewel.

They were surrounded by the vastness of space. The star shimmered around the planet like a beautiful mosaic. This planet system was amongst the richest throughout the galaxy. It was the trader center hub of the universe. Many influential people flocked here regularly. Deals were made on a regular basis, both legitimate and otherwise were struck between merchants and politicians. It was surprising that the jewel was not here. The place would be ideal to host such an object of immense power and desire. However, whoever made the jewels made sure that they would be found in the most unlikely places to avoid ending up in unworthy hands. The politicians here were tyrants and gaining more power would make them unstoppable. Despite the relative peace that surrounded the place, there were many people living in absolute poverty. However, they were banished into distant corners of the planet to avoid being seen by the public. This perpetuated the propaganda that this was the center of trade for the universe. Poverty would disturb the order of business and hence it was kept from the public eye.

The next jewel was rumored to be in planet Almeida. This was in the next solar system. It did not have any human inhabitants. It housed a reptilian species that spoke a tongue similar to humans. They protected and guarded the jewel with their lives. They were oblivious to the nature of the jewel, but they recognized that it was a very sought-after object and must be of significant value. They have successfully managed to thwart any attempt at acquiring them by the previous visitors. Ranthor learned that they were quite a formidable force. He was not sure how he would be able to defeat them. He decided that a stealthy approach would be best in this situation. The last battle had left him wounded and his wound just recovered. He did not want to imagine a scenario in which he would be wounded again. The search for the jewels wore him off as it did for the remainder of his crew. Luckily, they managed to reach so far without any fatalities. They were now faced with yet another enemy that safeguarded the jewels.

Chapter 7
The Journey to the Inner Depths

The ship was approaching the next solar system. Planet Almeida was the furthest planet in the solar system. There were several pirate ships waiting for them. The leader of the pirate ships communicated with Ranthor and told him that they were boarding their ship. Ranthor refused, which led the captain to fire a shot at them. It managed to damage the hull of the ship. The alarm started ringing and the escape pods were fired in anticipation of an evacuation. Ranthor asked Kendra to fire at the ship. She managed to shoot the deck, but the ship was barely damaged. They decided to let them board the ship and they would try to kill them while they were on board.

Ranthor allowed the ship's captain to board along with his other crew members. They looked menacingly strong for pirates, more like mercenaries. They were from one of the nearby planet systems. They would usually attack most of the commercial ships and pillage their loot. Their captain was a previous dishonored war admiral that was kicked out due to drunk and disorderly behavior. He was also known to be a gambler and used much of the loot to finance his gambling habit. He commanded the crew and trained them to perfection. They were trained in military combat skills and were extremely strong. Ranthor would find it extremely difficult to defeat these foes.

The captain boarded the ship along with his crew. They were looking for items to loot and sell as merchandise. The first thing that caught their eyes was the sight of the jewels. He did not know what they were, but they looked very valuable. They were heavily protected by the crew, and he was sure to get a good market value for them. He informed one of his lieutenants to gather the jewels and take them aboard the ship. He aimed his blaster at Ranthor and told him that if he tried to do anything, he would blast him with his ion beam. Ranthor complied with the instructions of the captain. However, they did not account for

Gideon and Kendra who were in the room behind the pirates. They snuck stealthily behind them and were preparing for a counterattack.

Ranthor was very apprehensive and feared losing the jewels. They had worked so hard to acquire them and were not going to lose them to some bandits. Kendra approached the pirate leader from behind and managed to strike him with her sword. Gideon blasted the other soldier with his blaster. Ranthor managed to finish off the two remaining soldiers. They had managed to salvage the jewels and prevent them from being stolen by the pirates. They dismantled the pirate ship and made sure that there were no more crew members there. They treaded carefully for the remainder of the journey, and they were on the lookout for any pirate ships. Luckily, the road ahead was not filled with any pirate ships. The journey was clear from there onwards.

The ship was now close to planet Almeida. They had finally managed to reach the solar system housing the next jewel. Ranthor and Kendra were brimming with joy at the prospect of finding the next jewel. Gideon was also happy that he was one step closer to reuniting with his family. Planet Almeida was a peaceful planet and was not the usual site for bandits. Hopefully, their next journey would not involve any bloodshed to acquire the jewels. Still, they were most probably guarded by the king or the royal guard and they would not surrender them easily. The king was not known for his military prowess, and neither were his soldiers. The task of getting the jewels therefore was going to be an easy one. The citizens of the planet were happy with their current ruler. Unlike the other rulers of the planet, they had been to the king here was loving and kind. He ruled over the people fairly and was respected by all his citizens. The planet had meagre resources and, unlike the other planets, was not a rich hotspot. However, it had a lot of land and crops which were exported to the other planets for their feeding. The planet also had many streams and was the holiday spot for many prominent politicians.

Ranthor was told that the next jewel will be in the mountainous region of the planet. However, he would use the other jewels to confirm the location. The ship was approaching the orbit of planet Almeida. Luckily, there was no welcoming party ready to attack them as they approached the planet surface. The planet cast a beautiful reddish hue that made it looked like a red emerald amidst a sea of jewels. It was the most beautiful planet in the solar system and the most inhabited by citizens. Most of them were refugees from other planets who sought political asylum. The planet was known for its tolerant attitudes to refugees and hence they comprised a significant proportion of their citizens. They lived here and had meagre jobs such as farming to support themselves. Some were in local politics and enjoyed the finer side of life.

King Regulus was the proud ruler of the planet and was heirless. People were worried about who his successor would be. The king was well into his eighties and despite his perfect health was quite old. The next in line to the throne was his defense minister Romulus. He was not at all liked by the people of the capital. He was ruthless and wanted to rule the land with military precision. He had good intentions but was quite inflexible which gained him a poor reputation amongst the people of the land. They campaigned against his succession to throne and had met with the king on various occasions to avoid him ruling upon his death. However, the king had held him in great regard and dismissed their wishes. He saw as completely unreasonable. The king trusted Romulus blindly with most affairs of the land and found him to be the most suitable for the job.

The ship finally landed on planet Almeida. They managed to land on a nearby abandoned landing strip. The first thing they had done was head to a nearby diner and enjoy their food. They were all famished from the long journey that they had endured. Kendra was digging into her meal and ate hungrily. The others were slightly more composed and took their time with the meal. Gideon was happy that they had stopped for food. His stomach was growling for the duration of their descent. He finally managed to grab a bite to eat and had felt significantly better. They decided to interrogate some of the citizens of the capital to learn about the mountain system. This would help them gather the necessary gear to help them with the ascension to the top of the mountains. They managed to gather some useful information and were going to head to a nearby shop to purchase supplies for the journey.

The marketplace here was not as busy as the other places they had visited. The people here would only purchase a few items and had designated a specific day to purchase all their needs. They did not have the luxury to purchase what they wanted. Therefore, the shops mostly had the necessities that most people would require. They had finally reached the shop to purchase the mountaineering supplies. Ranthor bought the equipment and paid the vendor. The vendor was extremely happy to finally make a customer today. Business was going slowly on account that the people rarely visited the mountain. The only customers were the miners that worked in the mountain. Their company only bought the bare necessities, and the orders were made to the number of employees that worked there. Occasionally, they would also purchase for repairs of the equipment. However, business was mostly slow. Ranthor managed to buy a lot of equipment and the vendor was happy that he decided to give some extra items to promote his sale. He did not realize that he was not a local, and hence would not become a repeat customer.

Ranthor made his way to the mountain top. He found it strange that the jewels did not start resonating yet. He wondered if the jewel was even in this planet. The jewels were bright when they came here at first. Perhaps someone managed to steal them. Still, this place was the most likely location of the jewels. Maybe they would be resonating when they climbed the mountain. He made his way to the mountain and started climbing the rocks. It was a steep climb to the top of the mountain. It was surprising that the miners did not create a path to the mountains to avoid climbing.

The climb to the mountain top proved to be difficult. Kendra almost slipped and injured herself on the footholds. Ranthor and Gideon on the other hand found the climb very easy. Both of them were used to mountain climbing and actually enjoyed the exercise. The journey to the mountain was quite easy for them and reaching the summit was not going to be difficult. They managed to help Kendra with the climb. They had finally managed to reach the summit and were preparing their camp in the event they had to stay overnight. Ooger was asked to be in charge of the camp, and he would remain there to protect it. Ranthor ventured into the mountain and made his way to the first set of caves. Gideon followed suit and prepared himself for a possible encounter. The journey to the jewels was always perilous and he did not expect this one to be different.

However, there was no one there to intercept them. The journey to the bowels of the mountain proved to be quite safe. There were no enemies waiting for them at the end of the tunnel. People here were not interested in finding any jewels and did not even know about their presence. They were too concerned about making ends meet that they did not concern themselves with the interests of the visitors coming to their land. The politicians were also nowhere to be found. They were free to search the place as they pleased. Ranthor was still surprised that the jewels were not resonating. He kept searching the mountains for any evidence of the jewels but did not find anything of interest. He searched every crevice and surface but did not even find a clue that would suggest the location of the jewels.

He reached the end of a tunnel where a chest was placed there. He decided to open the chest, and to his dismay he found it empty. This must have been where the jewels were housed. His suspicions were now confirmed that the jewels were stolen. Perhaps the king had ordered an expedition to search and gather the jewels. He decided that it would be appropriate to find the king and confront him to see if the jewels were in his possession. He left the mountains and headed to the market. From there he would make his way to the royal palace and see if he can get an audience with the king. The royal palace was around five kilometers from the center of the marketplace. Hopefully, the king would agree to have an audience with them. The people said that he was a reasonable man and would most likely honor the request of meeting with them. The people had audiences with the king to voice their grievances about the issues that were in the land.

The king was in his palace enjoying some music. He did not anticipate the arrival of any visitors. He had already held his meeting with his ministers and prepared the plan for his next battle with the opposing army. He was in his study listening to music and preparing to read one of his novels. The remainder of the day was going to be spent at the horse races where he would ride his trusted steed.

Ranthor made his way to the Royal palace and prepared for an audience with the king. The palace grounds were filled with every species of flowers available. The pavement was jewel encrusted and littered with various rare and precious artefacts. It was a breath-taking sight to behold. In the middle was a small pool of water and in it was a statue of a turquoise mermaid made out of green jade. The gardens were opened as a touristic site in the summer. This was because the king was at his summer estate and the place was used as a touristic spot. It managed to generate a good amount of revenue for the capital. The king was also happy that people had the chance to marvel at his garden. It was a powerful symbol of status that he used to exert his wealth. The people both revered and feared him for he was a ruthless ruler. He was benevolent, but if he was pushed in a corner his fangs would come out. He was not as corrupt as the other rulers, and not nearly as barbaric. However, he did not like to have audiences with the citizens and insisted that they meet with his ministers. He feared an assassination attempt. Despite the peaceful situation, a few people harbored an ill intent and wished that he was dead. His popularity was dwindling over the past few years.

Ranthor knew about the king's reluctance to meet with people. Nevertheless, he ventured into the palace grounds and was adamant to meet him. He was given an audience with his minister of interior, but he refused to meet with him. Instead, he marched into the main quarters of the palace and was headed to the king's personal wing. Strangely enough, he was not stopped by any of the guards. They did not register him as a threat. The king was a very private person and enjoyed most of his pastime in painting oil paintings and listening to classical music. He did not wish to be disturbed at this time. Ranthor was not happy at the lack of guards and took it as a sign of impending trouble. He knew of the king's reservations about meeting visitors and found it odd that he didn't try to actively prevent him from entering.

The royal quarters were decorated very lavishly in the latest imperial fashion. The carpets were imported from planet Odelphius, and the best silk was bought for the tapestries. The vases were decorated with golden lions, the emblem of the royal crown. The royal crest was seen in the canvases and murals. The king surrounded himself in all sorts of splendor and wanted this to be visible to all who come to his chambers. Silver candelabras lined the halls of the chambers. They were lit and cast a radiant glow onto the halls. The place was magnificently decorated and was well maintained. It had its own maintenance budget that the king personally oversaw. He made sure that the funds went into frequently. This was a behavior that was disliked by most of his advisors. There were more important matters to tend to both political and regional. The politicians of neighboring states were not happy with his foreign people and threatened to stage a coup should he continue the current status quo. The king did not pay them any attention and instead left the matter to his advisors.

The king left his room and was in the middle hall of the chamber. He is pacing up and down anxiously unsure as to why visitors were in his chambers. He decided to walk to them and address their issue. He was not happy about this unwelcome intrusion to his daily routine. Still, he wanted to get this done and over with so that he may continue his daily ritual. He approached them gingerly and looked at them from the corner of his eye. He wore a stern look and was gazing at them menacingly. Ranthor approached him and gave him an equally menacing look. The king cowered into the background, clearly intimidated by Ranthor. He decided that this was not an opponent to be trifled with. He decided to listen to them and assist them accordingly. He wanted to avoid any possible altercation. Ranthor looked at him approvingly and decided to ease up a little bit to allow his host to speak. The two of them went to the study and the king decided that was where they were going to deliberate.

"To what do I owe this unwelcome visitor stranger. As you well know, I am very busy man and would like it if we could skip the formalities and get straight to the point. I'm sure that you are equally busy and will appreciate the need for brevity. So, tell me what I can do for you?" Grunted the king.

"I appreciate your candor, and the fact that you are straight to the point. We have learned that you know about the jewels of Nebula. There is a jewel rumored to be in this planet and we would like to know its whereabouts," replied Ranthor confidently.

"The object you seek is rumored to be in the Loari mountains which are to the east of the planet. It is around 350 kilometers from here. I would advise you to take a guide with you there as the terrain is treacherous and the road is filled with beasts and bandits," advised the king.

Ranthor reassured him that he didn't need anyone. He asked him if there was a place, he can gather gear from. The king told him that there would be nearby shops. Ranthor made his way out of the castle and into the nearby market. The others followed suit and made their way into the open air. The gardens were scented with lilac and lavender. It brought a soothing quality to the place. Most of the people had a difficult time leaving due to the tranquility instilled by the place. However, Ranthor had a pressing mission to attend to and could not care for this. He was hurrying at such a rapid pace that the others could barely keep up.

They finally managed to leave the palace grounds and enter the main city. The town was quiet and there was not much activity going around. Most of the people either had lunch now or were at the pub. The latter were the friendly drunks of the town. Of course, the alcohol made them more merry and cheerful. The people in this town were frequently in the pubs and the business were booming. The restaurant was also a lucrative business for most of the investors. The capital had one of the best bistros in the planet and people came from everywhere to enjoy the food. Ranthor and others also decided that it was time for them to enjoy a nice meal.

Kendra was starving and welcomed the opportunity to enjoy some food. The others were also equally hungry. The bistro waiter came and served them juicy tender steaks and mead. They dug into their meals ravenously and had to order seconds. They enjoyed the meal heartily. Everyone was fed and happy. It was nice to finally enjoy a warm meal. The restaurant did indeed live up to its expectations.

Ranthor was feeling very confident about finding the jewel. His journey was finally going in the right direction. Hopefully, there will not be any interruption from any nearby intruders. His plan was so far working successfully, and he enjoyed the fact that he did not have to overcome any obstacles to reach his goal. This journey has been very daunting for him, and he could not wait to be back again in his father's good graces. Yet, he questioned whether he could use the jewels for his own good and abandon his father. He was wondering if it was worth it to return to the man that abandoned him in this hour of need. Was it worth it to return to such a failing father figure? Still, he wanted to reunite with his kin and the planet that he was born in.

They remained in the restaurant for a little while longer and decided to order dessert. They enjoyed an apple tart and crème brule. They then headed to the market to find gear for their journey. The journey to the market was quite enjoyable. Dusk has set a reddish hue over the horizon. The sunset in this city was beautiful to witness. Many people were gathered around the capital square to witness it. But Ranthor did not have time for such pleasantries. He yanked the others away and made his way to inquire about the whereabouts of the shops that sold climbing gear. He made his way into the far corner of the town and into the nearest shop. The place seemed deserted, but he still managed to find a single vendor that sold gear. The lady tried to convince him that she was a qualified guide, but he did not want anyone to come with them on their journey. He explained that this was a security matter and thanked her for her willingness to come. He purchased the equipment and made his way out of the market and into the mountains.

The journey to the mountains was quite an arduous one. They had crossed many streams and valleys on the way there. They had managed to pack some snacks for the journey so that they would not starve on the way there. The valleys were steep but luckily there were no predatory species or bandits here. It was a welcome break to avoid all the fighting. Ranthor was glad that the journey so far was going very smoothly. He hoped that this feeling would last, at least once just this time. Kendra also had the same feeling and was excited that they were getting on with their journey. She dug into the bag and opened one of the sandwiches. She was starving and managed to dig into her sandwich. The others were still satiated from the previous meal.

They had managed to reach the stream before the mountains. Ranthor grabbed a few bottles from their bag and filled them with water from the stream. The water was very clean that you could see your reflection through it. The others were sitting down and relaxing to prepare for the remainder of the journey. They had managed to cross a vast amount of land and were somewhat tired. Ranthor, on the other hand, was burning with energy and did not want to rest till he found the jewel. Regardless, he sensed that the others needed some respite and therefore decided to take a break here and gather their strength. He was eating one of the sandwiches just to pass the time. He managed to take a deep breath and take in the surroundings. The stream was actually quite beautiful and had not been for their current situation would have been a fantastic site to visit.

Ranthor packed the equipment and made their way to the mountain. There was not much left now. He could see the mountain from where he was standing. The climb was steep and would require all the energy he could muster. Nonetheless, he knew he had the aptitude for the task. He decided that he and Kendra would go up to the mountain and the others would stay as lookout. They had finally reached the mountain and were planning their ascent. The others agreed to stay as lookout and were going to alert them via intercoms if any bandits were approaching. Ranthor began his ascent of the mountain. He arranged his gear accordingly and swung the grapple hook at the nooks and crevices to gain a foothold. He then swung himself on top and managed to gain a footing.

He seemed to be experienced at this sort of thing. Mountain climbing came naturally to him, and he was maneuvering the mountain with such grace and poise. Kendra was also faring well, but was not as agile as Ranthor. Luckily, she was able to maintain her footing and travel at a reasonable pace. She just kept herself from looking down to avoid causing fear. She did not like heights much and usually felt vertiginous. However, she managed to muster whatever strength she had and powered on. The climb proved to be challenging but they both managed to cross foothold after foothold and gain a higher place. They were midway across the summit and were already starting to feel tired. They drank from their water bottles and rested a little bit before continuing their journey.

After they've regained their footing, they continued their journey onwards to the summit. The journey from here onwards was easier and Kendra was starting to getting the hang of things. Ranthor was almost at the summit and was ready to finish his climb. Kendra was also close to completing her climb. The climb was coming to end, and Kendra was actually happy she conquered her fear of heights. Ranthor was already at the summit and enjoyed another sandwich. Kendra followed closely afterwards and was panting as she reached the summit. Still, it was an accomplishment for her. She did not want to disappoint Ranthor by telling him about her fear of heights. Meanwhile, Gideon was on lookout duty and there was nothing suspicious so far. There were no bandits or beasts approaching them.

Kendra was searching for a way inside. She managed to find the entrance to the caves and made her way inside. Ranthor followed suit and they managed to enter the cave system. They managed to find a tree branch and wrapped a cloth around it and lit it to make a torch. They then ventured further into the caves to explore their surroundings. The cave was very damp and smelled of Sulphur. It was filled with woolly bats. This was a very docile species of bats that fed on berries. However, if agitated then can be quite lethal if provoked with fire. Ranthor made sure not to agitate them and left them in peace. The journey was going smoothly so far, and they did not run into any trouble. He was glad that they were interrupted but at the same time he was suspicious. Things don't usually go smoothly with them. Besides, the king was awfully quite helpful in assisting them with the quest. That didn't sit well with him. The jewels were known to be a well sought-after object.

The caves were very quiet at this time. However, the bats were awake and were feeding. They filled the cave and most of the remainder of the cave system. Ranthor traced the tracks that he had found near the entrance of the cave. He was searching the cisterns for any evidence of the jewel. He did not manage to find anything so far. Still, he continued his search and so did Kendra. Both of them searched behind every stalactite and stalagmite. They were a lot of gold specs but there was no evidence of the jewel. The jewel that was with them did not resonate or brighten yet. They were both disappointed that nothing had happened yet. Ranthor was getting disappointed that nothing was happening yet. Kendra, however, was optimistic that they will find the jewel. She continued to search the cave system for evidence of the jewels.

She managed to find a side entrance that was not discovered by any of the previous inhabitants. She motioned over to Ranthor to come and enter through it. The jewel started to resonate and both of them were happy that it did so. Ranthor was thrilled with joy that the jewel was close by. Kendra was equally pleased that they were finally close to their goal. They contacted Gideon through the intercom and told him about the new development. So far, there was nothing suspicious going on outside. Both of them ventured on further into the caves and avoided any contact with the bats. The caves were very damp and smelled of metal ores. This used to be an old mining cave that was frequently visited by the miners. However, the drilling used to agitate the bats which made them blood thirsty. Hence, this was abandoned to avoid any injuries to the miners.

Kendra managed to enter into the inner chamber of the cave. She had found a vault in the middle of the cave with an engraving inside of it. The engraving was a code to open the vault. All they had to do was find similar engravings and they would be able to open the vault. Perhaps it was the vault that housed the jewel.

She managed to find spokes that were engraved with the same markings. She moved it and it opened the way to a tunnel that had a box with a similar engraving. She opened it and found one of the keys that were required to open the vault. It was a simple steel key with a wooden handle. It fit the vault markings perfectly. All she had to do now was to find the other two keys and she would be able to open the vault. She was surprised to find that the task was going this smoothly. She did want to doubt this and decided that she was thrilled about the simplicity of the task. She continued her search of the cave for similar spokes to find the keys. She did not find another spoke in this room and decided to search another room.

The next chamber was similar to the other one. There were similar carvings on the wall, and this too was surrounded by bats. The place was equally damp and smelled of metal ores. She searched for the keys in the room. There was no spoke to be seen here. However, she spotted a lever nearby. She decided to pull the lever. She heard a nearby creaking noise and she decided to follow it. She managed to find a door which led to another door. She followed it and found a similar box inside. She opened it and she found another key. She then made her way out of the chamber and into the next. Kendra managed to avoid the bats with her torch and avoid agitating them.

The last chamber was bigger than the other two combined. She wondered what sort of contraption would be available this time. There were not very elaborate so far, and finding the jewel seemed somewhat simple. Still, she decided to take the win and agree that it might just be that simple. She searched the chamber for any evidence of any lever or other contraption. She did not manage to find anything despite thoroughly scouring the room. She almost gave up and decided to leave the room and search the others again. As she left, she stumbled on another lever. This one did not open a door and instead opened a hatch from which a rope hung from it. She pulled the rope and the box descended from below. She opened the box and managed to find the next key.

The way to central chamber was clear. Ranthor was scouting the room for any evidence of invaders. He did not find anyone in the room. Kendra came inside bearing three keys and told him that these were the keys to the vault in this room. She handed them over to him and he eyed them carefully. Both of them walked over to the vault and decided to open it. Kendra was shaking with excitement. Ranthor was equally happy that they will finally get a chance to reach the vault. They opened the vault, and they found a gem-encrusted key. Perhaps, this opened a door to another chamber that opened the way to the jewel. They decided to search for evidence of the lock that matched the key. They both kept searching for hours, but did not find any evidence of such a door.

They entered yet another chamber. However, there was no evidence of a door with a similar lock. The way inside the chamber was clear. There were a few silver and golden specs here which was evidence of previous mining work. Ranthor was looking intently for any evidence of the door but did not seem to find anything. The chamber was empty and there was no evidence of any door. They left the chamber and went on to search the others. It was beginning to turn dark outside, and they were surrounded by the light from the moon. The bats had finished feeding and were laying quietly in the stalagmites.

Ranthor entered the next chamber and he had finally managed to find the door. Finally, he could enter the door with the key. He ventured into the chamber and tried to open the key with the door. The door opened and he managed to enter inside. Kendra followed him into the next chamber. The chamber inside was less damp than the others and there was no evidence of bats.

The air suddenly became very still. The mountain air was very cold and bone breaking. Kendra was shivering and shaking violently. Ranthor did not seem perturbed by it. The main chamber was now within sight. It shone brighter than the others. There were many lanterns that shone bright. They didn't know how they were wired here or the reason for their existence in the first place. Were the ones who came before them expecting this company? It was a question that they would not get the answer to soon. Ranthor decided to venture further inside the chamber and approach the vault within. He was finally ready to open it and hopefully extract the jewel within.

He walked over to the vault gingerly. He expected that there would be a trap somewhere expecting to be sprung. It probably was attached to the vault. It was eerie, the absence of any sort of trap or hidden mechanism. He was not accustomed to things being this easy, and frankly he did not enjoy it one bit. This was a very coveted item, and it was laid out in the open. He managed to shake off the thought from his head and walk over closer to the vault. He finally reached it and gazed into its magnificent form. He was bewitched by the beauty of the inscription on it. He started opening the first key, and it sprung open with such ease that Kendra started squealing with excitement. She could barely contain herself that they were finally close.

Ranthor, on the other hand, was contained and maintained his composure. He started unlocking the second lock, and yet again the lock gave way to his hand just as easily. He was finally at the third lock and was making his way about opening it. Just as he was about to open the lock, he received an ion bullet. Luckily, it ricocheted off his blaster. This was a warning shot, and the person aiming it was clearly a skilled marksman. Oddly enough, he felt at ease that at least something was expected. It reassured him that the jewel was where it was supposed to be. Kendra drew her blaster and prepared for the oncoming onslaught. The other assassins approached them and were also preparing their weapons. The bullets clashed and brought some of the stalagmites careening in a downwards spiral. The cave, however, was maintaining its integrity and did not crumble from the shear brute force of the attack.

Ranthor managed to kill one of the assailants. Two more were soon struck down by Kendra's bullets. Yet the rest maintained their resolve and did not cower into the background. They did not seem to bear any noticeable insignia of any sorts. Neither of them recognized where these assailants hailed from, and they did not want to find out either. The only thing they needed to know is that these were their enemies. The best-case scenario would be that they were independent contractors, mercenaries of some sort, and that would not call for reinforcements. They wanted this ambush to end as soon as possible and did not want it to drag on further.

However, things rarely would go this easily, and whoever is ordering these fools knew too well about the jewels. It was also possible that this was someone they knew. Perhaps it was the king or maybe a remnant clan of the politicians that set up camp here. Either way, they had to be eradicated and a message had to be clearly made to whoever ordered this attack. It was the last straw. They were not going to tolerate another attack. Hopefully, they would not be wounded this time. They tried to avoid any incoming attacks as much as possible. Ranthor had barely recovered from the last one, and he did not want to retain another injury. Despite his frail constitution, his body was quite formidable and had excellent rejuvenating properties. It was a well-known quality about his race. This made them excellent at going to battles, and despite sustaining injuries would win the war.

Their opponents were giving them a run for their money. Clearly, these new assailants were military trained. They moved together with such a fluid precision that it felt as if a wave was moving against them. They barely lost a stride, and when they did, they quickly recovered their stance and managed to parry off the oncoming attack. Kendra was about to run out of stamina. She was tapped out and decided to let Ranthor continue until she recovered. In the meantime, she decided to study the battleground for any evidence of weak spots in their opponents' tactics.

Ranthor managed to take out another two of their opponents without sustaining any noticeable injury. The tide of the fight was going in their favor so far. Ranthor was also starting to get fatigue. He tagged Kendra and she continued the remainder of the fight. She took her sword and decided to take her opponents in sword combat. She managed to easily take them out. She realized that they were not good at close combat as they were at using their blasters. She managed to slice and dice them with such ease. They were now intimidated by them, and the remaining ones decided to leave the scene of battle.

Kendra started to rejoice as soon as their opponents fled the scene of battle. They opened the bottles of water and drank from them thirstily. Both of them were smiling at each other at their accomplishment. Ranthor approached the vault again and began hacking at the remaining lock. The vault give way and there was the jewel shining brightly in all its glory. Ranthor was teeming with excitement. The way was becoming clearer to them. The world was finally shining brighter, and Ranthor's heart was floating on a cloud of serenity. As soon as they escaped the cave, he would be soon greeted with a hearty meal of bison steak and gravy. He would even order dessert and would sleep soundly at night knowing that this insane search was coming to an end.

They contacted Gideon and let him know about the excellent news. He too was glad to hear that they had found the jewels. This had called for celebrations. The best part is that the way was becoming clearer for them now. Both of them exited the cave and were preparing their descent out of the mountain. The air felt clearer, and the moon was shining brightly. The night air was singing a very merry tune. There was nothing today that could change their uplifted spirits. They rendezvoused with Gideon and were making their way back to the ship.

The ship was finally close to their sight. Ooger was looking at them, eagerly expecting some good news. They entered the ship and told him the good news. He was ecstatic to know this and was preparing a meal to celebrate this new finding. The cloaking device was turned on and they enjoyed their meal in peace. They were going to make camp and leave the planet in the morning. It was good that they did have to proceed with such haste. It was a welcome break to get a good meal and sleep to recharge their journey for the upcoming journey ahead.

Ranthor did not want to rejoice just yet. There was still a lot for them to do and this was just the beginning of the journey. Besides, the mercenaries that escaped were going to report to their masters the findings of tonight, and that would mean that they would be on high alert. It was destined that there was going to be another encounter with these foes. Unlike their other adversaries, these individuals belonged to a much higher order. This order was not going to rest until the remainder of the jewels were found. Clearly, they knew about the extent of their power and would go to any length to acquire them. Little did they know that they were going to be met with their match. The crew was adamant to show them that they meant business and that they could not be easily defeated.

They were all sleeping soundly. Ranthor was finally calm, and his anxiety had abated with the sight of the jewel. He did not tolerate yet another derailment. Tonight, he could sleep worry-free knowing that he was on the right path to find the remainder of the jewels. He would soon no longer don the clothes of the battle hunter, and instead would wear the robes of royalty. He was still getting the thoughts of acquiring the jewels for himself. Perhaps, establish his own kingdom. Lately, he was thinking that he did not owe anyone including himself redemption. That he was entitled forgiveness, and that if his father could not see this, then it was not worth it going back to him. He did not want to feel the need to constantly have to prove anything to anyone. It was time to establish his own empire, one that operated with his own rules. No longer would he be shackled with the bonds of approval.

The next morning, they all woke up refreshed and ready to start the new day. The universe was theirs for the taking. No longer were they the underdogs that first started this journey. As of now, they were considered the silent underlords of the solar system. Ranthor woke up with a newfound vigor and was preparing the ship's coordinates for their next travel. They ate a quick breakfast and then began their ascent out of the planet. The way to the next planet system was planned, and the route was charted on the map. The engines were being revved up, and the ship zoomed quickly into the sky. They were out of the planet's surface and were into space. Kendra was talking quietly to Gideon about their dreams and aspirations. Both of were not directly involved with the jewels and had only come for the reward attached with the journey. They would then get back to their own lives and would forget about the harrowing ordeal that was involved in gathering the jewels.

Gideon had managed to contact his parents and let them know about the newest development in the journey. They were thrilled and excited about this that Ranthor could hear their excited squeals through the intercom. For Gideon, his biggest dream was reuniting with his family and living the remainder of his childhood with them. This was most important to him than all the jewels and precious gems of the entire universe. He was getting anxious to get this journey done. But even then, he did enjoy the little bit of adventure that he had got while travelling to find the jewels. It sure beat the dull atmosphere of the orphanage. It was something that one day he would tell his children and grandchildren. That he was seeking the legendary jewels of Nebula, and that he had met a lost prince. He was sort of feeling nostalgic that he would not be doing this anymore. His parents were not rune architects or adventure enthusiasts. Come to think of it, he did not know what they did for a living and did not think to ask them.

Chapter 8
Ghosts of the Past

The planet looked like a tiny speck of gold dust from below. It dissolved into the emptiness of its surroundings. Space was very peaceful and serene, it almost felt that it had its own presence. A creature of some sorts that was benevolent, but if provoked would swallow its denizens into blackness. They called the sea a cruel mistress, but space was the lord on high. No one dared upset the balance of space. A simple supernova was enough proof of that. Even the stars that were old as space bore witness to this. It was respected, revered, and greeted by the travelers that regularly made journeys here. Ranthor had only one thing on his mind and that was finding the next jewel. Kendra was pondering about the identity of the person that ordered their attack. Whoever it was, they had a means of tracking them.

The next planet was Planet Lozarius, one of the giants in the next solar system. There were no known humanoid inhabitants in the planet, and little was known about its fauna and flora. Finding clues was going to be challenging this time, but luckily, they had enough jewels to assist them in finding the next jewel. All they had to do now was wait for the ship to reach their next location. The remainder of the plan will be unraveled later. Ranthor was not much for strategic planning and took for using the element of surprise to manage his excursions. Kendra on the other hand was not content with this approach and often argued about the fact that it had always led them to the middle of an ambush. Trouble seemed to be always around the corner. She hoped that for once there would not be an ambush to surround them. Perhaps, the lack of sentient life forms in the planet was a blessing in disguise. Luckily, they had managed to pack enough food in the event that they had to stay for several days.

They entered the next solar system now. The ship began whirring and there was a weird sound coming from the ship's hull. Ranthor decided to go to the main computer compartment and get an analysis done of the system. He did not like that it made that sound. Despite not planning, he did not like that his equipment would start acting up all of a sudden. Hopefully, it was going to be something minor and would have to be repaired internally. The ship was equipped with a self-diagnostic and repair system that could fix minor mechanical and electronic issue. He entered the main compartment of the ship and began his descent towards the main computer. He entered the code, and the program began analyzing the deficit. He waited patiently as a report was being generated.

The report was finally prepared and indicated that the ship's cloaking device and shield system were down. It was extremely risky venturing without them onto the surface of the planet. They decided to descend onto the next planet and find a mechanic to repair the ship. Planet Tuvula was the next planet that they knew for sure was inhabited by people. They made their way onto the planet's surface and had finally managed to reach it. The ship began its descent onto the surface of the planet. Ranthor wanted to waste no time finding the necessary parts to fix the ship. He was furious at this delay and did not show any effort to hide it. Kendra was trying to calm him down but could not do so. She was equally frustrated that this was happening now.

Planet Tuvula was one of the ugliest planets they had ever come across. It was considered the spot where most of the prisoners, outlaws, and cast out political candidates were dumped. No one came here and the few people that lived here honestly tried their very best to escape the planet. Still, it was their only shot right now at fixing the ship. They didn't waste time finding a mechanic. He agreed to fix their ship and informed them that it would be done by the evening. Meanwhile, they decided to get something to eat. The food was surprisingly not bad here. They found a decent diner and had a nice meal. Kendra noticed that a shrouded figure was sitting two booths behind them. She was growing suspicious of the figure, but then she figured that this planet was suspicious as it is, and she did not need to read into the situation.

They concluded their meal quickly and decided to take a quick tour of the town center. Eerily enough, the hooded figure also made his way out of the diner, albeit in a different direction. Kendra was not happy about this and decided to stay on her guard. The best-case scenario was that he was a spy sent to track them. Still, it was very unlikely that whoever was tracking them would know about their technical problem aboard the ship. She dismissed the thought immediately but still decided to remain on guard in anticipation of any upcoming trouble.

They ventured into the market square which was covered in sickly green tiles and banners. Even the king' emblem was hideous, and it was rumored that he was too. The king was a frequent visitor of the market square. He enjoyed doing his own shopping and did not use the aid of the many servants that were under his employ. He did not care about the deplorable state that his capital was in, and neither were the citizens, who only cared about meeting ends meet, legitimately or otherwise.

What was striking was that the marketplace was quite empty. It lacked the regular hustle and bustle of the other planets that they had visited. Perhaps it was not a bad thing after all. They did not want the crowds to be here, especially in the event that something would happen.

They realized that the shrouded figure was still in the background. But whoever it was did not seem interested in them. He was making his way into a nearby alley. He was preparing for an exchange with one of the local criminals. Ranthor decided to tune him out and not get entangled in this mess. The others did the same thing. They had managed to take a quick stroll and were soon back in the mechanic's shop. They were all relieved to know that the ship was fixed. They could finally leave this sorry, sordid excuse for a planet and be well on their way to find the next jewel. Kendra was not happy about the cloaked figure. It was almost as if he had made it his business to throw them off his trail. Yet again, she decided to bury this thought deep in her mind and forget about it for the time being.

Later that evening, she sat in her quarters and was planning her attacks in anticipation of a possible upcoming battle. Ranthor was doing the exact same thing. He realized that they were both improving in terms of their skills caliber and agility. It was becoming slightly easier to fend off their foes. Hopefully, this was going to last and would be an advantage in any possible future encounter. However, he secretly hoped that there would be none. Despite being a trained warrior, he longed for peace and stability. He despised the fighting amongst the nations of these solar systems.

They were making their ascent out of the planet. Ranthor checked the computer and made sure that the errors were fixed. He then made his way into the cockpit and entered the coordinates. They were back on their way to locating the next jewel. Hopefully, the journey would be smoother from here on, but he knew better than to keep his hopes up. They would only be crushed yet again. Instead, he focused on being practical and planned a strategic plan for the next encounter with their opponents. He knew that finding the jewel would only bring more trouble their way. At least, it would be good thing to be prepared for the battle in advance.

Gideon frantically reached for the intercom and was making another call to his parents. He was reassuring them that he was still safe and sound. They rejoiced upon hearing his voice and had asked him when he would be coming back. He replied that it was going to be soon now. He then went and prepared a small snack for himself. He sat in his quarters and was playing with the nuts and bolts in his quarters. He decided that for the next journey he would ask Ranthor for something to do. He grew bored of lookout duty and decided that he could do more than just this. He had proved himself to be a valuable asset in their journey so far. Perhaps he could convince them to take him to fight their next opponent. Although, he was afraid of being injured in combat. He still longed for a peaceful, yet boring life with his family back home. He decided that it was best that he would help with locating and extracting the jewels. He would leave the fight to the grown-ups for the time being. Even though it pained him to do so, he realized that it would be best given his current circumstances.

The surface of the planet was now within sight. They were soon going to prepare their descent. All of them looked ambivalent upon looking at the planet. Compared to the previous ones visited, this did not look like it would house the jewel. It looked far too distant and deserted to keep the jewels. They had wondered if anyone had ever set foot in it. Still, it was worth the shot to explore it and exclude it as a possible spot to hide the jewels. Although, it would be an ideal place to throw off any casual amateur hunters searching for them. They would immediately dismiss it as a viable location, therefore keeping the jewels in safe keeping. Hidden in plain sight. It was a genius plan, one that was simple yet elegant.

Kendra was pacing up and down the corridor. She was very worried about followed by that stranger they had encountered on their previous stop. The clunk of her boots and the cadence of her stride was starting to distress the others as well. Ranthor decided to walk over to her and comfort her. He did not know how to do that, but he still will try, nonetheless. He owed it to her to give her the necessary comfort to power through the remainder of the journey. He did not even mind if she would sit this one out. He cared about the safety and welfare of his crew. Besides, they were fighting a fight that was not theirs, and it was important that they were kept out of harm's way as much as possible. Besides, he started developing some feelings towards her. He did not know what they were, but he wanted to explore them with her. He was not sure if the same feelings were reciprocated by her. Still, he wanted to at least find out.

He leaned over and sat beside her in her quarters. He brought a glass of water with him and offered it to her. She graciously accepted and thanked him for the kind gesture. They spent the evening talking about their fears and he managed to somehow calm her. Her leaned over and gave a squeeze on the shoulder. She did not resist and instead returned the embrace. She lay there in his embrace for the better part of an hour. It felt good to soak up that warmth. He too was glad that perhaps this was not an unrequited feeling. That maybe somehow something good was going to come from it after all.

Still, he did not want to overstep his boundaries further and decided to only embrace her. He felt equally safe in her embrace. He longed for the tender touch of a significant other. For so long, he had been living alone in exile that he forgot the power that human emotion had on healing wounds, and not only those of the flesh. He rarely exposed his vulnerabilities. In his business, that would usually mean death. Instead, he was usually walled off on the outside and remained cold. However, this encounter moved something in him that he could not understand. Was this thing becoming deeper now? He was actually afraid to know the answer. He was not comfortable with the idea of being intimate with anyone. Ever since he was exiled, he dismissed all forms of contact and decided to stay on his own. It was more peaceful and most importantly less complicated.

He left her quarters and bid her goodbye. She wished that he would have stayed longer. However, she decided to maintain her composure and return to whatever it was that she was doing. It felt good to feel warmth again, even if it was brief. She decided to head to the pantry and make herself a meal. All that pacing had made her quite hungry. She felt significantly better after having something to eat.

They were approaching the planet surface, and Ranthor was entering the descent coordinates. The planet had a beautiful crimson hue surrounding it. Perhaps, the beauty of it was not marred by the humanoid species that inhabited the other planets. It had a pure unadulterated beauty that was preserved in all its glory. It was also the home of several vicious beasts. The crew had to be extremely careful interacting with the local wildlife. They need to avoid provoking them in whatever way possible. Antagonizing them would ensure a sudden death. However, it was usually easy to steer well out of their way. After all, they did not seek to hunt these animals. Legends hold that their flesh had healing properties if mixed with some of the plants. The previous inhabitants used them for their medicinal properties before being wiped out. Nothing much was known about the previous inhabitants. The ship's log did not have much information about this. It was due to the fact that much of the literature surrounding them was obsolete and not updated.

They entered the atmosphere of the planet and already started their descent. Ranthor strapped his seatbelt and sat eagerly in his chair awaiting the landing. The others were equally keen to arrive at this mysterious planet. Some were anxious about meeting the wildlife here, Ooger for one did not wish to depart the ship. Ranthor understood and allowed for him to stay onboard. The others, however, were excited to disembark the ship. They did not wish to stay idle while Ranthor went on his search. Gideon was intrigued to learn more about this planet. He wanted to see the wildlife that inhabited the planet. He had learned about much of it from school and wanted to see in real life. The others were not as keen and wanted to stay as far as possible. Kendra was feeling less apprehensive than before and regained her appetite for combat. Although, she might not need it after all as there were no sentient beings here to combat. That was both relieving and distressing for her at the same time.

Gideon was surprised to find a paved road here. It was previously a remnant of the previous civilization. This place had not been inhabited by any humanoid species for the better part of three centuries. All of the evidence for the previous civilization either withered away or was consumed by the overgrowth of plants over it. The animals here were not used to any visitors. They had completely forgotten what people looked like. That might be dangerous as they may consider their presence as a threat.

The journey to the center of the planet was an arduous one. There were so many nooks, crannies, and crevices along the road that it was somewhat painful, and you had to maneuverer around them. Still, the weather was not too sunny and there was a cold breeze which made less insufferable. Kendra and Ranthor were powering through regardless of the condition of the road. There was nothing that was going to be stopping them from acquiring the next jewel. As for Gideon, he was fascinated by the sight and took his time strolling around the place. He imagined the flora here and took as many pictures of them as he could.

He also had a journal around and was jotting down a few things. His scribbles were barely legible, but they clearly meant something important to him. He stopped at every corner and took in the scene that was unfolding before him. Kendra wondered as to what he would do with it. She was going to ask him as soon as they were done with the mission.

Strangely enough, they found an abandoned hut by the river stream. It definitely looked out of place. The place was supposed to be abandoned for centuries according to literature, and yet this place looked at least 50-60 years old. Still, it might be holding a clue to the nature of this place, and possibly the location of the jewel. If there were sentient inhabitants, they sure were long gone by now. There was no sign of any intelligent life forms here. There were many birds in this region. Birds from every different species imaginable. The birds were somewhat large and had feathers of every color. The most striking was the one with the turquoise- and emerald-colored feathers. Gideon was eyeing it with such fervor that the bird realized it was being watched. Oddly enough, it seemed to like the attention and decided to approach Gideon. He petted it and it gurgled indicating happiness. It decided that it wanted to keep him company. He was happy with the new friend he had made and got food from his bag to feed it. The bird ate the food graciously and squawked happily. It was one of the oldest species of the planet. He did not expect it to be this friendly, but surprisingly it was. He welcomed his new friend as part of his crew and decided to let it walk with for the rest of the journey. Even Ranthor did not mind the presence of this new guest.

Kendra was walking very cautiously and kept expecting to run into the masked figure anytime now. However, there was no one in their nearby vicinity. She eased up a little bit and continued the journey. She was starting to become frustrated that the jewel did not resonate so far. She was wondering if they were going in the wrong direction or even if the jewel were in this planet. After all, someone might have come here before and took possession of them. There was that hut, and whoever inhabited it may have already taken the jewels. Despite this, she decided to remain optimistic and keep her hopes about finding the jewels. The journey to find them proved to be painstakingly difficult than she imagined. She never imagined it to be easy, but then again, she didn't imagine that it would take them to the furthest reaches of the universe. Whoever hid them was extremely clever and made it their mission for them to be separated across the vast reaches of the universe.

Ranthor was searching the hut for any useful items, but he did not manage to find anything of value there. He managed however to find an engraved machete. In it, a saying was inscribed the following:

Whatever you seek to redeem yourself. The answer lies at the end of the enlightened path.

He did not know what to make sense of this, but he decided to look for more clues. He did not find anything of value. He held the machete upwards and realized that it cast a beam of light. He then understood what the inscribed verse meant. He decided to follow the trail that it cast. He told the others and soon they were all headed in the same direction. Knowing that it was not going to be this easy, they were prepared to face any difficulties that lay ahead of them. Even Gideon was preparing himself for the journey ahead. There was nothing that was going to stop them from achieving their dreams. They have already travelled far and wide for this to fail. And they were going to be damned if they let a silly clue dictate their fate. Come hell or highwater they were going to get the remainder of the jewels.

Everyone was determined to contribute to finding this jewel. The combined effort of all the crew members was sufficient to find their current clue. Things were finally falling into place for Ranthor. Kendra was starting to ease up a little bit. She was finally letting her guard down and accepting that Ranthor would be there for her aid. She rested assured that he cared for her and would do anything in his power to make sure that all of them were safe. He was an excellent leader and had them kept safe and sound so far. He was also quite understanding and did not want to push them beyond their limits. She was going to do her best so that he will be reunited with his father once again.

The journey was getting easier now, but they were starting to get tired. They decided to stop briefly for water and snacks. The weather was hot, and they were sweating profusely. Each of them removed an article of clothing to cool off and splashed water over themselves from the stream. They felt a little bit better after having food and water. They rested next to the trees nearby and made a temporary camp to rest for an hour. The bird was also thirsty, and Gideon gave it a few sips of water. It gulped it down and its thirst was then quenched. It managed to find shade in the tree where it perched comfortably. It was surprising that it was still with them. It had gotten use to their company and did not seem to want to leave.

Ranthor was sleeping soundly knowing that the others were there to guard the place. He did not sleep well over the past few days and used this opportunity to catch some rest. He had insomnia over the last week or so. This was due to recurrent dreams of his upcoming interaction with his father. Part of him dreaded coming back home, if he could still call that place home after all. But then again, he did not want to spend his entire life wandering the universe. He wanted to settle down and relax. He grew tired of all the various conquests that took him to the furthest reaches of the universe. Perhaps, he would open a small restaurant after this adventure was over and he and Kendra could look after it. He was glad that she had reciprocated the same feelings. He could not imagine that he would be loved by someone that beautiful.

Meanwhile, in the ship Ooger was looking frantically at his surroundings for any signs of intruders. Despite the cloaking device now being active and armed, he still did not trust technology. So far things were peaceful, and he started to become bored of staying alone. He was regretting not joining the others in their journey. However, he was then reminded that this was dangerous planet and that he was going to be eaten by more than willing beasts. He decided to make himself something to eat.

The jungle surrounding Ranthor was providing some form of protection against the heat. He decided that it would be best to travel under the cover of the trees. The illuminated path was almost coming to an end. They would finally see the possible location of the next jewel. They finally arrived at an artificial door carved out of a boulder in the middle of a stone formation. There was a lever besides it. Ranthor pressed the lever and the door opened. Surprisingly, the mechanism was still intact and welcomed them into a very damp dungeon. They used a branch of one of the trees as a torch and ventured through the dungeon. Their vision was dim and there was barely anything to be seen. They kept lookout for any snakes that may be lurking nearby. This part of the jungle was teeming with them, and they were known to be extremely venomous.

There was no beast, no matter how big, that was going to impede the paces that were going through. Kendra was already at the other end of the door and Ranthor followed suit. Gideon seemed to be struggling with this part, so they both came to his aid and helped him get through. He was very grateful for the assistance. They now reached another chamber of this cistern which was equally damp and dark. They heard the familiar sound of the woolly bats. These creatures were found abundantly in this system. They could feed on almost anything, which made them adapt to any environment. However, these ones were somewhat different. They had a blue and golden coat which distinguished them from the other bats in the solar system. They were also more docile than the others and did not get as easily provoked. They were basically known for their laziness. Attacking people was not amongst the list of priorities.

The place was infested with bats, so much that they were almost indistinguishable from the walls. Their skin, however, set them apart from the wall, but only barely. For the untrained eye, it seemed as if they were ornaments and this managed to camouflage them well. This was a good thing for these very docile creatures who did not do much to survive. This place was amongst many of their dwelling spots. They managed to survive on whatever little shrubbery that was around them. They barely used to come out.

Ranthor was going deeper into the dungeon. Excited to find the next jewel, he almost fell into a nearby well. He quickly regained his foothold and went forward. He managed to warn the others in time so that they do not make the same mistake that he did. This area was surrounded by whirlpools. They needed to be careful, otherwise they would be swept into their certain doom. Gideon was preventing himself from looking below to prevent becoming afraid. He walked next to Kendra and held on to her as they approached the end of the pathway. He mustered enough strength to prevent himself from trembling. It was at this time that he was reminded that he was a child who was afraid and was clinging to the next adult for safety. However, he was to brush it off and like the hero he knew he was inside. He let go of Kendra and stopped shaking almost at once. He had found his inner brave self and was no longer afraid of the abyss that was below.

He went across the other end of the room where Ranthor was and caught up with him. He was excited to participate in this adventure. He held his head up high and walked across the damp chamber into the next one. He swung his head just in time to avoid the incoming bats that just woke up for a meal. His heart raced, and he rushed through to the other end. There was a gem-encrusted door at the other end with a similar lock system as the one in the cave before. They decided to split up and each one would find a key to hasten the mission. Then each searched a corner of the chamber in search of the key. Gideon managed to find the first spoke and turned it around to access the box containing the first key, which was behind a metallic gate. He eyed it careful and searched for any possible clues.

Kendra was moving to the other end of the chamber. She did not find anything here and decided to head to the next chamber. Similar to the previous cave, the mechanisms were interspersed amongst different chambers. This was frustrating, but unfortunately it had to be done. Whoever hid these jewels did not want them to be found at any cost. She wondered about what would happen when all the jewels were reunited. She had never thought of this before and had never thought of asking Ranthor. She was going to ask him the next time they would get time together. She was somewhat longing for some alone time with him. Perhaps this time she would take things to the next level. *Anyway, enough with that,* she thought to herself and decided to continue with the search silently.

She finally reached the next chamber and tried to look for the hidden mechanism. It seemed to be a set of spokes. She turned the first one and soon a mechanism sprung onto action. There was an hourglass that started dispersing sand. She moved on to the next spoke and moved it. It seemed that she needed to complete this task within a set time limit. Luckily, she was good at moving quickly and managed to find her way around these kinds of puzzles very easily. She moved around nimbly and quickly, managing to turn all the mechanisms around. A big round door opened, and a similar box was within sight. She quickly went over and opened the box. A similar key was placed there. She grabbed it in her hand and held very close as if holding a new-born infant. This key was important to acquiring the next jewel. Only one key was remaining to be found, and it left for to Ranthor.

Ranthor was searching for the next key in the last chamber. He was hopeful that he was going to find it. Finding the other two keys having given him a newfound faith in their combined efforts. He was happy that, yet another jewel will be within reach. The last key was suspended from a rope in the middle of the chamber. However, this time instead of spokes, the place was surrounded with deadly trap wires. They formed a lattice framework, and in the middle the lever was on one of the walls. He could not walk to it as this would trigger the mechanism controlling the wires, and that would spell certain doom for him. He decided that he might trying the lever, that in itself posed a risk of permanently of damaging the mechanism. He remembered that he carried a quiver of arrows and a bow in his bag. He removed it from the bag and aimed it at the lever.

He didn't manage to hit the lever from the first two attempts. His aim was not what it used to be. However, on the third attempt he managed to hit and move the level. This managed to make the tiles holding the trip wires flip backwards, therefore effectively burying them. The rope holding the key was lowered further downward. Ranthor now rushed to grasp the key in his hands. He was very eager to deliver the key and the others with it and open the door. He felt like he was going on a race against time. His heart was racing, and his palms were filled with sweat. He started feeling butterflies in his stomach. Kendra came towards him and asked him to take a seat. She took the key from him and attempted to open the door. It opened with relative ease, and this time it opened into another chamber. This was the inner sanctum of the dungeon. They had to descend a little deeper into the dungeon, where hopefully the jewel was housed.

Ranthor felt like he was being toyed with. The place looks like it was recently ransacked. The lights were smashed, and many objects were looted. He just hoped that the jewel was somehow stowed safely in a secret compartment. But he knew all too well that this would definitely not be the case. Whoever ransacked the place must have taken the jewel with him. His suspicions were realized immediately when he found the vault housing it empty. He clapped both of his hands angrily in the air. He was furious and was smashing whatever he could reach. Tears were rolling onto his cheeks. Kendra had not seen him in such a state of despair. In the heat of the moment, she realized that there was an insignia mark that was looked recent. It was carved onto the stone. Whoever did this wanted to be discovered. She showed to Ranthor, and he started feeling a little bit better. His face was less pale than it was moments ago.

Kendra looked at the insignia on the wall. It was a triangle with a circle inside. It was blue and gold in color. She realized that this insignia was well known to her. However, she was white as ash as soon as she came to this realization. The insignia belonged to an ancient order called The Monks of Eternal Solace. It was a well-known corrupt cell that turned competing kings against each other. They drove wedges and wars between kingdoms regularly. The incentives behind this were usually financial. However, in this case the incentives were not known to Kendra. She then connected the dots and realized that the mysterious figure that they saw previously was part of the same ancient order.

Ranthor drew a picture of the insignia, and he decided that he would use this to track the culprits. Little did he know that the Order was hiding in plain sight.

They were appointed politicians of every known capital state in every solar system. They flashed their insignia quite openly. However, they did not have a headquarter or a regular meeting spot. They decided to use the jewels they had in their possession to follow the next jewel in the hope of meeting them there.

They were going to start their search in the next planet of the solar system. This was planet Orarius. It was the biggest planet in this solar system, and the most densely populated. It was most likely where they would find any useful information as to the whereabouts of the monks. Ranthor had a score to settle with them, and he would not rest until it was done. He looked forward to grinding them into paste. The day when he met with them was going to be marked down in their memories forever. This was something that he vowed would be made a reality. Kendra was worried that he was becoming very vindictive. It was blinding the clarity that he had always possessed. That was going to pose problems for them down the line. They needed all the concentration they could muster in order to find the monks.

Planet Orarius was the hub of trade in this solar system. This was especially true for the trade of drugs and illegal opiate-spiked spices that were coveted by many of the royalty of the planet. There was a serious drug problem that afflicted this place. The worst part is that it was very much out in the open and the government was doing much in attempting to even cover it up. It was rumored that the king was also addicted to the spices. Those were regular shipment carts that were going to the royal palace on almost daily basis. He was never seen and would barely attend to his royal duties. The planet was run by his minister of state. Tyrant was an understatement to describe this man. Anyway, they were not planning to interact with unless there was a dire necessity to do so. Based on their luck, they would end up doing so anyway. So, they decided that as soon as they reached the planet, they were going to gather intel on him.

The planet was a casting a beautiful emerald hue on the solar system. Despite the corruption that surrounded it, it was actually one of the most beautiful planets that they had set their eyes on. Had it not been for the extreme industrialization process, it would have been one of the most wonderful natural reserves in the universe. Prior to industrialization, the planet held a vast array of rare plants and animal life. There were many sanctuaries and natural reserves that attracted visitors from the furthest reaches of the universe here. However, greed got in the way and soon it marred the beauty that once filled the place. Instead, the place was now a safe haven for any manner of debauchery the mind realized was possible.

They were now approaching the planet's orbit and plans were made to descend. Gideon gazed at the planet from the window and was captivated by its beauty. It sent him into a trance-like state that Ranthor soon made him snap out of. The descent coordinates were entered into the computer's mainframe and soon they were making their descent onto the planet's surface. Their systems indicated that the weather was moderate and that there might be a little drizzle on the way. Therefore, they were prepared and dressed accordingly. Anyway, being cloaked was probably good for them. Their previous escapades had gained them some notoriety amongst criminal circles and amongst the Order generals. Therefore, it was best that they were out of sight and out of mind. This allowed them to explore the planet as they pleased.

Ranthor was the first to disembark from the ship. He rushed over to the main square to try and gather clues about the mysterious Order. Gideon followed suit and was already on his way to catch up with his friend. The way seemed clear enough. The first thing they had realized was that no one was interested in giving them any information. People were extremely frightened to divulge any information about the Order. Even if they didn't know, they didn't dare utter their name for fear being killed or maimed. The ones that knew feigned ignorance. Still, they were quite adamant and were going to search till they realized that no one was going to tell them anything. Ranthor had made up his mind to punish this mysterious group.

The main town was deserted at this time of day. There were very few people around, and they refused to speak to anyone. The general demeanor was not welcoming one, even if the questions asked were not about the Order. This was usually the cases in big metropolitan cities. The remaining people rushed to their air cabs or headed to the nearest café. There was only one old man that was willing to help them out. He confirmed their suspicions that the minister of state was suspected to be a prominent member of the order. The key was to infiltrate the royal palace and see if the jewel was hidden there. This was not going to be an easy task. They were going to disguise themselves as one of the supply truck owners. It was one of the easiest ways to get in.

They had managed to find the warehouse where all the opiate spices were being held. It was a very heavily guarded facility. Many armed guards and armored vehicles were protecting the place. For once, they were planning to use stealth to gain the element of surprise to gain entry. There needn't be any blood shed to validate this experience. They approached one of the guards from behind and choked him. Kendra did the same thing with one of the female guards. They then donned their clothes and practiced what to say to the others to gain access to one of the vehicles. Hopefully, they would have kidnapped a few drivers. Otherwise, they would be arousing suspicion by commandeering the vehicles. In hindsight, they should have thought this through before deciding to asphyxiate the nearest guard they could find.

There was nothing that could be done now. Whatever damage that was done was already sustained. They entered the compound and approached the other soldiers. They asked for the whereabouts of the keys. They had explained that they were new drivers appointed by the company to deliver the spices. This ruse was actually believed by the others. They finally understood why. The sheer numbers of guards and hired guns made it virtually impossible to determine who was an actual member of the guards. Kendra managed to commandeer one of the vehicles and the engine was already revved up in preparation for a scheduled drop off in the palace.

The king was waiting eagerly for his spices. His eyes were blood-shot, and his temper was foul. No one dared attend to him unless solicited to do so. This time of the month was usually the worst. It was the time the company was making inventory of their supplies. This had meant that there would be a two-day halt on services. Luckily, that ended today. They were finally going to make the king pacified yet again and allow the minister to attend to more pressing matters. He was the one governing the country after all. The king was just a façade so as not to alarm the people. He had a slightly better popularity amongst the people.

Ranthor managed to reach the palace gate. He had held the credentials and documents required to access the palace. The guards let him in very easily. They were not going to be the ones to suffer the king's wrath by delaying the shipment. They did not even bother to inspect the back of the truck where Gideon was hidden. The journey was smooth from here onwards. Nothing now stood in their way of finding the minister. They were going to pry the jewel from his icy cold hands if they had to. Kendra was worried that he was getting very vindictive. This would have blinded him to reason, and that never was a good thing. She decided that she had better take charge in this mission to avoid any colossal catastrophe.

They reached the main grounds of the palace and had disembarked from the truck. They managed to stow away the truck in a nearby hanger. They didn't have much time before they were going to raise suspicions. The king was already waiting eagerly for his shipment, and this delay was going to sound the alarm. They had to move quickly and stealthily to avoid being detected. The way to the palace was not very far now. It was only a matter of time before they had reached the minister. Kendra told Ranthor that she was going to deal with the minister, and that in the event this was going to be difficult then he should intervene. He agreed, although begrudgingly, and made his way behind her to provide protection. He had managed to calm down a little bit and contain his anger. He realized that it was getting out of control.

Kendra rejoiced after realizing that he had regained his cool composure. She gave him a light kiss on the cheek to encourage him. That seemed to do the desired effect. He was now calm and collected, and most importantly ready to make a sound plan to reach the minister. The palace was heavily guarded even from within. They needed an access point or a vent which would lead them to the main quarters of the palace. They had managed to hide in the bushes and gather some visual information about their surroundings. The palace grounds were big and managed to hide them well. They hid in the shrubbery and the trees. The grass was knee deep and was hiding them from any oncoming guards.

They had managed to get close enough to the window that was part of the minister's personal chambers. Ranthor realized that they still had the gear they had used to climb the mountain. He managed to find a spot where none of the guards were looking after, a virtual blind spot. He then extracted the grapple hook from its holder and prepared for another mission. He hand Kendra her gear and asked Gideon to be on lookout duty for any guards. They managed to latch to one of the walls and used every nook and cranny to gain their foothold. It was much easier than the mountain, especially now that Kendra was feeling more confident that she had already practiced this. Her fear of heights had diminished compared to the last time they had climbed the mountain.

They were scaling the place with such ease. Finally, Kendra and Ranthor managed to enter through the window and gain access into the minister's quarters. This particular room they had entered had no guards. It was surprising that the window was unlocked. They started to suspect an ambush. The Order was already expecting them to come. It was only a matter of time before there was an encounter between them. The minister was nowhere to be seen. This was actually a relief as they were going to be able to search with ease and without any interruption. He had one of the biggest living quarters in the palace. The only one that was bigger was the king's, and it was only marginally so. They searched every inch of the chambers for proof of the jewel. So far, there was nothing to be seen. He was not going to keep in plain sight, especially considering that the servants went and came as they pleased.

Besides, they did not even know if he had kept it with him. After all, it was only a rumor that he was part of the order. Nothing was truly confirmed yet by anyone. Finally, they came across a mysterious looking painting in the room. Ranthor turned it around and a door swung open. It was leading to an inner chamber. The sconces that were by the sides of the chamber were immediately lit, and their glow showed them the way to the chamber. This definitely constituted proof that this man belonged to a hidden order. Why would a minister of state have a hidden room otherwise? They entered the room and began searching it at once. It was filled with many rare and very sought-after artefacts. But there was no sign of the jewel so far. They then came across a vault in the middle of the chamber. The jewels were resonating violently. Ranthor was filled with joy, knowing that he had finally found the jewel.

He was at a profound loss of words and did not know how to convey his happiness to Kendra. She understood what he meant without having to utter a single word. She shared the same feeling that he had. They managed to open the vault and extract the jewel. They were now going to make their escape. Their escape vehicle was safely stowed away from the main palace grounds in a nearby spot. All they had to do now was get to the truck and get the hell out of here. They did not want to suffer the combined wrath of the king or the minister. It was good to conduct a stealth mission. It avoided blood loss from either side. Not that Ranthor was soft, and he certainly did not care for his adversaries.

The journey to the jewels was coming closer to conclusion. They were already midway in terms of gathering the jewels. It was going to become easier now that they have more jewels. The chamber was closed, and all the evidence leading to it was sealed off to avoid bringing any suspicions that anything had went missing. They grappled back to the ground and prepared to reach the vehicle. It was only a matter of time before they had found their truck. They rushed in it and left the palace grounds. Both of them were grinning like two children who had visited the candy store for the first time. They rejoiced at the ease of this mission. Finally, it was the first time where finding the jewel did not lead to altercation and a definite injury.

The van was dropped off in an outpost very far away from the main town to avoid detection. They then entered a nearby pub and ordered drinks. They were celebrating their victory in the best way they knew how—booze. They also ordered a steak and kidney pie, fries, and sausages. They ate heartily and enjoyed the remainder of their night. It was nice to have some adult time away from the others and just enjoy a meal. The food was not bad as well, which added to the overall atmosphere of the moment. Their pathway was now clearer, both in terms of the jewels and their future plans. Ranthor wanted to ask Kendra if she would consider coming with him. However, he did not muster up the courage yet, and he decided that it was best to ask her this after finding all the jewels.

Kendra was looking at him with her kind doe eyes. For the first time ever, she was having these feelings for Ranthor. She didn't know if it was his companionship or the fact that she could open up to him about almost anything. She was concerned that this was going to derail her long-term plans. She dismissed the idea from her head and continued enjoying her meal. For now, all she had to think about was how much to drink, eat, and be merry. There was plenty of time to decide the other things. Her main priority now was gathering the jewels and collecting her reward. She did not consider any long-term plans for the time being, and she did not want to start doing so now.

They had thoroughly made sure that no tracks were left behind so that they will not be discovered. Now, they headed to the ship and were planning to leave the planet. It was time to embark on yet another journey. However, they decided to rest a little bit. The ship had to refuel again so they docked in the nearest planet to refuel. In the meantime, they all went out to eat and to breathe fresh air. They all rejoiced at the opportunity for some rest and relaxation time. This journey had drained them both emotionally as well as physically. They were all glad that it might end soon.

They all were happy and talking to each other. Ranthor got to know more about Gideon's background, and most importantly more about Kendra. This was the first time since the beginning of the journey that they all sat and talked for any length of time. For the majority of the time, the only conversations they engaged with together involved tactical planning and the jewels. Their journey together has strengthened them and made them more than companions, rather a family. All of them had looked out for each other countless times during their travels. For some reason, Ranthor was actually going to miss them once they had left. He had managed to develop a strong bond with them, one that is not there with his biological family. Sometimes family runs across blood relationships, across geographical boundaries and even across species.

Despite the food in the diner tasting average, they ate large quantities of it. Perhaps it was because they were famished or maybe because it was that they liked the company and wanted to take as much time as possible which included eating seconds to get to stay in this place. It was nice to be in a warm place for once. The ship was cold despite using the heating system. It was also dull and drab. Even Ooger seemed to enjoy himself for a while. He had missed quite a lot of the action, but he did not seem perturbed by this. He liked his quiet and invisible existence. He was used to his solitude and did not engage much in the conversations. Still, he felt a longing to this group of misfits and was wondering what he would do after all of this was done.

It was time to leave as the ship was finally refueled. The coordinates for the next planet were entered into the system. It had a weird constellation name, planet Epsilon. It mainly housed factories, and there were very few living species inhabiting it. The place was the industrial center of the universe. Literally anything mechanical, robotic, or electronic was produced here in mass. Many war machines were also created unfortunately on a daily basis. The emissions from the factories made it virtually uninhabitable except for the species that lived under extreme conditions. The factory workers were sealed off in bio-hazard suits. Ranthor wondered about they were going to overcome this issue. They had a few space suits in the ship. He had hoped that they be of use to avoid any injury sustained from the toxic fumes.

Chapter 9
A Welcome Respite

For the time being, all they had to do was sit and relax, waiting for the ship to take them to their destination. It was not very far away from their current location. However, it seemed like an eternity away. None of them wanted to enter that planet at any cost. But they knew that it was the only way. The prospect of going there was very daunting for each and every one of them, including Ranthor. Anyway, they did not have to think of it until they approached the surface of the planet. For the time being, they were just staring at the window, into space. Trying to muster whatever courage and patience they could for the next adventure. Hopefully, they would not be attacked by any of the robots. With their luck, it was definitely a possibility. Gideon, oddly enough, was excited about this strange adventure. He had a knack of liking weird locations. This was going to be yet another entry in his journal.

    He was documenting their entire adventure. Perhaps, he was going to write about the whole thing so that his children and their children will know about his travels. He was excited to let other people know about his travels so far. He kept his family regularly informed about what was happening. They did not like the idea that he was putting himself in harm's way, but they trusted Ranthor to keep him safe and sound. They also trusted Kendra and knew that he was well protected. He contacted them on a regular basis now that things were a little bit quieter.

    Again, they were back into the majesty of space. There was nothing that was going to make its way between them and Planet Epsilon. The planet was fast approaching now. Soon enough, they were going to reach there, and then would possibly find the next jewel. After this jewel, there were two more remaining jewels to find before heading to his father. The next jewel might be difficult to acquire. This was because Epsilon was heavily protected by the robots on the planet. Again, they would have to utilize stealth as a method to prevent an altercation with the robots. They were not like any of the foes that they had ever faced. They did not have as much exposable weakness that they could utilize to their advantage. However, after finding the jewels, Ranthor's confidence had increased significantly, and he felt that he could do anything.

He was preparing for the upcoming battle ahead. He did anticipate one, what with the robots having thermal detection software that would make stealth a difficult option. Nonetheless, they would first try it as an approach prior to using violence. That previous adventure was the smoothest that they had experienced so far in their journey. It was surprisingly good and managed to give them all a huge boost of confidence. Most importantly, they did not suffer from any injury. Ranthor and Kendra had managed to fully recover from all their previous injuries.

Kendra was looking over the horizon at the next planet, and she was considering whether she would stay with Ranthor once this adventure would end. She was not sure yet. But she would soon have to make this decision as there were only three jewels left to be found.

Gideon was nowhere to be found. He seemed to have vanished from all of existence. For some reason, one of the escape pods was missing. He did not leave any evidence about his departure. The others were surprised that he had left. He had shown so much resolve about staying and had convinced Ranthor of that. Part of him was sad that he had left suddenly without notice. They had managed to enjoy the journey so far. He was extremely helpful to them and did not mind the help that he extended to them. Still, they did not want to chase after him. After all, he had a family to tend to and they understood why he would do something like that. However, Gideon wanted to make sure that he knew how to get back home. He did not want to find him stranded over one of the previous planets they had visited him. He tried to communicate with the intercom in the pod system but did not get any signal back despite dialing multiple times.

Ranthor started to get worried and was concerned that something had happened to him. Luckily, the pod had a GPS system that was linked to the main ship. This had allowed him to detect the ship. It was actually close by in a nearby asteroid belt. Ranthor wondered as to why Gideon would end up there. The pod was easy to maneuver, and the only thing he had to do was enter the coordinates. Kendra was wondering if the Order was behind this. If that was the case, then the boy's life was actually endangered. Despite knowing that he could handle himself, he was only a little boy. He had to be protected at all costs. They had to get to him before the Order reached him first. There was nothing that seemed to endanger him at this point. However, they decided to rush there to extract him before things got messy.

They had managed to reach the asteroid system in time and decided to scout the area and look for evidence of other ships. Just as they had suspected, there were two ships approaching. Kendra prepared to board one of the ships. They reached the ship and managed to create a hole in its hull. This allowed them to board the ship and direct it towards the next ship in order to destroy it. But they had left one of the occupants alive in order to extract information from him.

As soon as he was captured, the mysterious figure managed to activate his cloak and a gas suffocated him alive. Clearly, whatever information he had was not something that his fellow members wanted to get out. Ranthor was furious at this current development of events, and he slammed his fist at one of the walls, managing to make a dent in the process. He had cared for the boy for the entire duration of this mission, and he had gone missing while under his watch. He used to protect all of the people under him. How did they not notice that he was gone? Were they far too distracted to notice the sound of the pod detaching from the main ship? He would not be able to forgive himself if anything happened to the boy. He had grown quite fond of him. So much so that he actually wanted a child.

This ship was empty, and there were no signs of Gideon being there. He went on to explore the remainder of the ship. Once he was done, Ranthor prepared to board the other ship. He managed to reach them and open fire. A hole opened, and he managed to enter through it. He found Gideon gagged and cuffed in one of the corners of the room. He was crying profusely and was begging his captors to let him go. Ranthor approached the men from behind and managed to knock them out with the butt of his gun. They were out cold, and Gideon was thrilled to see him again. He was untied and immediately rushed to hug Ranthor; tears were rolling on Ranthor's vest. He didn't mind it one bit. Actually, it made him feel as if he was some sort of a father figure to the boy; one that he clearly lacked. Both of them left the ship and made their way on board theirs. Gideon vowed never to leave again. Ranthor did not bother asking him why he had left; he knew that he was missing his parents badly.

The way to Planet Epsilon was becoming clearer now. It was going to be a few hours before they reached. Fortunately, this little detour did not take that much time. Ranthor was relieved at the sight of his friend on board his ship. He made sure not to leave his eyes off him again. Kendra also was worried sick about him. She scolded him a bit, but then hugged him and kissed his cheeks. She was relieved that they had found him in time. Who knew what those pirates might have done to him? Slavery was a growing business in the black market, as was child labor. Despite laws enforced to punish such criminal activity, they were growing at large. It was amazing what people were going to do for profit.

She was preparing a meal for Gideon and the others. It was her way of relieving herself of the stress. She barely cooked, but when she did, it was quite delicious. The others were quite worn out and would not even notice if there was something wrong with the food. All they cared about was that there was a hot meal that was going to be served. It was one of the few times during their journey where home food was being prepared. They had longed for it for quite some time. The food they had during their travels was not bad, but it was not as good as this. They were seated at their usual places, but this time, the atmosphere was much quieter than the last time they had been seated here. All of them exchanged worried glances at each other. They ate in silence for the majority of the time. None of them felt like uttering a single word.

The ship approached Planet Epsilon by mid-day. The place was almost deserted, save for the robots that patrolled the streets and operated the machinery. Many of them were created to greet the oncoming visitors. It only added to the eerie vibe of the place. There were only a few visitors per year, and most of them involved company executives that wanted to purchase parts and machines for their ever-expanding businesses. The rest were people who were sentenced for jail here. The planet was used as a penitentiary to house most of the dangerous criminals that were previously in overcrowded prisons. It was a testament to the increasing crime status in this part of the solar system. The planet was dull, drab, and extremely boring. Yet Gideon still managed to enjoy visiting it. He was interested in robotics and hopefully would be able to enroll in studying robotic engineering. He was looking at all of the robots with a keen eye and studying their properties.

Ranthor was holding the jewels in his bag. He inspected the bag every few minutes to check that they were still there, and, most importantly, to see if they were giving off their distinctive glow. He didn't know if he was moving further away from his quest or if he was lost. He felt disappointment in that this might be like a similar task where they were led astray into believing the jewels were there and ended up being ambushed. He brushed the thought off his mind and continued on the trail. There were no clues at the moment.

Kendra went to the local pub to see if she could overhear any of the local gossip. She did not find anything of value. All she learned was that there was a secret underground fight club where all the influential members of the society met regularly. It was scheduled for tomorrow night. They needed to get access chips in order to be allowed entry. There was a competition going on downtown in a nearby slum. The reward was two chips to access the underground club. They had to win those chips and gain access to this club; it was their only chance at acquiring the jewel, if it was indeed on this planet. Ranthor wondered what the competition might include. Most likely, it was a sparring competition to see who could get into the club. Interestingly, they had learned that it was an eating contest. As per tradition, the person who could eat the most pies would win the legendary chips. He was actually happier thinking that it was a fighting contest. Eating quickly was not amongst his fortes.

Gideon wanted to participate in this competition. From previous dinners, it was clear that he was the unbridled champion of the whole lot. Therefore, his name was registered amongst the participants. The others decided to sit this one out. The competition was going to be in an abandoned amphitheater nearby. There were people coming from all corners of town to witness this event. It was one of the few forms of entertainment that they had in this place. That is, if you could really consider this as entertainment. However, this was crucial for our heroes. The planet was deserted, save for the few people that they were seeing before them now. It was a sight to behold, seeing people on this planet. Most of them were out of jobs and reduced to these parts of the planet. The others, at the other end of the spectrum, were the engineers and designers who had wonderful lofts in the middle of the capital. They were not there most of the time, on account of business trips and holidays. Nowadays, most of the control and repair of the machines was done remotely, and they rarely had to come to inspect the place.

The competition was starting, and the pies were laid out in front of them. Gideon was in his designated place already. He had managed to eat three pies in the first two minutes of the competition. The others eyed him with awe and incredulity. There were both happy and shocked that this was the thing that would help them acquire the next jewel. Luckily, he had not eaten breakfast yet and had a light dinner last night; well, light for his standards. He was a growing young boy after all, thought Kendra. The others were equally cheering him on, seeing as he was the most likely candidate to succeed. He gulped down a fistful of orange juice and prepared to take on another batch of stale pies. Nothing stood in the way of his churning machine that was his stomach. He did not mind that the pies were a day or two old, at least. The juice seemed to compensate for the staleness of the pies.

One of the other competitors had already tapped out of the competition, he was panting and grunting. He did could not take it anymore. There were two other people besides Gideon who had an aptitude for this task. Both of them were twice his size and looked like they were capable of beating him and his two friends. However, Gideon was not even afraid in the slightest. He took on his competitors and defeated them in the competition. The chips were handed over to him, and he was hoisted on top of the shoulders of the citizens. They were happy to see someone new win the competition. He received his chips, and they made their way out of the slums.

They were making their way out of the slums and back into the city center. They stopped in between to get food from a nearby food carts. Surprisingly, Gideon still had an appetite for food. All of them wondered as to how much his capacity to eat was. It was as if a black hole was in the middle of his gut. Nothing seemed to keep him satiated.

They headed back to the ship in preparation for sleep. Although it was far from time to sleep, but they did not feel safe exploring the city at night. The place looked fabulous under the cover of the moon. It was no longer a horrible pile of machines and metal factories, but rather a beautiful painting of a starry night. Despite the industrialization process, they could still see some of the star constellations that were familiar to them. Ranthor was explaining them to Kendra and Gideon. In the meantime, Ooger was preparing dinner. He had been feeling like an unnecessary member of the team. He had grown bored of going on missions. Finally, he mustered up the courage to tell Ranthor about it. He allowed him to leave and gave him access to the pod so that he may return home. He rewarded him for his troubles as well. And so it was that he concluded his part of the mission.

They all had managed to sleep peacefully without any interruption. The oncoming beam from the sun woke them up with its warmth and brightness. It was time to get ready for the next day. The fight club would be conducted at night. They needed to get cloaks and masks to cover up their identities. They were now notoriously known across the galaxy for their adventures to gather the jewels. And seeing the sway and control of the Order over several planets, they decided not to risk detection. They kept escaping a hair's breadth away from death's grip and they did not want their luck to run out. Besides, there were rumors that the Order had tasked mercenaries to track them down and recover the jewels. A very powerful organization was hot on their trail, and nothing was going to stop them from reaching their goal. The time to throw caution to the wind was long gone. Instead, they had to make sure their footsteps were brushed off to avoid being detected.

Every misfit and miscreant on this planet had their eyes on them. It was even possible that there were people in the competition that were on the lookout for them. Their open presence at the fight club would be risky and had to be avoided at all costs. Again, Gideon seemed to be excited to attend an underground fight club. He was quite odd at times, maybe it was because he did not see this much action back at the orphanage. For Ranthor, he preferred the place to not be as discreet. At least, this way, there would be no witnesses. It was the only thing that was good about this location.

In preparation for tonight's event, they found a nearby shop to purchase masks and cloaks for the occasion. They had commercial items that had drawings of famous fighters; ones that would allegedly also meet at the club. This would help disguise them amongst the crowds as possible fight club enthusiasts. Hopefully, no one was going to recognize them and give away their whereabouts. The outfits looked very convincing to fool anyone. Still, they could not be too cautious. They had also purchased visors to cover their eyes to further avoid detection. Kendra was not happy about attending the fight club and decided to opt out, using the excuse that there were only two chips. Gideon was thrilled that he was the one that was invited. He hoped that there would be a lot of action, including them finding the jewels, of course.

It was already evening time, and a few hours separated them from the upcoming fight. Gideon left with Ranthor to have dinner at a nearby restaurant. Kendra stayed in the ship and made herself some tea. The location that they were given looked very shady, but it was, after all, an underground secret club. Hopefully, they would not have to be one of the participants and would be content watching from the crowds. Their seats were near the middle booth; this was both where all the rich and powerful people of the capital were housed. It was where they were going to find possible clues to the whereabouts of the next jewel. They ate their food hurriedly and then walked across the square to the location given to them. It led them to an abandoned warehouse far from the center of the city. The place was shady and looked like the kind of place where murders happened. Nonetheless, they continued onward and entered the place calmly. They were amongst the first to enter. None of the influential people had come yet. Perhaps they wanted to make an entrance to distract the people from the main stars of the show. It was not surprising, knowing that these rich people needed to be in the center of attention. It was addictive to enjoy fame and prosperity, legal or otherwise.

The ring was already prepared, and the first fight was going to start any minute now. The two competitors entered the arena. The crowds roared with excitement at the site of them. The fighters also enjoyed the rush of the fight, and most importantly the cheering of crowds.

The fight began, and both opponents were swinging at each other. There was no escape from the painful blows that each sent to the other. People were cheering, and blood was flowing onto the arena. Surprisingly, none of them felt tired or dizziness despite the blood loss. These were seasoned fighters who were prepared till death if necessary. The honor of the fight code made them do this. Some of them were previous military combat soldiers. The others were either militia or other hired guns. Both were equally strong, and equally trained. They had to undergo grueling tasks in order to reach the state that they were in today, and they prepared rigorously and religiously for their fights. It seemed as if the opponent in red was going to defeat his counterpart in turquoise. The latter had already collapsed to the ground, and the bell sounded, indicating that the fight had ended. Medics entered the arena and extracted the unconscious fighter to assess him for any possible brain injury.

The bell sounded again, indicating that the next fight was beginning. A simple injury, or rather a major one here, would not stop the fight club. These kinds of things happened here on such a regular basis that they were ignored altogether. The next opponents were relatively smaller in size compared to the ones before, but they were equally vicious. Despite their miniscule sizes, they were experts in close combat, and would even fare well against the previous reigning champion. The stage was prepared for this fight. Both of the fighters approached the center of the stage and prepared to attack. A punch was swung by one of them, but his opponent shifted his stance and avoided the attack. The other guy's fist hit the railing, and this made him howl with pain. Seizing the opportunity, his opponent swung a hit against him, which landed squarely on his loin, knocking him out on his stomach. He then jumped on top of the stage and came careening downward and knocked him out. The unconscious man was also escorted out of the arena, and his opponent was named victorious.

Multiple fights were going on in different corners of the club, in different arenas. Most of them were sending the other opponent straight into the infirmary or to his creator. The ones that survived vowed to come again next season, better prepared to fight. This was to face the abject humiliation that surrounded them for the year to come. The winner held ultimate bragging rights, wealth, and women. The women seemed to swoon at the sight of a barbaric fighter that would protect and provide for them. It seemed that these women did not support the feminist movement that was ongoing elsewhere, after all. Instead, they were content in being trophy wives and mistresses to the fighters of the club. This had managed to gain them notoriety across social circles, something that they deeply cared about. Of course, these marriages seldom continued due to the debauchery and infidelity of both spouses.

The last competition was starting now. This was between the first and second round winners of the competitions before. Finally, the guests of honor had arrived. The fighters were somewhat offended that they picked now of all times to come. The VIPs could not care less and resorted to batting their eyes at the competitors. Still, they were the ones sponsoring the event. Attending the event for them was a formality and a chance to catch up on some of the business of the week. They did not care one bit about the fights and found it too barbaric to continue had it have not been for the cash inflow it brought for them. After all, money was as important as oxygen to these people. It was the single driving force that had kept them alive. Well, that and the exotic beauties that they kept at the reach of the arm at this competition; a reminder that they were powerful and influential. The mistresses of the night, on the other hand, did enjoy the fight. They were hard-wired to enjoy power, wealth, and brutality. This wall their minds could compute.

The fight had finally ended. The scrawny fighter managed to win the battle. He was crowned the winner and a financial reward, as well the title bit, was conferred to him. A woman descended from the stairs to greet him, his possible next trophy wife. The guests in the middle seats were headed to a room inside the club. Ranthor decided to follow them and find out what it was that had to be done in secret. He followed them to the room and kept his ears pressed to the wall. He managed to hear parts of the conversation, but the sounds were mainly muffled.

"Listen to me, Gilderoy, we are fed up with your antics. The Order is expecting results, and so far, this heap of rock did not deliver us any. We have spent the better part of two weeks looking for the jewels. Either you find it or else we will decimate this planet and all of its inhabitants," snarled the stranger.

"It will be done, my lord. My soldiers have already found the location where the next jewel is expected. It will be a matter of days before we have our hands on it. You have my promise. You know that I serve at your pleasure, lord. For it is you that delivered me from certain doom, and I would pay with my life," begged Gilderoy fervently.

"Well, it just might if you don't find the jewel. I shall return within a week to check on your progress. Do not attempt to leave the planet. We have implanted a monitor and it is capable of stopping your heart from working should the thought ever cross your mind. Do not tempt me to use it," bellowed the strange voice.

Ranthor did not recognize any of the voices, but he was glad that this was the correct location. Furthermore, he knew at least that the Order was just as lost as they were. This gave him time to prepare a strategy. The first thing he was going to do was kidnap Gilderoy and get him to confess to the possible location of the jewel. Given that he was spineless, it was not going to be a difficult task to accomplish. He waited for them to exit the room, and the tailed him off to a nearby stand where he was talking about heading back to his house in about an hour. Ranthor decided to tail him and kidnap him once he had reached his home. He relayed to Gideon, and to Kendra over the intercom, what he had learned. Both of them were shocked to learn that the Order was here in Epsilon. It was the perfect opportunity to learn more about this mysterious group of individuals.

There were no public records held, and all people knew came from the grapevine. People rarely talked about them to avoid being kidnapped or killed. The others who were brave enough were taken in the middle of the night, and an example was made out of them. The ones that returned alive were left speechless, and no useful information could be gathered from them. It was, therefore, useless to interview anyone because they knew that despite being threatened, they would not give up any information or disclose any rumors that were secretly going on to outsiders. However, Ranthor had heard enough from the meeting to get an idea about what was going to happen. The only thing he had to do was convince Gilderoy to give him the location of the jewel. He hoped that this was going to work. The target he was following was as useless as possible. The only reason he was useful to the monks was his vast connections to the ruling family. With him, they could lay low without any law enforcement cracking down on them. They also had access to a lot of resources that were made freely available at his disposal.

Gilderoy finally left his seat and was headed home. The crew was tailing him to get to his location. He kept looking back and forth, anticipating being followed back. He was afraid of his own shadow. The man was as spineless as an Odelphian eel, but not as potent although just as bright. They hardly relied on him for any serious tasks.

Ranthor hid behind every wall, dumpster, and abandoned vehicles to avoid detection. He wanted to catch this idiot so badly and recruit him to his cause. It was either going to go peacefully or he was going to lose a limb; there were no middle grounds here. Time was ticking, and finding the jewels quickly was the utmost priority at this point. The road was quite long to the house. Gilderoy took the long route and kept changing it every ten minutes or so to throw off the trail of any possible intruders. He was finally at home and picked at the nine locks that he had kept as a further preventative measure. Ranthor wondered about the lengths this man had gone to protect himself. Who would care about this puny runt enough to chase him in the middle of the night? No one probably though he was of value. This was a good distractor to avoid unwanted attention to the jewels, and mainly to the Order.

Ranthor surprised Gilderoy from behind before he could pick at the last lock. He told him that if he moved or screamed, he would blast his spine with a gun and splatter it across the floor. Gilderoy complied and did not utter a single word. He was then told to head to his room and close the blinds. Ranthor asked him a series of questions about the location of the jewel. He said he did not know anything about any jewels.

"Listen to me, scum. Either give me the location I heard you mention in that room or prepare to be vaporized this instant. I am hardly in the mood to be toyed with. Now, before I count to three and splatter you guts on the floor, I would like to know about the place and a list of all your associates starting with the friend you met at the fight club," yelled Ranthor angrily.

"It is suspected to be in the catacombs in the outskirts of the city, about two hundred kilometers from here. Here is a map of the area. As for the name of my friend, even I don't know. We call him the Monk Master. That much is known about him. He keeps his identity a secret to the rest of the Order," replied Gilderoy with a startled look on his face.

Ranthor threatened to kill him should news of this conversation leak. He didn't want it to be known either. If The Order found out about this, he was surely going to be killed. They did not take kindly to divulging information, Ranthor left the house silently to avoid attracting attention and made his way to the ship. He and Gideon relayed the news to Kendra, who was sick to her stomach knowing that The Order was here. She thought that the last adventure was the end of them. However, things were rarely what they seemed to be. And their foes were extremely formidable, it was a miracle that they managed to get past them the last time. Just like their previous adventure, they planned on using stealth as a determinant for gathering the jewel. The Order was too strong a foe and fighting them at this point unprepared was not the best course of action.

The mysterious voice haunted Ranthor's head. He kept remembering the threats that he had issued his underlings. He wanted to know who this master was. He needed a name to pin so that he could target him and get rid of him once and for all. This person was the source of all their troubles and eradicating him meant that they could peacefully gather and return the remainder of the jewels. He was the only thing that stood between them and the completion of their goal. Ranthor vowed to himself that he would reveal his identity no matter the cost. He wanted this person gone forever. But for now, enough with the diatribe. He had more important things to do; finding the jewel for instance. They managed to reach the ship and started planning on how they were going to access the catacombs. They did not seem to have any idea.

They opened the plan of the catacombs and looked at it thoroughly. They realized that there was a back entrance that was not guarded. The only problem was the fact it was covered with dangerous plants and animals near the entrance. They would need to be very careful while they made their way to this entrance. They packed all their protective gear for the mission tomorrow. Each and every one of them dreaded this mission, especially knowing that the monks were involved in it. It was a miracle that they were not spotted. Gilderoy was probably cowering in his house and avoiding all forms of contact with anyone. That was probably for the best. None of them trusted him, but they did trust his lack of spine.

The sun quickly arose, and the sky turned blue again. It was time to finally execute the plan. They all packed the gear in their bag and purchased some vehicles to take them to the catacombs. They made sure that the mufflers worked properly to avoid any detection by the guards. Ranthor also equipped a silencer to his gun to avoid the impact should he need to use it. Kendra did the same thing but hoped and prayed that they would not end up in conflict, even if it was with only one guard. Even that one guard would be eventually found, and then it was a matter of time before they were located as well. Her mind was not clear today; instead, she was riddled with anxiety. She hoped that her colleagues' spirits were better so that this mission could go smoothly.

The vehicle managed to take them to their desired location in time for the drop-off of the jewel. They entered from the back entrance and were now inside the catacomb. The place was barely lit, and they could hardly see anything inside. However, they did not dare use a lighter or a torch due to fear of the sound and light attracting nearby enemies. Instead, they relied on their other senses and whatever light they could get to reach their desired destination. They had somehow managed to maneuver their way around the place. The jewels did not start resonating. This was not a good omen. The first thing that came to mind was that this was an ambush. It was possible that Gilderoy allowed himself to be kidnapped in the hopes of leading them to the catacombs. Then it would be his master's job to take them out or maybe one of his henchmen. Things did not seem to bode well for them at the moment.

The other alternative was that the jewel was not found possibly because it was deeper in the catacomb. All of them hoped and prayed that it was the latter. They did not want to walk into a trap, especially here. The place was littered with armored guards. Their mere presence frightened them; it could be likened to a wasp hive, the way they moved in complete coherence, the cadence of their boots moving in unison was fearsome. They were not like anyone they had ever seen, and hopefully not someone that they would encounter. For the time being, they remained in the shadows. Moving ever so slowly to avoid making any sound. They reached a tunnel and decided to enter it to get to the other end of the chamber. Perhaps there would be something for them to find at the other end. The jewels started to resonate and shine bright. This made Ranthor reassured that the next jewel was somewhere close. He continued moving through the tunnel along with the others and made sure not to attract any attention. So far, none of the guards were alerted to their whereabouts. The best thing was that they did not need to take out any guard on the way.

The tunnel was now becoming wider and merged into yet another tunnel system. They climbed through it and made their way to the next chamber.

They were now trapped between a rock and a hard place. The next chamber was leading to the guards' chamber. There was no way to get past without clashing with the guards. There were not that many of them, but if they decided to call for back up, then that would spell doom for them. They waited in the hopes that the guards would leave their station. They would enter during the time the shift changed to avoid detection. Hopefully, the wait would not have to be long. Any time spent here increased their chances of detection. There was nothing preventing the guards from entering the chamber and finding them there. They all prayed silently that they would not be detected. A guard approached the chamber, but soon turned around as he was called by his colleagues to grab a drink. Kendra's heart was in her throat. She almost fainted due to the fear. Ranthor was equally scared that they were close to detection.

The guards were drinking quite heavily but surprisingly did not get drunk. It was almost as if they were immune to the effects of alcohol. Most of them were chronic alcoholics anyway. This was the only thing that they could afford with their meagre wages. They started dancing and prancing, completely oblivious to their surroundings. Ranthor was going to use this to his advantage. Soon, they would pass out due to the sheer amount of alcohol they had consumed. They would then seize the opportunity and get past them. From there, they would use the jewels to guide to find the next jewel. They were saved by the failing social graces of the guards. The guards were still resistant and did not budge from their places. Finally, they succumbed to the effects of the alcohol and were fast asleep and drooling.

Ranthor and the others used this golden opportunity to get to the other chamber. The jewels were shining brighter than ever. Their joy was increasing with every increase in brightness. It was not going to be long before things turned in their favor. Life was playing to their luck. It was as if things were smoothing over for the time in a long time. Ranthor had spent many years of his life doing some meaningless jobs for a meagre fee. Finally, he was getting what he had deserved. The world was smiling for him. But he did not want to rush things just yet. The jewel was still not within their reach. It was definitely well guarded, and the vault was locked by stronger mechanisms than those that protected the other jewels. Still, they were not going to back down this easily. The Order was going to get what's coming for them. It was a matter for time before they got the jewel and dealt with the Order. It was the time for him to shine just as bright as these jewels.

The guards had just woken up from their stupor. Now realizing how much time had elapsed, they decided to scour the area. Luckily, the crew was long gone by then, and they didn't leave any sign of coming through the room. There were still snipers on the roof that would shoot at them if they came close to them. Ranthor made sure to avoid their stare by choosing a route that avoided the sniper's gaze. The troopers on the ground protected a golden encrusted box. It seemed to be of value. Perhaps it was where the jewel was hidden. Judging by the increased security around it, it definitely was. There was no sign of the Master of the Monks. He must have a private viewing area to see everything. He definitely was very protected owing to his status in the Order.

They were going to have to sneak without being detected. It was going to be a difficult task to do. Most likely, they had to take out some of the guards, and then they would wear their outfits. The best thing was that the visors would protect their identities. There were three guards in the next room with a similar body constitution to theirs. Now for the difficult task; how to they get them to turn their back so that they can gag them?

The guards did not turn their stare away from the entrance of the chamber. It seemed like it was going to be forever before they decided. Ranthor decided to do something innovative. He threw a rock across the other end of the room. The impact sent the guards searching for a source. They crept behind them and took them out one by one. They then donned their uniforms and marched over to the next chamber. Judging by the sheer number of guards, no one was going to recognize them. They advanced further into the chamber, take note all of all the measures kept preventing access to the next jewel. There were so many deadly mechanisms that would kill them in an instant. The Master did not take protecting the jewel very lightly. He was anticipating Ranthor coming and had prepared for a surprise his way.

Chapter 10
An Unexpected Reunion

The Master was in his chambers waiting to meet Ranthor. He wanted to have a formal introduction with him. He had known Ranthor for some time. This was a mysterious figure from his past that had decided to resurface now. It would bring old memories rushing back; painful ones especially. It was going to be an unwanted reunion between two unlikely foes. Still, the Master was interested to see Ranthor after all these years. He always loathed him, despised him for ruining his career back home. This was his ultimate chance for revenge. But part of him wanted to recruit Ranthor to his cause. After all, he would be a valuable ally to the Order. They could use someone of his strength, skills, and technical prowess. He could serve to train the next generation of monks. They would be a formidable force that no one could contend with, more than they already were now. But he knew that the unpredictable prince would never consent to such a task, not without some sort of threat anyway.

Kendra was sweeping the surroundings for any sign of the jewel. Her senses did not seem to pick up anything strange or unusual. The jewels stopped resonating, and they were worried that the jewel had been taken to another location. This opponent was clever and probably anticipated that there would be an extraction mission today. After all, they didn't trust Gilderoy to keep his mouth shut. He could probably weasel his way out of the punishment for disclosing the location of the catacombs. After all, he was still a strong political ally in this region. They could not find someone more willing to work for money, and, most importantly, dim-witted so as not to impede their plans. Ranthor had wished that he had killed him back when he had the chance.

They ventured further into the catacombs. This place was more suffocating than the remainder of the chambers, and it smelled faintly of death. They realized that there were many humanoid carcasses laid out in front of them. Kendra felt her insides making their way to her throat. She wondered what could possibly do something like this. Was it the work of man or beast? Either way, she did not want to know the answer. Hopefully, whatever did this would have perished with the remainder of the bodies. *The Order must have dealt with it anyway,* she thought reassuringly, but she was not convinced about her own thought. If this thing had managed to do this to these soldiers, then it must be quite strong and not easily subdued. They decided to lay low and avoid any encounter with whatever was capable of doing this.

A siren was blaring in the distance. The crew's hearts were beating heavily. They felt assured when they realized that this was a mock drill that was sounded to train the soldiers in the event of theft. Luckily, this had bought them time to explore the other chambers. This was because the soldiers that were stationed there headed to the main grounds for training. They managed to reach the main chamber. In it, they found a golden box that was quite heavy and looked expensive. The jewels were resonating heavily, and their color was becoming brighter. This must be where they had kept the jewel. Ranthor tried desperately to pry it open but to no avail. He was becoming frustrated with every attempt that he made.

He even tried shooting the box with his muffled blaster, but even that did not do the trick. He kicked the box violently. Luckily, no one noticed it because of the ongoing drill. He went on to explore the remainder of the room. Just as he was about to lose hope, he stumbled onto a switch that opened a tile housing one of the very familiar spokes. He managed to turn it and it opened the vault. The jewel lay there in all its glory. It was a magical sight to behold. He rushed over to get it, but just as he was about to do so, he felt a bullet hit him in the thigh. He was writhing in agony, disoriented as to where the shot had been fired from. Soon, he was gagged and cuffed, and so were the others. They were beaten senseless. They lost consciousness, and when they woke up, they found out that they were detained in a dungeon, their hands cuffed to the wall. There was no sign of their assailants.

Ranthor was the first to wake up; he was groggy and still disoriented from his injury, most likely due to the blood loss that he had sustained. He was moving violently, trying to untangle himself. He did not manage to free himself and eventually gave up altogether. Kendra lay there equally hopeless and confused. She did not know how they were found. They were disguised perfectly. Gideon was the last to wake up. He woke up after feeling like he was in a trance-like state. He was still not aware of his surroundings upon waking up. He cried immediately afterwards. He was scared and confused as to how this had happened to them. All of them were looking for something to use to cut their shackles, any sort of sharp equipment to use that would allow their escape. Alas, there was nothing that could be found in this dungeon.

They heard footsteps approaching. It was the guards informing them that their food was going to be brought. They also told Ranthor to prepare for an audience with their leader tomorrow. He wondered why would he be called for an audience. It was strange that they did not kill them, and instead decided to detain them. The monks were known to be ruthless and did not leave any evidence behind of their crimes. What could he possibly have to say to the Master of the Monks? He kept tossing and turning in his bunk, thinking of what the reason for an audience could possibly be only with him. At least, he would find out the identity of this mysterious figure.

Ranthor waited silently for the night to be over so that he could execute the remainder of the plan. He would be completely alone with the leader and would have access, albeit temporarily, to his private chambers. He needed to play this safe. Any mistake would mean certain doom for him. This was not the time for heroics; it was his only chance at saving his life and the lives of his crew members.

Dawn finally came, ending the ordeal of the previous night. Kendra was still in shock at their capture. She had not spoken since they had arrived. Instead, she was stuck in an expression of awe and wonderment. Nothing made sense for her anymore. Ranthor was waiting for his audience. He was rehearsing the plan silently in his head. He did not even bother to share it with his friends for fear that the walls had ears. He did not want to be complacent. This opponent was far too strong and cunning for them. They had to find a way to outsmart him, and they had to do it quickly; otherwise, they would soon be killed. It was only a matter of time until they realized that they had the jewels. Amidst the commotion of the battle, Kendra had managed to hide the jewels in her pockets and discard the bags. That was actually clever and prevented the acquisition of the jewels by their assailants. No one noticed her doing this as the ground was covered by rubble and smoke.

However, it was a matter of time before they were searched again. The clock was ticking and each of them looked at the other anxiously. They wondered who would be the first to be executed. Gideon was worried the most about this change of events. He spent last night tossing and turning in his sleep. This was the second time that he had a near-death experience. His feet felt like they were stuck between the two realms. He did not want to cross over just yet. There was so much that he had wanted to do. He kept thinking of his parents, the ones that he had just reunited with. He also thought of the friends that he was going to leave in the orphanage. He found comfort in the warm embrace of Kendra who was perched close to him. At least, he found some sort of comfort knowing that he was not alone.

It was time for Ranthor's audience with the Master. The guards came and removed his shackles from the wall. They transported him across the other end of the dungeon. He could see a well-lit room in the distance. That must be where his meeting was going to take place. He maintained his calm demeanor as he was being dragged across the other end of the chamber. He did not want to show any signs of weakness. That was the worst possible thing that he could do. His opponent would then gain advantage over him. Instead, he managed to calm his nerves with the knowledge that he would soon free himself from this prison. They finally reached the entrance to the room. The door swung open, and a mysterious figure emerged from the other end. It was a man well into his sixties, his hair as white as snow. He had a similar complexion to Ranthor. He was hunched over, but still walked with the grace of someone much younger. Ranthor was shocked after realizing that he knew this person. It was his uncle, Romulus.

Romulus motioned for the guards to take Ranthor to his chair. He stared at him with beaded eyes, angrily looking for an explanation for the theft of the jewels. The stare was returned to him with equal intensity. They both looked into each other without uttering a single word. There was lot of history between them. They were part of the same planet back in Planet Nebula. They led wars together and had each other's back on so many instances. It was strange to find them at odds with each other. Clearly, whatever relationship that was between them was now lost. They stood there, each thinking of ripping the other's throat and tearing him limb from limb. Finally, they decided to speak.

"How dare you show your face here, traitor? The jewels belong to me and me alone. You failed us several times, and if you think that this is your chance at redemption, then you are sorely mistaken. I should kill you, were it not for the blood bond that we share. Still, I urge you to repent and join me in my cause," spat Romulus angrily.

"I would rather die and have my carcass devoured by the rats than join. Besides, I am surprised at your audacity at calling me a traitor. After all, you are the one that is stealing the jewels for himself. I do not need your redemption, nor do I need it from Father. I seek no solace in knowing that I will return to that sordid, sorry excuse for a planet," bellowed Ranthor in fury.

"Then you leave me no choice but to kill you. Well, it would at least be fair to fight you standing. Unshackle him, you idiots, and hand him his weapon!" shouted Romulus.

Ranthor was the first to take a swing at his opponent. Despite his age, Romulus still had lot of strength and was able to parry most of Ranthor's attacks. He did not even stop to catch his breath.

He had managed to injure his uncle. Romulus backed away and was tending to his wound. He then swung his sword at him and managed to create an equal-sized wound. The two had similar fighting stances; after all, they were trained in this way. This made the fight even more difficult and led to its prolongation. Neither of them seemed to run out of stamina. They kept going on and on with no signs of the fight ending anytime soon. It was going to be a fight till death. Whoever survived was going to be the one that emerged victorious.

Ranthor noticed that the jewel was nowhere to be found; they must have relocated it after the recent intrusion. For the time being, his mind had to be focused on the fight. There was nothing that could distract him from a good fight, even if it was with his uncle. He managed to inflict yet another wound on his opponent. His uncle was now swaying violently backward and forward. It was clear that the fight was drawing to an end. Still, his uncle had not lost his resolve. Despite losing a lot of blood, he did not lose consciousness and maintained his stance in battle.

Ranthor was heaving loudly; he was starting to feel extremely exhausted. The fight went on for the better part of an hour with no clear victor emerging. His uncle finally gave in due to the blood loss; he had succumbed to his wounds and lay there motionless. Ranthor struck him in the neck with his sword and more crimson blood pooled over. With that, he remained there, cold as ice. Ranthor rushed over and managed to kill the guards that had brought him to the chamber. He stole their keys and made his way back to the dungeon. He had then managed to free his two friends. He told them about his meeting with Romulus. They were as shocked as he was when he had found out. They were consoling him and trying to comfort him. He reassured them that he could not care any less. He was glad that they were going to be rid of this clan once and for all. All they had to do now was find the jewel.

He managed to find the key to the vault after entering the room where Romulus was housed. He then hurried back to the main chamber along with the others. The vault was now relocated, and they did not know where it was taken. Ranthor was fed up with these constant failures that came in their way. He kept his composure and marched into the next chamber. They captured one of the guards and extracted some information from him. They learned that the other guards of the Order had managed to transport the jewel to Planet Odelphius. A new leader was also appointed to avoid the dissolution of the ancient order. The second in command was also headed to Planet Odelphius. They then killed the guard and extracted their gear. The crew left the catacombs and headed to their ship. Ranthor entered the coordinates and prepared for yet another journey to Odelphius. At least, it was a place which was familiar to them.

The journey was going to take a long time. They crossed a few solar systems during their travels. They were going to plan their retaliation thoroughly. Getting recaptured was not even an option. Gideon was scared and opted out of the next mission. Ranthor understood and reassured him that it was probably for the best. Kendra made him a meal and some hot cocoa to calm him down. He was still deeply perturbed by the last encounter. That must have scared the poor boy. After all, he was too young to be exposed to this type of violence. Ranthor thought of sending him home. Clearly, this journey was too dangerous for him, and keeping him here would endanger him and prove as hinderance to their plans. He would tell him later in the evening that he was going to take him home after Odelphius. The boy was clearly homesick anyway, especially after that stunt that he pulled with the pod.

According to the latest news, there was a rebellion going on in Odelphius. People were fed up with the tyranny that accompanied the rule of their leader. Masses were huddled at the royal palace demanding the resignation of the king. If he did not comply, they would publicly execute him. The king was holed up in his palace, unable to get out, and unable to show his face even to his most trusted advisors. At this point, he feared that someone from within the castle would attempt to assassinate him, or worse, someone had already infiltrated the castle and disguised himself as part of his entourage. He did not even want his wife to be with him. He had succumbed to paranoia and delusions, so much that it was impossible to get things done. This had further compounded the issue as none of the demands of the people were met. He was just adding fire to brimstone.

Meanwhile, the Monks were close to reaching the orbit of the planet. The jewel was stowed away safely in its compartment. Their leader was in the cockpit, enjoying his meal, and the others were on the lookout for Ranthor's ship. They knew that it was only a matter of time before they met again. He was a very strong foe, the likes of which they had never seen before. It was a mistake for the previous leader to allow him to engage in combat. He should have killed him there and then. This was a mistake that this leader was not going to commit. Especially since it was someone as weak and cowardly as Gilderoy. It was surprising that he was the next in command. He had recently been inducted in the Order and was now briefed about the details of their mission. His beaded eyes widened at the prospect of yet another encounter with Ranthor. He did not want to deal with him personally.

Ranthor was exhausted from the previous encounter and decided to rest, knowing that he was familiar with the planet he was visiting. Little did he know that there was no upheaval going on there. For the time being, he rested assured knowing that the journey was long and there was nothing that he could do about it. The others felt the same way. Kendra and Gideon were enjoying a nice conversation to get his attention away from the last encounter. He was clearly traumatized by the previous turn of events, but he was recovering slowly. He was a true warrior; strong and brave. His parents would be quite proud of him. However, he did include all these details so as not to worry them. They had just reunited again, and the prospect of losing him forever would crush their souls to bits.

For the time being, all they could hope for was that they will not experience the same trouble locating the jewel. Besides, with the Master gone, they were at least assured that their seize would have weakened. They only hoped that his successor would not be as strong. Little did they know that luck was in their favor. His successor lacked both the strength and charisma of his predecessor. It was only a matter of time before the Order was dissolved. However, Gilderoy was quite sneaky, and whatever he lacked in strength, he compensated with in guile. He would not have remained for so long had it not been for his trickery. The Master attempted his assassination twice before realizing finally that he was a valuable asset to their cause. With him at the helm, the Order would have an inflow of wealth from the capital. They would no longer have to resort to the meagre resources that they had amassed to, which was surprising as most of their work was illegitimate.

The ship had crossed one solar system and they were getting nearer to the jewels, but the journey still was filled with obstacles. The ship was fueled, and they did not have to stop until they reached Odelphius. Ranthor ran a background check to make sure that all the systems were operational before continuing with the remainder of the journey.

The coast was clear so far, and there were no enemy ships that stood in their way. They breathed a sigh of relief at this site; the only ships that were around were commercial ships that carried passengers across the galaxy. This next solar system was known to attract tourists. It was oblivious to the wars waged around it. Luckily for them, they did not participate in any of the political feuds that filled the other galaxies. It was quite peaceful here. Ranthor marked the location and thought that he might come and settle here after collecting the jewels. However, this dream seemed very detached from reality at the moment. They seemed to take two steps backwards with every step forward that they took. The others also sensed the number of colossal failures that they had faced before gathering the jewels. Had it not been for Kendra's quick thinking, they would have lost all the jewels. It was a relief that they did not think to search their pockets. Otherwise, this would have spelled their doom.

The ship crossed yet another solar system, and it was one more before they reached their destination. Ranthor was growing bored of the delay. His insides were burning and aching to destroy the Order, or in the very least, acquiring the jewel. The task seemed more and more difficult with every passing hour. He prepared the strongest weapons in his arsenal for the upcoming battle. To hell with stealth, he thought, he would blow the place to kingdom come should it be required. There was little that stealth had done last time. They were still discovered while they were in full armor and protective visor. He was still surprised that they were discovered. None of them spared any expense to remove their tracks. Unless they were already expected to come, and the guards had let them cross to the main chamber unaided. The latter was most likely true.

It was only a matter of time before the ship had docked. Planet Odelphius was two planets away now. However, that still felt like an eternity. Flashbacks came to Ranthor from moments during this mission. He recalled all the events vividly; the good, the bad, and the outright horrible. He reminisced on some of them, and the growth that had accompanied them. It did not matter to him now what the outcome was going to be like. He already came out of this a changed man, changing for the better. He had previously been selfish and self-centered.

He really cared about Kendra and Gideon. He felt a real connection with them, they were his family now. He almost was happy that the journey took longer than usual. Parting with them was going to be more difficult than the prospect of losing the jewels. But he was used to parting with people and the eventuality of the situation that he never made any long-lasting relationships. But for them, he broke his one cardinal rule.

They had finally reached Odelphius, and it was already night-time. The clouds were gray, and the atmosphere was quiet. The ship landed quietly, and they had made their way to a nearby restaurant to have dinner. They then left on foot to look for the jewel. They did not have much time to waste, and they did not want to spend the night sleeping. Gideon stayed in the ship and rested. Kendra went along with Ranthor to the wharf where one of the deals was expected to happen. The Monks were expected to meet a buyer there. He offered to exchange the jewels for a significant amount of money. After all, Gilderoy, unlike his predecessor, did not know or care much about the jewel or its actual value. He only cared about the monetary value that was attached to it. They needed to rush and get the jewel before it ended up in the wrong hands. It would be quite difficult to find it afterwards.

The way to the wharf was dimly lit. It was difficult to see anything with the poor lighting. They almost bumped into each other several times. There were no people around at this time of day.

There were no guards seen within sight, which was both distressing and relieving at the same time. Furthermore, the jewels did not react yet. They were both wondering if they were headed in the right direction. Just before they decided to switch tract, they noticed that the guards were two clicks north. They were carrying a large vault on a vehicle and transporting it across the other end of town. Ranthor was planning to use the element of surprise and attack the cargo. There were not that many of them and he did not need to resort to stealth. He could probably take them head on. Kendra wanted to use a less direct approach, but she could not convince Ranthor otherwise. They geared up their swords and pistols in anticipation for combat and walked right across to where the guards stood.

The battle started with the exchange of bullet fire. It was only a matter of time before they had managed to take out the guards. They opened the vault, and to their surprise and dismay, this was a decoy. They did not expect it to be that easy. The Order was far too intelligent to do this. They also did not want to use the strategy of disguising as soldiers. They had seen how that turned out previously and did not need a repeat of that fiasco. The search was resumed, and their resolve was stronger than ever. Kendra managed to find tracks leading to the jungle. It was another location worth exploring. They did not expect the jewel to reach the wharf, and it was most likely kept somewhere for safe keeping. They would locate it before it left for the exchange. It would be more difficult to tackle two foes instead of one.

They located a crate that was heavily guarded in the middle of the jungle. The jewels started acting up and became brighter with each step that they took forward. Finally, they were happy that they had found the jewels. They had to make it right. It was their last chance to do so. Nothing was going to stand in Ranthor's way in terms of acquiring the jewel. He did not hesitate to jump into action; however, Kendra pulled him away and urged him to formulate a plan. They found a back entrance to the jewels. It was not as heavily guarded as the front entrance, but it was a longer journey to the crate. They entered through it after taking care of the guards. They then advanced further and took out yet another group of guards. The was becoming clearer now, and thanks to the silenced guns, they were not detected. It was only after locating the bodies that they would be discovered. Therefore, they made sure to move as quickly as they could to reach the crate. There was only one room left in the way of reaching the crate. It had around five guards stationed there. They both agreed to wait until the guards made their rounds, and then took them out one by one. They headed to the crate and opened it. They located the jewel and added it to their collection. They then exited the camp in the same they had entered.

They rejoiced as they managed to leave the camp. The rush of adrenaline was still in their bodies. It was only a matter of time before they had the rest of the jewels. Time itself seemed to stop at this point. Their target was becoming closer and closer and was now in focus. The sheer strength that it took them to get through that maze was amazing. Ranthor and Kendra made an amazing team. They knew each other's strengths and weaknesses like the back of their hands. Both of them were jogging to reach the ship so that they could plan for their next journey. They had hoped that the map would be useful. Ranthor had noticed that Gilderoy marked the possible location of other jewels on his map. This was certainly going to be useful in locating the other jewels. There were now two remaining before this harrowing ordeal had would end.

Ranthor and Kendra finally reached the ship. Gideon was waiting for them patiently. He was happy to see them finally. It was time to leave this planet for good. The coordinates were entered for the next planet. Ranthor was already making plans for when he would find the last jewel. It was only a matter of time before he reached his goals. There was nothing that could stop him now. The ship was powering through the vastness of space. Kendra was also glad that this adventure was finally going to end. She was going to return to a peaceful life, away from the hardship of being involved in fights with different warring factions. She would use her share and retire to her planet with a nice beach hammock. There was nothing that was going to stand in the way of her happiness. Life was finally smiling for the both of them. Gideon was going to use his share to support his parents. He would also buy the many things that he could not afford at the orphanage. He was going to get the childhood that he never had.

The next planet that housed the jewels was Planet Taurus. It was in the next solar system. They were going to head there before the Monks managed to reach there. They were on a race against time. Ranthor was also preparing the plan for the next mission. Kendra was discussing with him the fine details of the plan. They anticipated the protection that was going to probably surround the jewel. Planet Taurus was one of the most dangerous planets in the solar systems. It was barely habitable, on account of the industrial fumes that filled the place. It was anticipated that within two years, all forms of life were going to cease. However, that was not their concern. The jewel was most likely located there, if it had not been located by the Monks and relocated to another planet. They had more equipment and manpower than Ranthor and Kendra did. Furthermore, their ships had better engine power. Nonetheless, Ranthor and Kendra had better intellect than they did.

The ship managed to enter the next solar system. They were now gazing at the planets in this solar system. The constellation of planets was shining brightly, giving it a beautiful crimson hue. Planet Taurus was close to them now. The ship was powering through to the planet's surface. It was only a matter of time before they landed on the planet. They noticed that the guards were circling the asteroid belt of the planet. They had to make sure that they would not cross them. Ranthor activated the ship's cloaking device. He then changed the thermal signal of the ship so that the thermal detector would not detect them. The guards had the most advanced detection software in the universe. This reminded him that he would soon need to upgrade the ship's anti-detection systems. For the time being, they had to use whatever resources they had to ensure that they were not discovered.

They managed to maneuver through the asteroid belt without being detected. Planet Taurus was within sight now. There were no more guards in this place. It was time to land. Ranthor prepared the ship for landing. He turned off the cloaking device and entered the landing coordinates. The ship was entering through the planet's acid rain-soaked atmosphere. The ship was resistant to the acid rain. It was designed for harsh environments. They prepared to wear the hazmat suits that they bought back in Odelphius. It was time to disembark from the ship. They moved into the main quarter of the capital to search for clues for the whereabouts of the jewel. Nothing was what it seemed here in this planet. However, there was nothing that was of any help here. There was a pub in the middle of the quarter. They decided to go on inside, but first, they had to remove the hazmat suits. Surprisingly, the atmosphere was somewhat tolerable. The place was jam-packed with customers. It was a place filled with all the scum in the galaxy. If there was a clue to be found, it would definitely be here. Ranthor ordered some food for them, and they found a table in the middle which would help them eavesdrop. Nothing was going on for the first few minutes. They then found a suspicious group of people that entered the bar.

The mysterious figure in the middle was Gilderoy. The other members must be part of the Order. There was also a buyer that accompanied the men into the pub. They were preparing for a meeting to discuss the jewel. The buyer was not keen on meeting them in such a public place. He also did not like Gilderoy's reputation for not delivering. The other buyers talk, and he was known for not bringing the items that were requested of him. Still, he decided to give him a chance to get the jewel. He gave him one week to find the jewel before he would go to another supplier. Gilderoy complied with the buyer's instruction.

They managed to gather enough from the conversation to know that the jewel was suspected to be in an ancient temple nearby. It was left there by the previous civilization that had inhabited the planet. The jewel was used by that civilization as a worship tool. No one knew what purpose it served, but they were sure that it was in their possession. Upon their departure from the planet, the jewel was still there, according to local folklore. The jewel was probably somewhere inside the temple.

Ranthor then made his way to the temple. Kendra followed close by and made sure that there were no tracks linking them to the mission. The temple was on the outskirts of town. It was located in the middle of a marsh and it was going to be difficult to enter. It was most likely that it was heavily protected. The Order was probably there already guarding the place. They had to end them once and for all this time. It was getting annoying how they managed to hinder their plans every time. Gilderoy was going to be more difficult to reach.

They finally reached the temple in time for the drop-off. The buyer was there along with Gilderoy. They were ready to explore the temple. The buyer waited in a tent nearby for the completion of the mission. He was not going to dirty his hands involved with whatever was going to happen in the temple. As for Ranthor, he made sure to find a reasonable entrance to the temple. The place was quite musky inside. The place was difficult to maneuver in the middle of the night. There was no lighting in the middle of the temple. Gilderoy was already midway across the main temple altar. Nothing was going to stop him from finding the jewel. He was then going to find the other jewels. He knew that Ranthor would follow him to the temple. It was a matter of time before he sold the other jewels as well.

The temple was eerily quiet at this time. There were many guards here, but they did not make a single sound. The operation was going on very quietly, but there was still nothing to be found. The jewel was hidden very well, if it was indeed here. There was no proof that it was in the temple after all. It was only the stuff of legend, passed down from generation to generation by the fanatics that believed of the magical powers of the temple. This was not reassuring for Gilderoy. Ranthor was not having enough luck either. It was very likely that the jewel was stolen. Just as he was about to lose hope, he noticed that the other jewels were glowing wildly. He headed to the next room of the temple. There was a huge mausoleum erected in the middle of the room. He didn't know who it was for; most likely, it was for the temple's religious leader. He must have ordered for the jewel to be buried alongside him upon his death. They would have to open the mausoleum in order to get the jewel. Gilderoy was right behind them. He decided to shoot at Ranthor. Luckily, he managed to dodge the bullet in time. He then swung his sword at Gilderoy and prepared to fight him. Gilderoy quickly left the room and a dozen guards entered after him.

Kendra was preparing her sword for battle. She managed to kill two of the guards. The others did not have a chance against them. They were picking them off one by one. However, the last guard managed to open the mausoleum in the heat of battle. He left the room and managed to hand it off to Gilderoy. Gilderoy managed to exit the temple in time before Ranthor discovered what had happened. Ranthor and Kendra managed to kill off all the guards in time to reach the mausoleum. He realized that it had already been ransacked. The jewel was no longer there. They didn't waste time looking for it. Ranthor knew that it was with Gilderoy, and soon enough, it was going to be in the greedy clutches of the buyer. The buyer was waiting patiently for the jewel to be handed to him. He was going to deliver it to the king for a hefty sum of money. He was trying to get the most of out of this jewel.

Gilderoy had already reached the tent and placed the jewel in its container to present to the buyer. The buyer looked at it and was amazed at this sight. Gilderoy was finally exonerated; his reputation that was tarnished by Ranthor's intrusion was restored. It was only a matter of time before he found the other jewels. He did not know that Ranthor had taken care of the guards. He was now coming for him and the buyer. The buyer departed for Planet Talinus. Gilderoy hung around longer to try and reach Ranthor. His eyes were set at finding the jewels. He would then meet the buyer at Talinus and hand over the remainder of the jewels. He had already shared the coordinates with him so that he could find him. For now, he had to end this crew once and for all. This was the last time that Ranthor was going to be a nail in his foot. He was going to make sure that this time, he was taken care of. His predecessor had done a poor job of taking care of him. Romulus was a powerful foe, but he cared too much about having a fair fight. Gilderoy on the other hand liked to fight dirty. He did not care much about the honor of battle.

Ranthor was just making his way out of the temple along with Kendra. They felt defeat yet again, and that the battle tides always seemed to go against their favor. But they could still hear the clinking of boots nearby. It was the scoundrel Gilderoy.

He must have come to plunder the remainder of the jewels, Kendra thought to herself.

Ranthor was preparing to slice him in half. Gilderoy came with his army of misfit soldiers. He had a blaster to protect himself. Ranthor charged at him and managed to separate his head from his shoulder. His face contorted in a single expression of shock before his soul left his body. The soldiers were soon taken care of. Anger had consumed Ranthor to the extent that it had blinded him. He searched Gilderoy's pocket for any clues. In it, he found a note scribbled with the name Planet Talinus. It must have been the place where the jewel was taken.

They had to travel yet again to a familiar planet. It was frustrating to return to these old spots. Ranthor was going to get the jewel if it meant losing his life in the process. At least they had managed to disband the Order now. Little did they know that there were other forces in the galaxy that were in search of the jewels.

There were many others scheming and plotting to find the jewels. Ranthor and his crew were now famous for having most of the jewels. News spread all across the galaxy of the jewels' possible location. Every mercenary that was worth his salt was preparing to reach Talinus. It was going to be Armageddon there. There was going to be so much bloodshed on the planet. Ranthor was dreading heading back, but he knew that it was the only thing that could be done. They were so close yet so far away. They didn't know anything about this buyer. The only thing they knew was that Talinus had a secret black market that used to convene every Saturday. Villains from all across the galaxy came to purchase drugs, child laborers, and countless other illegal things. The place was near impossible to track.

The journey to Talinus was not going to be as easy as the first time. The black market was somewhere where many people were killed. The bandits and mercenaries did not kid around when it came to purchasing the goods they wanted. It did not so much involve bidding and auctioning as it was bloodshed so that the highest buyer would get what he wanted. The place was located in the underground district. It was next to the slums. This made it easier to dispose of the bodies that were left behind after the purchases were made. No one dared to come or ask afterwards. Not even the brave soldiers of the local law enforcement agency dared to step into that place. The remainder were bought by the underground lords. The buyer belonged to one of the clans that ruled over the underground. It was expected that one of the king's agents were invited to make a purchase. The jewel was kept out of sight of the other criminals. It was solely reserved for the king. The transaction was already made prior to the beginning of the proceedings of the black market.

The king's agent was halfway across the solar system; he was speeding through the asteroid belt to get the jewel. He did not trust that buyer to sell it again; these thieves were an unpredictable bunch. He was annoyed that he had to cross the slums and head into the black market to receive it. Why couldn't he hand it over to him in Nebula? Unfortunately, these were his conditions. He did not wish to be discovered. He had a dozen galactic warrants on his head. The last thing he wanted was to end up back in a galactic level 3 prison. The conditions there were more deplorable than the slums were. He was part of the notorious Sigma Nine clan. It was one of the deadliest drug dealers and rare gem collectors in the galaxy. Rumor has it that they controlled the majority of the law enforcement task forces in the galaxy. They held so much sway in the politics of Talinus, the king was crowned because of them. No one dared openly defy them, not even the king. He steered far away from them. It was a surprise that the black market was not shut down. It was a well-known place. Almost all of the citizens knew about it. They might have set up a stall in the regular market. Still, it was barely acknowledged in conversations. People feared too much for their lives to speak openly of the subject. Instead, they cowered in fear of being killed.

Chapter 11
A Tale of Treachery

Ranthor had finally reached Talinus. He managed to quickly land his ship in a nearby farm, far away from any prying eyes. He could not trust any of the citizens. He was going to rely again on his eavesdropping skills to find about the black market. He managed to gather that it was next to the slums. A meeting was going to be held today most likely, considering that today was Saturday. The buyer was meeting with the king's agent to drop off the jewel. Kendra was loading up her gun in preparation to kill the buyer. She was too furious of all the games. Nothing seemed to go smoothly in this mission. She was going to end this vicious cycle. She was going to put a bullet in between the eyes of this meddling buyer. This was going to be done if it was the last thing she had to do. The buyer's face was ingrained in her memory, and she swore to take his life. Ranthor was going to aid her in doing this. He too sought revenge against this new enemy.

The road to the black market was riddled with people. There were many people in the main market square as usual. Realizing that they had plenty of time before the meeting, they decided to stop and have some food. At least, they were going to be well-fed before accomplishing their goal. It was going to take off the edge of battle. Ranthor took a swig of some unknown spirit which sent a fiery chill down his throat. He toasted Kendra to the upcoming death of the buyer. She seconded that and drank heartily thereafter. They didn't realize until now that they were extremely hungry. They did not have any appetite after their last fight and had not had anything to eat ever since they departed from their last conquest.

They had finally reached the back entrance. Luckily, the entrance was not guarded. It was impractical to guard this place as there were other activities besides the handing-off of the jewels. The other buyers made their way to the stands. The items were being prepared and the cages housing every illegal species were prepared. Most of these species were presumed to be extinct due to illegal hunting. Their prices soared off the roof. People came from across the galaxy to buy them. Ranthor was not interested in all this nonsense. The only thing on his mind was finding the buyer. His tent had to be here somewhere. The agent was already here. Ranthor recognized him from the time he was working at his father's court. It was yet another blast from the past. Nonetheless, he was not going to be overcome with sentimentality.

He had finally managed to find the tent that housed the jewel. The buyer was protected by many thugs that hung around outside the tent. He had given them a lot of money so that they wouldn't be easily bribed. That was the problem with hiring thugs; they could be bought with the right amount of money. However, it was not going to be long before he handed over the jewel, so he did not have to worry about being discovered. He opened the vault and was looking at the very coveted jewel. He found it difficult to part with it. It had a very intoxicating quality, a certain hold on whomever looked at it. He found it extremely difficult to avert his gaze away from it. He managed to muster whatever strength he had and managed to close the vault. It was no longer his for the keeping. Tonight, it was going to be on a ship headed to Planet Nebula. The agent made his way to his tent to examine the jewel. He rested assured, knowing that the jewel was in safekeeping. He took the vault with him and prepared to head to his ship for departure.

Ranthor's keen gaze located the agent and the vault. He decided to tail him to the location of his jewel. It was not far from where the black market was. He snuck behind the agent and with one bullet, he struck him squarely in the chest. He then advanced to the vault and opened it. He now realized that this was not the jewel. The buyer must have tricked the agent. It was not something uncommon to this clan. The Sigma clan was known for their deceitful ways. He made his way back to the black market where the jewel was probably housed. The buyer was still in his tent. The thugs had made their way to eat. There was nothing that was standing in the way of Ranthor and the buyer. He marched over to him and planned to put two bullets in his head.

"Listen to me, scum. You have about two minutes to spill your guts or else I will spill them for you on this nice rug. I want to know where the jewel is, and this time, I want you to avoid playing games with me. I have travelled across many damned galaxies to care about making to yet another one. I hope I am being perfectly clear with you when I say that I AM GOING TO KILL YOU!" shouted Ranthor angrily.

"You're too late. I have already handed the jewel to my leader. He is the king of this planet. The jewels are in his castle by now. You would not get past the guards. The place is well-fortified. I would advise you to head back the same you came from," snarled the buyer.

Before he continued the sentence, Ranthor planted two bullets in his head. He then decapitated him. He was burning with rage now. He was going to do the same thing to the king once he found him. Nothing was going to stand between him and his vengeance. Ranthor was not interested in making this peaceful or stealthy. It had become personal now; there was someone that made it so that he specifically did not reach the jewels. He was going to make sure that this decrepit old king would pay the price in blood.

Ranthor was making his way to the king's palace. He was going to storm the palace and get the jewel. The king had been looking for the jewels for a very long time. He knew Ranthor was looking for him, and so he increased security around the palace. The place was virtually impenetrable. No one got in or out of the place. All of the entrances were sealed. There were even snipers on the roof to protect the king from a possible attack from above. The king had three guards in front of his room in the event Ranthor somehow breached the perimeter. He was also armed as an additional measure. The jewel was stowed safely in a secret room behind the king's bedroom. It was under lock and seal. Ranthor was going to face an extremely difficult time getting this jewel. But that only served to increase his resolve. It was only a matter of time before he gathered the jewel, he thought to himself.

Ranthor managed to take care of the guards protecting the western wing entrance. The way was now clear for him to enter. Luckily, the western wing was the closest to the king, but, unfortunately, the most protected. He did not lose his resolve. The king was informed that the perimeter had been breached. He moved into the secret room to where the jewel was housed. He was sweating and panting heavily. He had clearly underestimated the power of this bounty hunter. He should have killed him the first time. He did not anticipate that he would stand a chance against the Order. Clearly, he was a force to be reckoned with. Ranthor now reached the king's private chambers. This was the most protected part of the palace. He and Kendra split to take care of the guards. It took them half an hour to finish them off. There was nothing protecting the king from them now. It was a matter of time before they gathered the jewel and killed the king.

The king was sweating profusely in the inner chamber; he made sure to be quiet to avoid detection by Ranthor. It was only a matter of time before they reached him. They were already in the king's chamber, the king's inner sanctum where he spent most of his time. The place had a lot of valuable items that many bounty hunters would kill for. The only thing that mattered to Ranthor now was the jewel. It was also the time to get rid of the final faction that stood in the way of their success. Life was giving him a run for his money; he just realized that it not useful to him to do this for his father. He decided that if this ordeal was over, he would use the jewels and harness their powers for his own good. They were rumored to give the person control over the universe. He did not seek control; however, he wanted to spread stability across the universe and become wealthy in the process. He would then fashion a peaceful existence with his soon-to-be wife Kendra; that is, if she agreed to marry him. His feelings for her grew day by day.

They searched everywhere for the king but he was nowhere to be seen. Did he leave the room? That was impossible considering that the area was protected, and they were near the western wing. There were no other entrances that would take the king outside. He must be hidden inside the chamber. Kendra was searching for a way inside to a secret chamber. There was no clue to suggest that there was such a room. She noticed that there was a partition between the two walls. There was a slight indentation indicating an entrance was nearby. He searched for a lever or a pulley that would work the mechanism that would open the door. She finally found a tile in the floor; she pressed the tile with her foot and the door swung wide open. The king was in there, hiding. Once he realized what had happened, he tried to exit the room. Ranthor hit him with the hilt of the sword, sending him careening to the bottom of the floor.

They forced him to open the door and get them the jewel. He quickly complied due to fear for his life. It was time to leave the building. They tied the king to the bed and made sure that he didn't escape. Ranthor promised to come back and kill him if he tried to follow them. Ranthor wanted to make sure that he forgot what happened. He hit him with the hilt of the sword, knocking him unconscious. He would surely wake up with no recollection of the event. He didn't trust him to honor his agreement, especially after what had happened with Gilderoy. There was one jewel remaining. Nothing was going to stand in the way of their conquest. He felt very ecstatic knowing that there was only one jewel left to take.

He felt like he was a god amongst men. Nothing could make him feel horrible now. The world was his oyster. Kendra was also happy that they had almost gathered all the jewels. It was a matter of time before they would reach the end of their journey. The ship was prepared with all of the jewels stowed carefully in their compartments. The last jewel was suspected to be in Planet Crimaceus. It was a giant planet that was three solar systems away. It was a planet that hosted a variety of criminals, miscreants, and exiles. It was a place that shipped weapons to other parts of the universe. Most of the warlords flocked there. Ranthor was already a target as it was. Many known criminals were on the search for him. It was good enough that he managed to escape Talinus without a single wound.

The journey to Crimaceus was underway. It was time to make repairs to the ship. A few updates needed to be made before being able to cross to the solar system housing the next jewel. The hull of the ship needed strengthening and new weapons needed to be installed in the event that they were going to be attacked. It needed to be as strong as any other military vehicle that was going to fire at them. All hell was going to break loose soon enough, and they needed to be ready. The nearest upgrade facility was two planets away. Planet Solaris housed most of the sophisticated equipment for ships and all modes of interplanetary transport. It was also where most black-market deals for ship weapons took place. They needed to be extremely careful taking the jewels there. They had gained a lot of notoriety ever since their last mission.

Planet Solaris was within reach. They made their way to land. The planet looked extremely deserted, and there was no sentient life force there. All of the shops were run by robots, and so were the factories. It was going to be difficult to negotiate with them the updates required for the ship. The robots were created so that they would limit the upgrades available. It was a measure imposed by the government to avoid the excessive use of military weapons. However, some people managed to override this mechanism so that the robots would do it at the right price. However, this was only available at the black market. There were close the entrance of the black market and the jewels were safely locked and stowed inside the ship. They did not want to risk being caught and the jewels stolen. The black market was deserted. There were no visitors today. No criminals were within sight and no drug deals were being made. The new ruler made sure to inspect all the areas, and the market had to be relocated several times.

There was the stall where the mechanic's shop was located. It looked menacing and was quite human-like. It was also a tough negotiator. He recognized Ranthor and Kendra and welcomed them into the shop. He learned about the plan to upgrade the ship. He would do it for thirty thousand kruats. Ranthor agreed and decided to give him the money he had made during his bounty hunting expeditions.

The ship was undergoing the necessary upgrades they required for their final mission. It was going to take the following two days to fix the ship. Kendra was headed to find a place for them to live for the coming two days. Most of the districts in Solaris were quite dangerous, and with the jewels around, it was going to be doubly so. However, she was going to guard the jewels with her life. With the upgrades paid for, the mechanics started working on them right away. This was the first time the ship was being tweaked. Ranthor regretted paying such a large amount of money, but it was for the best. The last jewel was within sight now. Nothing was going to stop them from getting it. The jewel was somewhere in a vault under the sea in Crimaceus according to Gilderoy's manifesto. The ship needed to be able to go underwater. The last jewel was going to be the most difficult one to acquire. All of the criminals were on the lookout for it. Word had probably gotten out that Ranthor was in Solaris, and they were going to make their way to take his jewels.

The jewels were stowed away safely in a vault in the middle of the room of the inn they stayed in. Kendra was going to stay in the room and protect them as an extra measure. She did not trust the vault alone. They were almost killed once and losing the jewels was not going to be an option. She would guard them with her life. No one made a move for several hours. Ranthor was headed to bring her some food from a nearby bar. Just as he approached the bar, he was approached by masked stranger with a handkerchief filled with an anesthetic agent. Ranthor fell down to the ground and was cuffed.

He woke up a day later on the main command room of a ship that was midway into space. He recognized the all too familiar insignia of the Order. They had somehow survived the onslaught that was delivered to them. They had found a new, more powerful leader to lead them through the next mission. The kidnapping of Ranthor was going to send a message to Kendra to get the jewel. She had three days to get to him before they would dispose of him for good. They managed to send her a holographic message via the ship's communication system.

Kendra was not sure what to do. The ship had completed the repairs. She gathered up the jewels from the vault and made her way to the ship. She entered the coordinates to the location given by the Order. It was only a matter of time before she rescued Ranthor. She was not going to hand over the jewels back to the Order; instead, she was going to use them as bait to reach the Order.

She was halfway across the solar system and ready to meet the Order. Her guns were stocked and loaded. Nothing was going to stand in the way of reaching Ranthor.

Ranthor was still dizzy from the last encounter. He tried to unshackle himself but was not successful. It took all the strength he had to even move a single inch. His captors did not watch over him. The shackles were quite strong and they did not think he could get out of it. Instead, the Order was waiting for Kendra to reach with the bag of jewels. It was only a matter of time before they were back to their business. It was soon going to be the new age for the Order of the Monks of Solace. Finding the jewels would ensure universal domination. The power they would summon from the jewels would be unmatched. No one knew what the jewels would summon. It was an ancient power that was unrivalled. It was rumored that it could destroy planets altogether.

Kendra was halfway across the galaxy and almost close to the location of the Order. She was headed at double speed to reach them. All she thought about was whether Ranthor was alive or not. But then rest assured as he was their bargaining chip. They would not do anything to him because he was their leverage. That didn't guarantee, however, that he was not living under deplorable conditions.

Ranthor was brought into the next room to prepare for his torture. The shock blasters were prepared so that he would receive his electric treatment which was followed by drowning. The videos were sent to Kendra which made her make haste. She was extremely worried about Ranthor. The Order was quite ruthless; it was not going to spare any resources to find the jewels. Under their new leadership, they were far more superior than ever. No one knew the name of the new leader. He had disguised himself, especially after what had happened with his two predecessors. He didn't want to interact with Ranthor or Kendra. He stayed in his chambers, out of sight and out of mind. He was going to make sure that this time, the jewels were going to be in his possession. For the time being, he was taking the time planning the next mission to find the last jewel.

Kendra had finally reached the Order's ship. She was granted access to board the ship. The first thing that she did was demanded that she be shown Ranthor. Seeing him somewhat alive made her rest assured. It was only a matter of time before they had killed him. After all, who could guarantee that they would keep him alive after they got what they wanted? They would most likely kill both of them after receiving the jewels. Still, there was nothing that Kendra could do other than handing them the jewels. After all, Ranthor was there all alone with no form of protection against his aggressors. She met with the intermediate agent who requested to see the jewel. He was satisfied that the jewels were in good condition. He examined them thoroughly for authenticity. After he was satisfied, he released Ranthor into Kendra's arms.

Then all of hell broke loose after they had exchanged the jewels. There was nothing to protect them now that there was nothing to bargain. Ion beams were flying everywhere they went. They were inches from Armageddon. The jewels were no longer in their possession. They were now back to square one. All of their work had gone to nothing. Ranthor was too disoriented to react. The only priority that they had now was to escape peacefully. They were going to come back for the jewels later. Ranthor was not going to get the Order have their way with his jewels. He had managed to kill the soldiers in the main room. They then used the pod to escape the Order's ship. Their ship was now within sight. They reached the ship and made their way into the cockpit.

The first thing that they did after reaching the ship was to engage their weapons. They fired the guns at the Order's ship and managed to breach the ship's hull, which burned through. Ranthor then boarded the ship, knowing that there was no one left alive. He headed to the vault where the ship was housed. He was surprised to see that there was a mysterious figure still guarding the ship. He didn't recognize him, but realized that it was possible that this was the leader. He was guarding the jewels with his life. He was actually going to do this even if it meant ending his life. Unlike Gilderoy, he cared about the jewels and not about their monetary value. He was going to fight them. The Master prepared his gun and sword for the fight. He advanced towards Ranthor and took the first swing. Ranthor managed to dodge just in time.

"It is finally my chance to meet you, Ranthor. Your reputation precedes you. Unlike my predecessors, I am not going down without a fight, and I do enjoy fighting dirty. Prepare for your eventual doom, vermin. I am going to make sure to destroy you this time. There is nothing that is going to stop me from protecting these precious jewels," bellowed the stranger.

"I am not going to let you have the jewels. Prepare to eat ion beams. You are going to be the last leader of this annoying Order. I will end you once and for all," retaliated Ranthor.

Ranthor fought to the death. He was hacking at the leader with his sword. He managed to open a gashing wound in his forehead. The Master did not back down. He managed to swing at Ranthor and hit him squarely in the shoulder. Ranthor writhed in agony. However, he managed to control the bleeding and get back in the battle. The fight seemed to go on forever with no clear victor emerging. The Master decided to fire an ion beam right across Ranthor's chest. Luckily, Ranthor managed to deflect the shot with his sword. It landed on a chandelier on top of the master's head and collapsed on top of him. He was trapped under it. Ranthor wasted no time and fired an ion beam between the master's eyes. He collapsed immediately. With that, he was finally dead.

Ranthor searched for the jewels and managed to find them in the vault. He then made his way out of the ship and back into his. They were now back on their mission. There was no time for them to waste. Planet Crimaceus was now two solar systems away. Time was of the essence. They figured out that the other criminal clans were in search of the jewel. Many more opponents were going to try and impede their journey. At least the monks were now out of the picture. However, that didn't mean that they were out of the danger zone yet. Besides, they realized that Ranthor's father was assembling a task force to get the jewels back. He planned to send an armada of ships to get the jewels.

The king expected to have the jewels within a week's time. His advisors had reassured him that was going to be the case. He didn't mind killing his son in order to get the jewels. He was cruel and heartless enough to do anything for the jewels. He was going to make sure that Ranthor did not have a place in his kingdom. He was planning to harness the power of the jewels to gain immortality. He would rule over the universe for all eternity. His plans for expansion of his reign were going on smoothly. It was a shame that he had to dispose of his son in the process. However, his throne mattered to him more than ever. His fleet were heading across to Planet Crimaceus. Prior to Gilderoy's defeat, he had managed to purchase a replica copy of his map. The king was planning to surprise them.

There was yet another faction on their tail. Ranthor did not have a chance to breathe just yet. He was healing from his wounds. Kendra had prepared him food to ease his wounds. Now that most of the jewels were found, Ranthor decided to relieve Gideon of his mission. He granted him access to the pod and made sure to protect it well to avoid another incident like the last one. He was going to reach his parents within two days. Gideon bid the others goodbye and promised to visit them as soon as their mission was over. He was crying for the fact that he was going to leave his friends. The only thing that was consoling him was that he would soon meet them again. However, he was happy that he would be reunited with his parents again.

Gideon updated his parents that he was making his way to them. The pod was stocked with enough food and water that would allow him to survive the journey back home. He bid the others goodbye and made his way back home. His parents had prepared his room. He was worried about Ranthor and Kendra. He wanted them to come back safe and sound. The last jewel was now within sight. Planet Crimaceus was the last planet in the solar system that housed the jewel. He wanted to know what would happen after all the jewels were collected. Where were they supposed to take them? It was rumored that finding the jewels would open a hollow map that would lead them to the location of the master jewel. It had the ability to harness the power of the universe's core. With it, the owner could rule any system that they wished. It also had the power to enslave the will of whoever they possessed. This kind of power would make its owner the most powerful person in the universe.

Ranthor was not going to make one of these criminals realize this goal. He didn't care much for universal domination. However, he was interested in gaining control of his kingdom. Kendra would be alongside him as queen. No longer would he have to suffer the tyranny of his father. He would be able to head back home, his head held proud. There was nothing that was going to stop him from realizing his mission, not even his own father. It was time to stop this decade-old blood feud. He was fed up with all the warring, the displacement from his home, and most importantly, the loneliness that followed. It didn't matter how he did it, even if it meant sending his father to the nether realm. He would do whatever was necessary to gain control of his land.

Kendra was there by his side to make sure that he completed his mission. She believed in him and trusted him with every fiber of her being. This woman was his biggest supporter. He could not care how this mission was going to end. As long as he had her by his side, nothing was going to affect him. He was glad to have found her. This was the only good thing to have come from venturing toward the ends of the galaxy. He would trade all the jewels in the universe for a life with her. He had to make sure that she was well protected. He did not want to lose her. He would be shattered if anything happened to her.

She exchanged a mischievous look across the other end of the room. Kendra came over and hugged him. It was reassuring to have her support in this crazy adventure. She had saved him countless times throughout their adventures together. He owed her his life and undying love. They were bound together for all eternity. But enough of all the romantic talk, they had a lot to do before reaching the next planet. He had to devise a plan to get the last jewel. Ranthor drew the schematics to Planet Crimaceus. This mission needed to be executed to perfection. He did not need a repeat of the other missions, but he knew that it was most likely going to be the same. He did anticipate a lot of opposition. He also knew that his father had caught wind of their little expedition, and he was not happy that he was not going to get the jewels. His father was a force to contend with. He knew that he would be after him with every weapon available in his arsenal. He would forget that this was once his son. He knew his father enough to know that the jewels were the only important thing for him. He would sacrifice everything for them.

There was only one solar system separating them from Crimaceus. The ship powered through using the additional thrusters that they had purchased. The ship's hull was shaking with the speed of the engine. It was a miracle that they were not caught in the middle of a blackhole. It started to mess up with the ship's navigation system. Ranthor reduced the speed to maintain the stability of the ship. He wanted to reach there in one piece after all. A little delay would not do much to hinder them. After all, they had all the other jewels. Whoever managed to gather the jewel would have to use it to reach them. He just hoped that it would be anyone other than his father. He was better equipped to deal with individual ships and not an entire fleet. He may have to acquire some allies before going on war with his father. Even after gathering the jewels, his father would not budge from the throne. He would need all the resources he had in his disposal to take care of him.

He wondered if it was a good idea to buy the trust of mercenaries. He didn't have any remaining funds on account that he had to use them to upgrade the ship.

There must be another way to gain allies, he thought to himself. He would think of it later once he had managed to find the last jewel.

The way to Planet Crimaceus was now within reach. They were about to cross the next solar system and gain entry to the one housing the planet. However, they noticed that two military-grade ships had followed them. Ranthor hesitated, deciding whether to shoot them or let them go on their way. He didn't have a choice as one of them started to fire a barrage of ion beams. He had managed to steer into a nearby asteroid field and use them as a shield to protect himself from the shots fired. He then hid there for a while, hoping to distract them. Unfortunately, the ships did not budge and instead, entered the asteroid field in search of him. It was going to be a very narrow escape now. Ranthor decided to tackle them head on. He fired a shot at the ship. It didn't seem to make the slightest dent in its armor. He was starting to panic now; there was nothing much that he could do.

Kendra thought of another idea. The asteroids were sturdy enough to breach the hull of the ships. She told Ranthor that they needed to trick the ships into colliding into the asteroid field. They were going to use their ship as bait to attract the other ships. They exited the asteroid field and signaled the ships to follow them. Their ship took a nosedive into the nearest asteroid. The other ship did the same thing. Ranthor then managed to steer his ship out of the way. The other ship, however, was not as lucky and crashed head-on into the asteroid. Fire and fumes were coming out the ship. It then exploded into nothingness. The other ship soon fled the scene of the crime. That did not feel reassuring to Ranthor. He was still being followed by someone. That ship could easily be going to report their location.

He steered the ship into the rubble. Perhaps, he would be able to find some clues about the soldiers that followed them. There was nothing left from the ship, everything had burned down after the crash. Ranthor left, angry that he could not find anything of importance. Kendra tried to console him, but it did not work. He bashed whatever his hands could reach. However, he finally calmed down and continued their journey. The security around the ship was increased to avoid detection. The cloaking device was turned on and their thermal signal was disguised. The ship also emitted a jamming signal to avoid detection by any nearby satellites. Hopefully, this would provide them an extra measure to avoid being found out. Ranthor was fed up. He felt like the entire universe had teamed up against him. He never had a break for a second from the moment this mission had started. This was going to end soon.

The ship was now virtually undetectable. Their only task now was reaching Planet Crimaceus and finding the jewel. No one seemed to follow them, or at least they had hoped. However, that didn't mean that there wasn't going to be any trouble waiting for them at the other end. If there was no one here, then that meant that there was an ambush waiting for them at the other end. Things were never as easy as they seemed. Both of them learned this lesson the hard way multiple times. This time was not going to be any different. They were well-prepared and well-equipped to tackle whatever came across them this time. Ranthor and Kendra had learned from their past mistakes to avoid whatever condition, trap, or natural disaster that may befall them. They were not going to be ambushed again. Enough was enough already.

Ranthor was excited to do a lot of skull-bashing once he reached the planet. They were now in the same galaxy as Planet Crimaceus. A few planets were separating them from their goal. So far, there was nothing obstructing their way. The way had been clear up till now. Ranthor disengaged the cloaking device and made his over to the cockpit. He searched the map for the planet's location and entered the coordinates into his ship. It was a matter of hours before they would land.

Planet Crimaceus was filled with marshes and wetlands. It was toxic, however, and travelers often got lost amidst the toxic plant species that were there. The dangerous animals would have taken care of the remainder of travelers that were brave enough to face the vile flora. And for those who survived this, there were armies of mercenaries and machines that haunted the surface of the planet and those that had protected the planet for centuries. These ancient thugs had formed an ancient knighthood, the knights of the Crimacean Sun. They were feared across the galaxy. If anyone had the jewel, it would be them, for sure. Getting the jewel from them would be a harrowing task. Ranthor was annoyed at this point to fall into yet another trap. He wanted to finish this adventure as soon as possible.

They had finally reached the surface of the planet. The landing coordinates were entered, and the ship prepared for descent. It seemed like time itself had stopped. The landing was taking quite a long time. Kendra's heart was beating heavily and Ranthor was trying to calm himself as much as possible. He had a tough exterior, but inside, he was just as scared. There was no assurance that the war would be over after the jewel was collected. The king of Nebula was still going to try to claw his way into their ship. He would then try to gather the jewels, if it was the last thing he had to do. It would be likely if he survived the onslaught.

Ranthor and Kendra were ready to disembark from the ship. Luckily, there was no one waiting for them. By now, they had been sure that someone was waiting for them yet the welcoming committee was not here to welcome them. Perhaps they would arrive later. Anyway, it was not the time to think about such things. They did not have the luxury of spending time pondering about any possible attacks. There was no time left for them to search thoroughly. The most likely place where the jewel was located was the palace of the knights. The king was very interested in finding the jewels. He had spent the majority of his rule trying to locate them. Rumor has it that he kept them in a secret dungeon in the middle of the palace. No one managed to reach this legendary dungeon. Ranthor was going to be the first person that might be able to complete this task.

They were planning to scale the castle. The main entrance was too risky to go through and the back entrance was equally as risky. The knights were familiar already with their approach and prepared beforehand for a possible breach. There were barely any footholds to grapple from. It was going to be a difficult task trying to scale the castle. It was made in a way that made it virtually impenetrable. The king also managed to upgrade the security to avoid any unwarranted access. He had heard about the previous strongholds that were raided by Ranthor and his crew. He did not want to end up as another statistic in the death toll that was brought on by Ranthor. The inside of the castle was equally fortified. Ranthor still managed to enter through a window on the third floor, and now he was looking at a schematic of the castle to make sure he knew where he went.

The king was holed up in the middle of his room. He was surrounded by several soldiers that he trusted. The third floor was surrounded by many mercenaries that were on the lookout for Ranthor. Each of them carried a thermal detection device that enabled them to see through the walls. Luckily, Ranthor came prepared and managed to find a spray that masked their heat signal. They were virtually undetectable now. The first thing they did on entry was to kill the first two mercenaries; it was not a difficult task. Ranthor managed to find the elevator that would take him to the king's quarters. It was going to be a few minutes before he reached the king. He would then find the key to the dungeon and make his way to the jewel.

The door to the king's quarters was bolted shut. It was going to be difficult to open the door. The mechanism to open it was controlled by the guards on the second level. Each of the three guards were assigned a lever that operated the mechanism to open the door, and each of them was protected by several mercenaries. It was going to be difficult to reach them. The first team of guards was protecting the first mechanism. It was the one nearest to the eastern wing of the palace. There were robots and drones hovering over the mercenaries. One of the drones managed to detect Ranthor and signaled for the others to join him. Soon, Ranthor was surrounded by several drones that were out to kill him.

Ranthor was shooting violently at the drones. He managed to take down the first one. However, the others circled around him and shot his gun. He was now left powerless against them. He had to make sure to hide from them. There were very few places where they could hide. He managed to find a garden outside that would protect them from the robots. The threat had subsided, albeit temporarily. They then planned to escape the palace and gather weapons. Their current weapons were not sufficient to protect them against the king's army. This was an encounter that almost led to their death. The planet hosted a few arms dealerships that were shady but still reliable. They housed some of the strongest weapons in the galaxy.

Ranthor and Kendra barely managed to escape the castle. They headed to the black market to purchase the weapons. Luckily, the arms dealers were not affiliated with the mercenaries. Similar to the mercenaries, they provided their services to the highest bidder. Ranthor managed to steal a few valuable items and gems from the king's castle. He was going to sell them on the black market for a considerably high price. This was going to afford them the guns that they direly needed. He would also buy a few hired guns to help him storm the castle. The palace was difficult to get through with just two people. They had to enlist the help of some ex-mercenaries. Most of them had a grudge against the current king and would do it for free. Ranthor offered to make one of them the king's successor. He managed to enlist six ex-mercenaries which were his private army. They then bought the latest weapons and grenades that were going to be used to storm the castle. Ranthor was going to wait for the cover of night to storm the castle again.

The king was still holed up in his room. He was informed about the recent developments that had happened. He was scared that Ranthor was not captured by his mercenaries so it was only a matter of time before he would come again. In the meantime, Ranthor decided to take a break and have some food with Kendra. They were going to wait till night-time. Hopefully, the second attempt was going to be better than the first. The castle was going to be more fortified than the last time they had entered. The mercenaries would be better prepared to fight them off. However, this time, they had more weapons and manpower. They could even storm the place this time. Anyway, it was most likely that they were not going to be able to scale the place now. The ex-mercenaries knew the palace by heart and knew every weakness in both the palace and the people that inhabited it.

It was time to storm the castle. Everything was prepared and the team assembled in the main square ready to storm the castle. Their weapons were locked and loaded; their souls filled with rage. For many of them, it was a chance for retribution. The king had robbed them of several things; their reputation for one was tarnished by him, and he ensured that they would not be employed again. For others, they had lost their loved ones due to the king's crazy missions. All they wanted was justice for the ones that they had lost in this ridiculous war.

The entrance to the castle was heavily protected by mercenaries and robots alike. It seemed virtually impenetrable for them to enter. Ranthor and his soldiers were advancing further into the castle. The soldiers in the entrance were taken care of easily by the weapons they had purchased. The entrance was clear for them to enter now. Nothing stood in the way of their mission now. The other levels were equally guarded by a group of mercenaries. At least now they knew the easiest way to the king's quarters. It was not going to be as difficult as the first attempt. The king had prepared an attack squadron on the second level that would take care of Ranthor and his goons. There was no time but the present to execute the attack. The first group of guards gave them a run for their money but went down like the others. They now advanced upwards to the king's quarters. It was only a matter of time before they had reached the king.

The king was prepared to meet them. He had a weapon arsenal of his own in the middle of his room. The mercenaries that guarded his chamber were armed to the teeth. Besides, they were carrying thermal detectors that was making them detect their enemies easily. These detectors were impenetrable to the spray that Ranthor used the last time. They had to face them head-on this time. The ex-mercenaries knew the weaknesses of these current mercenaries. They knew every Achilles heel that they possessed. The ex-mercenaries were on the front line for this part of the mission. The crew managed to take care of the first line of guards. The other group succumbed to their attacks soon enough. The king was now within their sight. He fought to the last breath before surrendering. He gave them the key to the dungeon to avoid being killed. He also told them about the location of the dungeon.

The entrance to the dungeon was now open in front of them. The ex-mercenaries were protecting the entrance to the dungeon. Ranthor and Kendra entered inside the dungeon to find the jewel. Something strange was going on. The jewels were not resonating. That was never a good sign, it usually meant that the jewels were nowhere near to be found. The worst part was that they were probably relocated or worse, stolen. Still, they decided to continue further into the dungeon and continue exploring the place. There was nothing to be seen for several kilometers. It was time to abandon the mission. However, they finally stumbled onto a box in the middle of the dungeon. Ranthor opened it with the key that the king had given him. Within it was a jewel. However, this one did not react with other jewels. He realized that this was a decoy kept in place to avoid finding the real jewel. Crimaceus was not the location housing the jewel. Gilderoy planted this fake jewel deliberately and marked it in the map to throw off the scent. He knew that Ranthor would find the other one and decided to hide the location of the last one.

Chapter 12
The Deserted Mines

Ranthor made his way back to the ship. It was time to leave the planet and look for the jewel elsewhere. He decided to head to the next planet in the system; Planet Lombargo. It was also suspected to house the jewel. Perhaps he would find a lead there. He did not lose hope about finding the jewel. There must be a way to find the jewel. Maybe he could attract whoever had the remaining jewel. After all, they too were in search of the jewels. They were going to use the jewels as bait to attract the owner of the last jewel. They made sure to give a strong enough signal that would attract the jewel owner. The coordinates were entered for Planet Lombargo and the ship left Planet Crimaceus. Ranthor was searching for the schematics of the planet to ensure that he found the possible locations where the jewel was housed. Planet Lombargo was now within sight. Ranthor prepared the landing coordinates for their descent. He wasn't hopeful about finding anything, but at least he wanted to give it a try. It was the last thing that he was able to do.

Planet Lombargo was the previous seat of the control for this galaxy. Most of the politicians used to flock here. Nowadays, it was a hollowed-out land that housed impoverished citizens that were stuck here. The planet still had a lot of natural resources, but the citizens unfortunately did not have the financial means to extract them. The previous establishment prevented the mining of the rare minerals and gems that were in the planet. They managed to bleed the planet dry before departing to the next solar system. It was in the one of these mines where the jewel was probably located. Ranthor went to try and ask the locals a few questions; the first being the location of the mining area. They pointed him to the location of the mines. It was going to be a matter of time before they reached the mining region. Ranthor prepared his equipment to enter the mines. He did not want to risk any chance of being shot at. He expected a surprise to be there when he arrived. The king was not going to let go of the prized jewels.

The last jewel was probably safely locked in the middle of the mining village. There were remnants of the previous civilization that created the mines. A lot of levers, pulleys, and other contraptions allowed them to cross the mining city. The city had not been inhabited for the past century and a half. No one knew if the mechanisms were even operational. It was quite dangerous to cross using them. They could either cross through or plummet to their certain doom. There was one access point to the mines. It was through a zipline that connected to the main square of the capital that was recently built by the citizens who thought of renewing the mechanisms that protected the mines. It was going to be a source of their livelihood again. All of them had grown tired of living in poverty, despite having the resources. Ranthor used the zipline to cross to the other end, to the mining city.

The mining region was deserted; there was no living soul to be found. It was also quite barren and did not have any form of wildlife. It hadn't rained in these parts for several years. This was the first time that someone came here for a long time. The citizens did not dare come due to the risk of the collapse of the cave system. At least they would not have any interference as they headed to gather the jewel. But it was not reassuring as the jewel would not have survived a hundred years without being discovered. Ranthor decided to continue and take his chances. After all, they were so used to disappointments that it didn't matter anymore. It seemed to be so random at this point. This was the best option for them now. The journey kept getting more difficult with every jewel collected. Whoever created the jewels did not want anyone to harness the power unless they were sure they could handle it.

The creators of the jewels used the jewels as a gateway to their planet. It was there that the doorway to the eternal source of power would open. The jewels were the key to opening the doors. Ranthor was trying to find an access point to the caves. He tried to use the pulley carts to get through. Surprisingly, they actually were fully operational and possibly could take them to the opposite side. They each took turns getting to the other side. It was better this way to avoid overloading the mechanism. It was made for people who were significantly smaller in size and height. Ranthor then managed to use the lever to open the door. He was now looking into the mine that housed tons of silver, gold, and rare gems. There was no sign of the jewel anywhere, nothing was seen within a few kilometers. He continued to venture through the cave system which seemed to divide into infinity. There were a few inscriptions written on the walls of the cave. It talked about an ancient jewel that was locked in a mausoleum. The ancients managed to find the jewel and hide it somewhere within this tomb.

The mines were filled with every rare metal imaginable. Kendra was in awe the sheer of amount of untapped riches that were in these mines. However, she managed to regain her focus on finding the jewels. She then continued her way to the other chambers of the mine. So far, the jewels did not resonate. There was nothing in the current cave system that indicated that the jewel was here. They were moving from chamber to chamber without any luck. All of the rooms had the same mechanisms, and all of them opened vaults that had decoy jewels. Ranthor was starting to wonder if this place had been recently ransacked. He didn't seem to find anything useful despite the long search. With every room they had entered, their frustration grew by leaps and bounds. Eventually, Ranthor decided to exit the caves. Just before he managed to do that, he found a secret entrance within the mines. He decided to follow his instinct and go looking for whatever might be in there. He was not hopeful, but he was also not going to be disappointed any more than he already was.

The jewels were not emitting their usual radiant glow. However, this room must have meant something; especially since it was hidden way out of sight. Ranthor realized that there was a huge sarcophagus in the middle of the chamber. It was gold and diamond encrusted, it had to be the final resting place of one of the ruling family members; such a burial was customary for them alone. The others were buried in less impressive caskets. He decided to open the sarcophagus and discover what was hidden inside it. It was difficult to pry it open, but he eventually managed to do it after many unsuccessful events. There was a purple receptacle in the middle. It had slots where the jewels were inserted. He managed to insert all the jewels successfully. There was one slot remaining for the final jewel to be inserted. However, he noticed that there were slots for three somewhat larger jewels. There was a written lore that indicated that once the jewels of Nebula were found, they would help lead their seeker to the three jewels of darkness.

However, the jewels of darkness were only a thing of myth. Still, Ranthor did not know why this receptacle had three extra slots. He had thought that his mission was going to be finally over. The addition of this complication did not bother him. He was used to this by now, and indeed welcomed a new challenge. For one, this was prolonging the time that he had with Kendra. He saw this as the light in his adventure. She was the best thing that had happened to him.

Ranthor was glad that she had accompanied him in his search for the jewels. Realizing that this was the only thing they would find, they left the mining city and headed back to the capital. They were at least glad to find this discovery. It must be some sort of map, but a map to where? He was soon going to discover after finding the jewel.

The planet looked like a small blob from space, this was the view that Kendra was fixated on. Something was telling her that this was not the last time they would visit Planet Lombargo. It had a lot to do with the jewels. Why else would that receptacle be there? Ranthor was looking at the map to see if he had missed anything. Nothing seemed amiss; he was quite thorough in his search for the jewels. As he was searching the map, he noticed that connecting the locations that housed the jewels pointed out to one of the planets. The location of the last jewel was hidden in plain sight. All he had to do now was decipher this location. The planet in question was Planet Delta 7. It was one of the planets that housed the ancient artefacts of the civilization of jewel worshippers. It was the home of the creators of the jewels. There was no place more conspicuous where the jewels could be hidden. It was the ideal location for hiding the last jewel. The creators must have ensured that the last jewel was buried with them. It was a long journey to the planet, but it was one which they would gladly make. Hopefully, it would still be there by the time that they would manage to reach.

The coordinates for Planet Delta 7 were entered into the computer's mainframe. It was good that they had made the adjustments to the ship. Most ships were not able to access that part of the universe. The conditions there would destroy any ship that dared to cross. The hull of most ships were not built to withstand the extreme conditions of most of the planets in that system. It was foretold that the ancients living there had a significantly different body build that could withstand almost anything. This had served them during the wars across the galaxy and made their planet virtually impenetrable to attacks. Ranthor wondered if there were still any inhabitants or were they wiped out during the war. After all, there were technologies created even then to penetrate the extreme conditions of their planet. They would soon find out once they reached the planet. *It would be interesting to find the ancient people of Delta 7*, Kendra thought to herself.

The journey to the furthest reaches of the universe was long and difficult. Ranthor was searching for something to do. There seemed to be nothing of interest to him. He had managed to map out and plan everything already. His obsession with the jewels almost drove him crazy. He just hoped that they would not hit any detour that would derail them from their mission. They could not afford losing the jewels. The last time this almost happened was a wake-up call that their security measures were not protective enough. The vault that was currently housing the receptacle was well-equipped with the latest anti-bombing sequences available. It was virtually an impenetrable protection device that would safely house the jewels.

Ranthor noticed something strange. There were ships with an insignia that he was quite familiar with. This was part of his father's fleet. They must have been sent to scout the area in preparation for the arrival of the entire armada. He recognized one of his father's generals, Ray. He was amongst the most ruthless men in any galaxy. He was quite impartial to torture and means that would get him virtually anything that he wanted. He served alongside him during many wars and almost died because of him. He kept disobeying orders, and this caused them to be captured several times. Ranthor kicked him off his task force entirely, and he was shifted to a different platoon. Ever since then, there was a bitter rivalry between them that never seemed to end. Ranthor avoided him as much as possible.

The ship's cloaking device was fully engaged and operational. Ranthor made sure that they were not going to be detected at any cost. He would rather avoid any collision with his nemesis despite wanting to bash his skull so badly. He fought every instinct that he possessed to remain out of their sight. The ship managed to pass by without noticing them. They did not pick their thermal signature as well. Kendra breathed a sigh of relief knowing that they were not going to engage in combat. Ranthor, on the other hand, regretted the missed opportunity, but he knew that it was the right thing to do. They did not need to cause unnecessary damage to the ship before they reached Planet Delta. It was still a long way and there was no repair shop nearby. Ranthor returned to examining his schematics.

The next solar system was virtually free of any enemy ships. Ranthor wondered what Ray was doing in the previous galaxy. There was nothing of value as far as he knew. Perhaps he was on another mission for the king. But he knew that it was far too coincidental, and it was most likely something related to the jewels. He had marked the location on the map in the event that they had to return to it. It would also ensure that his feud with his nemesis would end with one final fight to the death. He was still obsessing over the missed opportunity as he kept revising his plans. Kendra was fed up.

His reunion with Ray was going to be sooner than anticipated. His nemesis emerged from the rift between the two galaxies. The first thing that he managed to notice was the presence of an unknown ship. He decided to fire two warning shots at the ship and demanded to know the reason it was here, and, most importantly, who was commandeering the ship. He was hellbent on destroying them if they did not comply with his commands. Ranthor opened the intercom and prepared for a conversation with Ray.

"I am ordering you to surrender your vessel immediately. Your presence is a violation of the rules of the king of Nebula. Submit yourself to a mandatory search immediately or prepare to suffer the consequences. Prepare for me to board the ship at once. I am warning you that I will open fire in the event that you decide to disobey my orders!" howled Ray commandingly.

"Come on, board the ship. You will find that there is nothing for you to find. Anyway, the doors will be opening soon to admit your oversized carcass though, Ray. You always were as stupid as you looked. I wonder what meaningless tasks my father is giving you now. Does it include cleaning the stables? You were never of any use, anyway," snarled Ranthor.

"I should have known that scum like you would be the cause of such mess. You did not change one bit, Ranthor. You still speak before you deliver. It was something that you had learned from battle. You were always winning due to sheer dumb luck. You would soon realize that your lucky streak would not last," replied Ray rather sourly.

Kendra was not sure that antagonizing this clearly heavily armored foe was the best course of action. However, she trusted Ranthor's judgement despite not understanding it completely. Ray was now inside their ship along with two of his most trusted lieutenants. They searched every crevice and hole in the ship for signs indicating that the jewels were housed there. The ship was capable of making the vault invisible to even the most sophisticated of detectors. Ray was now satisfied that nothing was there. He left the ship but decided that it would be best to trail their ship. Upon leaving, he managed to install a tracking device inside the ship.

The tracker's signal was now visible in the middle of the device. Ray disappeared from sight and was nowhere to be seen. Ranthor did not trust that snake. He knew that he had many tricks up his sleeve. It was only a matter of time before they were reunited again. For the time being, they had to return to their journey and compensate for the lost time. Two galaxies now separated them from Delta 7. The ship powered through with as much power as it could possibly exert. Ranthor was in a race against some of the most powerful forces in the universe. They were not going to let him have his way with the jewels. But then again, he was not someone who was used to taking permission from anyone. His father was the last person that he sought approval from. He wanted so badly to separate his head from his shoulder. Nothing would please him more than the collapse of his kingdom. Ranthor was going to build the place again, on terms and conditions that would fairly apply to all of the citizens.

He had realized that he was daydreaming for the better part of an hour. It was time to make one last mandatory pit stop to refuel before they made their way to Planet Delta. It was going to be in the jungle world; Planet Arbourus. Ranthor managed to find a nearby refueling station and entered the coordinates. It was only a matter of time before the ship was fueled and ready for the mission.

The planet was filled with different plants and all sorts of wildlife. Other than the fueling stations, its beauty was not marred by the urban developments that surrounded the other planets. There were also many humanoid inhabitants here that survived and lived in complete harmony with the planet. Streams were running here with the clearest water that anyone could possibly find. You could drink from the water of this stream and see your own reflection through it. The purity of this water was not affected by the industrial fumes that surrounded the other planets. The usual Sulphur mushroom clouds that surrounded the other planets were not seen here. But it was important to note that this planet was not as advanced as the others. It seemed to lag a millennium behind in the evolutionary time scale, save for the fueling stations, of course.

The ship landed and reached the fueling station. Ranthor and Kendra did not leave the ship this time. They were both not keen on trying the local cuisine. Despite the natives having several places to eat, it was not their type of food. Both of them were quite used to having processed food that they did not trust anything else. They stayed in their quarter and prepared a meal for themselves. Kendra cooked while Ranthor prepared the plates. It was not going to be long before the ship was back in orbit. The fueling would take a maximum of one to two hours before completion. They had to do something else to pass the time.

There was nothing that was even remotely interesting on this planet. Kendra decided to take a stroll and Ranthor agreed to accompany her. The only thing that was noticeable was that the planet had several volcanic mountains. However, they were dormant for the better part of the century. They were both perplexed as to why the inhabitants would not proceed with industrializing the planet. Despite the beauty of the planet, it was difficult to live in this day and age in such conditions. Ranthor noticed that there were some carvings on top of the mountain. They featured the same receptacle and a temple. He wondered if this had anything to do with the legendary temple that used to be the resting place of the jewels. Legend had it that it housed the power of the jewels. It was the place that supplied power to the entire universe. Without it, the universe would succumb to eternal darkness. No one knew where the temple was or if it was actually real. The ancient did a great job hiding things as was evident by their recent travels.

They continued venturing across the planet in search of clues. There was nothing else of value to be found. Ranthor took a picture of the carvings and decided to add it to his map. There must be some clues in these carvings to help them find the last jewel. It was also going to help them find the three dark jewels, if they actually existed. Ranthor decided that they should take a small break. Kendra sat alongside him under the cover of one of the ancient trees. They embraced nature and basked in its glory. It was good to finally take a breath and recharge their energy. Both of them pondered at some point whether it was worthwhile to continue on this inane journey. It was a miracle that they had not lost their sanity yet. But they had reached this far, and they were not going to back down now, not at the last moment.

The fueling process was now complete, and they were free to get back to their ship. Ranthor paid for the fuel, and they made their way out of the planet. The ship was now back in orbit and headed to Delta 7. Kendra kept thinking about the markings she saw on the mountain and about their possible significance. She looked at the map to see if there was a temple, but instead found nothing. Perhaps the temple would be at the interconnection between the different planets. She would soon discover this after finding the last jewel in the sequence.

They were now separated by one solar system from Planet Delta 7. It was only a matter of time before they had entered the landing sequence. There was nothing or no one that could disturb their peace now. Little did they know that they were being tracked down by the king's soldiers. Ray was hot on their trail. He followed them closely without being detected. He was going to arrive soon in Delta 7 alongside them. The king was being updated about the progress of the mission as they were speaking. He was impressed at the progress that his son was making so far. He thought that he would be a valuable asset to him if he managed to coerce him to come back, but he knew that there was nothing that was going to bring him back. That ship had long since sailed. There was no chance of him ever coming back. Strangely enough, he was feeling nostalgic about having his son back in his army. He was going to ask him when the opportunity presented itself.

Ranthor was telling Kendra about his childhood. He was trained to be a warrior from the ripe age of seven. The children in their planet did not live the regular life a child would live. Instead, they entered the world of adulthood early on. The worst part was that they were introduced early on to the horrors of war. The first war that he had waged against an enemy was at the age of ten. He was with his father leading the battalion. His father told him that holding a sword and axe would make a man out of him. Meanwhile, children in other worlds were playing with toys and games. Their parents would enjoy sending them to school and ensuring that their learning would be complete. They were completely oblivious to what was happening around in other worlds. He wished that he had lived his childhood similar to the other children. He vowed that upon his return, he would outlaw the incorporation of children into the war regime, and most importantly, he would make it voluntary for the others to join.

This was going to ensure the prosperity and continuity of his people. He would establish industries and factories that would serve to employ the people that were going to leave their job as soldiers. He had just found the purpose of him finding the jewels. Ranthor would ensure the peace and stability of the universe. With the power harnessed from the jewels, he was going to disarm all the mercenaries and soldiers. It was time to finally end this Armageddon once and for all. There was going to be peace, stability, and prosperity in the kingdom that he would rule and the ones surrounding it. It was long overdue and a welcome change from all the horrors that surrounded them. The children were going to play together again.

These were all daydreams at this point. However, it was going to be soon easy to achieve them. Finding the remaining jewel and the other jewels of darkness would ensure their power would be harnessed. This would enable them to enter the temple of jewels and utilize its powers to aid them in their quest. Ranthor wished that the jewel would be located in Delta 7. It was possible that finding the jewel would open a map that would help in locating the remaining three darkness jewels. They were going to be easier to find than the other jewels. This was actually a relief as he was exhausted from this search. He had almost quit before, realizing that maybe this was not his war to deal with. Kendra managed to give him the necessary boost to continue on his path. It was this strength that enabled him to find the location of this planet. The ship was now within orbit of Planet Delta 7. The landing sequence was entered, and the ship prepared for descent. It would take around thirty minutes for the ship to land. In the meantime, Ranthor prepared their gear for the mission. Kendra was doing an inventory search to make sure that they had enough rations to last them should they need to stay longer. She did not anticipate staying long, but anything was bound to happen. The ship finally landed, and they departed the cockpit. They were welcomed by the whirring of machinery and the chirping of birds.

Planet Delta 7 was a replica of most of the planets in the same system. It did not have any distinguishing features besides the abundance of factories in comparison to the other planets. The citizens also looked similar to the other citizens. The same currency was shared as well. None of them were usual tourist spots; hence, no one cared about the lack of variability. Ranthor was now tired of walking and decided to find a vehicle. He managed to purchase a hovercraft from one of the vendors nearby for a reasonable price. He then used it to travel across town in search of answers. No one seemed to know anything about the jewel. There was, however, an abandoned landfill that was the last known location. This was told to him by one of the oldest inhabitants of the planet. It was the only clue that he had, and he decided to take whatever he could get.

The landfill was not very far away from the center of town. However, they needed to be careful as it was separated by an area filled with quicksand that would devour them whole if they were not careful. Ranthor was on the lookout for the quicksand. He would try to use the grapple hook and get a foothold on top of the trees to shield him away from it. The quicksand covered a significant part of the land. There were no trees within sight. Ranthor, however, found a metal wall with an anchor attached to it. He pulled out his grapple hook and used it to attach to the anchor. The first two trials were not successful. He managed to get it by the third attempt. He held Kendra close to him and they both swung across the quicksand. Kendra lost her balance, but Ranthor caught her in time and avoided her drowning in quicksand. They then traversed the area and landed in a nearby barren land. It was only a short walk from there before they reached the abandoned landfill.

They finally managed to reach the landfill close to midnight. Ranthor used his flash torch to search around for a possible sign indicating the presence of the jewel. He noticed that there was a building next to the landfill that was locked. He made his across to see if he could open it. The key was nowhere to be found. However, he managed to find explosives in the landfill that were left by the previous workers; he used these to blow a hole in the door. He then entered through and made his way to the first room. Ranthor searched for any evidence of the jewel. He was reassured by the fact that the sister jewels were resonating wildly. Something was definitely in this building. His spirits lifted up and he felt thrilled to be able to find the last jewel. He continued onwards in search of it. The first room did not seem to have anything of value. Ranthor entered the second room and found a similar lever. He used it to open the next door in the building. He then had to climb the stairs to the second floor. The second floor looked more complicated than the first. It had a lot of contraptions that opened a series of doors. There were three possible entry points which they could take. They split and took the first two entrances to utilize the time.

The first entrance led to a blocked way. There was nothing of value to be found. Ranthor retraced his steps and headed for the third entrance. Kendra was looking for something in the middle room. She too was not successful, but she continued to search the room for any possible clues. She found the box in the middle with a golden inscription. She found a key that might be useful to open some vault that was hidden nearby. She joined Ranthor after crossing the third door. There were two other rooms here that each had a vault of their own. She tried the first vault, but it did not budge. She then tried the other vault and there was another key there. She used the key to open the second vault. Lo and behold! There was the jewel inside the vault. Ranthor was thrilled to finally find the jewel.

Ranthor opened the receptacle and inserted the jewel inside. The device began to glow, and a holographic map was opened. It displayed the location of three jewels of darkness in each of their respective planets. They prepared to leave the building, but they inadvertently triggered a mechanism that trapped them in the room. The room was starting to quickly fill with quicksand, and there was nothing they could do to escape. Ranthor looked across the room for any possible clues that would help them. He found a trigger on the side of the wall.

He aimed his gun and shot it. The quicksand stopped and the entrance was cleared for them to exit now. They treaded carefully to avoid activating any more traps. Luckily, there wasn't any mechanism with death traps nearby. They exited the third door and were now in the main atrium of the building. From there, they walked outside to the landfill. Ranthor then used the grapple hook to cross the quicksand. They then made their way across to the ship. There were a few bandits waiting for them at the other end by the ship. They had to fight them in order to gain access to their ship.

The bandits did not get far luckily, and the ship was not breached. Ranthor managed to attack the first group and kill them off. Kendra dealt with the others. They called for backup and another group materialized out of nowhere. They continued to come and were now surrounding them. Ranthor decided to use his sword for close combat. He had noticed that this was a weakness of theirs. Kendra was using her gun to attack the remainder of their opponents. Ranthor was starting to feel fatigued, so she tagged in his place, and he was now firing the shots. He managed to kill several bandits with his gun. A few of them fled due to fear, but the vast majority remained and kept their ground. He didn't know where all of these bandits were coming from. They did not seem to end no matter what they did to stop them. He then pulled a grenade and detonated it, effectively killing a large group of bandits. The others fled to find a safe haven. This finally enabled him to gain access of his ship.

Ranthor did not waste any time entering the coordinates for the next planet. He turned on hyper-speed and zoomed out of sight. He was finally out of Planet Delta 7 and back into the serene, welcoming embrace of space. He paused to catch his breath. Ranthor realized that he was out of shape and no longer well-trained. He decided to spend this time training for the next mission. He spent a lot of time sparring with Kendra in preparation for any upcoming battles. He was adept at combat, but he found that he would become exhausted and out of breath after two or more rounds of combat. She taught him how to control his stamina and use his inner power to avoid being easily tired. The plan was to use the opponent's strength against him and therefore be able to topple him off balance.

It was a matter of time, but Ranthor finally managed to grasp the purpose behind training. He managed to execute the training exercises to perfection now. Kendra was thrilled to be able to teach him. He was an easy pupil to teach, listening intently to everything that she had to say. It was now time for supper. She prepared both of their meals and they ate in silence. There was nothing to do now but wait for them to reach the next planet. Ranthor was not familiar with the name of this planet. It was not in any known solar system that he was familiar with. This part of the universe was never explored by anyone. It was even possible that no one had ventured through it before them. Well, except for the civilization that had created the jewels. It was rumored that they possessed means of travel that were far more advanced than most of the ships now. Sadly, their civilization was soon dissolved after people discovered their power. The king of Nebula formed a legion along with the other rulers to drive them off. No one knew where this civilization was. Perhaps, there was a clue in the next planet.

Ranthor managed to find some ancient scriptures from his last expedition. It included some writings that explained the work of the civilization that came before; the creators of the jewel. They were called the Xenora, the bringers of light. This was the most ancient of the civilizations. The structure was further subdivided into three smaller sub-civilizations that served under one ruler. It ruled over this galaxy for the better part of the millennium. No one knew what happened to them. The scripture foretold of a great escape. They knew that they were going to be hunted, and, therefore, anticipated it. They had locked themselves in underground cisterns beneath the surface of the planet. Rumor has it that they had managed to survive. The first of the Xenora planets was nearby now. It was going to take a few days to reach there.

Kendra looked over the scripture as well. She was surprised that there might possibly a whole civilization underneath the surface of the planet. How did they survive down there and what supplies managed to maintain their sustenance? Ranthor was equally puzzled by this. He then remembered that this was one of the cleverest civilizations that lived. This underground facility was probably built at least a hundred years prior to the risk of invasion. It was probably stocked for the next several hundred years. They also would have found a way to grow crops without requiring sunlight. The ancient civilization managed to harvest and store the power of light to generate power that was sufficient to drive their agriculture. They were far more advanced in terms of technology, architecture, and agricultural technologies.

In order to cross to the planet, they had to access it through a wormhole. Ranthor prepared the ship to enter the wormhole. The ship's engines were powered to a hundred percent of their capacity. Upon entering the wormhole, the ship began to violently shake, but it managed to maintain its course with little to no damage to its hull. Ranthor anticipated this and prepared the overdrive that countered the shearing force of the wormhole. They were now stowed carefully in the middle of the cockpit. Finally, they emerged from the other end unscathed. The first of the planets was now within their reach. The ship was prepared for landing and Ranthor packed the gear for the mission. The land was surprisingly green. They had expected it to be barren on account that there was no one tending to its. However, there was an automatic sprinkling system that was set in place which relied on water drilled from the planet's core. Ranthor found a few fruits and gathered them so that they may eat later.

Ranthor then marched across the city center to find possible landmarks that might lead them to the first of the jewels of darkness. There was nothing that was remotely conspicuous or could indicate the location of the jewel. He relied on the map that he had which lit up as he went further down the road. It showed him the directions that he had to take to reach the jewels. He was reassured that there were no footsteps here besides theirs. At least, there was no clan or secret order that was on their tail for once. He could walk as leisurely as he wanted and would not be attacked by anyone. There were no vicious animals here that would try to hack at his flesh. The way was getting easier and easier with every passing step. He noticed that there was a mausoleum erected in the middle of the garden. It was for one of the prominent scientists on the planet. A statue was erected nearby with an inscription including his name and his accomplishments.

The man's name was Plearanus, the creator of the Nebula jewels. The jewels were used by the people to power most of the mechanisms of the planet and the surrounding planet systems. They had the ability also to regenerate discarded and damaged machines and provide rudimentary diagnostic tests to help fix the damaged machinery. Dr. Plearanus was the head scientist in the facility and controlled most of the work that happened there. He had died recently. Their species was known to live for centuries. It was one of the few advantages that they possessed over other species; that and their ability to heal themselves from virtually any wound imaginable.

Ranthor noticed that there was a switch next to the mausoleum. It was hidden behind the trees that had grown surrounding the mausoleum. He tried pressing the switch. This activated the mechanism that controlled the door by the mausoleum. It led to an underground tunnel that seemed to lead endlessly to nowhere. Ranthor followed the path that was laid out before him. He didn't know where it was headed, but he didn't want to waste the opportunity. It still might be an elaborate plan by the ancients to hide the location of the darkness jewel.

The pathway then bifurcated into two different ones. Ranthor had to make a choice between the two. Kendra was going to take the other one. They carried intercom devices that would alert each other if they had stumbled onto a clue. With this, they agreed to venture deeper into the tunnels.

Ranthor entered through the left entrance and made his way to the next chamber. There were no clues in this part, but he did not want to give up just as easily. The road seemed to go on endlessly. He finally managed to reach a room where two boxes were placed in the middle. He opened the first box and found a statue in it. He realized that there was a scale in one of the corners of the room. He put the statue on the scale. He heard the mechanism move but it soon stopped. He then found another statue in the other box. He placed it onto the scale, and this caused it to open a door on the other end of the chamber. This room had a box in it that contained a jewel-encrusted key. He figured out that this was of some significance. Realizing that there was nothing else in this room, he contacted Kendra to find where she was. She was in the middle of similarly designed mechanism. This was more complicated than the other one.

Kendra was struggling to activate the mechanism and gain access to the door. There were seven levers in that room. Out of the seven, only four activated the mechanism, the others would disrupt the sequence and close the door. Furthermore, they had to be activated in a certain sequence. Kendra tried multiple combinations but to no avail. She could not find the correct sequence of levers to activate the mechanism. There were no clues in the room to suggest the correct sequence of events. Nothing here was helpful to suggest how to solve this puzzle. Ranthor then realized something curious. The map that he had started lighting up as soon as he entered the room. They lit in a sequence in the direction of the levers. He now realized which of the four levers activated the mechanism to opening the door. With that, he pressed all the four levers and the door swung wide open. They were now in the middle of the inner chamber. A similar box was in this room and there was the key. All they had to do now was find out which vault opened with the keys.

They heard the sound of another door opening. Finding the two keys must have activated a mechanism that opened the door. They were now staring into the inner sanctum that was used to possibly house the jewels. The place was filled with fountains and a variety of plants. It must be the inner sanctuary of the ancients. Kendra wondered if there were still people living here. Her question was finally answered when she saw one of the people of Xenora. He was equally surprised to find her.

Chapter 13
The Mystic Realm

The door opened the way to the paradise of Xenora. There were multiple streams running there. Most of the inhabitants were Xenorans who had fled the surface due to fear of detection. They and their children now inhabited this part and were living in peace and prosperity. At first, they were alarmed at the presence of the two strangers that had found a way into their homes. But they soon succumbed to a wave of calmness as they realized that they did not want to harm them. The ancients gestured to Ranthor that they wanted to welcome them into their sanctuary. Ranthor agreed and decided to go in the same general direction that they were taking. The view here was quite breath-taking. There were many plants and animals that were thought to be extinct for several centuries due to industrialization. Nothing seemed to age here. The people lived in complete peace and harmony with the wildlife. Ranthor was impressed that the citizens did not resort to any form of hunting, and instead relied on harvesting fruits and plants.

One of the Xenorans indicated that they should sit in the seats laid out for them. A ceremony of some sorts was going to begin. The halls were decorated in crimson and green, and the priests wore similarly colored ceremonial robes.

"This must be one of their festivals," Kendra muttered to herself.

She was excited to see this. It also might give them a clue to help them finding the jewel. However, the Xenorans would probably be possessive of their jewels. There was nothing that could be done at the moment. All they could possibly do was wait and enjoy the show. A pit of fire was laid out in the middle and warriors came and danced around it. The sound of oddly shaped wind instruments could be heard in the background. The sound was somewhat pleasing actually, thought Ranthor amusingly. It was supposed make the listener fall into a trance-like state of happiness. The halls were decked with food of all sorts in preparation for the feast that would follow.

The next part of the ceremony was another dance festival that was performed by the elders. Everyone gathered for this part and displayed happiness and affection at this ancient ceremony being performed. The elders finally concluded their dance, and the stage was removed. The feast was brought in its place. The people were now eating merrily. Ranthor was getting worried that they were wasting a lot of time. He asked one of the elders about the possible location of the jewel. He told him that it was hidden in the temple nearby. The jewels of darkness were an item of the Xenorans, and they did not wish to part with them. The elder did not think that he possessed the necessary strength to wield them. Ranthor dismissed the idea and was planning to storm the temple at the earliest opportunity. He would wait for the cover of night to perform the operation. Kendra was not keen on going along, but she knew that she did not have a choice. She was worried about the Xenorans' reaction when they found out that the jewel was stolen. Ranthor reassured her that they would be long gone by then.

The festival concluded and the people were returning to their regular jobs. Ranthor was waiting patiently for night-time to arrive. He waited for several hours. There was nothing to do here so he eventually decided to take a nap.

Kendra was pacing backward and forward anxiously. She did not like the mission and thought that it was perilous despite Ranthor's attempts at calming her down. She had also finally succumbed to sleep and was now resting in its ethereal world. She woke up an hour later drenched in sweat due to the nightmares that she was having. Afterwards, she could not get back to sleep so she spent the remainder of the time taking a walk across the courtyard. The place was very peaceful and helped her calm down. The sound of the wind calmed her and so did the brushing of the trees against each other. Nothing seemed out of place here, at least it didn't now, she thought to herself. She could not help feeling that something was amiss.

Kendra always wondered as to why the ancients opened up to them quite easily. For a civilization that spent most of its time in hiding, this was a very unusual occurrence. She prayed silently that this was not a death trap in the making. However, she did not find any clues supporting her claim, and the further she walked down, she felt reassured that this was probably her paranoid mind playing tricks on her. The courtyard seemed to drag on for infinity. Each part was similar to the rest. Finally, she decided to get back to where she came from. Something caught her eye as she was returning from her evening stroll. She noticed that the same person that was Ranthor's nemesis, Ray, was here in this planet. He must have been tracking them somehow. He was talking to one of the village elders. That seemed extremely suspicious, especially since the same elder thought that Ranthor should not go looking for the jewel. Was it possible that this man was working with the king? She decided to lean in closer and press her ear to the wall to gather some information from their conversation.

"I trust our plans to get the jewel from the temple are going as planned. Remember the king is going to reward you handsomely for your troubles. He is also going to help foster a strong alliance that would enable your people to return again to the surface without fear of any attempts on your lives. Comply with my instructions and I shall make all of that possible for you. Fail to do so and I will annihilate you," ordered Ray menacingly.

"It is going to be a matter of two days before the jewel is extracted from the temple. Our people are working on it as we speak. You shall soon have your jewel and we will return again to our home. My clan does not approve of this, but I am tired of living this life of cowardice. We are one of the most advanced races in the universe. We should proudly live above ground and prosper just like any other civilization," reassured the Elder.

With that, they both departed their meeting place. Kendra was horrified to know that this meeting took place. She hadn't realized the whole time that Ray was following them. After all, it was strange that he did not attack them when he found them. He could have just stolen the jewels and went looking for the remainder. However, he chose a bloodless approach that would easily lead him to the remaining jewels. But how did he manage to gain the sympathy of the Xenorans? It seemed that the sanctuary had a lot of internal disputes. Ray simply used this to his advantage to sway the majority into helping him. Little did they know that he was not interested in repaying the favor. There was no guarantee that they would receive protection from the king once they had resurfaced. Kendra rushed off to warn Ranthor of this new development. He would know how to tackle this dilemma.

She finally reached their camp where Ranthor was fast asleep. Kendra woke him up and told him the whole story. He decided that they would defer their plan till two days from now. This would avoid creating suspicion that the jewel was missing. Especially now that Ray was able to track them. Meanwhile, he would search for the tracking device and disable it. If Ray could track them, then it was possible that there were others including his father that had access to this tracking technology. Ranthor searched every corner of the ship for tracking bugs. There was nothing that looked remotely similar. He continued his search while Kendra was still pacing. He finally managed to find the tracking device nestled between the mainframe computer and the cockpit. Ranthor then quickly used the computer to hack it and provide a different location for the device. He figured that destroying it would be suspicious. The best course of action was to derail the king's course.

The king was waiting patiently in his quarters in Planet Nebula. He had just contacted Ray to know the updates about the jewels. He conveyed to him what the elder had told him. The king was thrilled to know that their plans were going according to schedule. He then inquired about his son, Ranthor. Ray told him that he did not see him anywhere. In fact, his location had changed to Planet Odelphius. He wondered as to what he was doing there. The king warned to still stay on the lookout. It was possible that Ranthor was still on the lookout for him and may have discovered and tampered with the tracking device. Ray agreed and decided that he should be weary of any suspicious activity. The king then ended the conversation and returned to his meal. There was nothing much for him to do today.

He decided to take a stroll to his jewel vault; he had created a vault that would house all of the jewels. He could not wait until they were all in his possession. This moment was dreamt of years ago when he was much younger and capable of collecting the jewels himself. For now, he had to rely on his trusted soldier to gather them for him. It was only going to be a matter of days before they were in his possession. He still pondered as to what he would do if Ranthor refused to join his army. He was too much of a threat to be kept alive, but he did not want to kill his only son. *All of that will be decided in due time,* he thought to himself. The king was regretting removing him from his court. He had been a valuable ally, and ever since his departure, things were not always the same. He still was hopeful that he would be able to sway him back. Little did he know that his son had planned a rebellion against him.

The palace was deserted at this time of day. All of the soldiers were either guarding the entrances or had retired to a nearby pub after finishing their duties. The servants were in their quarters and were called readily should he require anything from the kitchen or elsewhere. However, he wanted to be left alone tonight. He was conflicted with his choices and wanted to remain alone and undisturbed. He had already had his supper and was preparing to head to bed. He received a knock on the door. He was furious at the messenger, but he decided to welcome him in anyway. It was news involving one of the minor regions that was under his control. They had staged a coup and reinforcements needed to be sent to deal with them. It was important to stop to prevent a full-scale riot in other neighboring states.

He discussed the plan with his advisor and with that, he called it a day. He retired into the night. He woke the following day to hear an update about the jewel. The expedition was going to begin at midnight to avoid any delays. Ray was already at the site as they were speaking, making schematics of the temple. The priests were inside praying and doing their regular rituals. The king was glad that things were going smoothly. He thanked his lieutenant for the update and shut off the intercom device. He could not contain himself and was riddled with joy. Nothing could ruin his day today. He then tended to other matters of state and tried to make himself busy to avoid thinking about the jewels. There was still a long way to go before they had acquired them all. He called for an emergency meeting of his counsellors to address this issue.

Ray was meeting with the priests to find the easiest way to access the jewel. They showed him a schematic of the tunnel system that led to the jewel. They also explained to him the traps that were guarding it against possible intruders. He was then ready for his mission. All he had to do now was wait for the cover of night and then he could execute his mission. He was growing bored of this planet that lacked the action that he was regularly used to back home. For him, the thrill of the fight was the most important part of his mission. Being confined to stealth and espionage was beyond his capabilities as warrior.

Ranthor learned of the meeting between Ray and the priests. He was preparing his gear for a mission to the temple. He had planned on following Ray to where the jewel was kept and then taking it. Considering that Ray already had access to the mechanisms operating the tunnels, it was going to be easier and less dangerous this way. Ranthor was going to then execute Ray to prevent any interruption by his father. He realized that he should have killed him when he had the chance. But then again, he would have still struggled finding the jewel.

The priests were not keen on helping him as there was no benefit incurred. However, it was going to be a matter of time before this feud between them had ended. He now had to focus on finding the jewel and then moving on to finding the remainder of them.

The tunnels had not been inhabited by any living thing for many centuries, except for the ceremonies that took place in the halls that were before the entrance to the tunnels. This area was considered religious grounds for the worship of the priests of Xenora. Outsiders were rarely granted access here, and there were not many of them around anyway. It was a challenging task to find this planet. The ones who had tried had perished in the process. This was mainly because their ships sustained severe damage crossing the wormhole which led to the mutilation of the crew. Ranthor and Kendra were amongst the very few that came to these parts since a very long time. There was no guarantee that even they would remain alive. The priests wanted to make sure no outsiders ever came again to endanger their peace. After deliberating amongst them, they decided that they would lay traps to kill Ranthor and his friend.

The priests were now leading Ray across the tunnels to where the jewel was housed. They crossed the first set of traps and managed to deactivate them. The path to the jewel was becoming easier with every passing step, but they forgot to turn off one of the mechanisms in the hallway. Luckily, they managed to duck just in time as the axe swung across them. That sent chills down both the priests' and Ray's spine. He scolded them for this nearly lethal mistake. The priests cowered in fear at the sight of Ray's gun pointing at them. They made sure that the remaining traps were deactivated before moving on to the next chamber. There was a puzzle in the next chamber that they had to solve. It was similar to the other puzzles, but instead of levers there were pulleys and weights. Each of the priests carried a weight and used it on specific pulleys to open the mechanism for the door. They were now halfway across the tunnel system. Ray's heart was beating at the sight of being closer to the jewel. He updated the king regularly of his developments. He did not realize that he would soon be followed by Ranthor.

Kendra and Ranthor entered the tunnel system and were lucky that the first set of traps was deactivated. They managed to find the footsteps of the priests and followed them to the next chamber. Again, they found that the mechanism guarding the next chamber was deactivated. They breathed a sigh of relief at this wonderful sight. This spared spending time trying to figure out the endless sets of puzzles that were typical of this place. They now entered the next chamber and made sure not to make a noise. Kendra found a place for both of them to hide. It was behind an abandoned crate that just managed to shelter them from detection. Ranthor was worried that they were going to be seen by Ray and the priests. However, they were so engaged with finding the jewel that they couldn't hear their footsteps. They waited for the click of the next door before moving forward.

The priests tried opening the next mechanism, but for some reason there was a problem with the mechanism. The machinery had acquired a lot of rust due to years of disuse. One of the priests used the anointment oil to lubricate the mechanism. This allowed it to spring back into action and open the door for them to enter. They were now in the central chamber that housed the jewel. Ray was shocked to see a countless number of rare artefacts and riches that filled this chamber. Had it have not been for the priests, he would have probably pocketed a few of them for himself. However, he needed the cooperation of the priests to find the jewel. Without them, it was going to be excruciatingly difficult to acquire it. They were near the vault now. The pounding in his heart was increasing by the minute. He could not contain his excitement any longer and decided to head straight to the vault. In his moment of excitement, he forgot about the protective mechanism. A wheel came careening downwards and landed on his foot. He howled with pain and had to walk with a limp for the remainder of the trip. He realized that this would be a fatal mistake should an opponent decide to attack him. He had left himself in a vulnerable position because of a stupid mistake that he had committed.

The vault was opened by the priests and the first jewel of darkness was now within sight. This had managed to reduce his pain, albeit temporarily. He walked over slowly to the jewel and caressed it in between his hands. The priests prepared to exit the tunnel. There was a passageway in the back that they had used to avoid detection. Ranthor now entered the main chamber and prepared to confront his enemies. They had seemed to vanish into thin air. He realized that there was a back entrance. He followed it and soon found himself against a dozen or so priests and Ray. He realized that Ray was now injured, and it was possible to tackle him quite easily. Ray panicked after realizing that he was a sitting duck. He tried to taunt Ranthor so that he would be off guard, but he was not successful.

"We meet again, old friend. I managed to follow you here to this planet. As you can see, I have the upper hand. I would suggest that you surrender and give me the remainder of the jewels. Do that and I will ensure that not only you walk out of here safely, but I will make sure that your honor is restored back home," bellowed Ray.

"I do not care for your so-called honor. I don't need the validation of your decrepit, senile ruler to determine whether I am honorable or not. Besides, you are not in a bargaining position yourself. I can see that you managed to sustain an injury. It would be easy to kill you. However, I would like to give you a fighting chance. Pick up your sword for battle and I would swing with one hand to make the fight fair. The victor takes the jewels, and the loser faces death as his penalty," replied Ranthor rather crisply.

The battle had begun between them and Ranthor seemed to have the upper hand. Even with his injury, Ray was a ruthless fighter. He made sure that Ranthor would not quit easily, he was going to give him a run for his money. The priests escaped the scene of the battle and were headed to seal the entrance. Ranthor would have to deal with them later. He attacked his enemy several times, but each attack was parried successfully by his opponent. The battle seemed to go on forever with no clear victor. Finally, Ray dropped a smoke bomb and fled the scene of battle. Ranthor was cursing under his breath.

The chamber was now covered with smoke and visibility was quite low. Ranthor had to hurry and catch up with the priests before getting locked down here forever. He managed to find the first group of priests and kidnap one of them. He agreed with great difficult to help them, that was after the threat of death. The priest showed them to the last chamber they had exited from. He opened the door to the next chamber. The chamber was empty. There were no signs of any other intruders or Ray. He continued the journey out of the tunnels as fast as he could so that he could reach his enemy right in time and get the jewel from him. It was a race against time which he was clearly losing. Nevertheless, he did not hesitate and sped through the mechanisms of the chamber. He soon reached the entrance and caught a glimpse of Ray's ship just as it was about to depart. He entered his ship along with Kendra and prepared to pursue the ship to wherever it was headed.

Ray realized that he was being tailed and increased the speed of his ship. Realizing that he was going to be out of fuel soon, he entered the coordinates to the nearest planet he could find so that he could refuel. Ranthor was following him neck to neck, never leaving the slightest gap. He noticed that Ray was about to land into an unknown planet, so he decided to follow him. They both managed to land. Ray found a refueling station and then disappeared out of sight. Ranthor decided not to run after him and instead planted a similar tracking device to the now unattended ship. He then decided to remain in the planet in the event that Ray returned to his ship. It had been a few hours, but Ray did not seem to surface.

Realizing the futility of the current task, Ranthor decided to return to his ship after spending several hours waiting for his enemy. He was going to orbit the planet until there was a sign of Ray departing the planet. He must have realized that they were after him and decided to lose them. Ranthor did not wish to run after him in this planet, and instead decided to draw him out. It was only a matter of time before he realized, although falsely, that the threat had dissipated. It was then that Ranthor was going to seize the opportunity and catch his nemesis.

Ray was just emerging from a nearby village where he had spent the night. He returned to his ship and prepared to leave the planet. There was nothing that was in his way. He prepared to use the jewel to find the other jewels of darkness. After that, his wounds would have had a chance to heal, and he would take another swing at Ranthor. He swore to destroy him, even if it was the last thing he would do. He admired Ranthor greatly. He was one of the few people that could give him a decent sparring match. All the others were nowhere near as strong and did not do much in terms of competition. He wanted desperately for Ranthor to join their army again. However, he knew that after the maltreatment and treachery that he had suffered from his father, that this was never going to happen. Still, he longed for another duel to prove his prowess in battle.

The ship was now in the middle of space. Ranthor located Ray and was now on his trail. He did not want to battle him in space and decided that he will let him land his ship and then execute his attack. It seemed like an eternity following his enemy. Ray did not know where to go and instead decided to search the nearest planet in the system for any evidence of the jewels. Planet Zeta S was the next planet in the system. Ranthor wondered whether if it was of any significance. Nonetheless, it was an opportunity to take what was rightfully his. It wouldn't take long to locate and acquire the jewel. Ray was still limping and was going to be an easy target. Ranthor decided that he will also play dirty. He would do whatever it takes to get the jewel. He was no longer to abide by the laws of combat and instead would do whatever it was in his power to win.

Ray's ship landed on Zeta S and so did Ranthor's. The atmosphere was filled with the all-too-pungent acid rain. The place did not have any living inhabitant for as far as the eye could see. Ranthor waited until Ray disembarked from his ship and then was on his trail. He did not know why he would expose himself by visiting a planet that was clearly of no benefit to him. Still, it was an advantage for him as he was a sitting duck. He would wait for the cover of night and then execute a sneak attack and kill him. The jewel would then finally be in his possession. It seemed far too easy, and he wondered if this was some sort of elaborate trap to catch him. Ranthor treaded with caution with every step he made. He knew that Ray was a tough adversary despite his injuries; he would definitely still have a few tricks up his sleeve.

Ray did not pick Planet Zeta S randomly. The ancient people of Xenora told him that this planet housed the map to the next jewel. Although the jewel could be located using the other jewels, this was a detailed creator's map that had all the mechanisms and traps outlined and was made for the ancients to use. The reason it had ended up in this planet was because one of the creators was killed here on his search for a rare metal ore for his machinations. Prior to his death, the Xenoran managed to send a video explaining that he had been badly injured, and that the map was located here. None of the Xenorans thought of getting the map due to fear of death. Instead, they relied on the knowledge that no one had come to collect the first dark jewel in the first place. It is this false confidence that had almost wiped them out in the first place.

The map was rumored to be in an abandoned mine just off the course of the city. No one had set foot in this mine for the past thirty years. The machines were still operational though, but most of the inhabitants had escaped to worlds with a better prospect of living. The only inhabitants were a few displaced tribes that had no means of transport out of the planet. Somehow, they managed to weather the harsh conditions and, in the process, had evolved both physically and mentally to enable them to live in these harsh conditions. Ray wore every manner of protective gear that he could lay his hands on. He made sure to avoid any injury this time. His wound was barely healing, and he was still walking with a limp from the last injury. He was glad at least that there was no evidence of Ranthor following him. However, he expected him to be trailing just behind him. He just needed more time to enable his wound to heal.

Meanwhile, Ranthor was exploring the planet that he had just stumbled onto. *There is nothing of value that can possibly be on this barren planet,* he thought to himself. Still, he realized that Ray must have come here for a reason. He opened the tracker device that he had set up on Ray's ship. He realized that it was next to an abandoned mine. He decided to follow the blip on the radar and locate his enemy. The journey seemed to drag on forever and Kendra was feeling bored. She begged Ranthor to allow her to return to the ship. He agreed and she left to go back to the ship. He didn't want to involve her in this feud anyway. It was between him and Ray. No one else needed to be injured in the process. Hopefully, this lifelong battle would end today, and a victor would be finally crowned.

Ray was now in the middle of the mine's underground system. He could not find any trace of the map yet. He figured that it was probably deep inside. The mine was not well-protected from intruders, but then again, it was not designed to do so. He wondered how the Xenoran managed to keep the location of the map a secret for all this time. This race was especially adept at hiding things at plain sight; it came as no surprise that they would be able to hide the map too. He was truly impressed at what this civilization had managed to achieve over the course of millennia.

The entrance of the mines did not seem all too welcoming, Ranthor thought to himself. He had finally reached there after preparing his gear and rations for this mission. Ray's footsteps served as a guide to help him maneuver his way across the mines. It wasn't like his enemy to leave such a sloppy trail. This was a bad omen for him; it further convinced him that this was indeed a trap. The entrance had now collapsed into nothingness, and they were both trapped in the mines until they managed to somehow find the exit. Ray was somewhat hopeful that he had at least some knowledge of the mines imparted by the priests, the same priests that rarely left their temple. He was sweating profusely, and his heart was beating with such great intensity. Ranthor, on the other hand, was unfazed by this sudden change of events. He had started getting used to difficult, unsolvable situations. They seemed to follow him wherever he went.

Ray finally reached the final chamber of the mines. He could see the map visibly perched on top of a pedestal. He went over to it and tried removing the map from its pedestal. As soon as he tried lifting it, sand began entering from the ceiling so rapidly that it was about to flood the room. He quickly returned the map to its pedestal and things returned to normal. Ray needed to find an object with a similar weight so that the mechanism that controlled the sands would not be activated. He searched the room frantically for any sign of such object. There was a discarded leather pouch that was around the exact same weight. He tried replacing it with the map and managed to stop the sand descending from the ceiling. A door now opened to the outside. He quickly exited through it and left the mines. He welcomed the outside cold breeze with the same relief that a prisoner would have once he was released.

In the meantime, Ranthor was trying to exit the mines. He had reached the final chamber of the mines and there was no evidence of either the map or of Ray. He realized that Ray must have discovered the location of the map and managed to exit the mines. The only thing that was crossing his mind was if this had been the only way out. He then realized that there was a small leather pouch on the pedestal. He removed it and soon sand flooded the room again. He transferred the things in his pouch to this pouch. Then, he left his pouch on the pedestal. Upon doing so, the door to the outside swung wide open. He also managed to exit outside the mines. Ray was nowhere to be seen and neither were the map or the jewel. Ranthor remembered that he was capable of tracking him. He then returned to his ship and prepared to leave for the next planet. He would then catch up to him and would get rid of him once and for all. This rivalry had to end finally as it was causing Ranthor significant distress.

Both ships were now trapped in the majesty of space. Each was trying to make its journey to the next jewel. Ray had the competitive advantage of knowing where the jewel was located. Ranthor was tracking Ray and, therefore, had the same knowledge by extension. In the beginning, it seemed as if Ray was going around in circles. However, Ranthor then realized that there was some logic associated with this madness. He was sweeping the area for other possible locations for the jewels. This way, he would expand his search to include the third jewel. This would save him a lot of time. Ranthor marked the locations that Ray was searching; including the location that he was headed toward currently. However, he decided that he will not try to bypass Ray and instead lay low and then steal it from him. This would enable him to take the jewel that was already in Ray's possession. This would make sure that Ray will not escape. It seemed like forever before Ray had settled on a planet to land on. He was not a pilot by default; the only thing he knew how to do properly was duel and spar. Ranthor knew all too well that no one wanted to accompany him on a mission due to his attitude.

Ranthor's ship was orbiting the space around the previous planet for the better part of an hour. His opponent did not make any plans to head to the next planet. This made him very skeptical and wondered if he knew that he was being followed. Regardless, Ranthor made sure not to lose sight of Ray' ship. There was nothing much that he could do at the moment besides wait. Ray was hoping that Ranthor would eventually grow bored and look for the jewel himself. He had deliberately allowed his ship's maps and schematics to be accessible to Ranthor. He knew that he would take the information and use it to find the next jewel. This would make the job easier for Ray; all he would do was take the jewels from Ranthor. He would then be left with the task of finding the last jewel of darkness. With the jewels reunited, he would be able to summon the power that was contained in them by the ancients. Legend had it that the person possessing the power of the jewels would be rendered invincible. No one knew for sure what would happen or if anything would materialize upon presenting the jewels.

Just as predicted, Ranthor abandoned his task of waiting for Ray and headed to the next planet in the system. Planet Exitorius housed the second jewel of darkness according to local folklore. This jewel was thought to be lost in time. The ancients did not know if it still existed. The creators did not leave any account regarding this information. It was going to be a much more difficult task locating this jewel. Ranthor did not have any information on finding it, and he did not know where to start. Adding to the complexity, the planet was littered with false jewels that were created to railroad travelers that ended up here randomly. The jewel, like its sister jewels, would react to the presence of the other jewels around. The false jewels would not display a similar response; this ensured that Ranthor would not take them. The false jewels were created to perfection, so much so that it was difficult to discern the difference. The Xenorans barely could tell the difference between them. The creator was the one who handcrafted them to match the same specifications of the jewels. However, he made sure not to imbue them with the same powers.

The ship was now landing in Planet Exitorius. Ranthor disembarked from the ship and started his search for the next jewel. Meanwhile, Ray was still hovering around orbit and patiently waiting for Ranthor to complete his task. Ranthor was not successful in finding any clues so far, but he did not give up his search. The planet was hub for tropical storms, and today there was a storm that swept across the entire planet. Ranthor had to hide for the time being to avoid the storm. He was going to resume his search after it had passed. Luckily, there was no one else here that could benefit from this impediment. Ray was still stuck in orbit and relied on the success of Ranthor to continue his mission. Ranthor activated the protective mechanisms that controlled his ship and provided him protection against this violent force of nature. He prepared a snack for himself and waited for the passing of the storm. He ate hastily, anticipating that things would soon return to normal, and he would go on to gather the jewel. However, the weather was ominous, and the tempest was still just as strong as when it had started. These storms would sometimes last days at a time. He hoped that it would be over soon. This had left him an open duck, vulnerable to any attacks by any oncoming foes.

Finally, the storm subsided and Ranthor could continue with his task. He exited the ship safely and made his way to the main quarter of the city. It had been abandoned several years ago, save for a few areas in the nearby slums. He went over there to interrogate the citizens for any possible information that could help him. They had been told that there was an abandoned quarry which might have the object he was looking for. It was the only remnant of the ancient Xenoran civilization.

The quarry had not been in operation for the better part of fifty years. It used to be the main livelihood source for over eighty percent of the population. The remaining twenty percent were the rich and affluent. They were the ones that owned the businesses, shops and the quarry that provided the sources of income for the remainder of the citizens. After the destruction of most of the planet, most of the remaining citizens retired to the slums and lived in extreme poverty. The planet, now in rubbles, was swept away by storms of acid rain. However, the quarry still survived and provided a good location for Ranthor to explore. He always wondered why the jewels of darkness were housed in industrial locations. He suspected that they were the reason these facilities were able to run at their levels of efficiency. The ancients must have used their powers to run their planets. It was strange to see their powers suddenly extinguished. The source of these problems would probably still be lurking in one of the nearby planets.

Ranthor arrived at the quarry and started his search. There was nothing on the outside that was of any value. He managed to unlock the door of the quarry. He entered inside and started exploring the main room which housed the workers' stations. There was nothing special in this area, no clue that would indicate that the jewel was nearby. He had hoped that the jewel would start resonating by now; indicating that there was something in this abandoned quarry. Alas, the jewels were as quiet as they were an hour ago. He continued his search despite the fact that there was probably nothing there, hoping that a clue would suddenly pop up in front of him. He did not want to lose hope, especially now that his mission was coming to an end. He will make sure to kill Ray once he found him.

The quarry suddenly came life and all the machines started whirring. Ranthor wondered as to how these ancient machines were working. There was no power source that was operational, both internal and external. The jewels in his bag suddenly lit up, and he realized that the jewel was somewhere here. He was excited to finally progress in this mission. The jewel of darkness was soon going to be within reach. His heart was beating wildly in his chest and his palms were getting sweaty. He mustered up the courage to venture forward. He did not know what to expect or if there are further dangers ahead. He expected that there will be dangers as such and prepared himself accordingly for any challenge. His goal was finally within reach; he was thrilled and yet sad that this brought him closer to the end of the mission, and the end of the time he would spend with Kendra.

Kendra was still in the ship looking over the manifesto for the jewels. Ranthor told her that he was close to finding the jewel. She was extremely excited hearing the good news. She ended the intercom transmission and was preparing a victory meal for Ranthor. She was also going to tell him that she was ready to live with him once this adventure was over. This mission had taught her several things; one of which was that some people were worthy of her trust. Kendra trusted Ranthor explicitly with every fiber of her being. She knew that it was the best thing to do and decided that she would remain with him after the mission was over. For the time being, she had to let him focus on the task at hand. He should not be derailed with a minor detail such as this now.

The planet was empty and devoid of any citizens. Kendra stepped out of the ship to take a stroll. She realized that there was no habitable place outside the planet. Having witnessed this, she decided to return to the ship and prepare a meal for herself. Unlike Ranthor, she felt incredibly serene and calm at heart. Perhaps this was because she had no stakes in this mission. However, she was relieved that things were finally falling into place. She would be able to finally continue with her normal life.

This was one of the few times that Kendra did not participate in this adventure. She realized that the next part of the mission involved Ranthor alone. Having respected that this was his path alone, she remained in the ship and waited for his return. There was part of her that wished that she didn't do that. Kendra was starting to get worried that something bad must have happened to him. But then again; she knew that Ranthor was very much capable of protecting himself. As for her, she dreaded the fact that she was not in the middle of a battle or an expedition. Being confined between the four walls of the ship was killing her. This was going to be the first and last time that she was going to be stuck like this. Nothing that Ranthor would say or do would convince otherwise. Kendra did not like her day off.

Meanwhile, Ranthor managed to reach the inner sanctum of the quarry. There was a small pouch inside one of the boxes. Ranthor opened it and the jewel of darkness was inside. He was thrilled to have found it. He could finally leave the quarry and go back to his ship. He contacted Kendra to tell her that he was on his way and that he had found the jewel. She steered the ship in his direction and was ready to open the doors for him to board. Suddenly, he felt an ion beam hit him squarely on the chest. He then collapsed and lost consciousness. Everything following this felt like a blur. Ranthor woke up finally from his coma and realized that he was stripped of all his belongings. He reached for his pocket to find the jewels but there was nothing there. He started to panic and sweat started to bead on his forehead. A mysterious figure was looking at him with a burning gaze. He approached him and was now looking at him closely. Ranthor gasped when he realized who was looking at him.

Chapter 14
Absolution

"It is unfortunate that we are meeting under such circumstances, my son. Unfortunately, you leave me with no possible choice. You should not have meddled in affairs that are far bigger than yourself. Ray was tasked with getting the jewels. Unfortunately, he had failed miserably. As such, I had to take action and take over this mission myself. Now you have forced me to attack and openly attempt to kill my only, albeit pitiful, son," bellowed the king.

"I'm surprised that you still have it in you to call me son. Especially after you had abandoned me for several years. There is no other father that would do something as cruel as you. Do you expect me to suddenly bow down and accept you as my sovereign again? I would rather you kill me first. There is no honor in a family that would feed you to the wolves once you are no longer useful. I loathe you with every fiber of my being, you decrepit sorry excuse for a father," shouted Ranthor.

The king felt as if his heart was torn in half. He did not expect redemption or forgiveness from his son, but he also did not expect being shunned. He was riddled with guilt for leaving his son, but he could not even get the chance to redeem himself. This was his only son and he had abandoned him in his hour of need. The king was clearly distraught at this sight. However, Ranthor did not care about the state that his father was in. All he wanted now was to be released so that he could take back the jewels. He could not even care about pursuing revenge against his father. He would not kill him; instead, he would leave him to ponder for all eternity about what he had done. Ranthor did not want the sweet release of death to absolve his father of his shortcomings. It was important that he answered to his mistakes, each and every last one of them. His father was to be held accountable for the current life that he was forced to live, for casting him out of home at such a young age. Ranthor did not have it in him to forgive and forget. The man before him was just another stranger that had meant nothing to him. The king was now kneeling besides him, begging for forgiveness. Ranthor did not even turn to look at him. Hatred consumed his mind, body, and spirit.

Finally, the king decided to unshackle him and attempt to have a conversation. He did not know that this was a very grave mistake. Ranthor was waiting for any opportunity to be released. The first thing he did was hold the king hostage and demand for his weapons and jewels. The king agreed to his demands and granted him his objects. Ranthor then let go of the king and disappeared into nothingness. His father was still sobbing in his chambers. He would have preferred his son to slit his throat and end his misery. Had the roles been reversed, he knew that he would not have the same level of humility that his son had possessed. The person that was before was much different than the son he had raised. Never did he imagine that Ranthor would display such an act of compassion and chivalry. He knew that he did not deserve this kindness. However, he decided that maybe he could mend things by giving his son the jewels.

Ray was still in the same place that Ranthor had left him. He managed to track the signal that Ranthor was emitting from his ship. Realizing that Ranthor was leaving the solar system, he decided to mark the same coordinates in his ship and prepare to follow him. He did not even know where he was headed, and neither did he care. It was only going to be a matter of time before he had managed to catch up to him yet again. His wounds from the previous expedition had healed completely. Ranthor would not be able to match him in power now. There was nothing that was going to stop him from ruling the universe. He decided that he would renegade from the king's mission and use the jewels for his own nefarious deeds.

The last planet that housed the final jewel was hidden from sight. Ranthor did not know how he would be able to reach it. According to Xenoran lore, there was an oracle that knew of the location of the planet. The oracle would give Ranthor the location in exchange for a blood bond. He would vow to help her in whatever conquest she deemed necessary. The oracle never asked her visitors to pay for the advice. However, should she collect the favor and the person could not deliver, it would spell out certain doom for them. The oracle of Xenora was one of the most powerful beings in the universe. It was rumored that not even the combined power of the jewels would make her perish. She had managed to survive the reign of many kings of Xenora before succumbing to old age. She would only grant Ranthor an audience after acquiring the second jewel of darkness; the jewel that was in Ray's possession. Therefore, Ranthor decided to pay Ray a visit. He would then acquire the jewel and plan for an audience with the oracle.

Ray was expecting Ranthor to show up anytime. He had prepared his arsenal of weapons for the fight. This time he would make sure that Ranthor was six feet under and no longer able to meddle in his affairs. He would then target the king and kill him too. He had long suffered under his terrible regime. With his newfound power, he would restore balance to his planet under a new, more efficient leadership. He already had the majority of votes to rule the planet. The citizens were fed up with the king and believed that he was quite senile to continue to rule. A young, capable leader was going to be at the helm. Ray was lost in a sea of dreams. The arrival of an enemy ship was the only thing that managed to wake him up.

The ship was not Ranthor's ship. It was one of the warring planets that they were constantly battling with. Surprisingly, the leader of the ship did not attempt to fight Ray. Instead, he contacted him to offer his services to get the jewels from Ranthor. However, that came with an attached price. In exchange for his services, he wanted to be named admiral of the new fleet under Ray's command. He also wanted to make sure that a peace treaty would be brokered between the two planets.

The alliance between the two would help cement the way for better stability and control over the galaxy. In exchange, Ray would ensure that the stranger would be entitled control over his planet. His name was Alamus, the high chancellor of Planet Tristar 7. This planet was at war with the Nebula system for centuries over the control of the galaxy. With Ray at the helm, a peace treaty would finally be brokered with the two warring nations. He would ensure the stability of the galaxy, and this would sustain his rule over it. The current king would be displaced to one of the distant prisons. This way, the saga that was the tyrannous rule of his would finally end. He was no longer amongst his people; especially after exiling his son. He was neither benevolent nor merciful, a quality that should always be possessed by a king. Luckily, Ray learned better than to follow the footsteps of his predecessor. His rule would change the ruling system in Nebula and leave him at the helm for decades to come.

Alamus knew that the conquest for power was amongst the many weaknesses of the people of Nebula. His intention was never to let Ray rule over, however, this was the only way that he could sway him to his cause. He would then use his influence to oust him and bring the Order back to the galaxy. It was only a matter of time before his name would be feared from the far east till the west. He would finally receive the reverence and respect that he truly deserved. Alamus had big plans for the development of the galaxy. The jewels would provide him with the first step to achieve this. He did not want to bloody his hands or reveal his identity early on in the mission. He was not a match for Ranthor's military skills. Therefore, he had to use his pawn Ray to facilitate the destruction of Ranthor, thereby, eliminating his main source of distress. The galaxy would then finally bow down to him.

Ranthor did not know about the interplay of powers that were in this galaxy. He was only concerned now with finding Ray and acquiring the first jewel from him. He would then proceed to the next planet and find the last jewel. Things were looking especially good now that he had found the second jewel. He guarded the jewels with his life. He had almost lost the entire battle, had it not been for his father's foolishness. This opened his mind to the fact that he needed better protection. This gave him the idea of securing a stronger vault for his jewels. Therefore, he decided to go to Planet Luminarus; this was the birthplace of all the master architects and smiths. They would create the best vault for his jewels. In this way, the security of the jewels would be restored. He could then rest assured that his most prized possession was well protected. He looked over at Kendra who had succumbed to sleep. He had dragged her halfway across the galaxy and for a moment it was going to be for nothing. He did not want anyone else to be his queen; that was something he was quite sure about.

Planet Luminarus was amongst one of the most protected planets in the universe. Its main attraction hub was private security companies and vaults. The companies served most of the kings in the neighboring states. Their blacksmiths were well-known across the furthest reaches of the globe. However, they were also known to be expensive. Ranthor was recently broke due to spending obscene amounts of money on the ship's latest repairs. Hopefully, he would be able to sell the ship at the end of this mission and recover the costs. He would use the money to buy a commercial ship. He learned of a private security mission in the asteroid belt in the system before Luminarus. The person that sent the distress signal offered to pay a sum of money for the rescue mission. Ranthor accepted the mission and entered the coordinates for the asteroid belt into his navigation system. He prepared his arsenal for the mission that he hoped silently he would not require. There was a trail of blood that followed him around across the galaxy.

The asteroid belt was commandeered by a pirating faction that ruled this part of the galaxy. The ship that had sent the distress signal was a commercial ship belonging to King Alveo the 9th, the ruler of most of the planets in that solar system. Ranthor was assured that he would be paid quite handsomely; the reason being was that the captive was none other than the king's own son. The king was riddled with guilt for sending him. He knew that no one would care to save him had it not been for the financial reward. Ranthor asked for proof of the reward before venturing onwards. It was only then that he had agreed to take it. He still wondered as to why the prince would come to such a place in the first place. There was nothing here that was either interesting or of value. Perhaps he did it as part of a dare.

Ranthor was furious that he was reduced to tasks such a babysitting an overgrown, spoilt prince who could not remain ten minutes without being kidnapped. He had learned that this was not the first time this had happened. The king was slowly growing tired to send his forces. He figured that they should be utilized to more important things, namely securing the planet from outside invasive forces. Had it not been for the boy's mother, he would have left the boy to the wolves. He couldn't care any less to deal with his antics anymore. There was a plan to formally disown him upon his return. This way, the king would not have any legal obligation to protect him anymore. His brother was already made the heir apparent; a move that the king thought was extremely wise. The outcast would be given a sum of money and an honorary role in some distant planet which would also serve his purposes of expansion. The king secretly hoped that his son would not be found and that he would not have to pay the ransom money.

The asteroid belt was finally within sight. It was the biggest one that Ranthor had ever seen in his entire life. He stared at it for several minutes, hoping to gather some clues about the kidnappers. They were hidden in plain sight in a virtually impenetrable fortress of asteroids. There were no signs of the ship anywhere. Ranthor tried to access their temperature signal, but this did not yield any useful results. They clearly possessed the same technology that he had which enabled them to mask their signal. Finally, he mustered the courage to enter the asteroid belt. This was probably a fool's move which had the potential to get him injured, but he knew that it was the only thing that he could do now. There were no ships within sight for the first two hours of the mission. He then realized the faint glimmer of a ship nearby. The ship had the royal insignia of the prince. Ranthor boarded the ship and was trying to find clues. The interior of the ship was huge and searching it was going to take a significant amount of time.

The prince did not bring many of his possessions on the ship. Ranthor noticed that there was no distress signal fired from the ship. This was an automatic function of the ship that was activated as soon as the inhabitants left the ship. He was wondering if the prince was actually kidnapped. There was also the possibility that he had willingly joined the pirates in their mission. After all, he did not get any respect from his father or siblings. It was most likely that he did it in retaliation. Despite that, Ranthor continued his search for any useful clues. There were no items that indicated the possible reason for the undertaking of this mission. The captain's log was empty. It was almost as if this mission was not chartered in the first place. Ranthor also noticed that there was a lot of alcohol and narcotics. The prince clearly loved to party and may have stumbled accidentally on this place.

Ranthor was becoming more and more confused as he continued searching the ship. There was nothing that was making any sense about this mission. He then realized that the prince was searching for the same thing he was searching, the jewels. He found a map in the cockpit that looked exactly like his. The final jewel's location was marked in this map. He took the map and stowed in his bag. Realizing that there was nothing of value on this ship, Ranthor departed the ship and was now back safely in his. He continued his search for the prince inside the asteroid belt. The search was going on forever. Just as he was about to lose hope, a dozen pirate ships seemed to materialize out of thin air. They were doing their regular sweep of the area to look for intruders. He followed them closely making sure to avoid detection. None of the pilots managed to detect his ship and he was able to follow them slowly into one of the asteroids.

The first ship landed there, and he could vaguely see the silhouette of one of the pirates. He was with someone that looked as if he was chained against his will. This was most likely the prince. However, Ranthor did not want to be hasty and decided to see how this event would unfold. He could vaguely hear the prince screaming for mercy and the pirate ignoring his pleas. He moved in closer to try and hear the remainder of the conversation. However, he stopped as soon as he realized that this was probably going to get him killed. Instead, he used a listening device that was in his pocket to amplify the sound. He realized that the prince was begging the pirates not to kill his father. The kidnapping was an attempt to reach the king. Little did he know that not only was the king reluctant to answer, but he also did not care whether he was found at all. Actually, the reward was for locating the prince. However, Ranthor decided that he would attempt rescuing him. He might prove valuable after all.

The pirate king continued tormenting the prince for more information. However, he did not manage to get anything of value about the king. He did not know the planet that he hailed from or anything that would help ensure that the ransom money would be delivered. He then threatened the prince that he was going to kill him. The prince did not seem utterly disturbed with this information. He told the pirate king that he would rather die than disclose the secrets of his planet. The pirate was adamant to find more information and so he decided to keep him alive. He knew that someone was bound to come for him sooner or later. Meanwhile, the other pirates took turns in torturing the prince. They eventually grew bored of this exercise; especially as the prince did not seem to care with what they were doing. Ranthor was surprised that this prince was not as spoiled as the ones he had gotten to know. He would make a fine addition to his team should he choose to accept.

The pirate ships departed the asteroid belt and left the prince there in his shackles. The pirate reassured him that he would come for him in the morning. Ranthor seized this opportunity and snuck up to meet the prince. The prince was quite alarmed that he was followed all the way here. He asked Ranthor if he was contacted by his father or any of his subordinates. He told him that he had responded to their distress signal and answered the call. Ranthor also told him that he was searching for the jewels. He offered him a position in his ship if he wanted. The prince said that he would think about it after reaching his home. The shackles holding the prince were removed and they were now making the journey back to his home. Things went over smoothly, and they managed to leave the asteroid belt without being seen by the pirates. Ranthor was finally relieved when they had exited the solar system without any signs of being followed. For once, trouble did manage to follow them across the galaxy. The exchange was made and Ranthor was given the money that he had requested. However, he still kept thinking about what a valuable asset the prince would have been.

Ranthor was now making his way back to the previous planet. His ship was going to get the necessary repairs that were required to get the next jewel. He also possessed the map that showed him the location of the third jewel of darkness. It was going to take two days to reach Planet Luminarus and start working on the repairs for his ship. It was only a matter of time before his goal of find the jewels was realized. Nothing was going to stop him from realizing his goal. The third jewel was now within sight. He was already imagining finding it. He wondered if the money that he had was sufficient to fix the ship. Anyway, he was going to take his chances and find that out when he reached. His mind was currently preoccupied with finding the last jewel that nothing else mattered now. Ranthor was going to use whatever resources available at his disposal for doing so.

He stared at space from the comfort of his window. The ever-growing darkness never ceased to amaze him. It was one of the many reasons that Ranthor had enjoyed long journeys ever since he was a kid. It also served to calm him when he felt stressed or angry. Kendra was now with him and managed to do this. He was extremely happy that she had still accompanied him. She was one of the very few people who understood what he was going through. However, she remained quiet for the better part of an hour. He asked her if there was anything bothering her. She replied that she was okay. She was only suspicious about going back to Luminarus. There were a dozen planets that did the same repairs for a fraction of the cost. He reassured her that they were the best of the best. He did not want to risk it by going to a second-hand dealer. She agreed with him despite not being completely convinced.

Their ship was now hovering over an all-too-familiar planet. It was planet Alvinus. Ranthor had learned that there was a combat competition that was hosted on this planet. The competition's reward was a hefty sum of money that he could surely use to finance his operations. He decided to land on Alvinus and register his name for the competition. Kendra was not too happy about this. The last thing they needed was some sketchy brawl to earn money. She was wondering if the search for the jewel was worthwhile after all. For the past week or so, she did not manage to get a glimpse of Ranthor. He was always rushing off to do the craziest task for whatever meagre amount of money that was offered for them. He was clearly deluded into thinking that the ship's upgrades were his best chance at gathering the jewels. They used the minimum number of resources to find the jewels. She felt as if he was deliberately prolonging the mission for another strange purpose. However, she did not want to confront him due to fear of him lashing out at her.

The ship landed at Alvinus and Ranthor registered his name for the competition. He eyed the competition and realized that this competition was going to be easy to win. There were a lot of amateur fighters in the first round. It was going to take the better part of an hour and a half to defeat all of them. The same went for the fighters that were in tiers two through seven. The final tier, however, had a lot of seasoned fighters that matched Ranthor in both skill and tactical planning. He was actually happy and amused that he would fight them. This would serve to prepare him for the final battle for the jewel of darkness that was in Ray's possession. He had just hoped that the competition would conclude quickly, and the victor would be crowned within a few days so that he could be back on track to find the jewel. The first two tiers were easy to defeat and were down in the same time period that he had predicted it would take to destroy them. Kendra came to see the remainder of the matches. She had initially abstained from doing so out of principle. However, she grew bored in the ship and decided to use this as a form of entertainment, which was sparse nowadays.

The next fighter in the third tier gave Ranthor a run for his money. He was an Odelphian brawler that was in the army for several years. He had managed to train several soldiers in the combat arts and had also trained the army in Nebula. Ranthor recognized him from a few of the audiences that he had with his father. The warrior standing before him was none other than the legendary golden Goliath. Goliath was the strongest warrior in his galaxy to date. No one had dared to battle him. Whoever did eventually was always maimed badly. Every king enlisted his help due to his military prowess and intelligence. The ones that could not pay the price at the end of training had perished into nothingness. Goliath entered the competition due to a shortage of funds. No one wanted to hire him on account of the maiming and the injuries that he had caused to some of the battalions. Ranthor was a huge fan of him ever since he was a child.

He remembered the days where he would stare outside his window on Planet Nebula and imagine himself as a soldier. Although he never met Goliath in person, he was always fond of him and admired him. His father decided to stop enlisting him for training after a few incidents with the soldiers. He killed an entire squad for failing to learn a combat sequence. He did this to prove to the others that they could as easily be killed. The king realized that he was too brutal to be kept in service. He was also not permitted back onto the planet. The king knew that Goliath was unpredictable and did not want him anywhere around him should he decide to take out his anger at him. Goliath had then spent years in hiding before being recruited to train the soldiers in his home planet. He had served there ever since without any known incidents. It was strange to find him on this planet and participating in the competition.

The first round started with a sword fight between the two combatants. Ranthor was not permitted to use his and instead was given a longsword. He found it difficult to wield the sword in the beginning but soon learned how to do the task. Ranthor decided to hide in the beginning and practice his skills. Luckily, Goliath did not manage to find his location. The crowd was booing him and then pointed his location to Goliath who smashed the alcove that he was hiding under. There was nothing that shielded him now. Ranthor trembled at the sight of the mighty warrior, but he was not going to back down from the challenge. He managed to swing his sword and hit his opponent squarely in the chest. Goliath was writhing in agony and had collapsed at the center of the stage. However, he managed to recover and get back into the fight. His resolve was now stronger than ever, and he vowed to himself to kill Ranthor. His mace was flailing wildly as he attempted to hit Ranthor. Ranthor managed to dodge every one of the attacks that Goliath sent his way. It was a matter of time before this battle was concluded.

Goliath smashed every wall, alcove, and precipice that could be used as cover. Ranthor was now trapped in plain sight. There was nothing that offered protection against the brute that was dueling him. He had used a lot of effort to prevent being hit by the mace. He managed yet again to injure Goliath. The second attack blinded him in one eye. Blood spattered everywhere and Goliath was screaming so loudly that the stage shook. Ranthor moved in and attacked his Achilles heel. The warrior collapsed to the ground and was soon pronounced dead. The crowd cheered on for Ranthor who managed to advance to the next warrior in the tier. Luckily, there was a break for an hour before the next fight. Ranthor needed to gather his strength for the next battle. He was very worn out from the last encounter. He was hoping that there was no opponent as big or as strong as Goliath. His wounds had just started to heal, and he was still out of breath.

The next opponent was significantly smaller in size but was equally as strong as the last one. He was one of his own soldiers from Nebula. Ranthor realized that he had trained this soldier. He recognized him from the tattoo that was on his shoulder. The soldier also recognized him and saluted him before the beginning of the fight. It was strange that many of these opponents were from his past. He started wondering if this was the theme of the tournament, and if other participants also faced the same ordeal. Anyway, it didn't matter as long as there was money involved in it. Besides, he had long abandoned his planet and no longer had any allegiance toward it. Fighting this opponent would be like any other he would face in the arena. His opponent did not seem intimidated either by the size of the competition.

Ranthor wondered how long this ordeal was going to go for. There seemed to be escape to the horror that he seemed to be facing. He was wondering if the king was going to be the next opponent, he chuckled silently. It was as if all the ghosts from his past suddenly decided to have a sparring match with him. Ranthor was at least happy that there was a monetary reward for this task. He could not imagine doing it for free. He would kill the theatre owner if that were to happen. The frustration was building up to intolerable levels. The competition was finally coming to the final rounds and Ranthor would soon emerge as the winner. Fighting this soldier would prove to him once and for all that he was above his father's court. It was the ultimate test of character that he could ever be handed.

The soldier was eyeing Ranthor rather suspiciously. He was worried about the king's reaction knowing that he had injured his one and only son. The only reason he joined the competition in the first place was to provide for his family and provide a much better future than that offered by the king. Planet Nebula was no longer the safe haven that it used to be. Most of the soldiers had managed to flee the oppressive regime of the king. There was barely anyone around to command the army. The king was looking for new recruits left, right, and center. There were even rumors that bandits would be recruited in the army if things continued to spiral in this direction. The remaining soldiers stayed because they were too old to be recruited elsewhere. The average age of their current intake was fifty years old.

The battle started in the middle of the arena with Ranthor parrying an attack from the soldier. He barely moved in time to escape the attack. They were now carrying axes instead of long swords. Whoever was controlling the arena changed the rules of battle. This was a strategy used by most arena masters to keep the crowds entertained. The arena master was sitting in a private booth in the middle and enjoying a nice warm meal. He was surrounded by many of the foreign dignitaries of this solar system who came to enjoy the fight. The booth also held an area where bets were constantly being placed. Considering that

Ranthor was the current reigning champion, people were rushing to bet on him. There were already bets that were concerned with whether he will be crowned the winner of the current competition. The arena master made sure to meet with Ranthor after the match. He wanted to sign him up permanently as one of the fixtures in the arena. Little did he know that he was going to be sorely disappointed.

Meanwhile, Ranthor and his former pupil were fighting till death. Nothing seemed to stop the flow of battle. Each possessed a unique set of skills that distinguished him from the others. Ranthor recognized that training was going on in a different direction than when he was around. The soldier was using a fighting style that was outlawed years ago. Luckily, the arena master could not care less.

The fight between the Nebula soldier and Ranthor did not seem to have a predictable end. The arena master realized that the crowds were beginning to feel bored. He decided to send a few of his distinguished fighters into the stage to challenge the competition. Perhaps this would stimulate Ranthor and his friend to be more aggressive. The new fighters were welcomed into the stage with a thunderous roar by the spectators. They lived for the fight, the arena was their home and the arena master their patron. Ranthor realized that he had actually started to like the attention he was getting from his fans. He considered coming back to the arena after the adventure was over and try to keep his title. The attention that he was getting felt intoxicating. It was as if a drug was pumping through his veins and electrifying them. It was also the thrill of the fight that had driven him to be one of the contenders for the championship title.

The soldier was exhausted from battle. He managed to get into a nearby bush in the arena to shield him from Ranthor's attacks. However, he did not account for the mercenaries that had descended onto the arena. There was nothing that shielded him from this onslaught of brute soldiers. He realized that he needed to trick Ranthor somehow into giving in. This way, he was going to maintain his current title and be crowned victorious by the arena master. He would then find a way to deal with the force that was unleashed before him. If he was lucky, then he was going to convince the arena master to dispose of them. He would be the conquering champion of all time. However, for the time being he focused on not getting killed. That was easier said than done. The soldiers did not seem interested in Ranthor. They found it easier to deal with him.

Ranthor was dealing with the welcoming committee that was sent by the arena master. He managed to pick them off one by one and dispose of them. The remaining fighters did not dare to deal with him. No one wanted to cross Ranthor at this point and turn into another carcass. They all fled outside the arena. The arena master was beside himself with fury. He decided that as a final measure, he was going to unleash the giants. He had never had to use the giants for any of his shows. He thought that he would keep them as an attraction for the next arena match. However, now was the time they could be used for a good purpose. The arena master regretted sending them in, but there was nothing that he could do to stop Ranthor from prematurely ending the match. It was the only way he had to make sure that Ranthor was taken care of.

The giants were released from their cages. They continued to howl at the denizens of the arena. Ranthor flinched at the sight of such monstrosity. He did not realize that such beings were present in the galaxy. There was a lot of folklore written about the giants, but no one believed it was real. He did not know how the arena master managed to capture them in the first place. The legendary creatures were intoxicating to look at. Ranthor felt bad that he might have to kill them for the sake of the fight. However, saving his life came as priority, and he would do whatever it took if it came to it. He would not be killed just to protect these freaks of nature. His soldier friend was still in hiding. However, the giants soon found him and devoured him alive. The only remnant of the soldier was his legs. The giants decided to discard the legs and left them in a nearby barn in the middle of the arena. Ranthor was shocked at the speed and precision of the creatures. They were at least ten times his size and almost fifteen times as agile as any of them were. It was a sheer miracle that he was still alive. He realized that the giants had no intention of killing him; they might even be trying to stage a coup together against the arena master. Ranthor had a wonderful idea, he would recruit them to his cause and gather the money in the arena's vault. The giants were instrumental to him.

The leader of the giants advanced towards him. He hoisted him towards the podium where the arena master was located. Ranthor was now face to face with the same man that thought unleashing a group of angry giants would serve as good friendly entertainment. The arena master cowered in fear at seeing Ranthor. He begged and pleaded him to let him go whatever the conditions may be. Ranthor told him that he wanted an increase in the prize money and for him to free the giants. He agreed to the first term, but he could not part with the giants.

Ranthor accepted the deal and went to the arena master's main chamber to collect his reward. He felt horrible for betraying the giants. However, it was the only way that he was going to get what he wanted. However, he would do whatever it took to help them out. He had planned on returning to them and saving them.

The giants were sent back to their cages feeling bitter from the betrayal of Ranthor. They howled and kicked at the cages that were housing them. The handlers faced a difficult time getting the giants to enter. However, they managed to trick them by providing them with their favorite meals. This trick had always worked with the previous inhabitants of the cage. The competition was now over, and the crowning ceremony had begun. Ranthor was ready to receive his title as the new champion. Most importantly, he wanted the money that was given to the champion. He would then complete the repairs on his ship and head to Luminarus after the end of the mission. For the time being, it was sufficient to continue his journey with the ship in its current status. Nothing was going to sway him away from his goal. Ranthor was exhilarated that this adventure led him to find love; a thing that he never thought for a million years was possible for him.

Kendra was looking at the window, waiting for time to pass. She did not want to be stuck in this state forever. There was nothing to be done on the ship. A part of her missed taking on adventures with Ranthor. She told him that she wanted to resume the field work and he was extremely thrilled at hearing this. It was not the same without her at his side. She would have probably torn each and every fighter in the arena mercilessly. He had told her the story about the giants and the arena master. She never thought that Ranthor was the type to be compassionate and caring. There must have been something that made him change his mind. Perhaps it was the fact that he was going to spend a significant part of his life with her. Whatever it was that created this welcome change, she was happy to support. She had always admired his fearlessness but now she was overwhelmed with the depth of emotions that he was able to display. A part of her told her that being with him was the right thing to do. She was going to tell Ranthor the news the following morning; after having enough time to mull it over in her own mind.

Change was something that neither of them were equipped to deal with. They had both experienced a significant amount of adversity in their lives. Adding this to the mix was not necessarily a solution to their overwhelming bundle of sorrow and regrets. It was good that there was still a jewel to collect; well, two, considering the one that was with Ray. This provided an excellent distractor to avoid dealing with the elephant in the room, the budding complex relationship that was developing between the two of them. The last jewel was not very far away from them. It was a few solar systems away and was actually within reach. Ranthor entered the coordinates into his system and engaged the ship. This was hopefully going to be the last time that he did this. Afterwards, it would always be the same route over and over for him. He was going to find stability and settle in one of the planets he had visited. He kept thinking of the Xenoran planet. It was one of the peaceful ones that he had visited, completely out of sight.

Chapter 15
The Mystery of Xenora

Both of them spent the entirety of that afternoon daydreaming about their life after the jewels. It was still a long way to go. After all, they had to activate and harness the power of the jewels at the temple. They did not know the first thing about doing that. None of the maps or schematics described the method for doing that. They would have to enlist the help of the Xenorans for this task. This was the same group of people that tried to kill them the first time they had arrived. Ranthor would try to bribe them like Ray did. Perhaps there was something else that they wanted. He also would assure them protection from any possible threat. That was sure going to win them over to his cause. The only thing left was how to battle Ray. Ranthor almost died the last time they both dueled. Even after Ray was crippled, he had a hard time. The best shot he had was to outsmart him. Ray would need to be lured into some trap and then they would pry the jewel from his hands.

Kendra was fascinated at the length Ranthor would take to collect the jewels. Ray used to be one of his father's most elite soldiers. He was also mentor and friend to Ranthor for several years. She was hoping that amends could be made between them. Little did she know that warring captains never held treaties. It was not the way the soldiers of Nebula operated, exiled or not. There was no possible way a truce was going to be brokered. The best that she hoped for was that they don't kill each other and instead settle for the shame of defeat. As for her, she was keen on finding about the last jewel. She was curious as to where their last adventure was going to take them. Unlike Ranthor, she did not yet face all her demons. She knew that there were not many of them. Kendra had faced all her demons a few years back. This adventure only served to reaffirm her belief that she could conquer anything.

Planet Epsilon gamma was the last planet where the jewel was housed. It was a very densely populated planet that was full of gambling and drug joints. The majority of the citizens were involved in a single illegal activity or two. It was quite a dangerous place to go to. Kendra was worried that they were headed to this planet. The jewel was probably with one of the smugglers. They must have heard that the jewel was important and decided to hijack the jewel. Ranthor was ready to take on whatever small thief there was to get the jewel. They would not know what hit them. Kendra was quite annoyed that some common thief was going to place a ransom for the jewel. She was ready to kill the vermin that had jewel with no questions asked. Engaging in dialogue was not an option for her at this point in time. The last thing on her mind was engaging in a conversation with a local drug lord about the price for the jewel.

The ship finally reached the solar system where planet Epsilon was located. The ship was now close to the place where it all would end. Planet Epsilon was emitting a radiant glow that illuminated the entire solar system. Kendra had already prepared their gear, entered the landing codes to descend, and arranged the map accordingly. She was still worried that there was nothing amiss going on. The jewels were very quiet in their pouch. It was quite unusual that they had not shown any sign of activity yet. If this had indeed been the planet, then something would have happened by now. Kendra was worried that the map's location was a false one. It was not going to be the first time that they were fooled by their enemy. The last time this had happened, they had almost lost the jewel. The next time involved them being kidnapped and chained to the wall of a dungeon. Hopefully, this was not going to be another trap. The Xenorans were master artists that liked to conceal things in plain sight. It was just frustrating to run around in circles looking for the jewels. It had to end at some point.

Suddenly, a fleet of ships that belonged to the Nebula system materialized out of thin air. Ranthor recognized his father's ship at the helm of the ships. He figured out that this map must have been planted by him at the last planet. He quickly steered the ship towards Planet Xenophius and prepared for the ship to land. The ship landed safely on the surface of the planet. It was one of the quietest planets that they have ever landed on. There was no criminal activity whatsoever on this planet. For the time being, they had to lay low until the ships were out of orbit. Ranthor did not know for how long this was going to be the case. Luckily, his father had not found out about them yet. His ship was just above theirs. However, he soon moved on to another planet. Ranthor sighed a sigh of relief that they were not discovered. There was gorge nearby that they managed to hide in. It was going to lose their signal until his father left the solar system. Ranthor and Kendra were searching the planet for any signs of life. There was no one on this planet for several kilometers. There was a village nearby that both of them decided to visit.

The village was the only evidence of any humanoid life forms. Surprisingly, there were still people that inhabited this part of the planet. The villagers greeted them and welcomed them into the village. A feast was made in their honor to celebrate the coming of new visitors into their planet. Kendra was glad that they managed to enjoy a hot meal in the meantime. She used this as a chance to bond further with Ranthor. Ranthor also enjoyed this welcome change to talk to Kendra. Things had changed now for the better between both of them. The villagers were singing to them and danced merrily. They then gave them drinks to enjoy the remainder of the journey. Kendra realized that they were wearing artefacts similar to the ones that the Xenorans were wearing. She wondered if they were one of their direct descendants. Ranthor asked them if they knew about the darkness jewels. The villagers surprisingly had a lot of information about the jewels. They told them that the jewels used to be at Xenophius. However, they were moved centuries ago from this solar system. It was Xenora Centra, the mother planet of the Xenoran civilization. The only way to access was with a map that was in this very planet. Luckily, the villagers were willing to give it them provided that Ranthor was to win their challenge.

Planet Xenora Centra was the seat of the Xenoran civilization. It was built to be evidence of the supremacy of their civilization. The challenge that the villagers had suggested was so that they could trust Ranthor with their most prized possession, the jewels. They had learned about him from the rumors that were surrounding him in the galaxy. They had also witnessed his performance live at the arena. However, they knew that he still needed to pass the challenge as was the common tradition of their civilization. Ranthor was ready for any challenge that was going to be thrown at him. He prepared himself for anything that the villagers were going to send his way. Kendra was going to be annoyed but she thought against it. At least there was a clue to find. She had grown used to dealing with disappointment on this adventure. She asked the villagers if she could contribute toward this adventure. However, they informed her that only one person that does the mission was the one in it. Ranthor still was happy that she was going to do whatever it took to help him in his mission. It was now time for the trials to begin.

Kendra was looking over at Ranthor from a distance and judging if his approach to winning this mission was good or not. She continued to monitor things using the intercom and helping him in whatever way she could. She realized at this point in time that Ranthor was the one that she wanted to spend the remainder of her life with. She made up her mind to join him when this was over.

The first part of the mission did not pose a threat to Ranthor. He managed to maneuver the first maze with relative ease. The maze did not pose a threat to him. Ranthor felt a sigh of relief at the completion of the first task. He did not expect that even this part was going to be this easy. The next part was a meadow in the middle of nowhere. He wondered what a meadow was doing there. There was no rainfall on this planet for months. It must be a virtual plane that was created by the citizens to give them the illusion of greenery. The second task was now within sight. There was supposed to be a key in the middle of the meadow. Ranthor had to find some way of locating it. Things would become much easier from that point onwards. There was nothing in the meadow that suggested the possible location of the key. There were multiple mechanisms that could trigger locating the key.

The first mechanism that he tried did not open anything. That spoke did not open anything. He then tried the next spoke but nothing happened. Perhaps it was not a spoke after all. Nothing seemed to be working and he started to experience despair. There was a lever in the middle of the room. Ranthor pressed the lever and a box appeared out of nowhere. The box had the key in it. He was happy that he had finally found the key. Now he had to find what the key opened. He tried the spokes again, but nothing seemed to be happening. He moved over to a nearby stream in search of possible answers. He decided that he would go for a swim. He was surprised at what he found at the bottom of the stream. There was a vault inside with multiple locks. He used the first key to open one of the locks. Ranthor realized that the meadow was only one of the areas involved. All of them eventually connected to the stream and the vault that was in it.

The vault was similar to the ones that were in the mines and the quarry. He wondered as to why the Xenorans went to so much effort to hide the jewels. Why couldn't they have destroyed them in the first place? He had asked the villagers this question. The answer he got was quite surprising. It was not that the jewels were difficult to destroy. They were created for a very important purpose. The Xenorans were amongst the many ancient humanoids in the galaxy. The jewels were a way for them to ensure that they would live for all eternity. Their civilization did not have a definition of life after death, unlike the other humanoids. Therefore, the jewels provided a way to ensure their survival. The destruction of the jewels would mean that they too would cease to exist. It was one of the reasons why the jewels were scattered across the galaxy.

The third part of the mission was now within Ranthor's site. It was a replica of the mining village. It even had the same traps. Ranthor knew the combination by heart and managed to get this key quite easily. However, as soon as he removed the key from the box, he was surprised by powerful soldiers that prepared to attack him. They all carried the same insignia as his father's army. The only difference was that they were clearly hired guns. His father was resorting to unconventional means to gather the jewels. The villagers warned Ranthor that some of the events he would witness were representations of things that were likely to happen. He realized after killing the first wave of soldiers that he was becoming much stronger. His time at the arena had clearly paid off. He managed to hack at all the soldiers and sending the remaining ones fleeing for their lives. Ranthor finally managed to leave the mine and make his way to the stream. It was difficult to locate the stream at first, but he soon found it. He then dipped into the bottom of the stream and unlocked the second lock guarding the vault. There were only two more locks that guarded the map in the vault. At least, he hoped, that there was a map. He knew that the villagers would perish if there wasn't anything.

The third task was quite an unpredictable one; one that he did not anticipate at all. At first, he thought that the quarry was going to be the next challenge based on the range of nostalgic places that they had visited. Ranthor was now in the middle of his father's court. It was the last time he was a prince in his country. The memory was very painful for him to take, but he still managed to maintain his composure despite this. The mission required that he proceed through and acquire the key. Ranthor noticed that his father was not seated at the throne. Instead, there were two thrones, one of which had Kendra seated on. The other one was his seat. This must be an alternative reality that Ranthor had created in his mind. This was his ideal scenario. The one that he had envisioned in his mind ever since he had found the jewels of darkness. He also saw that Ray was there by his side. He expected him to be killed, something that clearly did not happen in this alternative universe.

Ranthor entered the next room to look for the key. There was nothing to be found in the middle of the court. Ranthor found his father in the middle of a dungeon and was pleading his son for forgiveness. Ranthor's father was growing old, and he was going to die any time soon. Ranthor did not have it in him to forgive his father. The frail man was now withering away silently. After searching the dungeon, he realized that there was nothing there to be found. He moved to the other room where a box was located. He opened the box and the key suddenly appeared out of nowhere. The planet soon disappeared from view and he was back in the meadow again. Ranthor then continued to the stream. There was only one key to be found now. The stream was now in sight. He dived into the stream to unlock the vault. The next lock opened quite easily and there was only one lock that stood in the way of finding the map.

It was quite difficult to find the last lock in the mission trail. There was no magical area that Ranthor could easily connect with. He grew disappointed at the fact that the last lock did not reveal another memory. The quarry had now materialized into view, but Ranthor knew it wasn't going to be quite that simple. He moved on to the quarry to find the next key. He rejoiced at the site of having to thoroughly search the area. The quarry was amongst one of the most difficult tasks that he had faced in this mission. He contacted Kendra to tell her about the recent developments in his mission. He searched each and every part of the quarry but did not find anything, Finally, he left the quarry in search for the next area. Ranthor realized that there was a glacier beyond the quarry. The glacier was now within sight. Ranthor continued through the path and reached the glacier. He found a box that was suspended in the middle of a frozen lake.

The glacier was a very well-protected area, and the box was conveniently hidden there. Ranthor tried to blow up a hole in the middle and extract the box. That did not yield any useful result whatsoever. He then found a lever and pressed it. The lever opened the way for an ion beam that cut a hole in the middle of the ice. It melted as soon as the beam fell on it. Ranthor immediately swam and reached the box. The key was right there waiting to be taken. He quickly snatched it from the box and made his way to the stream to open the final lock in the vault. Soon, the map was going to be in his possession and the next jewel would be discovered. As soon as he reached the meadow, a few soldiers appeared in front of him. He prepared for another fight with the militia. He managed to kill them off. Ranthor then made his way to the stream. The meadow now disappeared into thin air. The stream was now within sight and there was no one there to deal with him. He reached for the stream and opened the last lock. The map was in the vault and was surprisingly dry.

Ranthor returned to the ancient grounds where the villagers were waiting. None of them looked particularly happy that the task was completed. The villagers never celebrated winning the task and had thought that the map would remain hidden at the bottom of the stream. However, as per agreement, they had to welcome the winner and congratulate him for getting the map out of its vault. The village elders presented him a ceremonial robe. There was then some singing and dancing involved. This went on for the remainder of the night. Kendra was thoroughly enjoying the ceremony unlike Ranthor who clearly wasn't fond of being the center of attention. The villagers were not fond of doing this either. They did not want to part with the map, but there was nothing that they could do about it. Ranthor bid them farewell and retired to the ship for the night. As for Kendra, she continued to enjoy the festivities. She enjoyed the company of the villagers and managed to learn a few things about the Xenoran civilization.

The Xenorans first arrived in this universe two thousand years ago aboard their ship. They trained the mechanics that were manufacturing the ships that were being created now. Their technologies are the basis most of the modern civilizations that ruled the galaxy today. However, their respective rulers finally realized that the Xenorans could not be kept alive. They were hunted across the galaxy and the vast majority of them were killed in the process. The ones that survived went into hiding for centuries. The last time they were seen was two centuries ago above the surface. Rumors stated that they were going to come back and take their revenge against the world of the living. However, Kendra did not think that the Xenorans were a particularly vindictive race. It was surprising what years of bigotry and killings would have done to them. They had a lot of hatred, particularly toward people from Nebula. It was one of the reasons that they were reluctant to give the map to Ranthor.

It was sad that they had to retire in these backward planets, trapped in here without being able to exercise their innovative minds. The place they were in was begging for a renovation. Kendra was wondering if she could help them change their mind about their plans for a full-scale invasion. The villagers were planning to take on Planet Nebula along with the other Xenorans. An alliance was recently brokered between all the Xenoran inhabitants of the galaxy. The king of Nebula was going to be their next target. He had tormented them for centuries and so did his predecessors who initially drove them out of their home.

They were going to drive him into hiding the same way they did. Kendra was just finishing up with the ceremony and was now also making her way back to the ship. By the time she reached the ship, Ranthor was fast asleep. It was only a matter of time before they left to go to the next planet. She wondered where planet Xenora Centra was located. No one had laid eyes on the planet for centuries. Kendra was not even sure if it actually had existed in the first place. After all, it was only a bunch of rumors.

The sun was shining as bright as ever. Ranthor woke up and prepared food for Kendra. He then entered the coordinates that were in the map. The ship's engine revved up with life and they were on their way to the next planet. It was going to be a matter of time before they located the final jewel. Ray was nowhere to be seen. Ranthor wondered where he had disappeared off to. They needed him for the final part of the mission. The jewel with him was part of the collection and the key to harnessing the power of the jewels. Both of them did not know what they needed to do next. The mission was almost over now, and they did not even know how to activate the jewels. They also did not want to part ways, not after they have found each other. Kendra tried to delay the mission with meaningless things to do, and apparently so did Ranthor. It was time for them to have a long talk about what they were going to do next. Kendra waited for the right time to tell Ranthor.

Ray was looking at the jewel that was in his vault and silently admiring it. He knew that this was his only bargaining chip with his former captain. This jewel would ensure his dominion over the entire planet and possibly the galaxy. However, he knew that Ranthor was going to defeat him easily in combat. It wasn't the same as it was back home when he could easily best his commander. Ray was now quite afraid of the possible fight with his former master. He had thought of surrendering to Ranthor and making amends. It was probably the best solution that he had come up with ever since he started his search. The jewel did not seem to lose its sparkle, unlike its master. He looked at the jewel again and decided that he still had some fight in him. He would take on Ranthor even if it was the last thing he'd do. He prepared his swords, guns, and all the weapons in his arsenal for the ensuing battle. Despite that, Ray was extremely worried about losing everything. Ranthor and Kendra were much stronger now than ever.

He decided to land his ship in one of the nearby planets and explore it. Ray was fond of this part of the galaxy. It didn't have the fair share of warlords, drug mules, and corrupt rulers unlike the other galaxies. He had thought of settling here possibly. He knew that the king had ruined Nebula, and there was no one interested in joining his army. He did not want to come back to rule that sorry excuse of a planet now. It was now that he had moved on further to bigger plans. He was now in a planet called Xernius, the crown jewel of its solar system. The planet was the market hub of the galaxy. Many people invested in multiple ventures and went on to become rich and successful. He was wondering if he could use the jewels to fund his operations. The planet was not very densely populated, and he could move around as much as he pleased. The jewel was in plain sight, and no one seemed to bother about it. The humanoids on this planet did not involve themselves in the race for power that the others were interested in.

The ship that Ray had arrived in was starting to act up. He took it to the nearest repair shop and started fixing it. In the meantime, he was exploring the planet and getting to know the basic culture of the capital. The reason the jewels were not that popular was because the people here existed far longer than the Xenorans. They had already created their civilization and did not require any assistance from them. However, things were starting to get worse over the past decade. The ruler of the planet was critically ill and was going to hand over the throne to his one and only son. He was quite as corrupt as the other rulers in the galaxy. The citizens were starting to leave by the dozens. The planet was going to turn into yet another uninhabited desert. There were rumors that the successor to the king was going to sell it to the Xenorans. It was going to be the planet that they were going to use to resurface.

The ship was now fixed, and Ray prepared to leave. There was nothing much left for him to do. He was going to return to the quietness of his long solitude. The only thing he hoped for now was that Ranthor would come for him and his jewel. Ray grew bored of the lack of combat. It was going to be a challenge to fight his master once again. He was going to make sure this time that he had killed him. It was a nuisance to wait for him for what seemed to be an eternity. Ranthor's signal disappeared from view, and there was no possible way of finding him now. He relied on the fact that he was still interested in the last jewel of darkness that was in his possession. He just hoped that he would not display the same cruelty that he had shown him. Had the roles been reversed, he wasn't sure that he was going to show him the same courtesy. Ever since Ranthor disappeared, he was gunning for his role back home. However, the king did not want to offer the role to anyone.

Ranthor was back in the cockpit of his ship thinking of a plan to acquire the jewel in Xenora Centra. He tried to figure out the possible atmosphere of the planet and how he would be able to find the jewel. Unlike the other maps, there was nothing in it to suggest about how to acquire the jewel. The villagers knew how to get it but did not want to share the plan with Ranthor. Kendra tried to get some information from them but to no avail. They did not want any son of Nebula to enjoy the power of their jewel. They may have been obligated to give him the map, but that did not mean that they would help him get the jewels. The villagers dreaded the fact that the jewels of Nebula were going to end up in the possession of the king. They would rather be dead and gone than ending up with him.

There was nothing that could be done now and Ranthor would have to come up with a plan on the spot. Xenora Centra was a planet that was thought to be non-existent. There was nothing in any of the maps, war documents, or local folklore to suggest the presence of this planet. All of the people that attempted to visit it either did not return or were somehow silenced so that they may not speak about it. It was one of the long-lost secrets of the universe, one that was very well kept. The Xenorans did not disclose the location to anyone and there was no possible way to find out from anyone. However, the map had the location marked clearly and it was only a matter of time before he got his hands on the jewels. The planet seemed to be nestled between two galaxies. Ranthor was not sure about how to get the ship there. He inserted the receptacle into the map and then the most surprising thing happened; the map transformed into a time rift creator. It had the power to create a rift in space and time, enabling them to cross the space between the two galaxies and reach the place of the jewel.

The time rift looked like a very expensive item that they had to protect with their lives. Ranthor realized that it had a port for charging. It took a lot of effort to charge, and he realized that he was not going to use it lightly. Only operating the first time used up a significant fraction of the battery. He kept it in the charging dock for the duration of the journey. This seemed to attract a lot of attention from some nearby ships. A few pirate ships were on their tail, but Ranthor managed to kill every last one of them and acquire their gear. From that moment onward, no one dared to attack them again. The pirates wanted to bargain with Ranthor for the jewels, at a decent price that they were going to propose. He managed to drive them off by giving them a deal on some of the rare gems that were in his possession. That had left them quite satisfied, and most importantly away from the jewels. They were now well on their way to the next galaxy and closer than ever to the last jewel of darkness.

Little did they know that the pirates were a vindictive bunch of people. They rarely left anyone alone after they discovered that there were some valuable items to be looted. They had already planned to ambush Ranthor soon enough. Kendra was sure that it was not the last time they would see them. She feared for her life and begged Ranthor to add protection to the ship. The cloaking device was activated, and their thermal signature was covered. There was no way the pirates would find them now. The ship had now crossed yet another galaxy and there were no possible enemies left. Ranthor was now enjoying a nice meal with Kendra and was daydreaming of about finding Xenora Centra. There was not much time left before they would reach the location. The time rift was now fully charged and ready to be used to create a hole in time and space. It was through this hole that they would cross over to the last planet housing the jewel of darkness. This harrowing ordeal was finally going to be over once and for all. Kendra called Gideon to update him about their successful mission.

They were now a galaxy away from reaching their goal. Ranthor was preparing himself for the mission and he extracted the map from his pocket. Just before he managed to do so, a distress signal sounded from the ship. It was Gideon sending the signal from his home. Kendra was quite worried as to why Gideon would be sending a signal now that he was safe and sound at home. She contacted him and indeed it was a distress signal. Their friend needed their help. The strange thing was that his signal was coming from Planet Odelphius. It seemed that his parents had taken him there for the holidays. They soon vanished and left him alone without any message. Gideon was quite sure that they were kidnapped and therefore sent the distress signal. He wanted his friends to come and help him search for them. Ranthor turned the ship around and prepared for a journey to Odelphius. He was soon near the planet's surface. He managed to land the ship successfully and was now headed to meet Gideon in a nearby square.

Gideon was quite happy to see Kendra and Ranthor again. Tears were rolling down his cheek and he looked extremely frightened. Kendra leaned over and patted him on the shoulder. She reassured him that they would find his parents and that there was nothing to worry. Ranthor also promised him that he would be reunited with them again. Gideon managed to smile and told them about the details of their visit. He told them that he wanted to visit one of the festivals in town. It was in celebration of the capital's harvest; one of the most important events of the year on this planet. It was going to be a nice trip with them. One that he was used to going on alone every year. This year was going to commemorate the occasion that he went with his family. He was always jealous of the children that used to come with their families. Finally, it was time for him to do the same thing. Gideon was now regretting coming here.

The last known whereabouts of his family was at a nearby inn that they rented. Their clothes, money, and all their belongings were there. This excluded the possibility that they had left on their own will again. Ranthor still had to explore that possibility. It was reassuring, considering that Gideon would be extremely heartbroken if that had happened to him again. He managed to dust off the prints from their belongings. The clothes were still warm; this meant that they were still close by. It was not going to take much time before they found them. Gideon was looking over them intently trying to decipher if they had found any useful information. Kendra realized what he was doing and suggested that she would take him for a stroll. He enjoyed the idea very much. This managed to take the edge off looking for his parents. Ranthor worked in the meantime to find them. The clues suggested that they were somewhere in the western quarter. He expected to hear from the kidnapper soon enough. However, he knew that Gideon did not have enough money on him. This must have been a trap to lure him in. He realized that he must be extremely careful dealing with the kidnappers.

Kendra was still enjoying a nice stroll with Gideon by the beach. Ranthor told her about the latest developments in the search. He also warned her to protect the jewels and take Gideon into the safety of the ship. She agreed and told Gideon that they were headed to the ship. Surprisingly, he was quite excited to enter the ship again. He missed the action and the fighting a lot. He recounted to Kendra the countless adventures that he had with his parents, but it did not measure up with the adventures that they had looking for the jewels. Kendra told him about the jewels of darkness and the mission finding the Xenorans. Gideon wanted to get back with them and search for the jewels. However, Kendra told him that he needed to stay with his parents until their ordeal was over.

Ranthor was now near the wharf at the western quarter of the capital. He was still hot on the trail of the kidnappers. He was going to find Gideon's parents and then get back to his mission of finding the jewel. There was no sign of anyone near the wharf. Strangely enough, no one had contacted them yet, telling them that they needed a ransom in exchange for the boy's parents. Ranthor was growing suspicious of this mission already. Nothing seemed to make sense, and the more he thought about it the less he could figure out if this was indeed a kidnapping. However, there was no reason for Gideon's parents to abandon him again. They were doing well financially and could definitely take care of him now. There must be another reason that they were kidnapped. He continued his search of the wharf which did not yield any results. Suddenly, a mysterious person emerged from the shadows and ushered him to follow. Ranthor followed him cautiously, avoiding getting very close to the veiled figure.

The man was moving very quickly amongst the shadows, he could barely catch up with him. The shadowed figure realized this and so he slowed down his pace. Ranthor was now able to catch up with him without losing his breath. He wondered where he was taking him. He decided to send a signal to Kendra to alert her in the event that he was attacked. After all, he was hovering behind someone who could possibly be a serial killer for all he knew. Whoever he was, he could easily take him alone. But he wasn't sure if he would be able to hold off any other goons that made their way to him. Ranthor was tired of dealing with ambushes; he hoped that this would not be one of them. He had acquired a liking for murder. *I would do really well as a hired gun*, he thought to himself. The figure motioned over to him to come up on the deck of the ship. He then removed his veil and Ranthor recognized him as Gideon's father. This assured him that this indeed was another trap.

Gideon's father explained to Ranthor the entire story. He had told him that Gideon wanted to abandon his dreams and stay indefinitely with his parents. They managed to escape for a while to get him to join Ranthor again. He was missing the crew sorely and had conveyed this several times to his parents. Neither of them liked the idea that he was going on another adventure, but they realized that Ranthor could somehow convince him to stay with them. Both of them arranged this fake kidnapping to reinforce this point. Ranthor realized that both of them were out of their minds. He did not know why they had orchestrated this madness just to convince their son of their intentions. They clearly learned about parenting skills from the same place that his father did. He did not envy Gideon for having this crazy bunch as parents. However, he decided to help them in convincing their son that the path that he wanted was not fruitful. Ranthor later realized that Kendra had convinced Gideon to stay with his parents.

However, there was something that they did not tell him. Therefore, he pressured them to spill the remainder of the story. They said that they gave Gideon money that was his trust fund. This was to help him in the event something had happened to them. He left them and headed back to his ship. Just as he was about to leave, he noticed that they carried very familiar communication devices. He remained in a nearby spot and waited for them. To his surprise, an image of Ray materialized from thin air. Gideon's parents were paid to lure Ranthor into this planet so that Ray could get his hands on the jewels.

Ranthor's first instinct was to kill both of them right there and then. However, he did not want Gideon to lose his parents, so he decided to confront them and utilize this knowledge for himself.

He went back for them and told them that he had heard the entire conversation that went on between them and Ray. They told him that Ray had told them to lure him in, otherwise he was going to kill Gideon. He understood that they were threatened to do what they did. He had a brilliant idea; it involved using them to lure Ray onto planet Odelphius. This would enable him to take the jewel before he went over to Planet Centra. It was the perfect plan. He reassured that he would not allow Ray to take Gideon. He was now safe in the hands of Kendra who could easily protect him from Ray and his tricks. Gideon's parents were happy that Ranthor had protected their son and would continue to protect him for as long as they lived. They sent over a communication to Ray that they had captured Ranthor. Ray prepared his ship to reach Odelphius within two days' time. He would make sure that Ranthor was taken care of this time. He would then handsomely reward the couple for their troubles.

Ranthor was hiding in the ship, he had managed to return by now and let Kendra and Gideon on in the good news. Gideon was beside himself with happiness, knowing that his parents were safe and sound. All he had to do was hide with Ranthor and Kendra until Ray's ship arrived. Gideon's parents followed Ranthor into the ship. They had their cuffs ready to present to Ray. They apologized profusely to them for their meddling. Ranthor reassured them that they had actually helped locate the jewel that he was desperately looking for. He gestured for them to follow him into the main cockpit. He was now training them for the moment when Ray's ship was going to land. All they had to do was hand over Ranthor to him. He would take over the rest when he was safely stowed in the ship. The cuffs that were on his hands would be loosely tied, and as soon as he entered, he would remove them and cuff Ray.

Kendra was not happy about involving Gideon's parents in this plan, but they were very keen to help them. Ranthor had done so much by reuniting them with their son. It was the least they could do to help him, and they were glad to do so. Gideon was resting quietly in the cockpit; he knew that his parents would be kept safe and sound. However, as a safety measure, he made sure to give them weapons to fend for themselves should things go south. He would lurk behind to protect them as well. He admired his parents for the noble act that they were about to commit. He was surprised that they were not getting cold feet. Ranthor was getting worried that the mission would fail. Would Ray fall into such a trap? He figured that he was desperate after all. Ray was still stuck somewhere in the middle of space. This was going to be the closest thing to an adventure for him and he did not mind being tricked in the process.

The sun was setting on the Odelphian sky and the ship's cloaking device was promptly turned on. Kendra returned from one of the nearby shops with supplies to make dinner. Gideon's mother helped her with cooking the meal. Ranthor was talking to Gideon and getting to know what he was planning to do after the adventure was over. He was happy that he was finally enjoying time with his parents. Unlike his, they did not have a lot of expectations from him. Some part of him envied Gideon and wished that he was in his place. Gideon was lucky to have them as parents, Ranthor thought to himself.

The ship's cloaking device started to dysfunction; there was nothing that that protected them now from the wilderness. Kendra was not worried at all, especially that they were on a planet as safe as Odelphius. There was nothing here that could attack them, save for a few overzealous politicians. This was the only predatorial species in this part of the planet, the mightiest of beasts.

Ranthor was guarding the perimeter of the ship and making sure that nothing was surrounding them. He retired to the inside of the ship and was waiting for the familiar resonation of the jewels that would indicate that Ray had arrived.

An elite task force was being assembled as they were speaking by both the king and Ray to kill Ranthor. They were not going to leave this to chance again. Ray had grown tired of the mess that Ranthor had created every step of the way. He had to give it to him that he was a tough adversary to contend with. He would have to pry the jewels off his cold, dead hands. Ranthor was also preparing to meet his adversaries; he was not afraid of any competition. He had fought different types of foes throughout his travels, and this was not going to be any different. The only difference was that Ray was not going to back down this time. It was a fight to the death; either one of them would emerge victorious or both would be left to meet their creator.

Kendra heard the news about Ray forming a super army to fight them off. She didn't know if they would survive the onslaught this time. The tide of battle was not in their favor. The odds were never in their favor in any of the battles they were involved in, but they still managed to emerge victorious almost every time. She didn't doubt Ranthor for even a second. Kendra would go to the ends of the universe for her love. However, that was not necessary at this point because the fight was coming to them. An armada from across the galaxy was making its way to them and preparing for Armageddon.

Ray was looking over his window, anxious to meet Ranthor for a final battle for the jewels of darkness. Not only was he going to emerge victorious, but he also had the support of the Xenorans to unlock the secrets of the jewels. He would in turn offer them his allegiance and ensure that they could come back to their home. He had promised to reunite all the Xenoran clans together and ensure that they would continue to live forever.

Xenora Centra was the crown jewel of the Xenoran civilization. It was the home of most the Xenorans that managed to survive the murders and kidnappings that occurred on their planet. The remainder were planning to reunite with their long-lost relatives on the mother planet. However, they needed to be provided safety to help with their crossing. The fleet that Ray commanded would make sure to make this a reality. The ancients rejoiced at finally being able to go home. The world around them was backwards and abhorred all sorts of technology. It killed them to live in this backwards civilization, unable to utilize the tools that were at their disposal. Nothing had prevented them before from leaving. But now they were sought after by every corrupt ruler in the galaxy to build their civilization. It was rumored that they could create more jewels, but they had access to that kind of technology only back home. It was one of the main reasons Ray had agreed to help them. With their help, his immortality would be ensured.

Ray was also coming to another attraction that was going to happen in Odelphius. The tournament of power was going to start soon enough. Warriors from all over the galaxy were going to attend. He would be able to recruit more soldiers to his cause. Ranthor would sure be interested to enlist his name as well. It would be good to be involved in battle again. The first thing that he was going to do was introduce the concept to him. The winner of the tournament of power would be the new master of the jewels and would control the armies of Nebula. The loser would have to suffer an untimely death at the hands of the winner. It was an offer that Ray knew his previous master would never miss. This was a rare opportunity for Ranthor to regain his honor amongst the people of Nebula. Ray was also interested in asking Kendra for her hand in marriage. Ever since he had set eyes on her, he envied Ranthor the love that he received from her. He might even spare him if she wanted to.

Chapter 16
The Tournament of Power

The tournament of power was one of the most respected tournaments in the entire planet. It was the second-most visited attraction after the festival of summer. Fighters from all across the universe came to fight in the tournament. The numbers had doubled now knowing that the jewel of darkness was the final prize. Even the pirates came to attend the tournament to support their clansmen fighting in the tournament. A few fighters from Alvinus came to fight. The giants from the arena master's collection were also brought as permanent fixtures for the events. The Odelphians were not sure if the giants were a necessary addition to the tournament. For many centuries, the tournament was the creation spot for many fighters wishing to be enlisted in the army of Nebula. However, no one was interested in joining that failed army, especially with its current leadership. Ray was worried that his soldiers were not up for the fight. This was why he had hired a few mercenaries to compete in the tournament.

It was rumored that the king was also coming to attend the event. He would select the winner to be part of his royal court. The title that Ranthor once held was still vacant and the king wished to fill it. He would need a foreign dignitary with military experience to be his right hand. Ranthor was not going to join even if he had one. The only way he was going to return to Nebula was going to be on his deathbed. The only thing he cared about was battling Ray. He knew that as soon as he won, the way to the jewels would be easier. It wasn't far from now before Ranthor possessed all the jewels. Planet Centra would open up to him and usher him into their golden arches. He would walk down there as king of the Xenorans. Perhaps this would finally win their trust and he would be crowned as their ruler.

The last adventure across the meadow made Ranthor think about the possible location that he would rest in. He happened to enjoy the technology that the Xenorans possessed and would make it his mission to live amongst them.

However, they would need to trust him first. He knew that he was not one of their favorites, but Kendra sure was. It was one of the main reasons that the villagers led them to the map. She might just be the key for them to live amongst the technological advances on Planet Centra. This way, they would be shielded from all wars and tyranny, far away from all the prying eyes. The villagers would be granted protection from any enemy that dared come across them. For the time being, Ranthor had to do one thing only, and that was to recruit fighters to match the legendary fleet that Ray possessed.

The first battle of the tournament of power began with two Odelphian fighters making their way across the arena. Ranthor was looking at them from across the arena and witnessing the fight. He was not much impressed with the fighting skills that they displayed, but he noticed that they were very agile. He would recruit the winner to be part of his team if they agreed. Ranthor's reputation preceded him amongst the fighters. A few of them offered their services for a price, but he assured them that he would pick the recruit by the end of the second round. He was now scouting for other fighters for his team. He was looking at the next fight to see if they would fare better.

The second fight managed to stir a lot of attention. One of the king's concubines participated in the fight against an Alvinian witch. Both had almost left the stage burning and almost killed half the audience. None of the other participants anticipated the fight to be this exciting. Ranthor thought of recruiting both of them on the spot. However, they both refused the invitation claiming that they were looking to be recruited with Ray's fleet and be part of a better, elite force to rule the galaxy.

Ranthor approached the Alvinian witch gingerly and tried to communicate with her. She was not quite keen on talking to him either. The witch had already heard of Ray's fleet and wished to join him. Ranthor tried to persuade her to listen to him, but the only thing that he managed to catch was the hem of her robe. He did not fare well with her opponent either. The other woman was not interested in talking to him, but she gestured to one of the other teams. She told him that he might be able to pitch to them. As for her, she was going to train for the next tournament of power. She knew that she wanted to join Ray in his quest for the jewels. Joining the army of Nebula would be an honor for her, especially since her father used to be a soldier prior to being claimed as a victim of the war.

The tournament of power was moving forward, and the contestants were piling to meet Ray at his ship. The winner of each of the competitions presented him or herself for inspection. Ranthor was watching from the stand at the crowds greeting Ray. The Nebula soldiers were respected all across the galaxy. At least, they were before the king managed to desecrate the tradition of hiring strong recruits. It was Ranthor's duty to select the best of the best. The king was not a military person and his expertise extended to the diplomatic relationships that were forged between his nation and the surrounding ones.

The final quarter of the tournament of power was coming up. The soldiers were preparing themselves on the stage for the next stage of the battle. The witch was moving to the next quarter. She was going to be the first contest, and she was paired with the warrior of Doom clan. It was unfair that she had to fight the clan alone, but she insisted that she would do it. Ranthor liked the spirit of that woman. It was a pity that she wanted to join a pitiful team such as Ray's. Ray was guaranteed his seat at the semi-final as was Ranthor. They were going to duel the winner of the quarter. The winner would then move on to the final fight to win the jewel. Ray joined merely because he was planning to win the other jewels from Ranthor. Despite the odds that were against his favor, Ranthor was going to make sure that the jewel was going to end up in his possession. Kendra was also wishing for that victory.

Nothing was going to make both of them happy than the sight of Ray losing the fight. They did not even care that they were the winners. However, losing the jewels to these strangers would cause a powerful shift in the tide of power. None of these soldiers knew what the jewels possessed. They were an object of magnificent power and glory. The witch and the warrior clan had a great potential for destruction. With the jewel in their hands, there was not going to be anything to stop them. Ranthor was going to make sure that he did everything in his power to make them lose. This was going to be easy, considering that the giants were going to be in the next match. The giants were going to kill both of the contestants, especially after what the arena master had done to them. Ranthor was also worried to enter the arena with them. He no longer had their support, and it was very likely that they would come to kill him.

The witch managed to torch the entire arena. There was no sign of the clan of warriors anywhere, and no one knew if they were alive or dead. Scouts were sent into the arena to see if they could be found. One of them found their bones near the giants' lair. At least the fire did not kill them, although it would have been a more merciful fate. The giants avoided the witch after the pyrotechnic show. They tried to reach for her in the beginning, but she managed to torch their lair and send snakes their way to attack them. However, she then realized that they might be a valuable asset for the next fight in the quarter. The witch made a pact with them and offered to save them in exchange for their allegiance. The giants would guarantee her a win in the tournament.

The next match had now started, and the other clans were fighting each other for a shot at the title. The witch was in the booth for the contestants that were moved to the semi-finals. Ray walked over to her to enjoy a talk with her. He tried to convince her of his mission to acquire the jewels. She seemed fond of the clan that Ray commandeered. The witch was Simeoni's sister and her biggest supporter. This was one of the reasons she disliked Ranthor. He was the reason that her sister was no longer with her. She joined the tournament to avenge her and bring honor to her family once again. Simeoni was the one that encouraged her to pursue her skills in witchcraft. This earned her a job with the king and a seat at the table. Ray was fond of her story and decided that he would recruit her no matter what the outcome of the fight was.

The clans that were fighting managed to rally a few people to their cause. One of them managed to kill one of the giants. The two teams were cooperating to kill the giants, and, hence, even the playing field. The tournament master witnessed this and decided to add a few more beasts to the fight. He was going to protect his main source of entertainment at any costs. There were no more giants in these parts anymore. He was not going to let some backward clan take care of them. Both of the teams were going to be disqualified. The beasts entered the arena and started devouring the contestants one by one. This was a message sent by the tournament master to anyone that thought about sabotaging his arena. He was not going to stand for any act of mutiny no matter how small it was. The previous match struck fear in the contestants' hearts and there were no more antics from then onwards. The next match went on smoothly without any interruptions. The clan won the title and moved on to the next match of the quarter.

The arena was closed temporarily for repairs and cleaning, something that the tournament master apologized profusely for. Ranthor used the opportunity to grab lunch with Kendra and discuss their strategy for the final match. It was only a matter of time before he would be on stage with Ray and that strange witch. He did not know which one of them he had regrets about fighting. At least Ray would deliver the jewels upon defeat. The witch was a useless distraction that was there on a vendetta quest. Little did she know that her sister was the one that intercepted their mission and almost killed them. Ranthor was going to make sure that both of them were dead. He did not need them interfering in the next part of the mission. However, he knew that with his luck, they definitely would manage to resurface and try to ruin his plans. The last jewel on Planet Centra was under lock and key as they were speaking. *It would only be fitting that the ghost of Ray would haunt me even there*, he thought to himself.

The quarter was resumed now, and the last match was underway. The last clan of warriors made their way to the arena to meet their opponents. The other soldier was the one Ranthor defeated in the arena in Alvinus. It was a surprise that he had managed to survive. The last that was known was that his body was splattered in one of the nearby craters. However, it seems that he had made it in one piece and was after Ranthor. It was interesting how one man had so many enemies in a lifetime. Ranthor was staring death in the eye with every fight. It seemed that everyone in the arena wanted to kill him; the remainder wanted to hand him over to Ray so that they may earn his favor. Ray was looking over the match with such an intensity that could only be described as religious. He wanted to make sure to recruit the soldier to his cause. After all, he was in the Nebula army and would want retribution against the king for cutting his wages. The king's days were numbered; it was only a matter of time before a new ruler was crowned as the king, thought Ray to himself.

The semi-finals had finally started with the fight between the two deadly clans. The witch was going to be the next contender. It was not much before she joined Ray's crew. After all, she was already guaranteed a seat at the table. The remainder of the tournament did not matter much to her because she was already guaranteed her win. The clan warriors were fighting for the second spot to rule beside Ray. The winner of this battle was going to move on the next battle with the witch. Both of them were afraid of her. She was known to poison and maim her victims. They were not going to be an exception to the rule. There was nothing that would stop the reign of Ray, not even the witch and neither were the clansmen that were searching intently for the jewels of darkness. The ancient people of Xenora were also enrolled in the competition. Their match would be the one following the clan's and the witch. They had somehow managed to secure a spot in the semi-final.

The witch was now enjoying a meal with a view on the top of the balcony. There were soldiers fighting amongst each other for the title. Ray was looking over his shoulder and observing Kendra's movements. Kendra was nervously looking over her shoulder for any signs of the competition. Ray came over from his quarter to talk to her. She did not anticipate him coming and saw this as a bad omen. However, she decided to listen to him and get to know his story. She realized that Ranthor and him were not always mortal enemies. Perhaps there was something that she could do to broker a truce between them. Little did she know that Ray was counting on her to try this approach. Ray was extremely well-equipped to fight Ranthor. The only thing that prevented him now from killing him was Kendra. He wanted to make sure that she believed in his intentions, no matter how nefarious they actually were.

Ranthor went to his ship to plan on leaving to Planet Centra. He did not want to continue with watching the fight. The tournament master would make sure to send someone to let him know when his battle would start. For the meantime, he would enjoy the view of the planet from the safety of his ship. He did not want to see any other clan member begging and pleading Ray to add him or her to his crew. Ray was attracting a lot of notoriety with his new order. The ports of Nebula were going to be filled with a different army than the one that currently inhabited it. This was going to be the end of an era for the king and his current entourage. Little did he know that one of his disciples was plotting against him, and most importantly against his own son. Ray knew that if Ranthor did not kill him then the king sure would. His mission only involved the collection and handing over of the jewels to the king. He was not, under any circumstances, to act as an intermediary and take the jewels for himself.

The king was now almost close to reaching Odelphius for the next part of the match. His seat was already prepared for the upcoming match. Ray was in for a surprise to know that the king was close to arriving. Ranthor recognized the king and his fleet from a distance. He knew that things would soon be over for Ray. However, it was somewhat worrying to see that his father had made this journey. It was going to making things especially difficult for him. The king was amongst the strongest warriors in the galaxy. The only reason he was not able to contend was due to an injury he had sustained twenty years ago. The king was given the title after a victory against the giants that plagued his country. The previous ruler was recruited as one of his generals. However, the current king threw a coup and killed his predecessor. He ruled the planet from that time onwards despite the disdain from his citizens. He managed to rule the kingdom with an iron grip and avoided multiple assassination attempts. Many skilled warriors tried to murder him over the years.

Ray was now looking at the conclusion of the third fight in the saga; the warriors in the fight both succumbed to a deadly nerve gas that was sprayed in the arena. The tournament was becoming more and more heated with every passing moment. The crowds had now doubled, and the atmosphere was suffocating. The tournament master was viewing the matches in his booth with the capital's elite. Ranthor and Kendra were both invited to the booth, but they kindly refused the invitation. Ray, on the other hand, accepted it gladly and went on to meet with the foreign politicians and forge new relationships with them. It was a bold move for Planet Nebula to have any intergalactic relationships with many of the states here, especially considering that they were still at war with some of them. Ray, however, reassured the ambassadors that with his election as sovereign the war would end. His reign would finally bring peace and stability to the region. Half of them were sold and a powerful allegiance was made between them.

The next fight involving the clan of fire and brimstone and the Xenoran ancient tribe began on stage. The Xenorans displayed great strength, creating a mudslide that swept the arena and all its inhabitants. However, the clan re-emerged from the mudslide and were making their way towards the Xenorans who seemed to have fled the arena. They soon found them and decimated half of them. The other half managed to protect themselves in a nearby tree. They were now holed in and stalling so that they may heal their wounds. The Xenorans were trying to find ways to escape the arena unscathed. Clearly, none of them were born to be warriors and they should be content with being the gifted inventors that they were. The tournament master accepted their plea to surrender and banished them out of the arena. The clan of fire and brimstone had won by exclusion and were now up against the witch. The witch did not even flinch after the announcement of her competition; victory was already assured for her. All she had to do now was continue with the match for the sake of appearances. It would serve her new master well knowing that she was as strong as she was clever.

The hounds of hell were also released into the arena to provide a source of entertainment. However, the witch managed to torch the place and kill every last bloodhound that roamed the place. The clan was the only remaining living thing that stood in the way of her plans. It was only a matter of time before she killed them too. Ranthor was going to come next, and then she would have avenged Simeoni. After that, Ray's head would come down rolling and she would rule the galaxy with the jewels. Despite leaving to Nebula not being ideal, she agreed to it so that she would gain the trust of her new employer. Prior to the tournament business was slow and this had been the only job she had occupied over the course of a year. She did not even mind that she was fighting on the wrong side of history; all that mattered was the flow of cold, hard cash into her pockets. The Nebula army was still one of the most powerful armies of the galaxy, there was no doubting that. It was the leadership of the army that was her main concern.

The match ended after the witch managed to cut a hole in the hearts of the clansmen. The tournament master came down personally from his booth to congratulate her for the victory. A celebratory dinner was going to be held in her honor today at his manor. He made sure that all the remaining participants were invited to the event. The remainder of the fights would resume after the dinner. It was rumored that this was where the tournament master crowned the next fighter that was going to join the arena. The best strategy always involved bribing the incoming warrior with food that he or she could not resist. This strategy was used by many before him for centuries.

The halls of the tournament master's manor were decked lavishly with gold from all across the galaxy. Various artefacts were laid out across the halls and knights in adamantine armor were protecting the halls. There was even an induction hall in the middle of the main chamber where the winners of all the previous tournaments used to be crowned. The tournament master himself was once a competitor in this arena. He moved on to this post to fulfil the wish of his father, the previous tournament master to keep the tradition alive. The Odelphian king wanted to shut down the arena had it not brought a significant inflow of cash into the capital. For the time being, he was content that it was reduced to an underground activity. Long gone were the days when the fighters were paraded across the town and the gate to the city was handed over to them.

The new regime ensured that the activity of fighting and tournaments would soon be banned forever. There was no place in the current leadership for such activities which were thought to besmirch the honor of the king. The people of the town were furious with the closing of the main arena and having to go underground. Rumor has it was that there was a coup staged against the king. The new king was very soft compared to his predecessors and they did not like it one bit. They also thought that he was one of the pawns of the Nebula king. He was always on Planet Nebula, desperately trying to climb on top of the king's robes. For all they cared, it was better off with his head on a pike. The king was warned several times by his advisors of the dangerous slope that he was walking on, but he refused to listen to them and instead continued in the same way. The Odelphians were fed up and time for a new leadership was on the horizon. It was only going to be a few days before the next king was going to walk the halls of the palace.

The tournament master welcomed Ranthor and Ray into his manor; he had just managed to convince Ranthor and Kendra to attend. Kendra was not keen to come but she did so to support Ranthor's mission. The tournament master was happy with the progress that they had made, bringing glory back to the arena. The spirit of the fight was very important for him, not only as a source of income, but as a way of life. He recounted the story of when his great grandfather opened the first arena in Odelphius around two hundred years ago. Ever since then, his family was in the business of creating the entertainment that was the arena. People travelled from far and wide across the universe to see the fights. The fights were not as dangerous as they were in this tournament, but they still provided happiness and entertainment, nonetheless. The kings of the planet had always attended the event to give their blessing. No king had ever tried to stop the tournament ever since it was started. This was a strange attitude that was started by the current ruler of the planet. One that was surely not going to be tolerated by the citizens any longer. The king was now holed up in his castle, waiting for the event to end.

The guests of the manor were now led down a hall filled with every dish imaginable. Ranthor was extremely hungry and wanted to devour everything that was on his plate. Kendra, on the other hand, was very suspicious of the gesture that was offered by the tournament master. She kept inspecting the plates for any signs of poison. There was nothing amiss so far and so she decided to enjoy the evening. She ate her meal in silence with Ranthor and enjoyed the little break that was granted to them. The best part was Ray was also delayed, so there was nothing to be worried about. Finding Planet Centra would have to be delayed for a day so that they may enjoy the festivities. Desserts were being served and all kinds of chocolate eclairs. It was a rare opportunity to witness a meeting between so many world leaders. The place was teeming with corruption that it was difficult to discern truth from the many lies that were circulating around.

The tournament master moved on from their table to one that had involved a group of politicians from the Stardust system. They were now money that was going to invest in some of his arenas outside of Odelphius. They were actually the main reason that was feast was arranged. He needed to have it under the pretense of the championship to avoid any suspicions of expanding his business. Grapevine moved much faster than actual news in this part of the planet. Nothing went past the king's notice. People would have been grateful that he would extend the same courtesy to listening to the problems that his citizens had voiced over to him instead of engaging in all this nonsense. However, little could be done about the king's whims, and it was best to avoid any sort of conversation with him as it led to a sterile argument.

The citizens of the Stardust empire were anxiously inspecting the manor for any evidence of good performing soldiers. They were also interested in enlisting the help of both Ranthor and Ray to their cause. Ray had assured them that his army would do the best protect them and that they were the best army that coin could buy. The investors were impressed by his offer and at the lack of a counteroffer made by Ranthor. He was completely oblivious to their presence and their influence across the galaxy. The money that he would have gotten from them would have sufficed for him to live securely for a century. However, he was done with the bounty hunter life for good and had long ago retired that hat. The only thing he cared about was to enjoy a peaceful existence with Kendra when all this was over. This was not going to happen with the investors because they required someone to work with them for the next twenty odd years or so.

The investors were now making their way back to the tournament master. All of them were interested about knowing how he managed to acquire the giants that were in the first part of the show. He told them that was a trade secret, one that he would not be able to part with no matter the sum of money that was involved. The investors were not happy to hear this, but they respected and valued his professional integrity. He would make sure to protect all of their endeavors with the same zeal that he had protected theirs. They talked things over amongst themselves and reached the conclusion that they agreed to the deal that the tournament master was offering. The remainder of the evening went on smoothly and an assortment of wines was brought over for the champions to enjoy. Ranthor was still in his booth with Kendra, enjoying a quiet conversation. He told her about the offer that the Stardust empire had offered him and that he refused it to stay with her. She did not seem that impressed; something that he found odd. He just promised her that he would let go of any prospect of profit for her love and she turned him down.

The tournament master came over to Ranthor and discussed with him the offer again. He wanted to know that if he was still interested, the offer was still standing. Ranthor reassured him that he was not interested in it. It would take a lot more convincing for him to engage in these types of activities for any sum of money. Despite the gravity of the consequences, he decided to stick with his decision and opt for a life of peace. Nothing was going to sway him from his goal, not even Kendra. He realized that these things don't last, and it was for the best.

Ranthor had an empire to command and an army to build from scratch. There was nothing that was going to stand in the way of his mission, not even Kendra. He had decided to give an ultimatum by the end of the evening, she was free to pursue her own path from now onwards. Her reward would be granted to her, and they could both part ways. However, he knew that this conversation was not going to end well for both of them. This was going to be the last time he saw her, and he did not want to remember it this way. Kendra was shocked at the way that he spoke to her, and she refused to come out of her room and listen to his explanation.

The evening had ended, and everyone was bidding the other goodbye. Kendra returned to the quarters provided by the tournament master, refusing to stay in the ship with Ranthor. He realized that this did not bode well for him. He did not know how he had managed to utter those words from his mouth. The only reason he did was to protect her from a life that was filled with adversity and danger. He would hardly be around most of the day and she would be reduced to another king's trophy wife. He knew that the life that she was about to embark on with him was eventually going to get her killed. Therefore, he risked everything to burn the bridges that had united them over the past couple of months. Little did he know that she was willing to live whatever life he desired of her, if that meant they were going to be united for all of eternity.

The journey back to the ship was quite a lonely one; one that Ranthor had not quite anticipated at all. He thought that things would be easily patched up after he was given a chance to talk to Kendra and explain the reason for the way he was behaving. He couldn't sleep on the account that he was riddled with guilt and ambiguity. He no longer cared for the jewels and would rather part with them than lose her. It was not the right time to speak to her. The maidens that guarded her room told him that she did not wish to speak to any visitor. He was turned away at the door; that was his cue to leave. Ranthor was going to try and speak with her next morning. Hopefully, things would have improved by then and he would get to make his case. Kendra could hear the click that his boot made as it contacted the floor. For a moment there she thought long and hard about forgiving him. However, she then decided to stand her ground and wait for a formal apology.

The arena was already prepared for the next match, the final rounds of the tournament of power. The witch was granted the honor of being the first contestant. Her opponent was none other than Ranthor, who was dreading the fight ever since the names were announced. He had hoped that Ray would fight and subsequently kill her. However, that did not seem like it was going to happen anytime soon. Ranthor did not want to fight the witch at any cost. It was not that he was afraid to kill her, but rather because he did not want to have another murder on his hands. This troubled and misguided soul had come for the pure purpose of exacting her vengeance. Little did she know that it was someone other than him that led to this vendetta in the first place. He was merely a pawn used to drive this woman and her clan to joining the Nebula soldiers' cause. They had resorted to worse means than this before.

The witch gestured to Ranthor that she would slit his throat. He was not intimidated by the gesture and instead welcomed it as an opportunity to rid himself of this nuisance once and for all. He already knew all her tactics and planned the perfect ambush for her. Unlike him, she did not have the element of surprise on her side and instead relied on sheer brute force and luck to win. Nonetheless, the witch was unfazed about heading into battle. She extracted a banner from her pouch and planted it firmly on the arena floor. She was marking the ground indicating that she had already foreseen the victory; *a bold move*, thought Ranthor to himself. He had grown fond of this lady and respected her mightily. It was a shame that he had to kill her at the end of the competition. He knew that if he didn't, she would be gunning for him without thinking twice. She was blinded by anger and frustration to the point where she was no longer salvageable. The king had gone to a new extent to ensure that Ranthor would not lay his hands on his kingdom. It didn't matter who died in the process. Nothing seemed to matter to the vicious ruler anymore, the only thing that did matter to him was to ascertain his power and influence on the citizens.

There was no ruler that was as power hungry or destructive as he was. All of them feared him or wanted to be him. The king maintained an iron grip for several years over his kingdom without as much as a whisper of opposition. He did not anticipate that all hell would break loose with the departure of his son. The entire army had pledged allegiance to his son and the kingdom, he did not realize that to them this was mutually exclusive. The king had to make sure that Ranthor returned alive or else he would lose all of his credibility. The ruler was now at the brink of a civil war and civil disobedience by the same man he sent on the mission to gather his most prized possession. This was the main reason that he had attended the event in the first place.

The king of Nebula was looking at the fight from his own cubicle. He was cheering on for both of the champions. Ranthor caught the sight of his father and soon felt that his insides had become as hard as ice. He loathed the man with every fiber of his being; he knew that his presence here could only mean one thing; the man was here to ensure that the mission was completed at all costs. Ranthor knew that he might try to recruit him once again. There was a reason he did not kill him before. He must still need him for something; that much was apparent to him. Perhaps he could use that to his advantage, thought Ranthor. However, he did not want to be involved with his father. It was bad enough that he had to leave his home and coming back meant that he would have to revisit all those memories again. All he had to do now was focus on the match and make sure that he would not be killed at the hands of the witch.

He did not anticipate the fight to last as long as it had. The witch was very adept at hiding in multiple places and flushing him out. There was virtually no place that he could hide from her and the deadly fire that she was spewing. Ranthor attacked her with his silver sword, but it did not even scratch her. She was immune to most forms of magic and mortal attacks. Ranthor did not know what could possibly wound her. He tried blasting her with his ion beam but that did not do anything. The witch managed to dodge every oncoming bullet that was directed her way. On the other hand, he was about to lose the battle. He was very worn out from being chased all across the arena. It was a miracle that the witch had not finished him off yet. However, he tried one last tactic. He aimed the time rift at the witch and managed to hit her. She fell onto the ground, collapsing with agony. The time rift was the key to kill her after all. The power that was emitted from it managed to effectively blind her for the better part of half an hour. However, the witch cast a protective spell around herself just in time to avoid another attack. This would at least give Ranthor some time to recover from his wounds and get back to the battle. The witch was tending to her wounds as well; wounds that were minimal and could barely be seen.

The time rift required recharging with every attack. Ranthor realized that the witch was actively trying to make him recharge the device and hence lose his competitive advantage against her. He had to give it to her; the woman was clever and would have served as a valuable addition to his task force. Ranthor would try to convince her again to join him and fight for the jewels. He would offer her whatever she wanted in exchange for her services. The first thing that he needed to explain to her was that her sister was sent as a spy to sabotage his mission. He did not attack her blindly and instead offered to spare her. Whatever subsequently happened was not orchestrated by him and he did not have anything to do with her from that moment onwards. He hoped that she would believe him. The witch decided to slow down and listen to whatever he had to say. She promised herself that she would at least listen and do nothing else. Ranthor accepted this strange turn of events and told her about the entire story.

He had learned from this woman that it was never her intention to become a witch and that this was only driven by this vendetta. He promised to do everything that was in his power to avenge her sister. After listening to the story to completion, she decided that she would willingly join his cause. However, they had to maintain appearances and keep the fight going on for a while longer. The tournament master would otherwise suspect that a pact had been formed between the two contestants and abolish the tournament altogether. Ray was looking at them from across the stands and was wondering as to why the fight had suddenly halted. Kendra was also tracking them with her eyes and noticed the standstill moment. Luckily, the others did not catch a sight of that, and the fight resumed normally. They both agreed that Ranthor would win, and he would move on to the next fight with Ray.

In the meantime, Ray was nursing the box that housed the jewels. He noticed that the king had entered his chamber unannounced. He was soon staring at the barrel of the king's gun and an equally angry stare. The king explained slowly to him that if he tried to ruin the match in any way that he was going to kill him and his entire family. Ray decided that he would gather the jewels for the king and let go of the dream to rule. He was, however, going to duel the king for the jewels as soon as they got back home. Ray managed to send a distress signal to his family to evacuate the planet. He would not execute the second phase of his plan before making sure that they were safe and sound. He did not want to compromise their safety at any cost and would soon abandon the mission than get them killed in the process. But he also wanted to make sure that his child would live in a world free of this kind of oppression. He was happy to know that both of his parents received the message and were on their way on a rebellion encampment that was far away from Planet Nebula. They were now virtually untraceable, and the king had no way of reaching them.

Ray had just received a message from his parents telling him that they had arrived safely at the checkpoint. He waited patiently for the fight between Ranthor and the witch to conclude. Unsurprisingly, Ranthor had emerged victorious from battle and the witch was spared. She made her way back into the stands and continued watching the fight. Ranthor managed to sneak in and tell Kendra the entire plan. She was not completely comfortable with trusting this stranger, but then again, she did not have a choice in the matter. The only thing she could do was protest the fact that she had almost killed them. However, she knew that Ranthor had much worse enemies that had become allies. Therefore, the history of this lady did not bother him one bit. Instead, he welcomed the opportunity to train someone of her caliber.

The witch turned out to be a great alley. She managed to stalk Ray's ship and figure out the location of the jewel. She knew the combination of the safe and where Ray hid the plans for the map. She would serve them well not only in locating it, but also in fighting off whatever monstrosity that was going to attack them back in Centra. Despite knowing that the mission was riddled with danger, nothing was going to stop her from heading out with them. Kendra tried to scare her with the best tools she had but nothing was working. Simeoni was too dear for her sister, and she would do anything in her power to destroy the people that had robbed her prematurely, even if that meant siding with them.

They learned that the witch's name was Cassandra and that she used to know the previous king of Nebula. She had sympathized with them and the cause that they were fighting. Ranthor recollected all his childhood memories and the quest so far. He also told her about the time that they met with Simeoni. Little did they know that a trap was set for them by her king. Their sole focus was to find the jewels of darkness and use the time rift to reach planet Xenora Centra. He also told her about his many battles with Ray, and that he used to be his mentor. Cassandra could not believe the chain of events that had surrounded Ranthor's life lately; she leaned in to try to comfort him, but her hand was slapped violently by Kendra. She did not tolerate Cassandra in the first place, and this was not going to make a lasting first impression on her. The tension between the two women was palpable that you could cut it with a knife.

Cassandra was going to dine with them today and prepare to leave to her home planet tomorrow. She had already given them what they required and there was nothing else that they needed her help with. Kendra was glad that she was not going to overstay her welcome after all. She did not like Cassandra one bit and wanted her gone from the minute she laid eyes on her. However, she had to hand it to her; she actually helped them a lot. With the information that she provided; the jewel of darkness that was in Ray's possession would soon be transferred to them. Ranthor was more of a match for Ray. It was only a matter of time before this ordeal ended. Kendra would then kick back and relax in a nearby beach and forget all about wars and feuds. Ranthor promised her that things were going to get smoother from this moment onwards. The king was the only person that they had to worry about. There was no guarantee of what he was going to do after Ray was defeated. This was definitely the reason that he decided to make an appearance in the middle of the tournament.

The king was now watching from the stands for the odd chance that either of them would slip. Ranthor could almost see the glow of the jewels in his scheming head. He did not want his father to get them even it meant for him to die. The king was vicious and would prolong his rule for eternity and then the people would not be able to do anything about it. Although he did not like Nebula, he also did not want them to be ruled by a tyrant for all eternity. The king was much worse than Ray ever was going to be. The citizens had grown bored of his constant searches and murders. They also did not tolerate the gang of militia that monitored the streets. At least with the soldiers, they knew that there were protected without having to fear that they might be robbed blind. There were a few instances of mercenaries attacking homes and pillaging what was in them. The king's popularity had gone down the drain after the last incident and the worst part was that he could not care any less. The search for the jewels blinded him away from his responsibilities to the people of the capital. He did not notice that a significant number of them had emigrated to other planets.

The proud citizens of Nebula looked up to Ranthor to lead them, but they were surprised to learn that he did not intend to return. Many of them took to the stands and in the surrounding tournament stalls to convince him to come back, but it was a fruitless effort. The king was amused by the scene and continued to watch from the safety of his balcony. Ray was preparing himself for the next battle and tried to create anxiety for Ranthor. It did not do anything except increase his resolve even further. At least he was not some pawn that was controlled and manipulated by the king. Unlike Ray, he was actually going to win this competition. The tournament master signaled for the handlers to unleash the next group of vicious beasts into the arena and with that, the battle began.

The crowds roared with excitement as the gates were lowered to reveal the next group of future generation genomically enhanced beasts that money could buy. Ranthor was unfazed by the beasts and so was Ray. After battling the giants and defeating them, nothing seemed to matter to them anymore. Ranthor swung his sword at one of the beasts and managed to slit it in half. It sent the others running for their lives. Ray was lurking somewhere close by, avoiding the confrontation with Ranthor. He was hoping for the beasts to cause an injury and that would be his cue to come forward. It didn't take much time before that plan backfired. He was now forced to come face to face with Ranthor. The former was looking at him intensely and calculating every move that he was about to make. Ranthor managed to parry each and every move that Ray was sending. It didn't take a long time before Ray was out of breath. However, Ranthor decided to spare him and give him a chance to get back on his feet.

The tournament master was gesturing to Ranthor and telling him that he should kill his opponent. Ranthor had openly defied him and that sent a fit of fury that was coming from the tournament master. He decided to punish both of them by sending another wave of blood hounds. However, he soon realized that none of the beasts were going to change the outcome of the battle. Therefore, he sent a few of the seasoned fighters to fight them off. That also failed miserably, and he was soon staring at another empty arena. The audience soon started to lose interest and most of them had left the arena. Just as he was about to lose hope, the two fighters resumed their fight. The people that were about to leave returned to their seats to witness this spectacle. Ranthor was now firing his gun at Ray in an attempt at a quick kill. He realized that the battle had dragged on for long enough and it was time to end it. Ray's wounds had finally healed, and he was going at Ranthor with all the strength that he possessed. They tore the stage with their strength and soon there was no place to hide for either of them. Ranthor wielded his longsword and made his way to the center of the arena. Ray did the same thing. They both approached each other and swung their swords. Ranthor missed a violent attack from Ray's sword by mere seconds. It would have split his spine into two.

The next hit was dealt by Ranthor's sword. It managed to hit Ray squarely in the chest and sending him collapsing across the other end of the stage. Blood was spurting everywhere, and he soon became unconscious from the blood loss. Ranthor moved in and he shattered his skull with the next blow. He then emerged as the new winner of the tournament of power. The last jewel was handed to him by the tournament master. Kendra was rejoicing at the site of the second jewel of darkness. Nothing was going to stop them from reaching the third jewel in planet Xenora Centra. At first, the king thought of intervening, but then he decided that it would be best not to cause a spectacle. Instead, he would wait for the cover of darkness and then follow Ranthor and his ship to the third jewel's location. He would only attempt to take the jewels once when they were all located. For the time being, he did not want to expose himself and therefore endanger what he was desperately trying to acquire for many years. The entourage of the tournament master was invited for a small ceremony before the festivities started. The king was amongst the guests that were invited. Luckily, Ranthor was not included in the list, and, hence, would not be alerted to his presence. He would leave after the party and lurk in the shadows until Ranthor arrived.

In a way, the king was not quite fond of the turn of events, but he was still hopeful that he could somehow intervene and get the jewels. He would have to travel to Planet Centra and Ranthor was going to be the one that would show him the way, his very own north star.

Chapter 17
A Light Borne from Darkness

The next ceremony was held in the honor of the winner of the tournament of power. It was again held at the master's tournament and involved the same assortment of wonderful meals that he had grown accustomed to. Ranthor was happy that this tournament was finally over. He had not rested for even a minute over the past two days thinking about the possible outcomes. Here he was now, the winner of one of the most ancient tournaments of all time. This served as a testament to his strength and resolve. He did feel bad about killing Ray, but he was taunting him for quite a while about the jewels. He did not need to involve himself in this mess, but he did, and the outcome was miserable for him. Ranthor did not see his father after the event. It was strange that he would just disappear the way that he did. However, it was probably for the best and so he decided not to ponder further about that anomalous thought. All he had to do now was feast and enjoy the evening for as much time as he could.

He spent most of the evening talking to many foreign dignitaries who had suddenly deemed him important to have conversations with. Ranthor was about to break into a headache due to the sheer load of information that these idiots were spouting from their mouths. He wondered how most politicians handled these people and he developed a new-found respect for them. He could not stand two minutes with this corrupt bunch of misfits, let alone two hours. He truly saluted the men and women that had the courage to deal with this on a daily basis. Ranthor would rather spend another decade searching for the jewels than do this. He was a warrior and did not know anything about the delicate affairs that maintained the balance between different member states. Luckily, Kendra was there to translate for him what they meant. He would have been completely lost without her.

In truth, she would actually do well as a politician, he thought to himself. Ranthor later introduced the concept to her and to his surprise, she actually accepted the offer. Kendra was going to be his advisor for political affairs back home. He would finally be with her by his side, explaining the incredulous things that these fat oxygen-sucking slugs were telling him. Ranthor decided that he would retire to the ship and sleep. He had enjoyed his fair share of conversations to last for a lifetime. He needed as much sleep as he could get for the final part of the mission. Kendra agreed to babysit the power-hungry philanthropists and politicians in the meantime. However, she told Ranthor that he owed her for the service, and she would come collecting the favor. He happily agreed to whatever she wanted as long as he could get some peace and quiet. He then bid goodbye and was already in his cockpit bed fast asleep. Ranthor was actually snoring by the time that Kendra had arrived. She wondered how a man with such a small frame could produce such a sound.

She chuckled silently while she watched him snore. There was nothing that looked more peaceful than this at the moment. Realizing that this was going to be a significant part of her life, she smiled and accepted it. In the beginning of their travels, she had thought that he was obnoxious and self-aggrandizing. However, she realized that she was very much mistaken about him. Ranthor was her friend and was always going to look out for her. Her mind was now wondering to the time they would spend on Planet Nebula. She realized that it was very far from her home planet. She also did not know how she agreed to join a career in politics. She did not know anything about international laws or treaties. However, she knew that she definitely possessed more knowledge than Ranthor and probably most of the politicians in this room. After all, she was probably the only non-corrupt politician in existence, not yet anyway. She was honored that Ranthor trusted her for this.

Their ship was now getting ready for departure and Ranthor was already midway across the night sky. It was still evening before he managed the departure from the planet. Kendra was looking over at the disappearing surface of Odelphius which was now only nothing but a speck. The night sky always made her nostalgic; it was a while since she contacted home. She managed to contact her family back home and let them know about what had transpired in her life. Her mother and father were finally happy to hear their daughter's voice. The journey took her away from those who were dearest to her. But it also led her to new dear ones such as Ranthor. It was only a while before the last jewel was found and their power was unlocked. Ranthor would soon stare into the new face of civilization and the dawn of a new ruler. Planet Nebula was going to see a change, the likes of which was not anticipated in the time of his father. Ranthor was excited to come back to a planet more tolerant and accepting of the diversity of citizens it had and not simply craving blind obedience and authority that the king was supposed to wield.

Xenora Centra was not a popular destination for travelers, even ones that possessed time rifts. There was nothing much to be done for anyone that was not looking for the darkness jewels. The inhabitants were long gone, and the machinery was left unattended. It would be a difficult task finding the next jewel. There was no one to tell them where the protection mechanisms were and guide them through. The ancients were never ones to desert their planets, even in the time of adversity. The ones that stayed on their planets were holed in underground, but at least they did not leave their homes. Ranthor did not believe that they would just leave their planet without any further notice. It was most likely that they were chased out by someone. The thought of that scared him. It just meant that the fight was not over, and he would soon be surrounded by yet another enemy. However, he had the moment for himself for now to savor and enjoy the view. Kendra was equally worried, but she managed to hide it well so that Ranthor would not discover. This was going to be the last time they were going to face an enemy. Did it really matter how powerful or weak their enemy was? After all their ordeal, nothing mattered anymore . Their only priority was to find the last jewel.

The time rift was sitting in its regular spot, waiting to be finally used. Ranthor wondered if it would be able to take them to their destination. He didn't know how to operate the time rift, but he had Kendra to help him if he didn't know what to do. She was a clever lady and always knew what to do in the face of a crisis. It was just two more galaxies before they reached the spot where they had to activate the time rift. Ranthor was now opening the maps and schematics to figure out a plan of action. He did not know what to make of the maps now that all the jewels were found. Nothing here seemed to make sense and there was no information about Planet Centra. He figured that he would figure it out as soon as he landed. Kendra reassured him that he was going to find the jewel just like he did with the others. The mission was soon going to be over and both of them were going back home after this.

Ranthor had to make a small pit stop to refuel for one last time. He managed to land in a nearby planet and refuel his ship. That did not take much time and they were back on their feet again. Kendra was preparing tea and snacks for the final mission. Ranthor's appetite was finally restored, and he enjoyed the meal that she had prepared. The time rift started to glow and resonate now which indicated the proximity of Planet Centra. It was going to be a few hours before their final journey had concluded. The rift's energy was starting to upset the ship and Ranthor had to silence it.

The ship was now halfway across the solar system, and it was only a matter of hours before they reached their destination. Planet Centra would not be difficult to find now that they had the rift. The only thing complicating the mission was the ship; they did not know if it would withstand the travel there, and most importantly, if they would arrive in one piece. Kendra did not want to know the alternative outcome if things failed. The last thing she wanted to imagine was being split in multiple realities and trying to gather the pieces. Part of her wanted to back down and call it a day, but then she looked at her friend and decided to continue. After all, she was not going to miss the adventure of a lifetime for nothing. Kendra was hoping to find other valuable gems on Planet Centra and use that to her advantage. Perhaps she would set up shop somewhere near Planet Nebula and offer her services as private security for the rich and famous. However, a career in politics was more tempting and rewarding for her.

Ranthor extracted the time rift from the pouch that was holding it. They were now finally at the spot which indicated the location of Planet Centra. He activated the time rift and entered the sequence required for it to operate safely. The all-too-familiar green light was activated, and they soon found themselves in another dimension. The ship swayed violently from side to side and parts of it were coming off. Kendra feared that their death would be during the crossing. Luckily, the ship managed to cross intact with no major damages sustained. Both of them were now staring at the other end of the universe. Planet Centra was in the middle of their view along with other planets in the system. The ship was now making its way to the last location of the jewels. Ranthor was glad that this was going as planned and so was Kendra. The remaining jewels were safely stowed away in their compartments and the maps were laid out to help them find a clue. They did not even guarantee that they would have easy access to the jewels. The planet was surrounded by a strong energy force field. This was added as an additional measure to prevent trespass.

The ship was now just above Planet Centra and prepared to make its descent. Kendra was looking at the place from her window and taking in the view. The planet was actually beautiful and had a lot of vibrant plant and animal life. Ranthor did not care for that and instead wanted the task done as quickly as possible. There was a problem with accessing the planet's surface; the energy beam barrier was not allowing them access. They had to somehow maneuver around it, but there was nothing in their immediate surroundings that could help. Therefore, they decided to visit one of the planets in the vicinity and search for someone or something that could help them cross the protective beam. The planet in their close proximity was one of the manufacturing giants, Zeldra 8. The planet was the site that created most of the vehicles that were used. This included ships and land transports. There were many mechanics that could help them fix their protective beam problem, for a small fee, of course.

The shops on Planet Zeldra were teeming with all sorts of parasitic life forms hoping to conquer the galaxy. There was a mechanic that was fixing every failed dream that was possible and adding different types of weapons to the armamentarium of this crazy bunch of misfits. Ranthor wondered about how all this would impact the war in the galaxy. It was because of these shops that there was a huge death toll. They were handing out weapons the same way his mother used to hand over candy after dinner. This place was more capitalistic than Planet Odelphius, and probably just as barbaric. Fights used to break out from time to time due to 'professional' disagreements between client and seller. The irony was that they used their own weapons against them.

The clerk took a look at Ranthor and knew what he had wanted immediately. He had already prepared an entire table full of designs for beam breakers. There were different models and designs with specifications that only an engineer would care to know about. Ranthor had to be careful and avoid being scammed by this man. He knew that he clearly was not someone well-versed in technological jargon. Ranthor contacted Gideon and told him about their current problem. He remembered that the boy was excellent at matters both mechanical and electronic. Gideon clearly told him which one to buy and the price that it was sold in most markets. The clerk realized that Ranthor would be a difficult customer and so acknowledged his desire to buy a specific model. The beam protector was then installed into the ship and tested to prove to the customer that it was in full working condition. Ranthor reassured him that if it didn't, he would make sure he was no longer in full working condition. The clerk chuckled hesitantly.

They still had time to eat food despite Kendra's reservations about having food in such a disgusting planet. Ranthor managed to find the only restaurant that was deemed normal by Kendra's standards. Both of them entered an ordered food and drinks. They were feeling relieved that they could now access Planet Centra. Kendra wanted to make her way there right now and end things once and for all. Ranthor, however, was not keen to do so because he knew that this would mean the end of the mission. To be honest, he tried everything in his power to prolong the mission as much as possible. This was the reason he participated in all the matches and tournaments. He was going to do it even if the jewel was not there. It was a lucky coincidence that it happened to be there. Luckily, this gave him an excuse to do these activities. Otherwise, he would have suffered Kendra's wrath; something that he did not want to be reintroduced to anytime soon.

Just as expected, the capital's welcoming committee had heard news that they had arrived and were now laying the red carpet for them. A group of bandits were skulking around their ship, trying to find the owner. Ranthor would enjoy tearing them up bit to bit. He had not gotten into a fight ever since the tournament of power. It was killing him to avoid any brawl and took this as an opportunity to sink his teeth into another fight. The bandits would not know what had hit them after this. He promised them that their heads would make a permanent impression on his ship. The bandits were not afraid of Ranthor and were already making their way to him. The first approached him and swung his sword at him, but he soon realized the mistake that he had committed. Ranthor parried the attack and hit his opponent in the middle of the face. Blood came gushing from his nose and he lay there writhing in agony. Upon seeing this, Ranthor decided to ease him out of his misery once and for all. A quick blow to the head seemed to do the job.

The other bandits looked at their fallen comrade and were terrified about what was going to happen next. Nonetheless, most of them stuck their ground and decided to continue with the fight. It was dishonorable to leave a fight once it had started, albeit in this situation more favorable to do so. They realized that they were stupid to remain in the fight and so one or two of them managed to slip unnoticed. The second group of bandits also received their fair share of beatings. It was only a matter of time before they lay in heaps and piles. People were cheering for Ranthor outside the bar and congratulating him for defeating the bandits. The sorry bunch was disliked by almost every citizen inside the bar; well, except for the bartender because they always brought him good business with their fights. The bandits were regulars to this part of the capital; well, they were anyway. It was very likely that they would no longer be skulking around here anytime soon.

The bandits were now defeated, and the way was clear for Ranthor to leave the planet. The bartender rushed to congratulate him on his victory and had brought two glasses of his finest drinks for his new favorite customers. He told Ranthor to stay and a meal would be prepared in his honor. Ranthor agreed to stay for the festivities for an hour or two. After that, he would have to return to his mission. He did not want any further delays to his plan than the delays that had already happened. He did not trust his father to remain in the shadows and not do anything. It was very likely that he would find a way to follow him here. After all, this was not the only time rift that was in their galaxy. The regulars told them that people from their galaxy used to come here very frequently. It was not after the restrictions and sanctions were laid out that this movement started to slow down, and unfortunately so did the tourism.

Planet Centra was the top travel destination to regular galaxy dwellers, a term coined by the bartender. It described people from other galaxies that frequently came to this part of the universe. Most of them were searching for the jewels, and so far, none of them had managed to discover the last jewel of darkness. There was nothing to guarantee that it had survived the past two centuries. Nothing on that planet was still in the same working condition. The departure of the Xenorans took a deep toll on the balance of powers on the planet. There were no longer any technological advancements and people retired to their homes after working in the factories. It seemed as if all progress had halted and there was nothing that could be done about it. The absence of a ruler in Centra led to the takeover of the planet by the flora and fauna of the planet. The place was now knee-deep in wild species of plants and was indistinguishable from a zoo. None of the original citizens lived there anymore.

Centra used to be the crown jewel of the universe and hosted a variety of events. There was not a year that passed by without a festival or a march. People came from all across the universe to witness these events. It was the envy of the other planets and the joy of its ruler. No one knew what had truly happened to him. It didn't make sense that he was ousted by his own people. After all, they had also fled the planet. Rumor has it that he was killed by the Order of Monks. The Order was known for mass assassinations. Prior to their disbanding by Ranthor, they used to control the ruling families in almost every galaxy. Centra refused to bow down to them and had paid the consequence. The legendary Order torched the place down and killed every last man, woman, and child in the capital. They laid the place to rubble and did not care that they had extinguished the seat of civilization and industry in the entire universe. The Order of Monk was now thankfully destroyed and incapable of performing unspeakable acts of destruction.

Dinner was laid out for both Ranthor and Kendra and they were enjoying their meal. The night sky was as quite as ever and all that was preoccupying their mind had disappeared from existence. They were now finally reunited and hopefully for eternity. Ranthor was no longer thinking of the jewel, a thought that was nested in his dreams daily ever since this mission started. He was now quietly gazing upon the stars and happy knowing that his wish was granted. As for the jewels, he would protect the ones in his ship until he managed to find the one that was currently eluding him. For the time being, all he wanted to do was bask in the glory that was the woman in front of him. Her presence made all the things in the universe trivial, and he could no longer care about his past. Ranthor was in a state of serenity that could almost be described as divine. There was nothing that could wake him up from the divine state that he was experiencing; well, nothing except knowing that this was all temporary. It was only a matter of time before it disappeared into nothingness. He would then be left alone yet again to face his demons, and he sure had plenty of them.

They had both managed to finish off their meal and dessert was now laid out for them. It was paired with a specific accompaniment of spirits and wines for them to choose from. Ranthor enjoyed the meal thoroughly and then went back to his ship to sleep. Kendra was taking a stroll across the pier and enjoying the ripple of the waves on the sand. This was one of the few times that she got to just catch her breath and be alone for a while. It was also one of the few times that she was ever going to be alone. The thought just hit her that the solitude that she craved would soon be lost. However, she did not seem overly perturbed by that. Instead, she was actually happy that she was finally not going to be alone. For the first time in decades, she was going to accept the presence of another person in her life, a significant other. She hated the words as soon as she uttered them from her mouth. This stroll was one of the few luxuries that was she was able to afford at the moment. There was no one else at the beach and she managed to go for a swim.

Kendra then went back to her ship, excited that she managed to get some perspective about what her life was going to be like. She prepared a cup of tea and sat in the middle of her compartment listening to music so that she could sleep. However, today she was not interested in getting as much sleep as she required. The journey to Planet Centra was going to take time and needed to get some sleep. For now, all she wanted to do was enjoy her tea and music. Ranthor remained asleep despite the cacophony of sounds that were outside his room. Nothing seemed to wake him up, not even an explosion. She envied this quality that he had to fall asleep on cue. He had the uncanny ability to remove all thought from his head and sleep. That was something that most people could not do with such ease. He managed to do it despite the many troubling thoughts that lived in his head.

Centra was now within full view of the ship, and it would be only an hour between them and landing. Ranthor activated the beam protector and made his way to the planet for another attempt at entry. Nothing was going to stop him this time from landing inside the planet. The ship approached the field and managed to enter smoothly without any difficulties. He was now inside Planet Centra and was preparing the landing coordinates for one last time. The ship was no longer air borne and Ranthor stepped out to explore the planet. Surprisingly, the atmosphere was very much habitable for him, and he did not need to use his suit. The ancients that lived in these parts were similar to any other humanoid species and lived in the same conditions. The planet was vast, and it almost seemed endless. There were no clues or things to indicate the location of the jewel. Any evidence of civilization was also wiped out; it was almost as if no one had ever inhabited this planet. Nature had reclaimed the planet as its own and, in the process, destroyed any evidence that there was life in Centra. Some of the ancient Xenoran burial grounds, or at least their remnants, were still visible from a distance. Even nature respected the dead and their resting places were considered sacred.

The Xenorans were not interested in life after death and dismissed the notion entirely. It was why they created the jewels in the first place; to ensure sustenance and immortality would be within their grasp. Their civilization collapsed, and they had to resort to living in the underground catacombs that were erected for their graves. Their children were deprived the opportunity to see the greatness that had once been a distinguishing feature of their empire. There was no

Xenoran folklore or stories to back it up as well, adding to the sense of failure they had felt.

Thunderous bolts started to sound out from one of the burial grounds nearby. It seemed that they have woken up a slumbering soul that did not wish to be disturbed and was now seeking retribution. The entire burial ground started to quake from the force of the thunder bolts and soon our two protagonists were trying to find shelter from this storm. The sky's color changed from its regular blue to a purplish hue and all the birds were no longer where they were supposed to be. Kendra was now frightened and had clung tightly to Ranthor for support. He was equally scared and was considering abandoning the mission. However, they did not come this far to be scared by some theatrics. Ranthor shouted and demanded that whoever was controlling this freak show announce themselves. Sadly, there was no one to answer his call and instead he was greeted with more thunder and lightning. The storm was predicted and was expected to last for at least two days. In the meantime, the two were confined to the ship until further notice. It was yet another opportunity to taste Kendra's famous cuisine that had taken the galaxy by surprise.

They were holed on the ship for what seemed like an eternity and the storm had almost subsided. The thunder, however, was a mere warning that worse things were about to happen. The ancient Xenorans that lived in those graves did not take kindly to visitors. They barely allowed their own to stay when they still inhabited the planet. The Xenorans were famous for their complete lack of hospitality. It was one of the reasons why a coalition was made to hunt and kill every last one of them. It was no longer worth to tolerate their haughtiness in exchange for their technologies and they had to be exterminated. Following the death of their majority members, they decided to comply with the rules of the galaxy they lived in. It was only then that they started welcoming people into their humble abode. The Xenorans now longed for another day in the sun, and it seemed that this wish was not going to be granted.

Leaving the ship left Kendra with a sense of refreshment and relief. It was the first time in two days where she was able to walk freely in a space that was not confined between two walls. Ranthor did not seem as bothered about being imprisoned in the ship as she was. He knew that he would get the jewel sooner or later. He only had a little time to savor before they would part ways. Staying in the ship was another way that he would ensure that this time was much longer. Their next stop was a bird sanctuary that housed the next clue. In the middle of the sanctuary was a box and it contained the first map in a series of maps. The map in the bird sanctuary indicated the location of the next puzzle. It contained a visual representation of spokes that were placed in a farm nearby. The map showed the location of the farm relative to the sanctuary and how to get there. Ranthor was soon back on his feet in search of the farm. It took him a day to find the farm, but he was finally there and ready to start the challenge. He was challenged by the all-too-familiar sight of the spokes that he loved quite dearly. Ranthor prepared his mind for yet another puzzle; hopefully, he would use more than sheer luck to solve this one.

The doors to the barn opened and a mysterious robotic figure welcomed them inside. He beckoned them to sit on the stools that were laid out for them. A presentation then played on the teleprompter device and indicated the nature of the challenge that they were about to be exposed to. The spokes controlled a mechanism that controlled the box above them. The box had one of the keys that opened the vault to the jewels. It also contained a fragment of the map to the vault to help them. All they had to do was turn the spokes and the box would descend downwards. However, the catch was that there was a time-limit to solve the mystery. Otherwise, it would be lost forever.

The barn did not contain any useful clues that would help to operate the spokes. Ranthor tried turning them both clockwise and anti-clockwise but that did not seem to do the trick. Kendra tried to search for another part and attach it. The reason for that was because there was an attachment in the spokes which indicated that there was a missing piece somewhere in the barn. She turned every stack of hay, every box and opened every cupboard but did not seem to find anything of value inside. Whatever was there to be found was extremely well-hidden to the casual observer. However, they were not casual observers. It would only be a matter of minutes before it was found. She just hoped that there was more to go by than some scribblings on the map. She noticed that inverting the map revealed a location to her in the barn. Kendra walked over and was awestruck to find the missing piece of the spoke.

She hurried off to Ranthor to tell him the good news. He was thrilled to find the missing spoke and quickly attached it to the other parts. He then moved it and soon a box descended from below. Ranthor lifted the cover that was protecting the box and extracted the key that was inside. The key was almost transparent and was quite heavy to carry. However, they came prepared and already made a pouch to carry it in. He carried the key and alternated the duty with Kendra, who was relieved to know that things were going as planned. They were now making their way to the second mechanism. There were no bandits or beasts to stand in their way. The forces of evil were not hovering close by. Neither of them believed their eyes at the simplicity of the task. Ranthor was actually wishing for a fight silently. He knew that if Kendra heard him, his wish for a fight would be granted. But then again, he also knew who the fighter would be in that case.

The second task was now visible from where he stood. It was the forest of Verdana. It was a place he knew all-too-well and was tortured in quite a number of times. The forest was amongst the biggest habitats for wild animals in the entire ecosystem. Luckily, the one that was before them was a miniature construct that could be explored in one or two hours. The actual forest would have required at least two weeks to just reach the other end. There were no clues in any of the nearby trees or the bee sanctuaries. There was a stream in the middle of the forest, an extremely foreign object that was not in the original forest. Ranthor realized that this was probably where the key was located. Judging from his experience with the villagers, it was most likely where it was kept. His clothes took a really long time to dry up after that dip. However, it was one of the most refreshing swims that he had ever taken for a long time, but it was one that he did not wish to repeat.

The dive to the bottom of the stream was not as bad as the last one. However, this stream did not have a hidden box. Instead, there was a pouch with a miniature map inside it. It held the location of the next key within the forest. The key was in a box in the middle of a hollowed tree as per the descriptions. The map also highlighted the possible location of the tree. All Ranthor had to do now was locate the tree. He followed the instructions of the map to the tree and soon found the hollowed-out tree. He reached and found the box that he desired. He opened the box and retrieved the key from it. There were two more keys left and then he would go on to find the last jewel of darkness. He was wondering about what fresh hell was prepared for him to venture through now. There were two more strange experiences that he was yet to witness. It might even have something to do with Kendra for all he knew. The Xenorans had a knack for unpredictability that could only be described as near divine. They were the masters of the element of surprise.

The next door led to them the quarry. It was the next place where the key was located. Ranthor knew the place like the back of his own hand, but there would definitely be a twist. They had to enter the quarry from the other end and most of the architecture was changed. However, the map in their possession indicated that the key was in a similarly shaped boxed that was in one of the peripheral chambers. The location was clearly marked on the map and all that he had to do was walk over to it. Ranthor reached the location and indeed did find the box. He opened and was surprised to see yet another map. The map had a picture of a room with a puzzle. He had to solve the puzzle in order to get the key. The room was not difficult to locate, and it took a few minutes before they were inside the room with the puzzles. The lights were suddenly dimmed to set the mood for the puzzle. The pieces were laid out in the middle and Ranthor had to find the combination so that the box would descend.

He tried one of the combinations that he had used before, but it did not work and instead the tiles burned down. Ranthor noticed that a timer was placed in the middle of the room, and they now had ten minutes to find the clue before everything disappeared. He used a light source over the map and illuminated it. The light showed him three possible combinations to operate the mechanism. He did not know what to do and was afraid to act randomly just like he did the previous time. He searched the room for clues to aid him in selecting the combination. He found that the room was pointing to the combination in the end, and he was sure that that was not a coincidence. He selected the final combination and luckily it was the correct one. The box descended from the ceiling and the key was there inside for him to collect. He managed to breathe less heavily and was elated at finding this clue amongst a difficult task. There was only one clue that was separating him from his goal now. He decided to rest and resume the adventure in a few hours.

Ranthor called for Kendra to join him for a snack in the middle of the forest. He enjoyed the view and found it very serene and welcoming. They enjoyed a nice snack of roast turkey sandwiches and an assortment of fruits and berries. The air was cool, and the sky was clear with no evidence of possible rainfall. He wondered as how this particular environment was recreated. Planet Centra did not have any wildlife, and it certainly did not have any forests, streams, or mountains. These places were created by machines that operated using artificial intelligence. The A.I. captured the essence of the person and created the environment that was most soothing for him or her. There were many versions of different places for both Ranthor and Kendra, but this was selected due to its lack of complexity. The other memory would prove very difficult to control by the machine and, therefore, multiple errors would arise subsequently. Being trapped in any of these virtual realities would be problematic as there was no Xenoran to help them out. Despite the sophistication of the artificial intelligence modules, they still needed a humanoid operator to maintain regular checks. This was deliberately kept in place to avoid a possible mutiny by the machines.

The creator of the artificial world was now dead and so were all the technologies that he had created over the course of the past century. There was no one that would be able to fix this if it malfunctioned. Ranthor had to be really careful about maneuvering across the next puzzle as any wrong step would spell his certain doom. He had dealt with enough danger and excitement in his life to last two lifetimes. It was finally time for him to play it safe. For once, he had to take care of someone else other than himself. He knew that Kendra would not forgive him if he endangered himself again another time. She was still recovering from the shock of the tournament.

The sky in the forest was lighting up with an unusual energy and time seemed to stop. The route to the next and final mission was now displayed on the floor. Soon, Ranthor would be able to cross to the final destination and gain access to the last box with the last key. He would then be able to get across and grab the last jewel. He was not sure as to what he would do after the jewels were collected. Perhaps, the jewels of darkness could be assembled in a similar way to the other jewels and open the inner sanctum to the source of their power. For the time being, he only needed to focus his energy on the box and the key. Kendra was also searching the place with him for clues. The last location was a metallic hangar, a ship hangar housed many combat ships that were very similar to his. It also had many levers and buttons that Ranthor did not know what to do with. He opened the map, but it did not show him anything useful.

The hangar was one of the worst places known on planet Centra. The architects faced a lot of issues creating this part of virtual reality. It managed to trap a few of the unfortunate souls that ventured through here. Some of them were lucky enough to escape, but some were foolish enough to return. There was a certain allure to the ship hangar to some of the military personnel. The battle ships reminded them of the wars that they waged with their neighboring states. For Ranthor, the place always seemed to spell doom and despair. He disliked the notion of having a ship hangar; the reason being that it reminded him of his humiliation back home. He mulled over his head, trying to think of a plan of action. There was nothing that came out, and he grew more and more despaired with every passing moment. He looked at Kendra for inspiration, but she was as blank as he was. They were both trapped in a giant metallic iron gate.

Just as they were both about to lose hope, a mysterious constellation appeared on one of the ships. The combination alerted them to the levers that they had to press in order to get the box. However, there were three possible combinations based on the designs on the shape. Ranthor still had not recovered from the last time they pressed the wrong lever. Would it show another ten-minute alert indicating immediate doom? That was a possibility he did not want to explore. He continued searching the room with Kendra for another sign to suggest which of the three combinations opened the box. The middle combination was the most likely one to open the box as far they figured. Kendra was sure that the second combination was the one and she decided to try her luck. She pressed the levers and turned on the spokes to the direction suggested by the combination, and to her surprise, the box descended from above. She gathered the strength to open the box and to her dismay, it had another map. This was yet another cheeky trick by the Xenorans to derail them from their goal. The map, however, was showing clearly where the key was. It was in the next chamber of the hangar and was marked with clear instructions on how to get it.

There were no mechanisms or tricks to getting the key this time. All they had to do was enter the chamber and extract the key. Kendra still expected traps and was still on her toes. Ranthor was also wary of yet another unwelcome surprise by the idiotic Xenorans. Ranthor wanted to kill every last one of them for the ordeal that they were both in because of their jewels. However, he knew that the jewels would grant him power and control over his people. He would no longer have to bow to anyone.

The last chamber had a box in the middle in the same place marked on the map. Ranthor managed to extract the key in the box and was now headed to find the last jewel. He connected the maps together and they marked the location of the last jewel. It was finally time for this mission to end.

Chapter 18
The Inner Sanctum

The king had managed to reach Planet Centra with a fleet of his own and was ready to meet his son. This was going to be one of Ranthor's worst nightmares. His father was about to destroy the entire planet in search of the jewels. He would not hesitate to exterminate everything that was in his way to get what he wanted. He mobilized the entire forces of Nebula for the task and left the planet unprotected. This was seen as a bold move by the army, but they did not dare cross him again. The last general that did ended up dead in the middle of his home. The king was now in the middle of the armada and ready to descend on the surface of Planet Centra. The landing coordinates for his ship were entered and it was going to be a few minutes before he would land on Centra. He was somewhat excited to meet his son again. He was not going to be as lenient as the others were with him. The king did not care about killing Ranthor and was going to do what was necessary to get what he wanted. He was going to kill Ranthor by his own hands if things got serious and was already mentally prepared for this. Part of him actually wanted to do it despite the outcome of the current expedition.

The path into the first room of the capital was in front of the king and his army. They followed in the footsteps of Ranthor and Kendra, taking care to trace each and every step that they took. The soldiers informed the king that it would be a matter of hours before they reached them. For the time being, he enjoyed taking a walk across the virtually created landscapes and taking in the technology of the civilization that he helped wipe out. The Xenorans were never sworn enemies of the king of Nebula. The war between them started out of nowhere and that was because the king wanted to expand his kingdom. The ancients of Xenora did not want to be involved with affairs related to Nebula, but the murders and the kidnappings forced them to develop a vendetta. The Xenorans vowed to kill every last citizen of Nebula once their uprising would start. The king knew that he had to exterminate the remainder of them.

Soldiers were now searching the quarry for footsteps and went to yet another one of the rooms. There was no sign of Ranthor or his friend anymore and they did not want to let the king know about the lack of any development. They feared for his wrath, especially knowing that he was on the lookout for Ranthor. The last jewel of darkness was now within his reach. It was either him or his son who would acquire the power. For the soldiers, all they hoped for was that they did not die in the middle of this conquest. The outcome was equally bad in terms of the ruling party; they only wished that the next ruler would still keep them under his employ. However, they finally found the tracks that would lead them to the current location of Ranthor. This made the troopers rejoice with glory at the success of their mission. It was a matter of minutes before the king would be reunited with his son for the last time.

The next chamber was unlike the others that were created from the creators' maps of virtual reality. Ranthor was amazed at the excellent design of the streams and mountains in this room. It was virtual recreation of the river of seven wonders and the mountain system that surrounded it. This was a place that was only rumored to exist. This was definitely the place where the last jewel of darkness would be located. The Xenorans were very creative to make this place the location of the jewel. It was one place which would be easy to hide any object; no one would dare search the streams and mountains; well, anyone but Ranthor. He never knew why the ancients were fascinated with streams. They seemed to hide plenty of things beneath the waters. It was going to be the last time they searched for a jewel. Kendra was relieved that the mission was finally over.

The inner chamber room was the stronghold of planet Centra and Ranthor was in the middle of the action. Kendra was exhilarated at finding the location of the last vault. She was searching keenly for the vault's location in the middle of the mountain system. There was no sign so far of the familiar vault and its lock. None of them were exhausted and neither showed signs of fatigue or boredom. The way to the first mountain proved to be the most challenging and Ranthor almost tripped during the journey. However, there was no sign of the vault at this point and there was nothing even indicative of its location. They moved out of the first mountain and into the plains to enjoy some food. The air surrounding the plains was clear and the water from the stream was clear that you could see your own reflection from it. Ranthor went for a swim down the stream, and he did not find any evidence of the vault inside. Unlike the other traps, there was nothing in this area that was helpful. The frustration and anger were starting to build up. Nothing that Kendra did or said quenched Ranthor's anger.

They were now headed to the next mountain in search for clues. The mountain was easier to reach, and it was only a matter of half an hour before they were there. Kendra was searching for the vault and had stumbled on another intriguing map. The map showed her that the vault was in the last mountain of this system. She rejoiced knowing the location of the vault. Ranthor was checking the keys in his possession and both of them were making their way to the final mountain. In the meantime, they didn't know about the welcoming committee that was waiting for them at the other end. Little did Ranthor know that his father was on his trail. The king and his crew managed to reach the first mountain and had located the trail that Ranthor made with his boots. The soldiers informed him that the footsteps were recent, and the print indicated that it was around an hour since they parted this location. The king was happy learning this information. He made sure to reward the soldiers with money and different types of rare items.

Most of the crew members were now exhausted from the search and had beckoned the king to give them time to rest. He agreed begrudgingly, especially that there was no way to convince them otherwise. All he kept thinking about was cornering Ranthor and taking the pouch of jewels from him. It would be easy for him as he had the manpower required to take the jewels. Ranthor would soon bow in front of the ruler of Nebula once again. There was no escape from the other end, and he would have to cross the king's crew at any point of time. The last mountain was going to be difficult to climb. It was amazing that the creators made this elaborate labyrinth from scratch. The mountains that they were now seeing were not from any solar system that they knew and was not a figment of the Xenorans' imagination. However, Ranthor did not seem to place where it was despite travelling most of the known planets in the universe.

The adventure was finally coming to an end and the vault was within sight of them now. Ranthor managed to locate the vault and was headed to collect the jewel. He opened the locks using the keys and the vault was now wide open. He extracted the jewel from its vault, and he was sure that it was the last jewel of darkness. Finally, the last jewel was in his possession, and he was soon going to activate the power that was trapped in it. He realized that a door had appeared out of nowhere. This must be the pathway to the power center of the planet. Collecting the jewel opened this door and it was now time for him to extract the power core. He opened the door, and he soon found the place that he was looking for. The planet's core was buzzing with power, and he noticed that there was someone inside. To his shock, this was the master engineer that had created the simulations. The man must have been over a millennium old. He approached him gingerly and tried to communicate with him. The creator was surprised to find someone after all this time and greeted Ranthor at the entrance and prepared to show him around.

The creator was the last of the civilization of inhabitants that lived on Centra. He explained to Ranthor that they were all annihilated by the forces of Nebula, and he was the only one that escaped. The reason that he escaped was because he was holed in the middle of his workspace. He saw the entire massacre from his monitor and was stuck there ever since. The creator was happy to see signs of life nearby. He showed them inside to the inner chamber of the power reactor, the source of power that fueled the entire planet and the entire Xenoran civilization. The jewels were brought here every century and used to power the mechanism. The power they would then possess would be used by the wielder to grant them a wish. The creator explained to Ranthor how he could power the jewels. He also told him that the powering event was scheduled to happen after two days from now and he would help him achieve that goal. The creator asked that Ranthor protect him in return and bring him back to his people. Ranthor agreed to help him out.

The power chamber emanated a significant amount of energy, enough to charge two solar systems simultaneously. Ranthor was excited to have the two days pass by as quickly as possible and then attend the ceremony. Kendra was gazing at the reactor with such awe and incredulity; she did not believe that this was finally going to be over soon. Her dreams and wishes would soon be granted, and she could get back to her regular life. They relayed the news to Gideon, and he was happy to learn about the good news. He was also just recovering from the last mission that they went on together. Gideon and his parents gazed into the reactor with the same amazement that Kendra was displaying. It was as if they were inside the reactor room and looking at it directly. Planet Centra would collapse if the power reactor was destroyed. This was the sole reason that the creator was still here. He had created a bionic replica of himself that was going to serve as his successor and operate the machinery.

The king had finally made his way to the inner chamber of the power reactor and was preparing to meet Ranthor yet again. He brought a few soldiers from his infantry to join him in the final expedition. He would make sure that he did not lose the fight this time. After all, he was not a match for Ranthor alone and he was not going to risk his chances. He watched as Ranthor was having a conversation with the creator about the ceremony to power the jewels. He was explaining to him the instructions for powering the jewels. There were slots for the regular jewels and others for the jewels of darkness. A central mechanism was there in place to charge the jewels to a maximum. The creator showed them the mechanism and gave them a mock description of how to operate the mechanism. He was going to be with them on the night to ensure that they did it correctly. He then bid them farewell and left them with the power reactor. It was a few minutes before king was going to make his appearance.

Kendra was waiting patiently by the reactor and was now prepared to leave after finally knowing how to operate the mechanism. She caught sight of the soldiers with the king out of the corner of her eyes. She alerted Ranthor to the presence of the soldiers and that they had to make sure that they were well prepared. Kendra reckoned that there were around twelve soldiers with the king, and they were armed to the teeth. The soldiers did not know anything about their opponents and the only thing they were taught was how to kill them in the most efficient way possible. However, the king warned them to attack Ranthor and Kendra only in the event that they showed any signs of opposition.

There was nothing to do now but wait for the power to erupt between the king's soldiers and Ranthor. Kendra's face was as pale as ash at the sight of the soldiers and was still wondering if they would get out of there alive. She just wished that the battle would start soon enough so that they would know the outcome. She raised her sword in the air and soon realized that it was being charged by the power reactor; an unpredictable move that she did not anticipate would happen. She took Ranthor's sword and did the same thing. His sword was charged as well and ready for the next battle. They had the competitive advantage against the soldiers now and this would at least even out the odds finally.

The soldiers were finally in the inner chamber with Ranthor and Kendra. They were led by the king who seemed excited about finally meeting his son. Ranthor's hairs were standing on their ends just as he was gripped with fear. The sight of his father brought a mixture of emotions rushing down the back of his spine. His first instinct told him to jump at him with all his strength and rip his head from his shoulders. However, he decided against it and thought of confronting the old king. He was not sure how he managed to get there in the first place. With Ray's death, there was no way he could be tracked. He then remembered that his ship was once part of the Nebula fleet and as such had to conform to the requirements of installing a tracker. The tracker was installed because there were several acts of mutiny that cost the king several ships in the process. Ranthor did not regret being detected by his, but he was annoyed at the fact that only one of them was to emerge alive. The king would not leave here without taking control of the power reactor.

"It's wonderful to meet you again son, it has been a while. Again, I am extending my hand in peace and offering your place back home. What do you say about that? I assure you that I am in dire need of your skills and power. Join me and you will enjoy a life of luxury again. Please do consider the offer that I am extending to you," offered the king sympathetically.

"After all these years of turmoil, do you really think that I would believe anything that would come out of your mouth? What sort of father tosses out his only son to ensure his control of the country? I would rather die than join you in any mission you take. I will make sure that you will not leave here alive, old man. I am giving you the opportunity to leave now and keep your head held high. Move closer and I will make sure to cut you into a million pieces," bellowed Ranthor angrily.

The soldiers marched across the battleground and prepared their guns and swords for the fight that was ahead of them. Ranthor was preparing his own sword and gun for them. The first attack was dealt by one of the soldiers who met his end shortly afterwards. The other soldiers tightened their control over their swords and shields. The second soldier moved in to attack and barely missed Ranthor. He then returned the attack which was swiftly parried by one of his partners. Ranthor barely escaped the attack and was now making his way to a higher ground. Kendra managed to kill yet another soldier. They were now afraid that the tides of the battle were soon going to be in the hands of Kendra. There was no other soldier that was able to take her on and she knew that all too well. Kendra's sword was shooting lightning bolts left, right, and center and she did not know how to control it. It was a miracle that she did not injure Ranthor or herself in the process. The battle would soon end with them crowned as winners and the ceremony would soon start.

Kendra realized that they did not have much time before the ceremony would start. The creator was holed up in his room, waiting for the fight to end. He wanted to make sure the king did not win.

The king was waiting at the other end of the chamber for his jewels and soon he would be at the helm of the ceremony to charge the jewels. Meanwhile, the creator wanted to make sure that the jewels would not fall into the hands of the oppressors. He, therefore, switched on the protective mechanisms of the inner chamber of the reactor. There were now metallic soldiers and drones that would aid Ranthor and Kendra in their battle. The soldiers were now up against Ranthor and the guardians of the room; therefore, the odds were now not stacked on either end. The battle resumed from where it had stopped the last time. Kendra and one of the robots moved in and managed to kill two more soldiers. The others were now out of stamina and were making their way into the makeshift jungle to hide themselves. Kendra was now scouring the area, looking for any signs of the king or his soldiers. She was going to rain hell on them at the first sight of them. However, she also decided to rest and plan her next move. Kendra guarded the power reactor and Ranthor, making sure that none of the soldiers got close to them.

The creator came out of hiding to meet with Kendra and wanted to let her know that it was only a mere seven hours before the ceremony would commence. She wasn't sure if they would be able to stall the king and his soldiers, but she was going to try her best. The creator returned back to his room and entered the sequence that unlocked the reactor's core. Kendra entered with him and was almost blinded by the sheer power that it emitted. The reactor's core chamber had not been opened for the better part of two centuries. The creator was surprised that the mechanism to open it was even operational. It was a relief too because he could no longer fix it even if he wanted to. This ceremony was going to be his ticket to leave this miserable planet. He was going to settle in Odelphius and be an advisor to the king for all the technical matters that were plaguing his planet. The creator would soon be heralded as another one of the Xenoran greats; a return to the glory of a once heroic civilization that brought technology to the universe.

The creator was the last surviving member of the Xenora ancient mechanics and was almost reaching the end of his days. The man had lived for the better part of eight centuries, creating different brilliant machinations that served the universe very well. There was no person, humanoid or otherwise, that could create the same machines or virtual reality simulators that were going to travel the galaxy. He would sure be teaching the Odelphians the various technologies of his people.

The battle resumed and the soldiers were trying to attack Kendra and the drones. Ranthor was also battling another platoon of soldiers. The king was calling reinforcements with every squad that was defeated. It seemed for a moment that the soldiers would not end, but then it finally was over. The soldiers collapsed in the middle of the battle grounds and so did their counterparts. Kendra was still fatigued from the final fight with the last of the soldiers. She was barely able to walk and there were only four hours to spare before the ceremony started. The king somehow managed to be spared of the onslaught. He was going to make sure to enter the inner core of the reactor with them. He was intent on getting inside and acquiring the power of the jewels. Kendra searched every corner of the jungle for the king and did not find any trace of him. *He must have escaped back home,* she thought to herself.

However, Ranthor knew that his father would not give up just as easily. He had to be holed up somewhere that was inaccessible to them, a place that was very far away from detection. Ranthor told Kendra to avoid the task of locating him; he would come to find them soon enough anyway. For the time being, they were listening to the creator telling them how to charge the jewels.

The creator was now priming the reactor for its final spin before he departed the planet for good. The jewels were inserted into their respective sockets and the ceremony was soon going to start. Kendra and Ranthor could barely contain their excitement. There was nothing that was going stop them, not even the king. His arrival would be instrumental for them to remove the remaining of the opposition forces. The jewels started vibrating, indicating that they had started charging. A charging bar was set by the jewels which showed the percentage the jewels were charged; it was still showing two percent. The jewels were emitting an energy that could either build or destroy planets. Ranthor would soon control a power that was contained by powers from across the ages. He would soon return as the rightful ruler of his land and would be hailed as God by his people. He would banish his father to the furthest reaches of the universe and rid them of his evil once and for all.

The ceremony was going on smoothly for the most part and there was no evidence of any opposing forces. The king was still in the inner chamber and did not make the slightest sign that he was somewhere nearby. He watched as the jewels were charged with power. Nothing he could do would prevent Ranthor from his goal. His only hope now was to trick his son that he was part of his team. He would try to sneak his way back and get the powerful jewels. However, he had to wait for Ranthor to exit the chamber so that he could get a chance to tell him. That didn't seem like it was going to happen. There was no one exiting or entering the chamber for almost three hours. He wondered what they were doing inside waiting for the jewels. After all, they completed their task and all they had to do now was wait. The king decided to wait for the cover of night and try to think of an alternative plan. He knew that nothing that he would say was going to soften the boy's heart.

The first jewel finished charging and was ready to be used. Ranthor was not going to use the jewels until all of them were charged. Even the power of a single jewel could help with the task, but he was not going to take chances, especially not after suffering in the process of getting the damned jewels. Kendra was concerned that Ranthor did not do anything but stare at the jewels. She beckoned him to leave the room for a meal. Luckily, he agreed, and they both exited the core reactor chamber and were headed back into their ship for a snack. The food was already on the table and ready for them to eat. It was time for her to tell him that she wanted to stay with him. Ranthor listened to what Kendra had to say and he was glad to hear the good news. It was only a few hours before they left this miserable planet. The best news that he received today was that he was going to be reunited with Kendra after this mission was over. It was more important than all the powers of the universe combined, and he would gladly give them up if he had to choose between the two.

Ranthor has grown around power and was always surrounding by a great deal of strength and a greater sense of needing to have control. For the first time in his life, he had learned to give up all the control and trust Kendra. This trust had paid off finally when she decided to continue the remainder of her life with him. He was excited to take her back to his home planet of Nebula and make her his queen. The only thing that was standing in their way now was the charging process of the jewels. The creator contacted them and informed them that the charging process was now seventy-five percent complete. It was only a matter time before they would be back in orbit to Nebula.

Kendra was now listening intently to Ranthor's description of the planet and the citizens. He told her about his pastimes and what he was missing about the planet. She could listen to him for hours without being bored; she barely understood what he was saying, but she could not care less.

The creator had run into a little trouble in the programming of the charging dock and was now furiously hacking at the device trying to fix it. He reassured Ranthor that it would be up and running in a few minutes. There was nothing that should worry them; these things sometimes happened, and they were lucky to have the most qualified engineer at their disposal. He called them back again to inform that things were back in working order. Ranthor was glad to hear the good news and went back to his cockpit. Kendra was in the other room and was looking at the maps for possible hiding places that the king would be using. They were both on the lookout for him to ensure that he would not get to the core reactor room. There was nothing that was protecting the creator now from any imminent attack. The arrival of the king would compromise their plans and would doom the mission to failure.

The other simulations started to fade away now as the power reactor was temporarily disabled. They returned to working order as soon as the mechanism was fixed. This brief interruption allowed the king to remain camouflaged in his hiding place. He was now within the creator's line of sight. Ranthor and Kendra were busy mulling over their long-term plans to notice that he had advanced inside the inner chamber to where the power reactor was located. The scream of the shocked creator woke them up from their stupor and sent them to the core chamber looking for the source of the creator's worry. Soon enough, they discovered that the king had managed to make his way into the inner chamber where the jewels were now reaching ninety percent charge. It was going to be his time now to get the jewels. Nothing was going to stop him from executing his mission. Ranthor was now beating the ground with anger; this would not have happened if he wasn't distracted. He blamed himself for mishandling the situation and was now apologizing to Kendra and the creator.

The king was looking at the jewels, trying to figure how to dismantle them from the charging dock where they were located. He did not know how to dislodge the jewels and nothing that he did was doing the trick. In the meantime, Ranthor managed to sneak behind him and gagged him. The king was now tied behind one of the poles. Ranthor was holding a gun to his chest and warned him that any sudden movement would result in his death. He was now fed up with chasing his father and he would put a bullet between his eyes if he dared to even speak. The king complied with his instructions and was now sitting quietly, avoiding any sort of eye contact with Ranthor or the creator. He did not want to let out as much of a squeal. Ranthor looked at him furiously and tried with great difficulty to prevent himself from killing the man. All of his emotions were now back to surface, and he remembered every offense that was uttered to him by his father.

"I'm sorry, son, I know that I haven't been the ideal parent, but I hope that you find it in your heart to forgive me and set me free. Please give me the chance to make amends. I no longer want to rule the planet; that can be yours for all I care. I implore to spare the life of this old man and let him live the remainder of his life in misery and I will no longer be in your way," begged the king eagerly.

"You know that you would not have granted me the same courtesy if I was in your position. Still, I don't wish to kill you, old man. You might actually prove to be a valuable asset to me after all. I will set you free on the condition that you head back to your ship. Here are the coordinates that I want you to head to. If I find out that you disobeyed me, I will come back to kill you personally," Ranthor reassured his father. The man nodded in agreement.

The creator just informed Ranthor that the charging process was now complete, and they were to go to the core and collect the jewels. It was finally time for them to head to the jewels and extract their power. The king was also waiting for them intently to reach the chamber so that he could make his escape. Despite promising Ranthor, he knew that this was his chance to escape. He radioed his remaining soldiers and asked for them to extract him from the chamber. The soldiers were now in the middle of the chamber and ready to take the king back to his planet. Kendra found the group there and with a few swift movements of her sword, she managed to kill them all. The king collapsed in the middle of the floor, dead from a heart attack. Having witnessed the defeat of his soldiers was the final straw for him. He could not bear the idea of another defeat and decided that he needed his departure. With that, Kendra returned to the inner chamber to witness the remainder of the ceremony. Ranthor was waiting for her to come.

The jewels were now fully charged and functional. They were stowed into the same receptacle that had initially carried them and were now making their way outside of the chamber. Ranthor led the expedition, and the creator was invited back to the ship. He made himself comfortable in the cockpit and prepared a meal to eat. He was surprised that such a backwards technology managed to survive all these years. He suggested to Ranthor to make a few adjustments, ones that he would gladly do for him if required. Ranthor kindly refused the offer, stating that this ship was the main reason that he found the jewels in the first place. There was no technology in the entire universe that was going to change his mind about that. The creator silently nodded in agreement and continued daydreaming about his life in Odelphius. Perhaps, he would create new robotic fighting devices for the next tournament of power. Rumor has it that the tournament master was a big fan of Xenoran technology.

The creator had also thought of retirement; after all, he was in his eighth century now and his bones were far too brittle to survive working in the factories and workshops. Retirement seemed like an excellent idea for him; it would be a great opportunity to visit the places in the universe that were manufactured by his people. There were many kings that could use his help as a consultant. He could still do what he wanted without the trouble of creating any machines. The job was very sought after and many kings were on the lookout for a Xenoran to advise them on their technological problems. It was after many years that he managed to leave his hiding place and enter into the world of the living again.

Ranthor returned to his home planet Nebula as the new ruler and was welcomed back by his faithful servants and citizens. The people rejoiced that their previous ruler was now dead, ushering in a new age of enlightenment. The jewels were used to power the industry of the planet and soon enough the planet was ready to accept all sorts of visitors. Kendra was the advisor general of the forces of Nebula and chief political advisor to the ruler. The job was becoming boring and both of them longed for the next adventure. Ranthor assured her that there was going to be another, more exciting one soon enough.

The End